Pownall, David,
1938-

The white cutter

$18.95

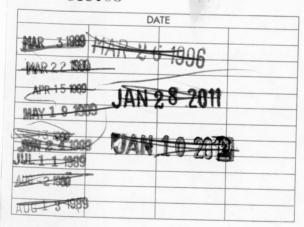

DATE		
MAR 3 1989	MAR 2 6 1996	
MAR 22 1989		
APR 15 1989	JAN 2 8 2011	
MAY 1 9 1989		
JUN 2 7 1989	JAN 1 0 2012	
JUL 1 1 1989		
AUG - 2 1989		
AUG 1 3 1989		

THE
WHITE
CUTTER

THE
WHITE
CUTTER

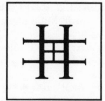

DAVID
POWNALL

VIKING

F

2-89ST 1900

VIKING
Published by the Penguin Group
Viking Penguin Inc., 40 West 23rd Street,
New York, New York 10010, U.S.A.
Penguin Books Ltd, 27 Wrights Lane,
London W8 5TZ, England
Penguin Books Australia Ltd, Ringwood,
Victoria, Australia
Penguin Books Canada Ltd, 2801 John Street,
Markham, Ontario, Canada L3R 1B4
Penguin Books (N.Z.) Ltd, 182–190 Wairau Road,
Auckland 10, New Zealand

Penguin Books Ltd, Registered Offices:
Harmondsworth, Middlesex, England

First American Edition
Published in 1989 by Viking Penguin Inc.

1   3   5   7   9   10   8   6   4   2

LIBRARY OF CONGRESS CATALOGING IN PUBLICATION DATA
Pownall, David, 1938–
The white cutter.
I. Title.
PR6066.0995W4   1989   823'.914   88-40269
ISBN 0-670-82579-4

Printed in the United States of America by
Arcata Graphics, Fairfield, Pennsylvania
Set in Bembo
Designed by Sarah Vure

FOR ALEX

The stone knows the form. . . .
Ezra Pound

Men of sense are really of one religion . . . and
men of sense never tell it.
Anthony Ashley Cooper

```
┌─────────┐
│         │
│    I    │
│         │
└─────────┘
```

Perhaps I should describe Bert, my father, first. Later on I must delve into his character (part of myself perhaps?) so the urn of all these strange fragments is important. He had a body and head that were famous within the craft of all white cutters in northern England. It was a shape that struck at the eye, a tar-barrel of a body strutting about on short, stout, curvilinear legs; arms that seemed to be as long and thick as beech boughs, always waving, waving; and hands, oh my father's hands, mole-paws, digging-hands, spades that could clip and chisel tight and hold on to a gale-tossed mullion twirling on a rope sixty feet in the air in semi-darkness. His hands had great beauty for me, even the hardness of them, the thick pads on the finger-ends and the balls of the thumbs where he held down the saw, right then left, switching the strain as the slow, smoking blade tore back and forth.

His head — more than any person I have ever seen in my travels — belonged to his body: it was *of* his body, an extension, a chapel, an apse of his bulging nave of a torso. There was no neck to speak of, only a joining-place where the broad, heavy shoulders slid into his skull in two ridges of muscle. Black, wispy hair covered all of his head and face except for the dark, frowning, heavily-browed eyes that were always bright with anger or humour. His nose was a Lancashire nose, a tombstone in memory of form and beauty, a relic of the one Adam had when it was punched by God in the garden. Many falls, many fights, many dropped hammers and falling stones had carved that nose. But now I must tell the story of his smile. If his hands were beautiful to me, his smile was a miracle. It was rarely on his wide, red mouth but when it came it was a revelation of his inner self, of his strange spirit which he had striven to keep clear and clean. In many days of mud and disappointments, after collapsed walls and broken blocks that had sundered near to the last saw-stroke, after lost tools and thefts of equipment, no pay, late deliveries, jeering priests, incompetent clerks of works, drunken colleagues (when he was sober), might come a magical smile for me, even after my worst

7

wickednesses when he must have cursed the day that he had decided to keep me and bring me up himself rather than hand over his appalling progeny to the church to become a whimpering monk.

His voice I will leave till later.

It has been a long voyage home from the last of the three penitential pilgrimages the Abbot of Iona laid upon me for the sin of killing my dear father: primum, he said, you must go to Santiago de Compostella in Spain; secundum, you must go to Rome in Italy; tertium, you must go to Jerusalem in Palestine. I was a youth of fourteen when I set out on the first of my three great journeys: I return as a man of forty-eight, my atonement completed except for the final part: quartum, the abbot said, you must write out the story of your sin in all truth and detail, then destroy it before the altar here on the isle of Iona.

We are beating up the Narrow Seas towards Winchelsea but the ship's master says the tide is against us. We passengers are desperate to get on dry land and who can blame us? Those on board who have seen the skills in navigation of these sailors all the way from the Holy Land have much to complain about. Having to spend the last hours before harbour stuck out at anchor with the ebb-tide bringing the lovely aromas of old England to us will be agony. The fish can keep the sea, say I.

I have come back penniless. I own nothing but what I stand up in, my tools and my writing materials. This is the state of a child, of a student. All the money I have earned while on my three pilgrimages has been spent, stolen off me, or given away. It will mean a fresh start for me but I have the strength and wit to make it, God willing. On the abbeys, churches, cathedrals, castles, mosques, palaces and tombs of the world — from Muscovy to India, from Cadiz to Danzig, from Athens to Avignon — you will find my mason's mark, H across H, ╪ , Hedric Herbertson, and what work you find it on will be the finest. This is not pride, not at this stage in my rebirth, but a craftsman's honest estimation of his worth backed up by emperors, popes, princes, sultans and generals of all persuasions whose truths are never flatteries.

The sailors are even more salt-mad than the passengers. These lads have been at sea for nine months and pilgrims are not their favourite cargo. Since the early hours they have been urging on this vessel, (foul, leaky, floating sewer that it is!) to make a landing during the

8

hours of light. They have scooped the air with their hands and their hats, to drive the ship on faster!

Now we have sight of the coast. The gulls are turning to wait with us, having observed the anchor plunging into the waves. We will clean out here where the water sweeps the sandbanks.

The water is warm enough to bathe. These scars on my body are not from one story, but from many. They hail from battles, accidents, attempted assassinations, love-making (God forgive me for carrying such memories home with me!) tortures (what's worse than love?), punishments and ritual markings from tribes that have taken me into their heathen bosoms. Not all of my scars are on the outside.

The women passengers have long since given up averting their eyes as the men bathe. No one on this wretched ship has any sense of privacy left at all. The three big dames from Northampton will come to the side to poke fun at me. Before we land I will be importuned for the fiftieth time to tell them how I got that writing in Arabic around my cock. The ladies have only been on board since we called in at Pontevedra in Spain to pick up pilgrims returning from Santiago de Compostella and Saint James's shrine — my first but I walked it, there and back, as the abbot ordered, only taking ship from Iona to Paris. One thousand miles. According to my book I worked on thirty-nine buildings during the nine and a half years that my first pilgrimage took, and I earned fifty-four pounds, twelve shillings and fourpence, all currencies rendered into the English equivalent at the proper rate of exchange where ascertainable. (I still have no idea of the true value of the Basque *groque*.)

I can stand up in the water. This is English soil, I suppose, this fluid sand that is shifting through my toes: my homeland. Not that the word *home* means much to me, except in the broadest sense. There is no place for me to go to, only Iona where I must go to burn this book which I now begin in order to end. From there? I have no family or friend. I will go to London. King Edward is not the great builder that his father, Henry, was but he does a bit here and there and he will be glad to have the best white cutter in the world working for him. Certainly I will be looking to get at least eightpence a day, that's a farthing for each of my years of penitence. My dad's last wage was fourpence back in twelve hundred and fifty-three and rates for top-class men have risen a lot since then.

Yes, ladies, it still means what it meant in the Bay of Biscay, off the

9

Cape of the World's End, près de Madeira: the Arabic reads, "to the tower of the rose, my love, be always prominence and providence".

How they laugh, the dears. Ah, at my feet I feel England's strong tide turning. Venus shows herself low down in the evening sky.

When I was born there were plenty of building jobs in the north. My dad, Herbert of Garstang in the wage-books, was working at Cockersands Abbey on the Lancashire coast. My mother was a labourer on the site. Her name was Joan. Whenever Bert talked about her in later years he would say that he only took up with her in order to keep warm. The small, desolate Praemonstratensian abbey was set in a low field by the howling mouth of the Lune estuary. The abbot had insisted the construction work be pushed on well into the winter months. Bert and Joan retreated to Lancaster for the worst of the weather and came back in March when the gales dropped. I came along in August, born in the lee of the white cutter's lodge.

My father recalled on many occasions his two years with my mother. She was not like the other female labourers, he said. She tended to the slight side whereas they were usually large, cumbersome creatures. When I was of an age to understand — six, if I remember correctly, Bert told me that my mother had lovely breasts. Many times after they had parted and lost touch for ever, those lovely breasts had got my father into trouble. He would put them on every female figure he ever carved; the Virgin, Mary Magdalene, apostles' mothers, Herod's daughter, any one at all. The prior of the black Augustinian canons at Lanercost made a complaint about this repetition and Bert was forced to do them again. But they turned out just the same, only a fraction smaller. When Bert taught me how to do breasts they were, of course, based on those that had suckled me. This was, all at once, a satisfying, nostalgic and disturbing lesson.

I did visit Cockersands once again during my early years. Bert was working on the priory church in Lancaster and he sent me down to Kirkham with a cart to pick up some stone from a ruin. The shortest route was by Garstang, Dad's old birth-place, but that road was menaced by border raiders who had been with us all summer. So I was advised to go by the coast road and cross the Wyre near Towbrick. My progress was slow, the horse being an old nag whose strength I had to save for the more arduous return journey loaded up with stone. As I was fording the Conder not far south of Lancaster I saw sheep carcasses floating in the river, all ineptly and wastefully butchered. The old horse shied away from the carrying current, nosing the air with flared nostrils. So I went westwards instead of southwards until I reached the sands at Cockerham. Along my route I encountered many signs of old and new slaughters for this area had been devastated annually. It was a miracle to me that the crops still grew and people remained. Their resilience was strangely obstinate, but then I remembered the determination of my own people who could not remain in their homeland, as these farmers had, but had clung on to life after massacre, plunder and rapine had conspired to eliminate them. All their crops had to be of thought.

As I rode in the cart towards the lonely monastery in its field by the sea where I was born I was able to see it from a great distance, the sands being so flat and the air dry and clear. It was a dark pile, occupied by a few unhappy men, outcasts, fifth and sixth sons, half-idiots, men gathered together to praise God for their infirmities. My father scoffed at them as he scoffed at all Christians. He made their houses for them, he constructed their castles and churches, their spires, towers, mountains of craft — he prostituted his skill (and it was born in prostitution) — only in order to live. Bert would never be allowed to build his own church for his own faith. As the old nag plodded over the wet sands towards my engendering and my birth I thought about my father back in Lancaster with the ill-tempered prior; a man notorious for his haughtiness and insolence. My father had to take all his abuse then go back to the work-place and make something beautiful for a Cretin. This was the skill he had brought me up in — praising one god while appearing to praise another, the secret worshipper of a separate truth who must live his life according to the laws of an alien creed and keep his own beliefs quiet. Without this pragmatism any one of our faith would be dead.

This appeared to trouble me differently than it did my father. He was a man of perpetual rage. While I pondered about all the inner agonies of our craft, how we could never be ourselves while serving our main customer, the church, Bert did not argue or struggle in his mind. All his frustration came out in his work, in his furious battering at the stone, in his hacking at the dead, dangerous world. Around me he had built this gloomy, windswept mausoleum in sight of a grey sea.

"Built to last," he always said about his work. "Even the Devil won't knock that down." As I looked across the fields at the abbey I knew why. As far as Bert was concerned everything he built belonged to the Devil who would never destroy his own works.

If I say I was brought up without a mother then I would be giving a wrong impression; for I had mothers, many of them, but none lasted long.

It was my father's habit to find a woman on each site where he worked; not in the town or village nearby, but from amongst the female labourers. So they were always mates as well as lovers; not that I came across very much love being lost between them.

None of them could stand living with my father for very long (Bert found it difficult to live with himself, never mind another), and the women either moved on or went to more congenial men, if one could be found in a company of builders.

In my memory there is a blurred, composite face which has arisen as a design emerges from countless scratchings on the tracing-floor: it is my mother, this vague, indistinct female; an overlaid image of gentle outline. She has sad, dark-ringed eyes from much imposition — Sarah's slant-eyes, Margaret whose eyes dipped at the corners, Jane whose eyes were red-fringed slits in a broad ox-head of rusty hair — so many of them, strong, bad-mouthed women who smelt of earth, all going to make up my mother in my mind.

None of them could tie my father down let alone understand him, because they had no access to his inner life. As a white cutter goes from place to place seeking work he takes his world with him, and it is a secret world. He must avoid entanglements when he can, keep his encumbrances down to a minimum, and be wary of sharing his confidences with outsiders. These are severe restrictions to a man who loves easily, as did my father, and, I believe, he would have attempted chastity as a means of reducing the hardship on his heart, if he had been capable.

Which he was not.

To me this aspect of an itinerant white cutter's life has always been a great sadness for I am like my father but more so: I find much joy in women and I consider them to be closer to our craft in spirit and shape than we men. They are our source of energy and inspiration but we must keep them out of the sanctum or they will destroy it for inner reasons of their own.

Ah, women! If my mother had been a mason and I had come into this world from a male inspiration matched with a female incarnation, what a creature I might have been. I could have transformed the art of building instead of merely tinkering with it. As Prince Daniel Romanovich said to me in Moscow many years ago, "Hedric, there is a woman in you somewhere. You have a dome-shaped soul." Well, what the old fellow was saying, I suppose, was that I always yearned to bend the vertical. And have bent it, by god!

But my education was Bert. Though I am drawn to ferret out as much influence of the female as I can in my make-up, I have to return to my dad for the moulding. I was part of his tool-kit. In fact he carried me as a baby in his leather bag with the chisels chinking under my bum. Wherever he went, I went. If he was working in a high tower, I was tethered somewhere at the foot of it. If he was barrowing stone, I was in the barrow with it. When the winches hauled up a canvas bucket of cement, I was in the bucket. Bert had taken a decision long ago. If I was to be taken on as his inheritor, as his future, as his eternal promise in an evil world, I would be kept as close to him as his own self. Not that this attitude of his did not bring perils of its own. I have already mentioned the scars accrued during my three great pilgrimages, and there were broken bones in plenty as well, but beneath those scars and breaks there are older ones of childhood, of tumbles, treadings and trappings when Bert forgot where he had left me or assumed that I had more nimbleness than I was gifted with: death, he told me, had sometimes come close. That may be why now, in my prime when I am even closer, it does not frighten me. Here, on this earth, I was left by Bert. I might just as well be still in his tool-bag for all the distance I have got from him.

II

No one should be incredulous when I recount my life from the moment of my birth. It is not that I am claiming a total grip on my personal history, nor an ability to reassemble all the responses of my senses from that earliest of moments; but what I can maintain is that I was aware of the forces acting upon me. Is it surprising that a man who has spent his life fashioning matter into the fulfilled shapes of pure spirit should be able to remember the fashioning that made him? Especially if that buffeting, that crude carving was at a time most tender and vulnerable? For being a mason is only that story — a man at the focus of forces that hold this world captive as it grinds on. I was who I am now — the son of a son of a son who was a mason, going right back to the Romans and further, so Bert said. We never had the wit to do anything else, he alleged. One day someone put one stone on top of another — probably to hang himself.

Those very early days in my life were deeply rooted in Adam's Dust. Although I had life, I was most like that which has ruled my career ever since — a thing of grit, grain and crystals. In my mother's arms I was a stone being carried to the foundations to be built on but, pause here, first there was a father to shape me. Bert called me fond names from his trade — what else would he lay tongue to? — and so I was his *bosol*, his *orbilon*, his lile *ashlar*, and when I was cleaned off at both ends, his fine *parpent*. Could these names mean anything to an unformed infant? No, perhaps, but when he handled me as if I were a composite part of a column or a block of stone smoothed off at two ends, ah, that was teaching! That was the beginning of my education. Touch and usage are everything to the very young.

In my arguments with my father over the craft at later dates I would quote these times to him, even some of his actual words and phrases. This irritated him a good deal as it made him blame himself for seducing me into the business, the cruel business, he called it, of white cutting. He often claimed that his ambition for me was that I should become a carpenter, for wood is softer, he would say, and you can work faster.

Not that this little jelly was completely uncritical of the world that he had been born into. The divine spark that I was able to infuse into so many structures over the face of Christendom later on kept my eyes open and my sense of perfection alert from the very beginning.

What was I doing here in a land where it never stopped raining; where a winter-stabled horse grew moss on its back; where cloth, leather, wood and stone were always damp and the only real warmth was within? My father always contested these memories, claiming that I had made them up in retrospect. He had no recall of such a wet world. In those days, he said, the summers were better, the winters whiter, the springs more sudden. He was wrong. They were days of mud and rain until a day three weeks after my third birthday. I can remember that milestone of a morning very clearly as it ushered in a decade of good weather. But I must deal with this first period of my existence — the Damp Days when the seasons of England congealed around a windy, wet March that went on for ever repeating itself through all the months of the year: Christmas was Easter; Whitsun was All Saints. It was a time when I was like silt in water, swirled by my father's soul-currents, seeing through his vision within this cloudy incompleteness. Yet I grew and grew, struggling out of one bog into another.

During those first three years I could not speak or write, or express myself except through simple smiling or crying: but I knew the conditions we lived under. Bert raged on, cursing our existence and we traipsed from site to site in the north: I heard him wish aloud for death as an end to it all, but in his luggage was another mind — me — and I was dreaming of beginnings. Hungry? I was, often. Battered by the jolting of the horse when we had one, I was. Cold when the blankets fell open and he was too deep in misery to notice or hear my cries, wet when the rain got through the string-pulled neck of the bag and streamed down my face, pooling in my own mess for I was not bag-trained till five (a source of shame to me and indignation to Bert). But neglected? Never. I can say in all truth that when Bert was with the world, not in love, despair or drink or furiously hollowing out a gullet for a gargoyle, I was uppermost amongst his concerns.

However, he was not equipped to give me comfort. That comes from women. Warmth and care of that kind no man can manage, no matter how hard he tries. As my tender frame endured the denial of the in-built needs of babies it was my mind that took up the challenge.

Bert's idea of what an infant needed to survive was simply an extended form of his own requirements — after all, I was Bert as far as Bert was concerned — a new start, a quintessence, but, in the sporadic dullness afflicting his intelligence as he dived in and out of his black moods, he failed to remember that I was only as strong as the strength put into me in the form of nourishment. Once he had split up with my natural mother he forgot the most essential function she fulfilled — providing me with milk. Bert assumed that I was weaned simply because Joan was no longer there.

Within the first fortnight of my removal from Joan's breast I nearly died. Bert kept stuffing various bits of solid food into my mouth, often straight out of his own after he had chewed it up for me: I remember lots of rabbit, old brown-bruised apples and stale bread he had softened up for me. This diet and the continuous shaking I endured as we travelled along put me into a bad fever.

Bert had received a recommendation from the prior of Cockersands to work at another Praemonstratensian house high up on Shap in Westmorland. It was an isolated, dreary place which needed a zig-zag journey to reach it, forcing us to dodge in and out of the Lune Valley to keep away from the Scots and the criminals who had found a wild haven far away from the king's justice.

At the height of my fever we were caught in a freezing gale just south of Penrith. Bert begged shelter with an old woman who had a hut she had built in a cleft of rocks near the river. The crone was near-mad but when she nosed my breath and told Bert that if I did not get milk I would die he was forced to believe her. She carried the marks of many children and men on her and if there was one thing left in the world that she knew anything about, it was nursing babies. However, she had no milk to offer — no cow's, sheep's, goat's or even mare's. The only source of milk she knew of in this wild district, so she told Bert, was a vixen raising cubs in a wood on the other side of the river.

Bert absented himself from the hut overnight, in the worst of the gale, and I was left with the crone who could not stop tittering. In the morning I was wakened by a thin, high scream. Looking up I saw Bert framed in the entrance, a red, writhing scarf round his neck and five cubs nipping at his heels. I will not attempt to describe fox-milk to you, nor the problems that accompany nuzzling an angry vixen, but merely announce that it was there and then I decided I was weaned and would never depend upon milk again. Unfortunately I could not communicate this decision to Bert because I was, as yet, unable to speak.

When we reached the abbey at Shap in its cauldron of wind and water by the River Lowther, my father asked the grim canons for cow's milk for me, begging them to save my young life. I have a clear recollection of the kitchen with its sweating walls, the fire of slow-burning wood surrounded by the brutish, gleaming features of the canons, the stench of their fouled robes, as I spat and vomited out the cow's milk they were ladling down my throat. Eventually they used a funnel normally employed on orphaned calves and I was held down on the table and drenched, but no matter how much they poured down they could not get past my gullet. That night Bert was allowed to sleep by the fire with me in his arms while the canons included me in their prayers for they thought I would die. Such an obstinate child, they murmured, he would have made a religious, once broken. Many were of that temper themselves, sold into Christian slavery by exhausted parents. At breakfast they came to bury me, fresh from mass, spring flowers in their grimy fists, in holiday mood for it was seldom that anyone so young died amongst them. But I had frustrated their midnight fantasies and I was not ready. As my father had slept I had shinned down his leg and fed myself by licking the fat-encrusted spits and gnawing a hole in the barley sack with my gums. I suppose a rat took the blame.

I never touched milk again although it took my father several months to realise I had taken a decision which anticipated that which nature would have taken for me in the normal order of things. I would have liked some response from him, some amazement or admiration. Whoever our ancestors had been I was sure that there had never been a child such as I. When he dandled me before bed-time, whether it were in camp by some savage, freezing beck, or in shelter and warmth, I would look into his eyes to find some recognition. "My son," I wanted him to whisper, "you are a prodigy." But he never did, even when my prodigiousness was obvious to everyone. Such is the abyss between one soul and another, seldom bridged except by rainbows of promise. Bert could not delve into my decisions because he thought I was only a babe. Yet he spent his working life creating images of a babe who exceeded all imagination, who conquered the West. He could believe it of Mary's son but not of me. To him I was just a helpless baby, a little animal not yet fit to take its place in a terrible world. To myself I was already an adjunct of Bert's soul, a room which his spirit strolled through sometimes to tell its secrets. Not that I could respond with speech; that was a barrier that I lusted to break through every time he talked to me as if I were his equal: "Hedric," he'd say, "I've had a bad time of it. The mortar wouldn't set. I've snapped my best chisel in half. Again I've been doing Moses when it should have been Abraham. My vine leaves looked like cabbage. I must leave this business. If I had any sense I'd give up and despair!" Then I would put my little arms round his neck and cover his face with kisses, belching and farting as my stomach churned over the sour bread and thin ale he'd given me for dinner, jumping up and down on his lap as I waited desperately for the first words to come through to comfort him with.

The trouble was my father would say anything to me — dark, dangerous things that he would never have shared if he had known how I had developed so precociously. Some of them were so miserable and demented with unhappiness that I would flop down between his knees and howl. Then he would do the worst thing possible: he would pretend that I had understood and laugh it off. In this way I became truly and falsely an extension of him — his minor self and his fool. The habit of opening himself right up to me never left him. At the point where I was putting one word after another (and I was a latecomer in that direction) my father was too far gone in our intimacy to draw back and be more reserved.

What a man will say to a child he has engendered when there is no one else listening is not only luminous with truth but it is also desolating: if the child is his own responsibility, a burden for life, the fruit of a despairing fling after warmth, later regretted, then the man will tell all. He has nothing to lose. It is only a smaller version of himself that he is talking to: a version that has the advantages of innocence and unpollutedness. Not many men would enjoy the thought that any such one-sided conversations should be recorded, but such is the power of my memory in any detail to do with my beloved father, that I am able to reproduce his lonely addresses to me verbatim. Within my adventures have occurred moments — indeed periods, such as when I have been in prison or captivity — when these excruciating and honest soliloquies (or so he imagined them to

18

be) have come in very useful in terms of keeping my sanity and strength.

Now is the opportunity for me to describe my father's voice as it carries the painful wisdom of his talks to me in my memory. It was soft and gentle, a round tone that was almost indolent but audible in it, deep down somewhere, was the cat-whine which could double him up with anger, make him hiss with fear, snarl with derision. He could lull me almost to sleep during his immense confessions — which sometimes lasted for two days and two nights without either of us shutting an eye — and then pounce on me with an outburst of grief which could not be consoled by one so young and speechless. Then the cosiness fled, the music was stilled and he stared at me with his screwed-up, tortured face of the lust-racked, god-forsaken.

"Do you expect me to endure this life much longer? Only for you, you ape! You thief! Yes, to frustrate you! To thwart you! What, you will push things on? Whittle out a new world from this rotten stuff? All I pass on to you is your place on the arch of suffering. Do you want it? You will not flower any better than I have. Chances are that your achievements will be less than mine as things go from bad to worse in this accursed land. No Creator imagined that even a pauper's hovel might be erected in England. Why else will nothing ever dry out, or the land be properly drained? Everywhere we want to build is the home of the willow. England? A sponge! We build on a swamp, son. Our work floats on a lump of sedge and mud fit only for toads. That's it, shake your head and suck your thumb, you little leech!"

Many times I thought he would strike me. He would prowl around my crib — whatever it was, a box, the bag, his upturned saddle — and scream out, suddenly lunging at me with his fist or boot. But when his need for violence was great and not to be denied he always turned it on himself, beating at his head and thighs with all the ferocity I had seen him apply to his stonework. My defence was always to laugh which drove him into even worse frenzies that became so extreme his body would protest and shut him down with a fainting fit. Oh, the recriminations when he came round! Why do I do this to myself? What is the matter with me? When will I find peace in this world? A new sound was in his voice then, one I loved and learnt from, one that has guided much of my philosophy.

So that is how he raised me in the green gloom of the Damp Days — stumbling from crisis to crisis, always asking himself why he had

19

taken on the task. He could not admit I was the only part of the future that attracted him. His own work would never really emerge from the toils of his mad melancholy — if the King had made him the *magistro cementariorum regis* for all his building works it would not have made my father happy. His only true occupation, once the decision was taken to keep me, was the creation of a freemason who would eclipse all others. Bert could never admit this was his intention. Indeed, he could not own up to the desire that I should be a better mason than he was (which didn't take much)! It was as if a generative, noble power had started up in his spirit without his knowing — an altruism that offended him in his bad moments and astonished him in his good. In all our years together he never once told me it was his goal to see me wear the garland. As things turned out he would have been more inclined to snatch it from my brows and then regret the impulse. Yet I was his model far more so than he mine. Looking at each other is a deep part of the inner mason's craft.

We were at Monkwearmouth up in Duhram with the black Benedictines and Bert had entered into a contract for a *Massacre of the Innocents*. Bert's imagination being slow and sluggish, I had to be every Innocent, sitting, lying, being skewered, even standing! (I could barely toddle.) The abbot seemed to approve of this uniformity — the souls of all children are equally pure, he told Bert, the ignoramus. He? Uniform? After living with Bert for eighteen months? Oh, I knew shades and passions, I knew moods and migraines. And I knew bad work when I saw it. When I fidgeted, yawned or cried Bert would place me firmly back into the pose of the suffering infant he required and started battering away, muttering to himself. And when he was carving the hands of the soldiers as they grasped their swords, it was his own hands he copied from. Towards the end of the contract I noticed that one of the soldiers had my nose: a sign of things to come, a token of his acknowledgement of my superiority, and his fear of me.

III

As I said, the weather changed. It was as if we had begun to live in
another country. The Damp Days drifted away into history un-
mourned, leaving behind a trail of architectural disasters requiring
repairs and remedial work for years. As the land dried out it altered its
levels and consistency and foundations shrank: churches that had been
well socketed into wet ground were being strangled below the surface
as stones shifted. Many of these contortions brought my father
running from his hideaways and sulking-corners, me at his side,
wide-eyed as I bent my brain to understand how good news became
bad news then good news again — for it was the good weather that
ruined the monasteries and made the white cutters prosperous again,
for a while.

Much of the work Bert was given should have been done by other
masons who had defaulted on contracts requiring them to restore any
damage due to subsidence or tilting. These men fled the kingdom to
Scotland, Ireland or France in order to escape these penalties and so the
number of people employed in the trade was reduced and the skilled
white cutter became much in demand. Bert's occasional hostility to
the situation arose from the fact that he was for ever sorting out other
men's *deficient creations*. This was a touchstone he used with the monks
and priests whenever he could because he thought that it inflamed
their doubt.

Creation was a word they reserved for the Almighty. Bert used it in
connection with his equals, his brother masons, and therefore,
himself. The defects he found in buildings were the defects he had
discovered in Christianity: the points of tension were not balanced,
the stresses and thrusts were wrongly aligned, bad, cheap materials
had been employed, and there was no overall, coherent plan. Yet
within the failure of that faith was an older, more resilient and
satisfying creed. As Bert mended the crippled abbeys and outbuild-·
ings and set them right he invested them with his own truth much as a
doctor takes over part of a patient's existence if he effects a cure.

Bert's delight in this type of work was lessened when he had to repair and correct structures he had raised himself. Here, then, was a disappointment for me: Bert was a short-term thinker, a man whose struggle for self-improvement would always be limited to one phase. Not being able to return to one's failures and create success out of their rubble means a restricted entry into the higher levels of achievement.

As I grew up this lack of self-criticism in my father pained me considerably. He was too ready to disparage the work of his fellows without applying his standards to himself. No mason builds alone. His creations are always part of a joint effort and his work must always harmonise with that of his colleagues who are alongside him. Displays of outlandish individual expression are destructive as they wreck the impression of inspired togetherness a great piece of architecture depends upon for its effect. It must feel as though a whole community had picked up its tools and talents and raised the thing, not one wayward mind in pursuit of self-glorification. But I run ahead of myself. These are thoughts from a later stage in my life when my father was coming under stricter examination from me.

Not long after my sixth birthday — the third of April, feast of Saints Burgundofara, Pancras of Taormina and Richard of Chichester and other Christian charlatans — Bert took me over to Yorkshire where we spent the summer working at Kirlees, a convent of Cistercian nuns. The Cistercians were not a popular order with the white cutters because they tended to train up their own masons and do their own building work, favouring a more austere style that required less decoration and, therefore, less really skilled freestone carving. The abbess of Kirlees had asked for help from the Cistercians at Jervaulx and a couple of brothers who had been trained up as masons had gone over to the convent and caused trouble amongst the nuns. Believing that secular outsiders with no privileges from within the order might be a safer bet, the abbess had made contact with Bert through the Cistercians at Holme Cultram in Cumberland who knew of Bert via the Black Augustinian canons of Carlisle for whom he had done some major reconstruction work on a squeezed transept arch.

Bert did not like the Cistercians, nor did he like working in convents but the chance to rehabilitate a slumped retro-choir beneath an elongated barrel vault was too much for him. As an intellectual problem it had all the appeal of arguing with the Almighty: put one foot wrong and all would be lost. The female Cistercian architect —

"some stupid tart who could dream a bit", Bert had growled when he first saw the building and its condition — had tried to construct a roomy, airy space behind the altar that could be used for what the women at Kirlees called "wandering prayer". People locked away from the world come up with some odd ideas and they develop strangely within their own isolations. These nuns lived in a wooded valley full of huge wild pigs and the women had never been able to go out much for fear of them. Over the years they had tried to incorporate the woods, and the beauties of the same, into their convent rather than attack the question of the pigs or bring in huntsmen to clear them out. So the retro-choir was full of slender pillars resembling young ash trees and the abbess had allowed discreet lines of foliage to be sketched around the bases and the capitals, even twisting around the full length of the pillars; a heresy of over-adornment to the ascetic Cistercians. Instead of walks in the woods with their hearts full of desire for their common husband, Christ, amongst the foxgloves, the nuns wandered in and out of the pillars of the retro-choir running their fingers over the stone foliage, seeing colour where there was none, hearing blackbirds where none flew, and feeling caresses from the window-draughts. For the earth-tremor that shook the north in February 1245 to have disturbed this pathetic pretence for these women and brought their arboreal phantasm close to destruction was a cruel return to reality for them. The abbess was faced with a female dementia: the nuns refused to curtail their "wandering prayers" in the retro-choir, even with the pillars under threat of breaking as the thrust of the vault pushed them outward. Even when it was reported that the same earth-tremor had caused all the wild pigs to move out of the valley on to more open ground to the east, the nuns refused to switch from the artificial wood to the real one that had now become safer for them. They were addicted to their semblances and the stone wood of Kirlees was growing in importance for them as fast as the green wood was growing in nature. It was their trysting-place, their bank of love, barren though it was.

If Bert had been abnormally honest with himself, and the abbess, he would have admitted that it was this horrifying weakness of soul that attracted him to this task. The Christian confusion between the art of imagination and the art of God irritated him. As we all know, the Spirit has no imagination, it only has power to do anything it wishes — and those wishes do not come from imagination but from omnipotency. It is only Man who has imagination and that is because he needs it. How else will he transform the material world into a reflection of the Spirit? How else will he finish the Spirit's work for it? Nevertheless, what Man achieves will only be such a reflection of light, not the truth. We masons have been charged with this enterprise — to make the inanimate pay homage to the Spirit in shape, and from shape essence and substance may follow.

The abbess was a silly woman. Her only strength was that she had not been taken in by the "wandering prayer" cult, mainly because she had kept herself at some remove from the other nuns by dint of her position and a natural inclination towards an idle solitude. Be this as it may, it was certainly her responsibility to clear the nuns out of the retro-choir so Bert could start work on the repairs. Instead she left it to him and went on a visit to a sister convent in Lincolnshire. As Bert said at the time, the women had virtually appointed him as her deputy, requiring him — a simple craftsman — to solve the greatest problem of her administration.

A bachelor man with a six-year old son is left in charge of a house full of warped women. All he has to do is drive them out of their twisted tabernacle, knock half of it down, rebuild it, then deliver their illusion back intact — his own intactness, and that of a defenceless (though interested) juvenile, is of no consequence. I should be asking for danger-money, Bert said as he watched the abbess ride out of the gate into the pig-free wood and away to the south.

Our room was in the convent guest-quarters, a commodious building built right on the bank of the river. The Cistercians always have large accommodation for visitors and encourage the wealthy and powerful to stay in order to obtain bequests and gifts from them; the Benedictine policy of amassing power at court and using political influence being alien to their ways. When we arrived at Kirlees we found that the "wandering prayer" cult had attracted a host of curious nobles and scholars who remained in residence when the abbess left the convent to the government of my father. While they occupied whole suites of rooms and had preference in the kitchens we lived in a damp cell near the point where the main sewer discharged into the river. Once this gaggle of onlookers became aware of Bert's situation they followed us around like an audience at a street-play. They were amused at the thought of this unkempt, angry commoner being left in charge of a band of their class's cast-off daughters, half-mad with rancid loneliness and lusts that should have been long abandoned. All their own indulgences and despairs, their corrupt feelings, were in the slow dance of the nuns under the dangerous roof of the retro-choir.

For two days Bert got nowhere. He could not make a start in the retro-choir because it was always needed for the "wandering prayer" and the crowd of spectators was permanently encamped in it, having food and drink brought over to them from the refectory.

Bert was undaunted. He had only contempt for the audience and pity for the players. Possessing a craftiness that was not always limited to his trade, he took me into the abbey church with him on the third day. It was just after nine and the nuns were gliding about between the pillars. The guests were already crowded around the entrances to the space, gently applauding the early dances for the women had now devised steps and figures to their "wandering prayer" between the buckling columns and they hummed and sang tunes to these dances which sounded distinctly secular. I was enjoying the spectacle, and the singing, which was very sweet, when Bert suddenly hissed into my ear:

"Cry!"

I looked at him enquiringly and received a savage pinch on my arm that made me shout with pain.

"Go on, cry!"

As soon as the women heard me bawling they stopped their "wandering prayers" and came over to where I was standing. Maternal concern shone in their mad, vague faces. Bert hovered on the edge of the cluster they made around me, urging me with his eyes and leaping eyebrows to put more into it; so I howled, I yelled!

One crowd is drawn to another. If the actors in the play start watching a play themselves, the audience stop watching them and watch the play within the play. They get sucked into the deceit inside the deceit. Soon all the gawping nobles, scholars and idle ecclesiastics in the crowd were gathered round the nuns who were gathered round me — and I was now shrieking as if under torture.

The sound of a child in distress was designed by the Good Spirit to pierce any female heart. No woman can resist it. Those nuns cradled my head on their bosoms, they clucked, they stroked, they sighed, but I refused to be quiet. Bert was still there, now standing on a tomb and glaring down at me, whirling his arms around at me to signal that I should scream even louder. As I increased the devilish noise I was

25

making and the nuns worked frantically to soothe me, Bert disappeared from view. A moment later there was a tremendous crash and the air filled with dust. The nuns scurried from the retro-choir with me in their arms and the crowd followed them, bellowing with fear.

Bert appeared a minute later. He was covered with dust but beneath his beard I could see that he was smiling.

"We've got a partial collapse up on the east wall there. The rest is shaky but it can be shored up while we get working on it," he explained. "Truly, I am sorry if it puts you busy folk to any inconvenience."

The nobles demanded to know the cause of the collapse. Their lives had been in danger.

Bert called me to him. I ran over and stood by him, holding on to his leg. I could feel the crowbar he was holding under his coat.

"My guess is as good as yours. The place is insecure. But I have noticed that high-pitched sounds can unsettle a structure poised at too fine a point. It may have been the boy's crying. It may have been the singing of these good women. Whatever it was, she's down and no one must go in there until I say so."

Having given his orders Bert took me back to our quarters and left me there while he found timber to block off the entrances and exits to the retro-choir. The sightseers hung about then went off to pack their bags. One old nun came across to our room and found me sitting by the river. She stood over me, her robe billowing around my head.

"Are you all right now?" she asked.

"Yes, Mother," I replied respectfully. "I'm fine."

"Can you remember what was the matter?"

Without waiting for a reply she walked away towards the woods and shortly afterwards I heard her singing her "wandering prayer" with the blackbirds. Within the hour she was joined by all her sisters.

It did not stop raining for the whole of the next three months. During that period the cult of the "wandering prayer" at the convent of Kirlees died what might be called a natural death and we completed our work undisturbed.

IV

At Seaton-near-Bootle in Cumberland Bert fell in love with the wife of the Furness lodge's magistro and ran off with her to the Isle of Man. This action of his dominated the end of my sixth year on earth and most of my seventh. The husband, a very experienced and sagacious white cutter with the most genial temperament (before the event), turned into a vengeful pursuer, taking an oath at the altar-rail of the Gilbertine convent of Old Malton that he would behead my father and mortar his bonce into a jakes' wall once he had caught him. The woman was certainly not worth it, though she did have a gloomy Iberian beauty, all hair and sulkiness. Compared to the tough bawds of the building-sites who most often shared my father's bed, Romana was, indeed, a flower. On the sheep ship we voyaged in my lady was sick almost to death. Once you have seen a dark beauty go green and long black hair encrusted with vomit then you tend to prefer the native fair. This preference of mine did not always apply, though every dark woman whom I have loved (and I have adored many, many, some to the point of sublime distraction, and some of these have been as black as jet from tip to toe) has, at some time in our passion, turned into Romana and haunted me from that gale-tossed cockleshell we sailed in from Ravenglass to Poolvash Bay. It was, I think, the way my father cared for her, nursed her in the most womanly manner, holding her as he had never been able to hold me, without awareness, without thought. Whenever I was in his arms he knew he was holding someone who could not be contained or consumed — an exploding future, if you will; with Romana it was different. She was limited to their mutual madness. It had to end and they both knew it but chose not to care until the time made itself plain.

Our arrival in Poolvash Bay was fraught with peril. A gale was blowing from the south, an unusual direction for hard weather in this sea. The effect was to funnel the tempest between both horns of the bay and drive the waves right up the shallow beach to a height of thirty feet or more. The master of our ship was a fool (and a Manxman, does

27

it need to be said?): he assured us that it was common practice amongst the sailors of this island to ride the crests of these huge waves which could tenderly lower the vessel on to the shore once their strength was spent: "like a mum wi' her bairn". To all of us within this scene of wildness it was obvious that such a scheme would never work so the farmers on board immediately started throwing their sheep over the side thinking that they would rather give them a chance of survival in the raging sea.

I do believe that my father would have followed their example except that neither I nor Romana could swim: when I say that I could not then that is an assumption, for, like the sheep, I may have been capable of instinctively reacting to the danger and learning fast — instantaneously, as I hit the water — but not that sack of sorrows, Romana. She had surrendered herself to terror and hung around my father's neck begging him to save her life. It was impossible for him to take any other action than to remain on board and submit to the master's navigational lunacy. As the farmers followed their sheep over the side — all to perish — Bert lashed us both to the mast, his tool-bag tied round my ankles, then put his long arms around us, clasped his hands and prayed to the Good Spirit. A massive breaker hit us and we shot forward like a suicidal seal.

It is part of my fearless nature that I never close my eyes at times of threat. When I was about to be executed in Pferrungsamen in . . . when was it? '72? I refused the blindfold and actually looked the headsman right in the eye. Similarly, as we bounded towards the shore, I gazed over Bert's shoulder at the fantastic sea, admiring the glassy curves and arabesques, the sweep of its arches and the crazed entablatures of foam. It would be dishonest of me not to admit that there are fine buildings studded along the lengths of my pilgrimages which owe their inspiration and impetus to the demented waters of Poolvash Bay.

Our craft moved at such speed as it spanned the abysses between the waves, at times shot through the air, hawsers whistling, the sails flapping like wings. The Good Spirit must have had a hand on the rudder — ostensibly under the control of the mad Manxman, a man not close to the divine judging by his subsequent behaviour in the alehouse. When the final wave had us high on its back and was heading for the hard, rocky, shore, suddenly a narrow river estuary appeared beneath us, a channel no wider than twenty yards, and our hull slid

28

steeply down into it as if we were a settling gull.

The master claimed this to be a form of landing he was forced to make more often than not, the Irish Sea being the brute that it is. To me, even as a credulous child of five, that smacked of sheer braggadocio.

Most buildings are raised on the ashes of their predecessors: even the very stones may be the same, refashioned to suit another style, another age. Temples spring from the destruction of superannuated shrines and chapels, often of the same faith that has blossomed or become bloated. Like the flower and the tree, it is decay that sets architecture on, nourishes it and forces the new forms upwards.

This is true of all civilisations, ancient and modern, except that of the Erse-speaking people. If they build it must be from nothing and in their native stone — granite.

After a month in which we had to shiver in sheepfolds and beg our bread, my father gained access to the chief who governed the south of the island. He lived in a very small fort at Ballinardredd. It was small because the builders had become exhausted with working the local granite and had given up, their tools broken and blunted, their spirits defeated by this difficult, formidable stone. The Lord Lambfell Goby Corrage — for that was his name — ordered them to scale down their plans to a more modest expression of his greatness, paid them a tenth of their contract — in diseased sheep — then kicked them off the island.

This was the man whom my father faced a week before Christmas in '46, me on one side and Romana on the other. It was a pitiable sight, I should think, but it failed to move Lord Lambfell.

The chief had a blind hatred of all things English. This could be attributed to the frequent raids that were made by the English on the Isle of Man in retribution for the raids that the Manx made upon the coasts of England, but balance and fairness were not dominant qualities in his lordship's mind. Within his system of logic it was not only his function but also his duty to be a pirate. That was the tradition that he had been brought up in. In order to follow it he was forced to live an insecure existence in an inhospitable environment and dwell in a small house.

"I want a palace, not here but up on higher ground, and it must also serve as a monastery, a church, a prison, fort and farmhouse and have

29

accommodation for six hundred warriors," he said, using the interpreter, for Manx lords have no English as a point of honour. "I'll offer you one hundred marks in silver, and it must be finished by the end of the October apples in two years' time."

Bert refused immediately. What Lord Lambfell was asking for was a Herculean task that would take two hundred white cutters, layers, setters, carpenters, smiths, plumbers and labourers five years to complete in granite. The cost would be nearer to two thousand marks if prices remained stable (which they didn't on the Isle of Man as it had a robbery economy).

"Then you'll go to prison, having built it for me first — unpaid," Lord Lambfell replied with a grim smile. "You have no choice. But I'll tell you what. Let's leave the final price to be further reckoned. I'll pay you fivepence a day to do what you can. All my warriors will help you. I'll get some captives from . . . well, Wales will do, it's nearest . . . and we'll see how we go along."

Bert refused again, even though it was obvious that he needed to buy time. I have faced up to many potentates who had minds as childish and impractical as Lord Lambfell, who wanted the best of my genius for next to nothing. My strategy has always been to appear to agree then start work, chipping away at their thick heads as I went forward with the structures and all the real problems. In this way I have found one can eventually win the right price. But Bert would not compromise.

We were stuck in a sea-cave at Geinnagh Doo to teach Bert the wisdom of coming to terms. The tide came into the cave twice daily and we were forced on to a narrow ledge at the back until the sea ebbed. All we had to eat was mussels. The only fresh water dripped from the roof. After a fortnight of this Romana was half-dead, too sick even to complain, certainly too sick to be made love to, and I was having hallucinations. Bert would have held out but one of the guards begged him to surrender to Lord Lambfell's will. He was an English lad who had been captured during a raid on the Wirral when he was only seven years old. He had been brought up as a Manxman and spoke Erse but enough of his mother tongue had survived in his memory and he delighted to speak it as an alternative to that throat-clearing the Manx call a language.

"You have to understand his lordship and the way he works," the guard explained during one low tide, sharing his handful of barley-bread with us. "He never means what he says. All is flux with him. He aspires to the kingship of Man but he knows, in his heart, that there is no true way to it. It will emerge, perhaps, like a path through a forest. So he must flounder. On the raids we flounder. We flounder in estuaries, in marshes. We flounder around the countryside looking for houses, monasteries, to rob. Most of the time we don't find anything. Amongst the men Lord Lambfell's raiding-season is known as flounder-time. He is floundering with you, trying it on, casting about. He knows what he has asked of you cannot be done: but what he can't stand is that you have said so and won't flounder along with him a while."

I can see that gaunt, flaxen-headed youth's face now, his sad eyes hooded in the light of the driftwood fire, his long hands laid in repose on the helve of his axe. In all my experience of this world I have never had a better analysis of high statecraft put before me.

Bert sent a message to Lord Lambfell that he was ready to start work — on one condition: that his woman should receive the attention of the best doctors in the Isle of Man. This was granted and Romana was dead within a week.

Thus far I have refrained from giving a physical description of his lordship as it provides me with a problem of conscience. I have no wish to praise such a person: in fact I believe that it is folly to laud the wicked and witless in any aspect of their beings. However, as a detail of record, and interest, perhaps, I have to put it down somewhere that Lord Lambfell was the handsomest man I have ever seen. Not that I was immediately aware of this as his lordship was well covered with hair and beard during our first interview with him but when he appeared at the site chosen for his new five-pence-a-day city in the hills to discuss the plans with my father, he was clean-shaven and shorn.

Lithe and short in stature — barely making five feet — he had that intense attractiveness which carnivores have when they are in their prime: their eyes are the focus of strange laughter-lines around the brows; their nostrils flare and flutter with life; their teeth are statues of death that glitter with death's dreams. Behind it all there is the lively guile of the hunter but in the space beyond, where the thinking mind is housed, there is a vacant lot. In all his vitality and nimbleness, this lord was as stupid as a lion.

I can see him now as he pored over Bert's diagrams in the mud on the hillside, his beautiful forehead knotted as he tried to follow the basic ground plan. He had chosen a westward-facing situation for his capital at a place called Cronk ny Frey Lháa. Granite quarries were close by. The prevailing wind would howl straight through all apertures: (the Manx adore draughts, it gives them the impression that they are moving intellectually). Niarbyl Bay was in full sight of the watchtowers that Bert would build to a height of at least sixty feet to give the alarm when the English came streaming over the sea to exact revenge for Lord Lambfell's floundering. Was it any wonder that my father wore a permanently bemused expression that New Year? He was in the middle of a nightmare. Lord Lambfell made things worse by starting to like Bert. He moved us into his fort at Ballinardredd, gave Bert an Irish slave-woman from Donegal, and began to spoil me: all this before a single block of granite had been laid.

Whether I like someone or not has always been more important to me than whether someone likes me — or not, as the case may be. Once this Manx lord had taken us into his heart we found that life was much easier, provided that we never thought of the future. Bert insisted I should encourage Lord Lambfell in his attentions towards me, I should play tag with him, cup-and-ball, anything that he wanted. Lord Lambfell was without children, a failure attributable to him alone as he was randomly promiscuous amongst the island's womenfolk. He yearned for a son. I was at an age when the man in my future was becoming visible, perhaps in the most appealing way it would ever present itself. I had all the outlines, the sketches of my potential but the power had not yet arrived. Lord Lambfell would have resented that power because it makes his kind look ludicrous.

I had several arguments with Bert at this time as I believed that he was hoping Lord Lambfell would adopt me. Bert denied this but I had worked it out for myself that should my adoption precede the inevitable failure of the new city at Cronk ny Frey Lháa Bert would stand a better chance of survival if I were, by then, already Lord Lambfell's son and heir. When I first raised these doubts Bert got so furious that he cuffed me — an unusual thing for him to do as he was always more bark than bite:

"You little prig! And here's me doing every damned thing to get us home." (Don't ask me where *home* was!) "I have to listen to this madman as if he had some sense. I have to accept his invitations, put up with this flea-bitten bitch in my bed," (an arduous imposition I can assure you; Donegal Orla was twice the size of Bert) "and all you can do is suspect me of planning to unload you!" (Now the first cuff, a real ear-stinger.) "Here I am, in a hopeless position, no help from anyone, and my own son turns against me!" (Here the second cuff which caught me on the cheek and made my eyes water.) "How long d'you think it will be before he tumbles to the fact that we're playing for time? He's thick, all right, but not that thick! With the tools and labour I've got here it will take me a day to cut one block, another to transport it, there's no bloody cement, no carpenters, no glaziers. . . . D'you know what's keeping us alive? His dream!" (Here the third cuff right across my mouth which made my lips burn.) "Dreamers are killers. Ask anyone in this business."

I retracted. Donegal Orla — who had been watching the argument — nodded her huge red head with satisfaction and came across to boot me, believing that Bert had been showing her the way. I will not indicate what depths my meaner side can sink to by describing Bert's reaction to this liberty she took, and my enjoyment of her punishment. All I will say is that she wailed for a week and chewed her food with difficulty for the rest of her life.

January and February brought some of the worst weather that the storm-battered Manx could ever remember. Even they were subdued by the ceaseless fury of the northerly and westerly gales and the cold that poured over them from the east. It was impossible to go out. Cutting turf for the fires was a sentence of death as the poor slaves would freeze before they could get their blades into the ground. The work at Cronk ny Frey Lháa could not get started under these conditions and we spent our time in the fort huddled under skins and blankets, joining Lord Lambfell in his dream. My father had drawn up the plans for each part of the new city on sheep vellum and his lordship spent hours poring over them by the fire, asking questions, adding a section here, a room there, a new tower, an entrance, a garden. The dream swelled like a bladder as he blew into it. With each day the project became more and more impossible and Bert more committed to its construction.

One day in mid-January Bert was lying alongside Lambfell who had me on his back and was looking at the plans for the monastery. Bert had avoided asking too many questions about this area of the dream as it was the most unnecessary and the most costly. However, cost and necessity are not the concerns of the mad and magnanimous and Lambfell had suddenly become deeply interested in how the monastery would be set up once Bert had built it.

"A new order of monks and nuns is what I'm after here," he said sombrely. "I've seen the existing ones at close quarters — the Benedictines and the Cistercians and the others: it isn't in me to respect them. They're French, Spanish, Italian — and I don't think they're right for the Isle of Man. We can't accept them like the English did, without question. It goes against the way we live and think."

Bert was silent. Sitting on Lambfell's back, my heels in his ribs, I was tempted to spur him on to a further explanation: but I desisted, catching the sardonic gleam in Bert's eye as he stirred the peat ash with the point of his drawing-compass. Being able to catch his mood and slip into his mind I joined him in contemplation of Lord Lambfell's qualifications for founding a new monastic order; after all, the man had spent every spring and summer since boyhood plundering the effects of the existing ones.

"My idea is simple," Lambfell continued. "The new order would have no vows. People don't need to be monks or nuns for life but just now and again. They can come in and go out as they please providing they pay the fees. Now, take myself, after the raiding season I could do a spell. The Isle of Man is perfect for the monastic life. It's hard on the flesh and the spirit. Why no one has founded a monastery here before I don't know."

Bert stared into the fire, unwilling to be drawn further into the deranged thoughts of this pirate. He had had to deal with many men of cruel commercial instinct — some of them churchmen — and he knew the rule: expect the worst for it will surely happen. In the faith he adhered to, our secret, persecuted truth that has been forced to shelter within Christianity and the white cutter's trade since the terrible twenty years of our agony, we have been sustained by an invisible church which cannot be corrupted because it only exists within the minds of its members. That all cathedrals, churches, abbeys and palaces we build are to the glory of *our* Gods, not exclusively to Christ and his holy mother etc, is a further advantage inasmuch as we do not have to declare it but we know it. When we see our best work standing bold in the sunlight, that blessed element, we are proud of our genius but this must be tempered by the shame we feel at our deceit. How we would love to throw our hats in the air and cry out for all to hear that this mighty beauty has been raised up for the Good and Evil Spirits and their wonderful war.

With the trials and agonies of his forebears uppermost in his mind it

34

was not difficult for my father to smile at Lord Lambfell — a brilliant, soft, mocking smile that went with a familiar pat on his lordship's shoulder as he whispered into the interpreter's ear.

"Ask him if he thinks that any self-respecting providence would allow such a monastery to function in its name. Make it a joke, if you will."

"God accepts sin which comes and goes," Lambfell replied, "even though he doesn't like it. What really offends God, I think, is consistency: and what appeals to him is rhythm: in and out. In and out."

Theology such as this does not merit any man's serious attention. Anyone trying to follow its logic will understand how much we suffered that winter as Lord Lambfell sent his muscular mind on raiding-parties into the infinite, always returning empty-handed after much floundering.

V

By the time the winter gales had died down the granite quarry on the slopes of Sleian Barrule had flooded to a depth of twenty feet and more and a landslip had carried away a portion of the site at Cronk ny Frey Lháa. Even without these impediments Lord Lambfell would have become unenthusiastic about his new city. His dense, smoky brain was already throbbing with one thought: the raiding-season had started. As if to illustrate this fact a succession of Irish attacks took place on the north coast. The King of Man called his lords to a council where Lambfell and his peers spent many happy hours soaked in drink planning their response to this Hibernian impudence.

Bert and I had become part of his lordship's household — and part of his dream. As that dream had been abandoned (not an unusual fate for expensive, long-term projects in the building business), we assumed that we would be released from what he called his service, our skill not being required any more. When Lord Lambfell returned red-eyed from the King's council and announced that a major retaliatory raid would be made on Dublin within the next two weeks we expected to be told that we could now return to England. The worst that could happen would be the extraction of a promise from us to come back when better circumstances prevailed — a promise that we would break without any hesitation having seen Lord Lambfell break thousands during the course of the winter. Besides, any oath taken to achieve the impracticable in a mason's terms is an oath taken on a false altar.

Lambfell gathered his men about him and put them into training. They exercised on the shore and on the hillside. The fort rang with the sound of steel and the hall stank with sweat during meal-times. We watched these preparations with joy hidden in our hearts.

One day we were down at the beach where Lord Lambfell's two ships were being got ready for service, having been laid up all winter. We watched the sail being re-rigged, the hull timbers caulked, preparations that stirred Bert and touched off a typical burst of impatience. Against my advice, he raised the subject of our departure. Lambfell did not reply but I saw displeasure in his face. The following morning a party of axemen frog-marched us down to the beach with orders for us to work on the hull-scraping. Two weeks later Bert was given an old leather shirt, a steel cap and a rusty sword and told that he was going to Dublin on the raid.

Bert protested long and loud. His objections were argued upon the fact that he was not Lord Lambfell's sworn man and thus not committed to fight in his cause. His lordship got rid of this quibble by forcing Bert to swear an oath of fealty at the end of a rope. When he further complained that he was no good at fighting Lord Lambfell re-entered the intellectual arena and, for once, he didn't do too badly.

"You fight with stone all the time when you're working," he said with a leonine smirk. "You batter, you hammer, you stab and poke and prod and swing and smash. Look at the way you're built! I wouldn't be surprised if you turned out to be almost as good as I am in a fight."

As the interpreter staggered through the monstrous morass of Manx into English, his eyes rolling with the effort, I tugged at Bert's hand. He was getting angry and I needed to deflect it before he wrecked our chances. Whenever anyone made a good point to Bert his answer was to resort to passion. But I was too late.

"I'm a creator not a destroyer!" he roared. "I battle with the dead, not the living. What d'you think I build with, blood and bones? You stick to thieving, your lordship, I'll pay my way and keep my pride."

The interpreter's eyes bulged as he worked out what Bert was saying. He was a slight, effeminate man who had come to me many times for comfort during the dark days of winter. All he had asked of me was permission to sit close so that the pent-up energies of the warriors who pursued him for the purpose of torment and teasing could be turned aside. I had often held his hand and, once, when Bert was not looking, played with his genitals. Now he could repay the favour.

Staring straight into his nervous eyes I firmly shook my head. Bert was nonplussed when Lord Lambfell's response to his outburst was to clasp his hand and utter Erse that even I had managed to learn. It meant "thanks a lot" and "welcome aboard".

When Bert went to Dublin I was left behind in the care of Lambfell's

37

steward, an old man called Rosin. He was a lazy, frustrated fellow, always claiming to be ill and put-upon, and no lover of children. Most of the time I was shooed off to the women whose company I preferred. They seemed to understand how hard it was for me to be separated from my father for the first time since my birth. They found our relationship peculiarly interesting as all their children were ignored by their fathers whereas I was completely dependent on mine for everything. They knew Bert by now and could not work out the reason for the way we were. Two of the slave-women — including the vast Orla — were pregnant by Bert and there was much gossip and speculation as to whether Bert would take those children into his exclusive care as he had done in my case. It was not in my real interest to tell them that it would be over my dead body. It took Bert all his time to cope with me and me all my time to cope with him. Having competition within would put our little family under stress. Also, we couldn't afford it.

Rosin got it into his head that I should begin some kind of formal schooling with the other children. In the Isle of Man this did not stretch to any disciplines that a boy might expect to study in England but to much simpler things such as what you could safely eat, how to rob a gull's nest without breaking your neck, how to deliver a lamb that was being cunt-throttled and things like that. I spent much of my time with Lord Lambfell's herbalist who was having to spend all day out in the hills gathering the plants he would need to treat the wounds of the warriors when they returned from Dublin. Witnesses to his skill in the past were to be found all over the south of the island: cripples at the gate; amputees eking out a living down at the sea-caves expert in one-armed crab-catching; the blinded and brain-damaged huddling against the walls of the kitchen; they were everywhere. Lambfell was not a man to indulge the disabled and the winter had seen many of these poor oafs put under the sod — when a spade could be got into it.

It was while I was on Bradda Hill picking white anemones that I saw one of Lambfell's ships returning. His long brown banner streamed out from the mast-head in a sign of triumph and I heard the bohrans being beaten as the vessel was rowed into Port Erin Bay. I ran all the way down to the landfall. When I got there I saw the wounded being unloaded, many of them half-dead, encrusted with brine, and I checked to see if Bert was amongst them. The warriors indicated to me that a great victory had been won. When I asked where Bert was they pointed to the west. I later discovered that he had been kept behind by Lord Lambfell with the other ship. His instructions were that I should be brought over to join him as Bert was now working on the west end of Dublin cathedral in fulfilment of one of the conditions in the new treaty between the King of Man and the King of Leinster.

It was useless to argue. My only interest was to rejoin my father wherever he was. While he had been away my sleep had been troubled with nightmares in which Bert deserted me and went his own way, glad to be shut of his burden. Sometimes, in his rages, that is what he called me: his burden. It was a left-over from the early days when he had carried me in his tool-bag.

On occasions there had appeared fatigue, dislike and irritation in his eyes. Having taken on the responsibility of bringing me up, doing his duty for the faith, there were times when I could see that he regretted it. As he had walked on to that ship to go to Dublin there had been a lightness in his step that had worried me. As the ship was pulled into deeper waters he had raised his steel cap to me and smiled — a luminous, liberated smile like that of a man let out of prison.

Fair weather arrived on the Isle of Man in the week that I set out for Dublin in Lord Lambfell's warship. As the men rowed her out of the haven I suddenly became aware of the beauty of the place, full of spring flowers as it was, and I regretted hating it so much.

For the first time in living memory the Irish Sea was becalmed and the warriors were forced to row the entire distance. Our journey took four days longer than had been calculated by Lord Lambfell so when we arrived at the Manx camp on the Binn Eadair peninsula overlooking Dublin Bay, his lordship was no longer there. Along with two other lords he had become impatient with the Irish who were procrastinating about the payment of the agreed buy-off treasure and had gone into Dublin to teach them a lesson. When I asked about my father all I could get in response were gloomy looks. Lord Lambfell's impetuousness was not popular with the King of Man as it appeared to be wrecking chances of the treaty coming to fruition. It was the opinion of his chamberlain, as expressed to the commander of our warship who took up my enquiries for me, that Bert had the same chance of survival in Dublin at that moment as an oyster at a lecher's supper.

"You're an orphan, son, by the sound of it," the commander told me through Fingan the interpreter who had been sent out in the original invasion fleet. "Best thing you can do is stay with the ship till we get back. Lord Lambfell will look after you."

Straightaway, I believed what he said: no questions, no clinging hopes. Maybe it was because of my nightmares, or working with the herbalist on the wounded back in Ballinardredd, or the chaos and confusion of the camp, but my world trembled uncontrollably. Before this moment I would never have believed that Bert could be dead without seeing his corpse: now, the ground having been prepared, I sucked in the pain as if it were medicine. I saw his body floating face-down in the phosphorescent sea. I saw him hanging from the rafters of a half-built hall. I saw him headless on the street. My imagination flared up as blue and poisonous as the gas from a battle-grave.

That night I had no sleep. I wandered between the beached ships and the camp-fires receiving the curses of the sentries until they saw that I was in grief and let me roam like a lost dog looking for its master. I did not know what to do with myself. Tears did not come. The ache in my chest would not blossom. My mind just kept repeating images from Bert's farewell: the raised rusty cap, the freedom-loving smile, goodbye, boy, you're on your own now.

Dawn found me far from the camp. Throughout the long night I had heard bells coming from the west, a sound I knew well from all our working days. I was drawn towards it and as the sun came up I stood beside a darkened abbey knowing the strange mechanism of prayers the Christians would be running behind the black walls. For the first time I thought outside the beliefs Bert had taught me: I begged that huge church to hurl its tedious petitions upwards, sidewards, anywards to preserve my dad. I didn't care that it was not the truth they were muttering in there: all I wanted was the force of their faith. As the bells tolled again for Terce I pressed my face against the wet stones and urged everyone within to bring one man to mind and entreat the universe for his life.

Then I realised that I was still in a foreign land. The abbey had made me forget. I was not in England. Its shape, the sound of the bells, even the way the fields and gardens were tended, had led me to think that I was at home — that these shapes and sounds *were* home was a conclusion I was, as yet, too young to comprehend. Nevertheless, comfort had been given. When three black-robed Benedictines rode out of the main gate talking in Norman French much of my fear left

40

me. With so many familiar things around I began to be optimistic. If Ireland was like this then Bert might have survived, somehow. Keeping my distance I trotted behind the Benedictines, following them through the morning mist as they headed north then west. Knowing their ways I guessed they would be going to Dublin — where the power was.

There is something eternal and all-embracing about a boy of eight running along a road. He will be left to his business, whether it be errand or mischief. No suspicion will be aroused, nor will anyone feel the need to ask where he is going, what he is thinking: he is a boy running along a road, as innocent as the breeze. I wore no sign of where I had come from. Too young to be an enemy, too witless to be a spy or a saboteur, I ran through several camps of warriors and the shore where the Leinster fleet was drawn up. It was after noon when I arrived in the city proper and I had been running for five or six hours but I was not tired. The Benedictines split up once they had crossed the Liffey and I chose the wrong one to follow. He went to a small house near the sea and stayed there. After an hour I retraced my steps, anxious to find the cathedral of Christ Church to look for Bert. I found it surrounded by a crowd of warriors and townsfolk who were listening to an address by an Augustinian canon who spoke a language that was close cousin to the accursed Erse. From my sketchy knowledge of important words such as "give", "gold" and "sacrifice" I could deduct that the Augustinian was asking these Dubliners to contribute to the Manx exactions which were part of the treaty, and getting nowhere. As he spoke I looked above his head at the west front. There was English stone up there, stuff from Dundry and Purbeck that I recognised. I scanned the work, hoping to see something that was bad enough to be Bert's.

There was nothing. Entry into the church was barred and there were signs of unrest in the vicinity. I decided to go and find some food then come back later. The Augustinians might help me if I could think up a convincing story as to why I, an English boy, was in Dublin alone. As is often the case, the truth would be of no use at all.

Wandering around the city I was surprised at the amount of English I heard spoken. The people were a mixture of bedraggled, kilted folk who wore a lot of braids and wire in their hair and others whom I might expect to see in any English town. Although the city was virtually under siege from the sea — the King of Man's fleet being in command of Dublin Bay and its approaches — food and supplies were coming in from the west. I had little trouble begging a cup of milk and some bread from a troop of horse-warriors by pretending to be dumb and letting them mock me to the point where they felt ashamed of themselves.

When I returned to Christ Church there was a riot in full swing and the Augustinian had disappeared off the steps. I skirted the edge of the brawl (which seemed to be between those who were willing to contribute to the Manxgeld and those who were not) looking for a way into the cathedral. En route I got battered and knocked out by some youths who had joined in the disturbance for the purposes of exercise and entertainment. I awoke in the church porch, my nose streaming with blood, an Augustinian trying to stem the flow with a cloth. Other than that I was uninjured. The uproar had subsided, leaving only a few casualties behind to be repaired by the canons.

There was blood in my hair, all over my clothes and I must have looked worse than I was because the Augustinian carried me into the infirmary. As I was put on a pallet between two old canons who were wheezing with lung-fever, my mind was running ahead making up a story to explain my presence in Dublin.

No one spoke to me for hours. It was not until evening that food was brought round and I was invited to sit by the fire with the other patients. Some of them were damaged rioters who were as nervous as I was and they were not inclined to be conversational. The sick canons were so ill that they did not come to the fire but lay on their pallets being spoon-fed by their colleagues.

Eventually a pot-boy came from the kitchen to collect the dirty plates. I spoke to him in English and he replied easily enough, not making a great deal of it. His name was Gerald and he was the son of one of the canons' brothers who was on a campaign against the native Irish lords in Munster that the English had mounted — for Dublin, I discovered, was really an English city and had been so for years.

I asked Gerald if he knew anything about my father, feeling that I could trust him. In the back of my mind I imagined that Bert might have been looked upon as a Manx hostage and therefore a Manxman — one of the enemy. I was taking a risk by identifying myself as his son should he have escaped.

Gerald laughed when I told him who I was. Bert had made himself popular with the canons for the few weeks he had worked on the building — an interior section of the west front, as it turned out — and they had been sorry to seem him go when the prior used him as part of a trade for a parcel of land in Wicklow. Subsequently, the prior had found himself in dispute with the Dublin English lords who had demanded compensation, insisting that Bert was their hostage *in body* and that the deal with the prior simply meant that he had the use of Bert's skill for the length of time it took to pay off a loan that the Canons Regular of Saint Augustine had made to the city for the purchase of mast-timber from Baltic merchants. The rate of repayment agreed was two pence a day: an insult even to a craftsman as limited in ability as Bert. The further insult was that he was now mere currency.

Gerald recounted the full details to me with warmth and interest. It was his ambition, he told me, to study Law when enough of it arrived in Ireland. With all this detail stored in my informant's mind it was not difficult to ascertain where Bert had been sent. The person who had concluded the bargain with the prior had been the Cistercian abbot of Vallis Saultis in Baltinglass, Wexford, but Gerald knew that he had immediately used Bert in a further series of negotiations with the Franciscans at Ennis in Clare to buy fishing rights on Lough Inchicronan.

It occurred to me that this process of rolling barter might not have come to a final halt as far as Bert was concerned so I asked Gerald if he could follow the chain through to the point where Bert could be located. He did not have to be asked twice. As soon as his duties in the kitchen were completed he went out into the city to those places where he knew such business was done, recollected and gossiped about. He looked upon this garnering as part of his legal studies.

While Gerald undertook this research for me (it took several days) I thought it wise to remain in the infirmary. The canon in charge was anxious to be rid of his lay patients and I was forced to employ a ruse to be kept under his care. As it was my nose that had got me in there I was driven to the painful device of punching myself on it to make it bleed. He became so irritated with my nose and the failure of my blood to clot that he made me stand up all day, arguing that this would reduce the pressure in my head.

When Gerald finally came up with the news that my father was almost certainly over in the deep centre of Ireland working on the abbey at Clonmacnois on the banks of the Offaly Shannon, the King

43

of Man attacked the city again in revenge for the killing of Lord Lambfell and his friends who had over-extended themselves both in their strategy and at the end of Irish halters. Dismay and regret coloured my feelings when I heard this: I did not like to think of that man dying in such a way. It made as much sense to me as hanging a cat.

The attack was successful, so much so that the Augustinians decided to abandon the cathedral and retreat into the Pale outside Dublin until the invaders were driven back. This did not seem to worry them much and I got the impression that it was part of the cycle of their lives. As I now had the information I needed to find Bert I stopped punching myself on the nose and the Augustinians put me out in the street, advising me to leave the city. Gerald had filled a sack with provisions for my journey and left it round the back of the kitchen. Slinging it over my shoulder I followed the crowd of refugees heading towards the western gate.

The Christians consider that all things are ordinary when compared to their god's uniqueness. No event or circumstance makes them marvel. That is what makes them dull and incapable of great creativeness for they leave it all to their supreme being. Here I was, a tender child of eight, fatherless, motherless, swirled along by danger, but I had our framework of truth to hang on to; it supported and sustained me. War is the echo of evil above. If we are in peril it is only the peril of our Gods. We will not be saved by blaming original sin. The original sin was the creation and its incompleteness which keeps the Powers in turmoil.

The city was on fire. Over my shoulder I could see the great clouds rising from the houses along the shore. This did not terrify me. It was the ruddiness of my love's cheek, the spark in its eye. Inconflagration, consolation.

44

VI

To get to Clonmacnois directly meant traversing the great Bog of Allen. If a drought ever came to Ireland it would take fifty years of it to dry out this swampland and, even then, it would be congenial only to frogs. Many travellers skirt the Bog by going south-west to Athy but I was in a hurry and not wishing to be on the trodden path in case I encountered the wrong company. The Bog was vast: whole armies lay in the depths, I was told later, their shields and spears coming to the surface when the mud was convulsed during eclipses and the flights of comets. To be small and light of foot in such a place was greatly advantageous.

While my food lasted I travelled quickly. Gerald had advised me on my route as far as the edge of the Bog but from there onwards I guided myself by my vague notions about where the sun might be rising and setting, the sky being continuously overcast. Fixing my position by the stars was a skill that Bert knew and had passed on to me as it was incorporated into our cryptic principles of architecture. I think no one had seen a star in the Bog of Allen. If Bethlehem had been there then the shepherds and the three wise kings would be still wandering around somewhere in Connemara, their gifts covered with moss.

Once I had removed myself from the environs of Dublin and got through the outlying districts I saw no one. The land was not cultivated nor cleared and my progress was slow. As the forest turned into bog and the ground levelled out I became aware of the hugeness of the sky. Until then all my life had been spent amongst hills. There had never been a time when I could not look up to high ground and see how it possessed part of the air as a building does. Here, in the Bog of Allen, it was sky and water. Anything that was built here would be sucked under and lost.

Having spent my first full day wending through the reeds, getting from island to island of firm peat or rushes, I settled for the night in a clump of willows, sharing it with a host of owls. My only cover was the food sack — now empty — and I lay on the damp ground shivering

45

in the cold west wind as the birds sailed in and out of the willow boughs above at their hunting. They were like sad ghosts, pale and mournful as they hooted to each other, but in their claws I knew they had the grip of pincers raising a block of stone; in their wings the power of pulleys to lift great weights. As I lay on my back and watched them I imagined bigger and bigger creatures struggling in their talons: from voles to rats and rabbits to dogs to calves to horses and, finally, with an owl clutching each of his four limbs, came Bert, his hair flying, eyes wild, and I slept.

After four days in which all I had had to eat were young willow shoots I was very sick. It did not seem to matter which way I went, the Bog remained the same. Even my footprints disappeared the moment I made them. With a fever in my blood, a delirious thirst that forced me to drink the dark water, I dragged myself on to some firm ground as night fell and just lay in the reeds convinced that I was going to die. There was no strength left in me.

I heard voices. That did not excite me at all: I had heard all sorts of voices over the last four days but I still had the sense to know they were all in my head. These voices were speaking in English: more evidence that they were part of my hallucinations. When I heard the reeds being crushed underfoot and listened to a long discussion between two men about using a live green frog as bait for pike I remained persuaded that I was undergoing a terminal phantasm and sat up in order to view this final *ignis fatuus* of my life. A spear was immediately thrust through the reeds at me and I cried out, ready to admit that this, at least, was real.

A peculiar hiatus ensued. The spear, which was a trident, then moved from side to side until it made contact with my leg, then two heads appeared between the reeds: still no words, no threats, questions or challenges. I gave them a greeting and received no response. They pushed through the reeds and stood over me in a staring silence.

These men were Carthusian monks. Their evening conference about green frogs had been the only verbal intercourse allowed to them that day and they were eking it out when I disturbed them. As they poked and prodded me, turned me over, felt my brow and pockets, they did not speak — similarly, as they carried me back to their settlement, doctored me and put me to bed, they maintained a speechlessness that bewildered me, innocent as I was of their régime.

46

The Carthusian is supposed to live off his own garden, alone but on a compact estate of small houses, each having its own portion of land. Their churches are generally not large or adorned to any degree. I have seen many such establishments in France and Italy though it has not yet caught on in England as an idea. My mutes in the Bog of Allen were men who had found Saint Bruno's Rule appealing with its emphasis on silence and self-help but they had not been able to interest the English bishops or the King sufficiently to get permission to set up a Charterhouse of their own. On deciding to go to Ireland they had encountered nothing but hostility and misunderstanding and had been driven to found their own illegal monastery here in the Bog where a garden was an impossibility. Instead, they divided up the water and each brother fished his own section, thus preserving Saint Bruno's concept of independent existence within the community. What might have troubled the founding saint of this movement was that these Aquacarthusians used every available bit of parler-time to swop hints about tackle, bait and other riparian trivia.

For heroes of this spirit they were the dullest men I had, as yet, encountered. I could not help but admire their determination to get close to Christ but why they had decided he favoured those who had been marinated in the Bog of Allen escaped me. Their books and blankets were perpetually damp; illness and discomfort hung in the air: their constant diet of pike, bream, roach, tench, chub — the dullest food that fresh water produces when it is fresh, brought about a grey pallor in them, further discoloured by livid rashes.

For Christ to be the sole recipient of the learned conversation of these fools made me pity the poor Galilean. Certainly, as a sick child, I resented their refusal to speak to me. I craved company, maybe a little coddling, but these stern, tight-lipped English fanatics would give me nothing but casual care and a few scraps of food. Being with them made me realise how much I missed my father who, though he had many failings as a parent, always talked to me, sharing the world as he saw it. Whenever the Carthusians came close to me I would think of Bert and deliberately throw great questions at them, questions he had asked time and again in my presence: why is the creation so imperfect? If the proper home of the spirit is heaven what is it doing stuck down here? If our earthly existence is a test then is it fair to assume that nothing really works as it should?

My interrogations proved to be so unpopular with the Carthusians that they left my food outside the hut as soon as I was able to drag myself that far to get it. Not one of them ever dared to answer. It amused me to imagine Bert engaging these sour, taciturn men in dispute on essential issues. They would not have stood a chance. Not that Bert could answer all the questions he asked me, but at least he was prepared to show his ignorance to a child, and tackle all the monsters of metaphysics.

As I got better I took to sitting just inside the door of my hut so I could shoot queries at the Carthusians as they put my food outside. The effect of this was to make them put the food further and further away. As I got stronger my voice got louder until I was bellowing questions about the eternal verities over a hundred yards or more as my dinner was pushed towards me at the end of a long pole.

So intrigued have I been with my memories of the awful Carthusian silence in the trackless, soundless Bog, that I have omitted to record that I was chained from the first day of my arrival. Other animals at Clonbullogue were chained — the water-hounds, the geese, the herons that the monks were trying to train to fish for them; and all the books. Chained cages of fish lay deep in the reeds around the settlement being fattened in monkish experiments. One of my largest questions to the Carthusians was how they had known to bring so many chains with them on first migrating to the Bog, for there were no smithies within miles. They never answered as was their wont but one day I saw why: one of the monks had taken off his robe. He had a chain wound round his waist. These men had walked all the way from Dublin carrying many times their own weight in symbols of slavery. Wherever they might go this metal monastery would go with them, each link a prayer.

In spite of the conditions at Clonbollogue I got better. The skies cleared and some warm, bright weather arrived, bringing out all the flowers of the Bog. As the water heated up with the daily sun the fishing improved and the monks spent all their time out with their rods, saying their offices amongst the reeds.

It was three weeks before I realised that I was their prisoner and not their patient. Until then I had been content to wait. My sickness had frightened me and I remembered the conviction I had had on the day I was found by the Carthusians: I had been dying: another day out in the Bog alone would have been my last on earth. Placed alongside the realisations that occur in any child's mind at that age — mortality being the most overwhelming — it was not surprising I had become cautious with myself.

However, it took more than my own prudence to explain why I was being kept in captivity long after I was fit to continue my journey. As the monks always ignored my questions on any subject — theological or not — it was impossible for me to get an explanation for their behaviour. All I had to go on was the treatment they afforded me — which was minimal — and it was my interpretation of that which convinced me of their real purpose.

Each day saw an increase in the amount of food they gave me: efforts were made to cook and present my meals in such a way as might encourage me to eat more. Having nothing better to do I consumed everything they put in front of me with the result I started to get fat. Meals were served more often. The Carthusians braved my cross-examinations to come and look at me, to prod me with their fingers and feel my flesh. No matter how hard I taxed them on major philosophical issues and matters of the *penetralia mentis*, how widely I foraged in their fuddled doctrines, they bore it with equanimity. Silence and tight little smiles were their weapons of defence.

The Christians eat fish once a week for a good reason: it has nothing to do with Friday and the crucifixion but everything to do with fish being the most tedious food known to us. All fish taste the same. If the different species could have flavours as separate as their appearance then all would be well, but that is not the case. Fish-flesh is merely an extension of water's tastelessness.

The Carthusians of Clonbullogue ate nothing but fish year-in year-out. It is a well-known medical fact that such an exclusive diet turns the mind. People who live on lake and sea shores are often more deranged than inland dwellers: witness the low intellectual abilities of the average sailor. Also, fishing is not a pursuit that exercises the brain. It can be done, and perhaps is best done, in a state of trance.

The manacle around my leg started to pinch as I got fatter. One evening I was sitting down to a feast of glazed tench, holding forth to my audience of Carthusians about how I found it difficult to reconcile religion with altruism, when I noticed that one of them was drooling. His attention was not focused on the fish but on my leg.

My heart seemed to stop beating as the truth sank in. Although my hand shook as I continued to feed myself I did manage to disguise the shock of the moment. When I had finished eating I bade the monks good night and went to my bed, covering my manacled leg from their eyes. It was plain that they estimated the readiness of their victims for slaughter by the degree to which the steel pinched the flesh.

That night I worked on the pin that held the end of the chain. It had been hammered deep into the central support of the hut and all I had to work with were roughly-cast links in the chain itself, using them like a file. By dawn I was still a long way from being able to loosen the pin. When they brought me my breakfast I did not sit by the entrance to talk as I usually did, but stood with my back to the pole to hide my handiwork. This did not fool the Carthusians. One of them pushed me aside, examined the pin, then went out and returned with a hammer with which he knocked the pin deeper into the recess I had made. Shortly afterwards I heard a lot of new activity amongst the huts: the clang of iron pots, the sharpening of knives, the building up of fires. A cloud of woodsmoke hung over Clonbullogue.

A monk had been left to guard me. As the Carthusians had never made introductions or addressed each other in my presence I had baptised them myself: this one I had called Ralph Rabbit because he had big front teeth that stuck out beyond his lower lip. Ralph Rabbit was a thin, excitable man of about thirty with large hairy hands. He had some eminence amongst his brothers by dint of his skill in making lures for fish out of feathers, wire and cloth. As he watched over me Ralph Rabbit worked on one of these, picking threads out of the hem of his habit and wrapping them round the shaft of a hook.

"Can you find it in yourself to agree with this?" I said to him in a shaky voice. "Surely, as a Christian, you must condemn murder, never mind cannibalism."

Ralph Rabbit sniffed, took a heron feather out of the folds of his garment, cut a few tufts of it off with a little knife, then started to tie them to the hook.

At this moment I regretted having asked so many weighty questions on previous occasions. This was one that really mattered to me. However, I failed to impress Ralph Rabbit with its importance. He kept winding threads around his lure.

"Have you eaten other people who have come to this place? What does this say for the duty that you have towards travellers? Hospitality is the oldest virtue we know. It goes back to ancient times. . . ."

My voice trailed off as the other Carthusians entered the hut carrying an anvil and a couple of axes and a hammer between them. My manacle was broken off. As the hammer rang on the anvil my leg went into a convulsion and I lost control of my bladder. Two of the brothers picked me up, wet as I was, and chaired me outside.

"See if you can stand," one of them said.

My bladder did it again and my bowels followed. The shock of being addressed for the first time by one of them was like being saluted by Death. As they let go of me I fell to the ground. I looked up: the axes were raised.

"Not here. Take him down to the pike-hatchery so we don't waste any of the blood," the one I had called Tom Turtle said with a beatific smile. "They'll go mad for it."

Now it was my turn not to be able to speak. As they bore me down to the water's edge I groaned and whimpered but was hardly heard above the cheerful chatter of the Carthusians who had obviously declared this to be a feast-day.

Terror has been part of everything I have ever built: it is in the curve that fears my circle; it is in the straight line that fears my beginning and end. No arch of mine was ever raised but that it sang of my fear of falling into death. My best work was born out of peril. When I see the impossible achieved in stone it is the dead saluting the living, the inanimate expressing its envy of life. No truly great work exists without the stimulation of danger. It will squeeze the best out of a supple soul. In its pure form it is the teasing of the Gods. Out of it may come indignity, abasement, surrender, the complete dismantling of a man's pride — or, if he is open to the sharpest, most acute provocations of this existence of ours — an opportunity to stand on tip-toe and stare right into the eye of the Creators. What will he see there? What I saw that day on the banks of the Figoil river at Clonbullogue: sunlight flashing on a blade. Marsh marigolds. Lesser celandine. A dark barge loaded with stone lying deep in the water, its crew standing along the side, poles in hand. They sang. They sang. Oh, even now I can hear them singing! Tom Turtle lowered the axe then made as if he had been ready to use it to adjust the frame of the pike hatchery. The men poled the barge over to make a landing, shouting questions as to their whereabouts.

I sat in the mud and cried.

The barge was laden with black Purbeck limestone that had been

51

sailed over from England to beautify Clonmacnois. The stone had been unloaded on to the barge at Limerick then brought up the Shannon through Lough Derg and Portumna but the master had made a wrong turn during a night passage and gone up the Brosna river instead of following the main course upstream. How he had got from the Brosna into the Figoil was a mystery to everyone as the two were not connected. A flood was the only explanation that was offered. Meanwhile the transport of several tons of expensive English decorative stone remained a problem: Clonmacnois was forty miles away to the west and the Figoil flowed east. The bargemen spent the day discussing their predicament with the Carthusians. I sat within earshot, keeping my own counsel, allowing my heart to leap every time I heard the word Clonmacnois. It took me close to Bert. It was that strange word that had saved me. The stone was going to him, to be under his hand. He would be responsible for the stone and I would be part of it, delivered unto him like Cleopatra to Caesar.

I was conscious of the watch the Carthusians were keeping over me during their day with the bargemen. As the prohibitions on verbal intercourse had been suspended for the feast they employed themselves readily in conversation, using the precious opportunity to the full. I knew the monks were aware of my interest in the destination of the stone: during my weeks of captivity I had told many of them where I was headed and why, having no reason to keep it secret. I reasoned that they would expect me to either ingratiate myself with the bargemen in order to beg permission to accompany them, or I would stow away when the barge left. Their intention would be to keep me from talking to the bargemen. As they took no immediate interest in me this was not difficult and I was prevented from meeting them, being pushed further and further to the back of the company. The Carthusians believed that as long as they could stop me complaining to the bargemen, or getting to their vessel, I would be forced to remain at Clonbullogue.

The most intoxicating drink is conversation after loneliness. The mouth becomes drunk on its own motion: the mind spins and weaves wonders. Warmth and comradeliness come to the fore of even the cold spirits amongst us.

I sat on my own and watched the Carthusians at their bacchanal of talk. I saw their eyes begin to glow, their cheeks flush, their limbs become animated. The bargemen were amused by the conversion of these phlegmatic, pallid pedants into such vivacious companions. The

Carthusians could not forbear from touching the simple inland sailors, putting arms around their necks, pinching their cheeks. Both parties became enchanted with each other and the talk bubbled out of them like water from a hot spring.

When the orgy of oral communication was at its height and the Bog rang with laughter and back-slapping I slipped away unnoticed and hid in the reeds a good distance downstream, choosing a place from which I could keep the barge in sight. Terrified that I might miss it if the bargemen moved at night I took one of the Carthusians' fishing-lines and stretched it across the main channel, one end tied round my waist. In my soaked clothes, shivering but elated with new hope, I sat and gazed at the barge willing it to move.

Towards sunset the crew went aboard and took up their places. I untied the line from my waist and got ready to swim out. A trailing rope from the port side was my target. If I could pull myself up on it and slip in between the Purbeck blocks without being seen, I would stand a chance.

With horror I noticed all of the Carthusians bringing out their crude, flat-bottomed fishing punts to accompany the barge as it moved away. They had obviously discovered my escape.

I got angry at this refusal on their part to admit defeat. Knowing enough about Christians by now to be certain that the bargemen would never believe that a monk would contemplate eating a child, any attempt to enlist their support would be pointless. They had assumed that I was a slave of some sort. The Carthusians would have told them that I had run away and asked for their help in recapturing me.

My plan was changed. Inside my head a cold, iron-hard mechanism began to turn. I was not prepared to give up my passage to Clonmacnois and reunion with my father. That barge of stone had come for me, having found its way over impossible terrain. How it would find its way back into the Shannon I had no idea: neither did the bargemen as it turned out: but I was sure, in my heart, that it would. Nothing was going to stop me getting aboard.

One of the Carthusians was a cripple. He had been a soldier in a previous life, perhaps, and had lost both his legs in battle: whatever was the cause (and I could only guess as they never spoke to me), he had only stumps and propelled himself along on his hands. He was well fitted for life on the water but he abjured the use of the pole and paddled himself along with his palms. My name for this monk was Sam Spider.

I waited in the reeds until the barge came level. Some of the Carthusians were ahead of it, scanning the water. My prayer was that Sam Spider would be in the rear as he usually was, his hands not having the effectiveness of the long poles when it came to speed.

Sam Spider was at the back, and on my side of the flotilla. I submerged myself, the fishing-line in one hand, then swam under water until I was alongside Sam Spider's punt. As his left hand dipped in to paddle I grabbed it and pulled him in, winding the fishing-line around his throat, then hung on as he threshed about, putting all my strength into strangling him. We went down several times until I thought my lungs would burst as my only chance was to hold on to his back, his hands being abnormally strong. He fought to get his fingers beneath the line but I kept it too taut for him.

After what seemed to be an age, a chaos of spasm and agony, Sam Spider went slack and we started to sink. I pulled him into the reeds, hoisted him to a position where he would not go down, then swam off to retrieve his punt. Stripping off his habit I put it on, got into the punt and paddled, dragging Sam Spider off the reeds after me. Once in the main channel I released my hold and he sank.

By now the barge was disappearing ahead between the reed islands. I paddled as fast as I could, sitting cross-legged to look as much like Sam Spider as possible. Within quarter of an hour I had caught up with the rear of the flotilla as it scoured both sides of the Figoil for me, the monks calling to each other, not wasting their last hours of parler-time. I hung back in Sam Spider's usual position, making the occasional foray into the reeds, but mainly keeping my eye on the barge as the dusk came down. I knew there had to be a point where the Carthusians would give up the hunt and return to Clonbullogue. I had to be out of sight by the time that decision was taken, but still in eye-contact with the barge or I might lose it in the Bog as night fell.

The Carthusians fell back in the last glow of evening when they knew their return could be made with some light. I edged the punt into a pool at the side as if continuing the pursuit to the last minute. The monks called out to me to give up and get back as they poled past. I watched them slip away into the dusk then set out after the barge, paddling frantically through the falling darkness.

I had not far to go. The barge soon loomed up ahead of me, its bows pushed into the reeds. Candles had been lit in the stern where there was a simple shelter made of canvas. As soon as I saw the barge I stopped paddling and tried to work out what approach I should make to the crew.

Taking off Sam Spider's habit I tied its ends together in a knot and buried it as deep as I could in the ooze beneath a reed island. In terms of any explanation I might have to give them, the punt was less of an embarrassment. If I told the truth, leaving out what I had done to Brother Sam Spider, the bargemen might accept that I had been forced to steal the craft. However, theft was theft. They might be very law-abiding people. Besides, I still had no idea of what story I could tell them that would attract sympathy.

Shivering out in the Figoil in the punt I put my brain to the problem: I had to lie. The truth was not going to win over the bargemen. Even if it did — an impossibility — then their immediate response might be to return to Clonbullogue to punish the Carthusians for their unnatural appetites: a course of action that would not only slow me up but could result in my recapture. There was no guarantee that the Carthusians would not defeat the bargemen and then eat *them*!

It occurred to me that I did not know the characters of the men I was proposing to deal with: my only contact had been via their meeting with the monks, and their discussions with them. I had noticed how the laity reshape their behaviour when in the company of the religious: they do not show their true selves but what they believe the religious would like them to be. Once out of their company the average person reverts to his old habits of mind, which might include a positive hatred of all priests and their pretensions. My best plan was, therefore, to spy on the bargemen and try to calculate how they would receive me in all the several guises I could adopt.

It was an easy business to paddle the punt up to the side of the barge and listen to their conversation. They were not men who spoke in low voices. It sounded as if they were used to calling to each other across great distances, over the crash of quarry-work, jetties, docks, carts in the street. Somehow they had made a fire in the stern of the barge and I could smell bread and meat cooking.

Clenching my jaws together in order to stop my teeth chattering I sat bowed in the punt, one hand holding on to a bunch of reeds, listening in the dark. Their fire made a soft rose of light which was spangled with stars from beyond. I could not see the speakers, only hear their voices.

55

". . . all over us like a herd of heifers," said one.

"The stink was terrible. Can't stand old fish," said another. "Pah!"

"If they hate the world then they hate us," said another. "It follows."

"Don't talk out of your arse, Roger," said another.

I sighed with relief. There were allies aboard. Up until then I had been worried that the entire crew might be made up of severe Christians who had been forced even deeper into Cretinous obedience by being lost in this watery wasteland: men who would be desperate, far from home, feeling betrayed. Only if you have been lost in the Bog of Allen with a load of limestone can you say that you truly understand perdition.

"Nevertheless, they must be serious folk. No one gives up everything and lives like that for a joke. At root they must be good. . . ."

"Most monks are running away from something."

"You mean they're criminals?"

"Not necessarily. They may be running away from women."

"If there were no monks there'd be no monasteries."

"Roger worked that out all on his own, didn't you, son?"

"What they find to do with themselves beats me. I'd get bored."

"They're thinking about God."

"Does God care if they do or don't?"

"Well, you don't know, do you? I've had prayers answered."

"You're burning that sausage, Roger."

"No matter what happened to me, how miserable I got, how much I hated the world, I'd never think of becoming a monk."

"They wouldn't have you, not with your vices. I've seen you making eyes at a dead horse."

"What's vice then?"

"The opposite of virtue."

"What's virtue then?"

"The opposite of vice."

"You're asking to get thrown overboard, Roger."

"I'm only as good as the next man. That's all I'm saying."

"That's me at the moment."

"Then there's room for improvement."

"Which way tomorrow?" said one, changing the subject.

"Follow the river. What else can we do?"

"We're two weeks late already, and this river seems to be flowing east. We should be going west."

"Your piece is bigger than mine. Cut a lump off."

"They must be worth a few pounds at Clonmachwherever it is if they can send all the way to England for stone."

"Let's hope they'll pay up when we eventually get there. At this rate that might be Christmas."

"The Irish are poor, don't you think?"

"No poorer than the English. My aunt died of hunger in Romford last year. At the end her mouth was all green through eating dock leaves and nettles," Roger said.

"Saw her, did you?"

"No, but I heard."

"Don't believe all you hear. Does your mouth go green when you eat cabbage?"

"It might if I ate nothing but cabbage."

"The farting would kill you. Is that how your aunt died?"

"Pass the bottle, Geoffrey."

"I should think that mason up at Clonmacwherever it is must be cursing us by now. He's waiting for this stuff."

"Well, he'll just have to wait, won't he?"

"He's a famous man, a genius, they told me in Limerick. The abbot thinks he can do no wrong. Pays him what he asks for. No expense spared. Only the best. Spent years getting him to come across from England. They say he's the top man in the whole business, home and overseas."

"What's his name?"

"Don't know. All I've seen is his mason's mark. They had it in Limerick on an order for lime. It's like a fence."

"A fence? What's a fence like?" Roger asked.

"What d'you mean — what's a fucking fence like? A fence is like a fucking fence, isn't it? What d'you expect a fucking fence to be like?"

Unable to stop myself I paddled the punt into the light of the fire, shouting at the top of my voice with excitement.

"The mason's mark that is like a fence is this and it belongs to Herbert Haroldson, my dad!"

As the bargemen came to the side and looked down at me I raised my finger and drew this on the flame-lit air.

VII

There were explanations that had to be made to the bargemen. From the moment I realised what I had done by appearing so precipitately out of the night my mind had to work very quickly. I started talking before I got on board, not giving them a chance to ask questions. As they pulled my wet clothes over my head, I talked: as they rubbed me down, I talked. As they tried to put food in my mouth, I endeavoured to talk. No, I *babbled*. Somewhere inside my child's mind a tap had been turned tightly off for all the weeks I had been with the Carthusians. I was not connected to the reservoir of speech — I had talked long and loud *at* the monks whenever I had the opportunity — but to that fount of shared responses, comforts and kindnesses we hold ready for those who might like us. I was determined that the bargemen should like me, love me, weep for me!

My lie is worth recording as its relationship to the truth sheds light on my character at that young age. What I emphasised to the bargemen was neither the abominable designs of the Carthusians on my body, nor their cold taciturnity, but something I thought the bargemen would hate. I told them the Carthusians had driven me out because I was too much of a nuisance: that they had given me the punt and sent me after the barge, saying, "Go with those fools. They're used to brats like you. We demand higher standards."

"Did you wish to become a monk, lad?" Geoffrey asked. He was a large fellow with a shock of wiry, white hair and an expression of wistfulness on the perimeter of witlessness. "You seem too young for such a venture."

Here was the first question. Geoffrey had managed to get himself heard as I gulped for breath before rattling on. How had I got there? would be the next question so I must cover it in my response.

"My father thought I should spend some time with a monastic community as part of my apprenticeship. Most of his work is for the Church . . ." I said, groping for the next chapter of the lie. "He arranged with the abbot of Clonmacnois for me to come to Clonbullogue . . ."

"And they threw you out?" demanded a small, fierce man whose hair was parted in the middle and clipped down with copper combs. I was later to know him as Thomas of Eye, or Tommy. I thought I had struck the right note with him as he seemed so angry with the idea. I was to learn that his indignation was a fixed state of mind.

"They did, sir," I replied meekly. "I was reckoned to be unfit for the rigours of their intellectual life."

"Intellectual life?" said Roger scoffingly. "We spent all day jabbering about how to catch perch with dragonflies!"

Roger was to become my friend so I will spend a little time on him. He was of the old Saxon stock, very squat and strong in the leg and hip with sloping shoulders, a long neck and a head that was not quite big enough to balance the bottom half of his body. His voice was high and querulous. At my first encounter with him I was aware of an urge to slap him down, a feeling the other bargemen had to struggle with every time Roger opened his mouth. He was no more than twenty at this time; blithe, vacant and intense in waves.

"Shut your face, Roger," growled the barge-master, William de Waus by name. "What will a small boy know of an intellectual life? He's just repeating what he's heard, aren't you son? You don't know what an intellectual life is any more than I do. Don't listen to Roger, whatever happens. Did those monks molest you in any way? Don't tell me. I can guess. Your father will see that they're sorted out."

William de Waus was the oldest of the bargemen and he had the least natural authority. With his bald, narrow head, beaked nose and mouth full of bad teeth he had few physical advantages over his crew. He was certainly the weakest of them and seldom stirred himself, spending his time seated on the stern making waspish remarks. His power over the other bargemen came solely from the fact that he owned the barge.

After an hour of my account the audience began to droop. The odours of the Bog were rising in the night air. They were already dreaming of another day. I was well satisfied with the reception of my story. No one had doubted that the fabulous mason of Clonmacnois (where had that reputation come from?) was my father. If there were any misgivings about the rest of my tale then they would be clarified when we got the barge safely to the monastery and discharged its load of Purbeck.

59

I had to share Roger's blanket. He took me under his arm and allowed me to lie close to him for warmth. Out in the Bog nocturnal birds were screaming and whirring as the bargemen, one by one, fell asleep and started to snore. I was aware that Roger was still awake and bursting with questions.

"Tell me something about the freemasons," he whispered after a while. "Do they really have the right to say what they like to the King? Why can't the Pope touch them?"

"Shut up, Roger," murmured Thomas of Eye. "Let the boy sleep."

"He'll tell me tomorrow," Roger said, sighing, "won't you?"

Holding on to Roger, feeling his young heart beating, enjoying his warmth, I would have told him all the secrets of the universe if I had known them. It had been a long time since I had felt safe, longer since I had not felt lonely. Roger, although unaware of it, was flanked by a devoted servant, one who worshipped him for the best things anyone has to offer: the inside of their presence, the boon of their body, the heat of their human heartblood. As I drifted off to sleep in Roger's arms I knew that tears were running down my face but I did not bother to wipe them away.

The next morning brought a wind from the south that quickly purged all chill from the air. By the time the bargemen were up and about, plying their long poles in the bed of the Figoil, the sun was at play in the Bog, changing its colours, lancing its dankest corners, altering its mood to summer. Without my knowledge June had come to the calendar and this glorious day was the first sign of it.

William de Waus was not the sort to waste anyone's labour. He saw that it was not practical to employ me on the pole as I was too small but there was a job he had to do now and again that he found onerous as it got him up from his seat in the stern. It consisted of sounding the depth of the water ahead with a stick that was as long as the barge's draught. After an hour I discovered why he had been so anxious to be relieved of this work: it was not only that it disturbed his repose but that it made him unpopular. The barge was so heavy that every time its bottom grounded in mud it took immense efforts by the polers to get it off. As a result of their odyssey in Ireland the arms of Tommy, Roger, Geoffrey and the rest were like the thews of bullocks, twisted and bulging with muscle built up by this strenuous exercise. Every time I got the barge stuck I expected those arms to be raised against me but my companions proved to be more patient. Apparently William de Waus was even worse at this job than I was.

"Don't you worry, boy," Geoffrey shouted as I guided them on to the tenth mud-bank that morning, "you're doing all right. We'll have her off in no time."

Unused to such kindness I turned my head away from him in case he should see the tears in my eyes for I had not done with weeping. Each consideration I received from these simple, good-hearted men affected me deeply.

"Where to today, master?" Tommy said as he heaved on his pole, bending it like a bow. "Any idea?"

"We'll keep to the river," William de Waus muttered, his eyelids fluttering as he dozed in the sun.

"It's going south now," Tommy shouted. "Do you want to go south? I thought we wanted to get west."

"It was going east yesterday," William de Waus replied wearily. "So we're improving, aren't we? We'll get there."

"Getting broader too, master. We'll be able to get a good speed up soon. Do we want to go south that fast? If we knew where we were headed it might help."

Tommy's bantering had no effect on the master. His old head had fallen forward so his chin rested on his chest. It was as I was looking at him that I saw the Carthusians coming up behind us in their punts.

My first instinct was to jump into the water and drown myself.

I was gripped hard as I tilted forward. Looking up I saw Roger's eyes. They were stern.

"You're one of us. Leave it to Willy," he said firmly.

The Carthusians came alongside. They stared at me in silence. William de Waus was awakened and stood up.

"What do you want?" he demanded. "I don't like being followed."

Bound by their oaths of silence the Carthusians pointed at me. Ralph Rabbit held out a roll of vellum on the end of his pole. William pushed it aside.

"Don't waste my time with that. I can't read, neither can any of my crew."

The Carthusians went into a dumb-play that the bargemen could not interpret, but I could. It was to do with the disappearance of Sam Spider. At the end of it William de Waus was in poor temper.

"Don't stand there waving your arms about. Tell me what you

want or be on your way!" he shouted irritably. "If you could talk fourteen to the dozen yesterday you could do the same today if you wanted to. State your business or depart!"

The Carthusians pulled themselves right up to the barge and started to clamber aboard. Without a word Tommy swept his long pole sideways and knocked them back. The other bargemen prepared to do the same. William de Waus searched around under his seat and came up with a battered half-sword. He held it over his head, showing it to the Carthusians.

"There're more of these where this came from. Any more trouble and I'll arm the crew," he snapped. "Pole on boys. Leave these dummies where they are."

Seizing a spare pole himself William de Waus drove it down through the water. Once they had recovered from their astonishment at seeing such animation in the barge-master, the crew followed his lead and we moved forward.

I kept my eyes to the front. Some of the Carthusians poled themselves ahead of the barge and looked at me with hungry hatred as I passed, then they fell back.

In my memory I still have the image of the sun on the water with the darkness of those savage men rearing up on either side, their robes outstretched like the wings of hellish birds. I have often thought of that sun as my God and theirs: that they adored its light as much as I did on that day. Yet they had found a way of keeping it out of their lives. To them it was no more than a coin on the water, the purchase-price of pain. Now, in my riper years, I pity their memory.

By noon we had reached a point downstream where the current was strong and the barge moved faster. We saw the first signs of a settlement on the banks. The Bog had been left behind by now and the land was firmer with more forest. Sometimes we thought that we had seen a field on a slope but it was never sharply defined, just a change of hue in the swarming, sunlit green of a great plain. There were a few old fish-traps hanging from the banks, a couple of abandoned weirs, the turf walls of a hut, an abandoned garden. We sat on the black stone, guiding the barge with the long poles trailed in the water, and waited for the first sight of people.

We did not make camp that night. William de Waus was confident that

62

we could safely take the barge down the broad river in the dark; it kept to a southerly course, there were not too many deviations, and he was beginning to feel that he might be making headway in his search for a way back into the Shannon. As they had had a lazy day of it the bargemen did not complain. We glided along under an awe-inspiring dome of stars not even needing the absent moon. Everyone was in a good humour. The river was sound. It would take us somewhere, anywhere, away from the Bog.

Watches were set and the remainder of the crew settled down to sleep for a few hours as the dawn began to lift the starry dome off its earthly moorings. I could not think of sleep, my mood clinging hold of me, enchanting and delicious as it had been all day. I sat on the bows, legs dangling, searching the stars and the dark waters for proof that this pleasure would last. I saw a mother otter and her three cubs. I saw water-rats and voles, creatures so small that the strength and penetration of my eyesight astonished me in seeing them. Fish flung themselves at the stars, crashing back into the river with showers of mercury that seemed to take an age to fall. Even the tiny insects that buzzed around my head and tickled my bare feet were a delight. But my greatest pleasure lay in the sounds that kept the remembered Carthusian silence at bay — the grunt and curse, the word, O the precious, life-giving word! Any human noise that said: "We are doing things that will not hurt us. Our journey, somewhere along the line, will make its point without pain," was a healing comfort to me. I had killed a man. I had put out his light. My will told me that guilt was too dangerous a drug for one so young. I would not feel it. I would feel the beauty of the future. Sam Spider would have to have his share in that.

As I saw the first huts of Athy in the dawn I became conscious of how alone and strong I had been that day — able to reach out without fear to others, brave enough to remain within an elation that mystified and frightened me. But a more thrilling and important awareness had me in its grip: I realised that since that axe had been raised over my head I had not had a single thought about Bert, my father. In his absence he had failed me. My love for him was chastened and changed. I no longer *needed*.

Jumping to my feet I shouted out: "We're here! We're here!"

"Where's here?" Tommy murmured grimly, eyeing the stockade and the sharpened stakes that lined the bank. "Looks like nowhere to me."

★

Our reception at Athy was cold. We were not allowed to moor the barge but ordered to stand off in mid-river while the chief was roused. This meant a great deal of difficult work to stop the heavily-laden vessel slewing round in the current. By the time that the chief had come to the gate of the stockade we were a quarter of a mile downstream, having had to pull in to the left-hand bank to get out of the current. The chief mounted a horse and rode down on us with a party of shaggy warriors, their swords unsheathed. Several of them notched arrows as they drew up alongside the barge. The chief was young and lively and the warriors evidently hoped for some fun at our expense.

William de Waus was nervous. He tried to step off the barge to pay his respects to the chief but he was waved back. The chief then started to harangue us in a hotch-potch tongue that was the gleanings of England, Normandy, Ireland and hell; a language designed for use by the unfriendly. For his archers to let fly would not have taken more than one raised eyebrow. What he wanted to know about was the stone. Was it a floating wall? A barricade? An engine of war? A portable bridge?

With the help of Roger and one of the Irish crewmen, William de Waus explained that the stone was for a church. Where? demanded the chief. Clonmacnois, replied William de Waus. The chief snorted into his beard and slapped his horse's neck with the flat of his sword. Clonmacnois already has seven churches, he bellowed. Then it may be going to have another, our master said.

The chief got down off his horse and came towards the barge. Liam, the Irish crewman who had been helping with the interpreting, held out his hand to help the chief across the gap between the barge and the bank. With a sweep of his sword the chief knocked the hand aside, giving Liam a gash across his palm. The poor lad was so surprised that he fainted on the spot.

The chief stepped aboard, got up on the Purbeck and walked on it. Then he turned on William de Waus and called him a liar. He said that Clonmacnois was a hundred miles to the west and the river went nowhere near it. So what were we doing here? This stone was obviously not going to Clonmacnois. It was going to Carlow to be used by his brother-in-law to fortify his castle. "Can you deny this?" he demanded. When William de Waus attempted to the chief shut him up with a fierce glare. "You're hand-in-glove with my brother-in-law and I should kill you if I have any sense." On and on he raged and rambled, tapping his leg with his sword's blade.

"I wonder why he wants black stone for his castle?" he said. "Ah, I know. So no one will see what he does to my poor sister Belle at night."

All the henchmen started to laugh. We on the barge did not. It was plain to us that this chief was nothing more than a brigand. The mad callousness of his nature was further revealed when Liam came out of his faint and sat up, clutching his hand and crying. I went to help him, thinking that a child would not alarm anyone. The chief snarled at me like a guard dog and I scuttled back, leaving Liam to staunch his own wound as best he could.

I shook with rage and disgust. If I had had a hammer and chisel against the barbarian's brow at that moment I would have driven it home with joy in my heart and carved his cranium into some meaning. Instead I had to watch him swaggering and smirking, enjoying the hold he had over us, parading his paltry *puissance*. Then he looked at the sun, observed the people who were walking from the stockade to satisfy their curiosity, sheathed his sword, took a scoffing look at Liam's wound, leapt back on to the bank and mounted his horse.

His warriors watched him closely: every grimace, every glance, every little movement of his hand. The chief sat on his mount, shoulders slumped, staring to the south. He sighed a couple of times and rubbed his nose, muttered something to himself.

Aware of his audience he tugged at his long upper lip and mused, his eyes fixed on the downstream course of the river. Any movement in the crowd made him twitch with irritation. As the minutes passed all the people held themselves perfectly still, not wanting to disturb their leader's massive pondering. It went on and on. The horses became restless. The warriors had to scratch their fleas. Flocks of birds passed overhead on their morning forays for food and we saw them return to their nesting-places much later as we stood and waited. When he did begin to speak in his barbarous mess of a dialect we all jumped with the shock of it.

"You have taught me something about my enemy," he said with a sharp wave to the south. "He is richer than I thought. If he can afford to bring stones from England to build his defences then he has become too strong for me. Go to Carlow and tell him that I am coming in to

65

submit and be his man: but tell him that I should be treated with respect as I could still do him damage if I wanted to. Also, I am his relative by marriage."

Before the last word was out of the chief's mouth, William de Waus was bowing to indicate his immediate acceptance of this arrangement. He told Liam to tell the chief that he would pass on his message if he would be so kind as to let him have the name of his brother-in-law. Liam took some time to get started, stumbling over the words, his eyes fixed on the deck as he nursed his hand. When he had finished interpreting the chief rode his horse right to the edge of the bank and leaned forward over its neck.

"How many people are building castles in Carlow?" he roared down at William de Waus, then galloped off, his warriors trailing reproachfully along behind him, giving us many a backward glance.

Under the eyes of the silent crowd we poled off into the current. They stared at us with neither hostility nor amicableness. If the chief had had us cut to pieces for a breakfast entertainment they would not have regarded us differently. That day, in their talk, we would be the stone-men. If there was anything worth remembering about our visit to Athy it would be how a cut was put across a helping hand.

VIII

We had hoped to pick up supplies in Athy as our food was running low. William de Waus was not inclined to halt our progress to the south even though he knew that Carlow might prove to be a worse place to get through than Athy had been. His barge was at risk. We could not dawdle. If we approached any other settlement for flour or meat we might be in greater danger than if we encouraged the favour of the chief's brother-in-law by bringing him news that he wanted to hear. Then, again, he might be the sort of man who would brush aside our explanations, take the stone, steal the barge and sell us all into slavery. Either way we had everything to lose. So we fished, we gathered green stuff from the banks, we found a few duck chicks and roasted them. William de Waus kept us moving.

The man who was least afraid of the future that gaped in front of us was Roger. He was not like the rest of the crew inasmuch as he put a great value on his own thoughts. His obedience to William de Waus was an observation of duty but it did not prevent him from thinking around the predicament we all shared. William de Waus forbade us to be cowards, or ever to contemplate abandoning his precious vessel and taking our chance in the countryside, but these prohibitions served to excite Roger's intellect.

"Willy has over-reached himself this time," Roger confided to me as we floated between an avenue of overhanging aspens. "I've worked for him on and off for two years and this is the deepest trouble he's been in. We've delivered stone, glass and timber up and down the south, east and west coasts of England. We've delivered lime to the Welsh at Saint David's. It hasn't been easy but he's made a good profit. Now, suddenly, at his age, he takes a contract from an Irish bishop who's known to be off his head, has to move into leasing ocean-going vessels and transporting his barge over a huge, dangerous distance on tow — a dicy business I can assure you — and all for what? I can tell you: a killing. He's charging the abbot of Clonmacnois a fortune for this job. But he could make the same money by doing three less risky trips up to York or Ely. So, why has he done this at an age when he is supposed to have accrued wisdom? Can it be only his cash-craziness? I say no. It's something else. What Willy wants to do is leave his mark. The most impossible job for the most impossible money in the most impossible country. It's his last challenge before he retires and settles down in Swanage."

"Stop polluting the child's mind with your chatter," William de Waus growled from his seat in the stern. "If I listened to the likes of you in my life I'd be in poverty. No one wants his neighbour to make money. A lot of the time they don't even want their neighbour to live."

Roger rested his pole, glad of the encouragement to enter into discussion. He winked at me as if to say: listen to this. It will help you to understand.

"This venture of yours will probably cost us all our lives," he said blandly. "None of us will object. We have to work. Your mistakes are part of the destiny we have chosen by serving a man who doesn't see beyond his pocket. We have the comforts of our religion to sustain us. You have the thought of all the money you've made out of us to keep you happy. When the chief at Carlow puts an end to us all there will be music in heaven for us and your wife can rattle your purse in memory of you."

William de Waus sniffed and gave Roger a look that was both hard and fond.

"To think that I was once thinking about adopting you as my son and heir, Roger," he said. "What a reward I would have got for my kindness. As God has seen fit not to give me children he has also made me incapable of judging a true friend. I was not made for fatherhood or amity, it seems."

"Here," Roger replied, pushing me forward. "Here's a friend. He'll believe anything you tell him because he knows no better. But not me. I've got opinions of my own."

William de Waus laughed and shook his head. The sun was now at its noon height and the river was clad in a clarity of such distinct hues that it hurt my eyes to look at it. The sky was completely within the water, blue for blue, bounded by the rolling green reflection of the banks. Above and below us was a casement of colours that moved with us like a second barge, the vessel of our fates.

"Boy," William said ruefully, "if you do not see your father again I am sorry. To be the son of such a famous man must be a great joy to you. As you grow up — if you get the opportunity — you will know more of the true world that we were all intended for; that world of wealth and power your father moves in. It is my belief that old Paradise was such a place. It was a court, a palace, not a peasant's plot."

I had to turn away to hide my smile. William de Waus did not know my father as I did. To him he was a creature of fable and legend, a divinely gifted craftsman, intimate of abbots and lords, marvel of the mighty. To me he was still just Bert and no matter what had happened to him at Clonmacnois (could it really be much better than Athy?) he was not going to have changed all that much. Nevertheless I was somewhat shocked to discover that I felt resentful William de Waus should have an inflated idea of my father's worth. To be irritated by such an enjoyable inaccuracy — or so it should have been for me! — was worrying. Bert might have already saved my life. If the bargemen had not found out that I was the son of an important man in their lives — the customer, no less — they might have disposed of me already. Thus I conjured with conjectures as we slowly wound our way towards Carlow.

We entered Carlow on the afternoon of the second day after leaving Athy. The crew had resigned itself to some form of maltreatment, not finding it credible that they should escape twice in succession. If the chief of Carlow was merely a larger specimen on the Athy model then his malignancy would be that much greater and our chances that much smaller. It surprised me that no one had attempted to desert the barge under these circumstances and, more curiously, everyone had become more cheerful within their fatalism. By the time we encountered the chains across the river which guarded the town we were ready for anything.

We pulled ourselves in on the chain to the left bank as that was the side most built up. A fort made of timber and turf stood on a piece of rising ground above the roofs of the huts. Having made fast we braced ourselves, not even bothering to take shelter or keep the stone between us and bowshot.

No one came.

William de Waus walked up and down the deck. He called out in a light, dry voice a couple of times: not too loud but enough to be able to say that he had given warning of our presence.

There was no answer.

The chain was held to the bank by a simple hook set into a rusty hasp. It would have been an easy matter to remove it and be on our way, replacing the chain behind us so no one would know we had passed through. But William de Waus decided to be more cautious. He sent Roger into the town to reconnoitre, taking Liam with his bandaged hand and myself along to deflect suspicion and attract sympathy should we bump into anyone. Roger protested to no avail. We left the barge and went into the maze of narrow, muddy streets.

There was no hearth-smoke over the town. No dogs barked at our approach. We peered behind the door-hangings of some of the hovels and found evidence of habitation but no people or livestock. As we advanced we began to feel the coldness of the place. It went beyond the morning chill of the river valley into the realm of the spirit, a frost of the soul.

Beside the turf fort was a large paddock full of horses, many of them dressed with ornaments. Beyond that was another paddock full of cattle, pigs and sheep. No one stood guard over these animals. We stood by the barrier of thorn branches and scanned the walls of the low fort. Nothing stirred.

Roger led us round the fort's perimeter. He had decided not to be at all surreptitious.

"Walk boldly," he said, "don't look afraid or guilty. If they are forced into fear and trembling by us three then we might as well keep them worried."

He put his hand on the pommel of the battered half-sword William de Waus had lent him and strode ahead. We followed along behind, listening for an arrow's sigh.

On the other side of the fort was a church, also made of turf. A cross of ash-boughs stood drunkenly on the roof. The door was open and we saw the backs of people who had crowded in, filling the entrance. As we paused lots of dogs started to bark inside the fort. We looked at Roger for guidance and he pointed to the church.

"We can only go there, God help us," he whispered.

In spite of the dogs we remained unchallenged as we crossed the area in front of the fort gates to the church. When we were standing next to the people crammed into the entrance Roger tried to make our presence felt by coughing, hemming, even clapping his hands. No one bothered to turn and look at us. We could hear voices raised inside the church and I recognised the tum and bamus banter of Latin.

Made confident by the total indifference of the crowd to our arrival, Roger put me up on his shoulders to see what was going on inside. I have never seen so many people packed into such a small space. It was a lesson in the real relationship between our body volume and the space we can occupy if pressed. They were like piglets stacked against a sow in there, not an inch between. At the other end of the church there was colour, the blaze of pure white against the overwhelming bog-browns, a feather or two, and the encrustations of gold wire, jewels and embroidery. I saw the high headdresses of women of rank and the odd drooping bonnets of men of distinction. A priest was raised above them supported by a host of red-haired altar-boys who clustered round his feet like robins.

"What's going on?" Roger hissed.

"Sssssh!" the people in front of us hissed back.

"It's not Sunday, is it?" Roger persisted.

"Will you shut your gabbin'?" the man directly in front of us said, giving us a glance over his shoulder.

I bent down and whispered in Roger's ear that I thought it was a wedding or a christening involving people of high station. He pulled my head down and whispered that I should especially check to see if there was a coffin to be seen anywhere. I assured him that there was not.

Roger walked away from the church entrance and set me down.

"All we can do is wait for someone to take some notice of us," he said, folding his arms. "Stand here and look brave."

We stood and looked brave for another half-hour before the church started to empty. The people backed out of the entrance, tumbling, falling over themselves as they were violently pushed out. I could hear voices loud as herd-boys inside. The people spilled out in a sunken silence, picking themselves up when they fell.

As they turned in our direction we stood as firm and straight as we could, Liam's arm in his sling hung before us like a banner of helplessness; my meagre height and years positioned next to Roger, my hand in his as a sign of good nature. We looked into the eyes of every person who passed, man, woman and child. Not one of them gave us a nod or a glance as they hurried back into the town.

Our little show of courage went unnoticed until a group of warriors in mail came out of the church pushing the last stragglers with their sword scabbards. One of them strode over to us.

71

"You'll be off the English boat," he said. "You," (he fingered Roger's cheek,) "go and tell your fellows to sit tight until we can deal with you. These two can stay here with me."

Roger let go of my hand. He wanted to speak but the warrior gave him a nudge in the direction of the river.

"We have a busy day. Do as you're told."

All the colour I had seen clustered at the east end of the crude little church came out into the sun. It expanded as it hit the air. Robes were flung open; hats were doffed; hems were swung; sleeves were flapped. By now I had shifted my hand into Liam's and I felt the sweat in his palm.

"What's the matter?" I enquired. "No one's hurting us."

"It's the company I fear," Liam whispered. "That's the Musgrave of Urslin Glebe."

He indicated an absurd figure dressed in a violet cloak. The man had the benign expression of a high-nosed sheep and a round-ribbed stature to go with it. He looked innocuous, if over-dressed.

"Why are you afraid of him?" I asked.

"He's the cousin of the King of Leinster. This must be a very great affair or he wouldn't be here," Liam gabbled, jigging his wounded hand in the sling. "Sure we must be trespassing on their time. Willy has ignored a warning sign on the river or something. . . ."

The bride and groom came out of the church accompanied by the priest and the most gorgeously dressed guest of all. All the people had left by then and only the rich were left in their splendour. I was struck by the ugliness of the bride who was small and dark, her face cross-hatched with lines that could have been from laughter or temper, also the beauty of a woman by her side, a waiting-lady perhaps, whose fairness was marred by a black eye. The groom was a short, tubby man with a fuzz of golden hair left in circlet round the back of his head, his bald dome painted with a mark that I could not yet decipher. He smiled a great deal showing a set of fierce ivory teeth. Yet none of these kept my attention more than the gorgeous guest. He glittered like a dream.

The wedding-party's horses were brought to them and they mounted up. We stared as the jewels flashed and the air brought us the reek of magnificent perfumes. With an official carrying a gilded staff at the head, the cavalcade set off and proceeded towards the fort gates which were opened to admit it. The whole journey was no more than fifty yards.

As the last horse went through, the warrior who had previously accosted us came across and told us to follow him. We entered the fort and stood in the courtyard while the wedding-party dismounted amidst more gales of scent and laughter. As we waited William de Waus and the rest of the crew arrived with Roger. They were told to stand with us.

The gorgeous guest was no horseman. I had noticed how much trouble he had hauling himself into the saddle, even with the help of a groom. The man's broad vat of a body was not made for riding, nor for walking. There was something ape-like about it under all that finery. As he dismounted he lost his balance and crashed to the ground uttering a stream of tremendous oaths.

My heart stopped as I listened. The hat of the gorgeous guest had fallen off during his tumble and there was the wispy black hair above the pendant pearl ear-rings. Behind the jewels in his beard was the mouth I had kissed. It was not smiling now but as the grooms rushed to help him to his feet I heard the famous laugh and the wonderful smile followed soon after.

"Dad!" I cried, rushing up and hurling myself at him. "It's you!"

The grooms dragged me away immediately, beating me about the head. Bert stared, unable to believe his eyes.

"Stop!" he commanded. "Don't hit him."

"Bert!" I shouted, jumping up and down, "It's me, Hedric!"

"You're too fat to be my Hedric," he said carefully, his eyes roaming all over me, "though I know that voice."

"And you're too fancy to be my father," I replied, "but I know the way you fall off a horse."

Bert rushed forward and swept me into his arms. He whirled me around, kissed me and hugged me until I was breathless. The wedding-party were delighted and let out shrieks of enjoyment.

"I've brought you luck, Herbert Haroldson," the bridegroom declared. "Glad I am to have brought joy to such a man as you. This is, indeed, a great day. We will celebrate two times over. I, Ranulf the Clement welcome you here, child."

As he bent over to offer me his hand to kiss I saw that the sign painted on top of his bald head was this: **H̅H̅**

When we found each other again that day in Carlow our instinct was to go away to somewhere quiet and find out how much had happened to us. That was not to be. Suddenly we were the centre-piece of the wedding-feast. A celebration that had been marred by coldness and fear was now made warm by our happiness. No one would leave us alone. I was cosseted and cuddled, having to spend all my time on the knees of men and women who were not used to holding children, enduring their caresses and wine-laden breath while I longed to be with Bert. There were so many questions that I wanted to ask him. Many strange emotions were at war in me. As I watched him swagger around the tables in the hall I had to stop myself laughing while, I observed, the crew of the barge watched him in admiration. The more that the bridegroom and his guests deferred to Bert the more I wanted to pull him down to the man I had last seen in the Isle of Man — a prisoner, a conscript. Oh, I could not bear this butterfly with his powder-bright wings! It was not true of him.

The feast went on all day and night. I was not allowed to have any time with my father at all and he made no effort to seek me out beyond the occasional pat on the head as he circulated amongst the other guests. The crew were given places at the end of the hall and I eventually managed to rejoin them. Together we watched the high table folk get drunk, something they did with absolute unawareness of the lower orders crammed below them. If the men wanted to urinate they did so on the spot, using vessels off the table. If they were sick they merely leant over sideways and coughed it on to the floor. The women ate little and drank less, sitting stiffly beside these roaring clowns, their faces impassive.

It was with regret that I watched my father sink into the debauch. Remembering how desperate I had been over the last couple of months, how much I had missed him, this was pain indeed for me. By the time evening came I was too miserable to disguise my feelings and I wept.

"Don't cry," William de Waus said softly. "Your father is only doing what he has to. They're all only doing what they have to. Sit it out."

"But I want to talk to him!" I mumbled fretfully. "He's just ignoring me."

"If he's Lord Ranulf's best friend of the moment, then he has to watch out. They told me in the town as we came up that his lordship

74

loves heartily and swiftly," William de Waus went on, his eyes set straight ahead as if he were not talking to me. "See that fair woman three places to his right? The one with the black eye? That's his wife up until yesterday. She's the sister of the chief at Athy. They told me in the town that she has bruises all over her body, poor creature."

I looked at the fair woman. She had the frozen look of the condemned. Her hands lay on the table in front of her and she stared at them as if they were part of the feast.

"How is she not his wife today if she was yesterday?" I asked William de Waus.

"The Pope has granted him a divorce on the grounds that members of her family follow an older religion."

"What religion is that?" I said, my voice shaking.

"Oh, something to do with trees."

Bert started waving his arms around in a gesture that was familiar to me but now terrifying. He rocked back and forth, he whistled and whooped. I recognised this as a presagement to a major change of mood. Shortly he would start arguing with someone. He would get into deep water. I got off my seat to run to him.

William de Waus held me back.

"Let him be. There'll be time enough," he whispered.

"He's going to start a row with someone," I explained, trying to shake off his restraining hand. "He'll get us all into trouble."

How wrong I was. Bert was merely beginning to tell the bridegroom about the church he was going to build for him; of its beauteous proportions, its inner geometry, its meaning. "The face of your beloved will be in its ground plan," he promised. "Where you worship will have the die-stamp of your power, your existence under the supreme *creators*" (how cunningly he slurred that word-ending, I thought). "I must not speak of death on such a day as this but once you have gone, Lord Ranulf, your life-adventure will remain emblazoned here, in Carlow, in the church that I will build for you."

I sat open-mouthed as I listened to this bardic incantation. Lord Ranulf shared my admiration for Bert's eloquence but not my amazement. He had, I reasoned later, probably heard it before whereas I had never seen Bert in such command of either self or language. What had happened to him at Clonmacnois? Had he sat at the feet of the greatest Offaly poets? Was there an hallucinatory herb in his drink?

"You do me well, Herbert Haroldson," Lord Ranulf said, "and I am not a man to be impressed easily. Not another man in Carlow has been to the Port of Glory at the shrine of Saint James at Compostella as I have; not another soul has knocked his head against the head of the statue of himself that the mason put there so all would recall his triumphs. By that knocking I have the echo of his bedazzling brains and I know my building mysteries, yes I do. If I were not who I am I would be a mason and a good one too. I love a good mason. I love you, Herbert Haroldson . . . (here he clasped Bert to his bosom and bent his bald head for it to be kissed in veneration). . . . In my head there is a city! Its walls are not of turf but of marble! Last night I dreamed of it and I dreamed that you, Herbert Haroldson, my friend, built it for me in a year and a day. You put your mark on the place where my dream came from, with love and respect, I'm sure . . ."

Bert bent to kiss the spot again. Lord Ranulf pulled him down for more, tears streaming down his glistening red face.

"I have been to Santiago de Compostella! Who calls me a liar?" Lord Ranulf roared, thrusting Bert away. "I have seen the head of Saint James. He smiled at me!"

Everyone in the hall nodded or grunted affirmations of this obvious truth. Bert sat down, his hat askew, his knees apart, sweat darkening his clothes. I could see that he was exhausted. Later on I was to be given a full account of the run-up to Lord Ranulf's wedding.

His lordship had journeyed across to Clonmacnois to receive the Pope's verdict on his application for a divorce from Belle d'Athy, the chief's sister, and to obtain permission to marry the ugly, monkey-faced woman who was Edna of the Thousand Children, a courtesan from Armagh (and one of the loveliest natures I have ever encountered). Belle had proved to be childless, hence the ill-treatment, but Ranulf had adored her still. His solution to the dilemma was to divorce Belle and keep her as his concubine, marry Edna (who was as fertile as a foxglove) and thereby recruit an army for the future — her thousand children — all of whom would be legitimised by papal decree. While at Clonmacnois Lord Ranulf had met Bert who was kicking his heels and waiting for the load of Purbeck to come up the Shannon so he could start building. He had become a favourite of the abbot, an otherworldly man of Celtic feyness, by dint of his facility with the science of the spirit — a corner of thought much occupied by people of our clandestine persuasion. Bert could talk about the invisible in a way that none of the monks could: he could build in the air! It was this religious wit, this ease of movement in the universe of light, that convinced the abbot Bert would be a master of material. The more Bert talked, the more the abbot became astonished that a layman, a base, secular creature, could have such sensibilities.

Meanwhile, Bert had not laid stone upon stone, nor (and this I find more significant) did he feel that the abbot really wanted him to. As with all Christians, it was failure that the abbot feared. He had come to venerate Bert's skill with the free spirit but he dared not believe that such intuition could manifest itself in stone. (Can it ever? I ask.) So, the building plans for Clonmacnois were an agreed fantasy. It was a case of the barge that never landed, the mortar that was never mixed, but the myth that became supreme. By the time Lord Ranulf arrived to hear the result of his suit this myth was as flamboyant, obvious and hollow as a pageant-head and both men were glad to break it. The abbot dropped his feyness for long enough to do a deal with Lord Ranulf whereby the divorce and the permission to remarry were included in a cross-transfer of land-rights in Kilkenny and Athlone and Lord Ranulf took up some of the abbot's war-service responsibilities to the King of Leinster and guaranteed a bequest on his death of fifteen hundred marks, plus the building of a church in Carlow more in keeping with Christ's dignity. The abbot gave Bert to Lord Ranulf as a free gift to help with the church. Because he had got him for nothing Lord Ranulf loved Bert immediately. Since they met at Clonmacnois they had never stopped talking or been sober.

Although I was not aware of all this history at the time of the wedding-feast it saddened me to see my father taking part in such a charade. The bonhomie was false. His lordship's love was not worth a halfpenny. My father danced like a bear on a chain of fear. He had not worked properly since we fled from Seaton-near-Bootle and had lived off his wits and unkeepable promises for too long. What little skill he had must be crumbling inside him, I thought as I looked at him quaffing again; his hands will be soft, his eye uncertain, his nerve brittle. I must get him back to England soon or he will die the white cutter's death, the hammerless agony.

Belle d'Athy left the high table and came down to where I was sitting. Servants followed her and stood protectively around as she found a place at our table. She shooed them away with a flash of her beautiful slender arms and I saw the reddened knuckles of her hand in a pink blur. The black eye stared at me with a bloodshot anger but the other one was meek enough.

"Boy," she croaked.

"My lady?"

"You have met my brother, I hear."

"We have," I replied as calmly as I could.

"What did you think of him?"

I thought for a while. William de Waus contrived to warn me off from being too outspoken with a squeeze under the table.

"He refuses to make his mind up in a hurry," I said.

"That is one of his qualities. The other one is that he is rash, cruel and inconsiderate."

"Those are three qualities," I replied, hoping to make her smile. She did so, revealing two broken teeth on her upper right jaw.

Unwilling to be outdone in the matter of child-charming, Edna of the Thousand Children left the high table to the roaring of the drunks and picked her way down to join us. As she got closer I saw she was not, in fact, ugly. From a distance her face was as knotted and dark as thornwood but it cleared into petiteness and merriment as she got closer. Her eyes were very deep brown under a jewelled scarf of wheaten colour and they warmed as they looked. If I were a courtesan then I would want eyes like Edna's. They would be of more use than the most beautiful body in the world.

"You are talking to the mason's son, are you not?" she enquired pleasantly. "It would be true to say that the child needs his hair cutting and his clothes washing. He has lived with dirty men for long enough though I swear I've never seen such a handsome lot beneath the rags they're wearing, I have not, I have not."

As she made the strange little sing-song repetition at the end of what she was saying, her head bobbed like a bird's and her eyes flickered as if on a spring behind her forehead. She caught me looking at her and my frown of consternation. I blushed beneath her gaze that was, at first, fiercely haughty, then deliciously amicable.

"Ah, you have noticed the symptom? 'Tis nothing to be ashamed of, boy. Too much coquetry in my younger days. Too many wee affections for the menfolk. Now it is nothing but a tremor of remembrance of my old loves, it is an' all, an' all."

"An' all, an' all, an' all!" her servants sang in gentle mockery from their places against the wall. "'Tis only the symptom."

Our conversation (which, I must confess, I was enjoying) was interrupted by a huge altercation breaking out on the high table between Lord Ranulf and the King's cousin, the Musgrave of Urslin Glebe. The Musgrave had offended Lord Ranulf by getting so enthusiastic about church-building and my father's legendary skill that he had offered Bert a massive bribe to come and work for him instead. Lord Ranulf gave my father no time to answer. Wrapping the Musgrave's violet cloak around its wearer's head he poured ale over him. Although both the offer to Bert and the dousing were claimed as jests later on it was a killing matter at the time. What prevented harm from taking place was the entry of Belle's brother, the chief of Athy, with his band of warriors. They had come into the fort unchallenged. As they stood in the entrance of the hall I could see another long period of thought descending upon the chief. In about three hours he would work it out that the enemy had been completely at his mercy.

He took in the scene at the high table; our presence, the black eye his sister was wearing, and shrugged.

"I'm your man!" he called out, then knelt down, beckoning his warriors to do likewise.

"Ach, it's too late for that, brother!" Belle called out. "Why in God's name can't you do things when they're most of use?"

"Go on, away with you Belle, your brother is too stupid to understand half of what's happening to him," Edna retorted with a knowing chuckle. "It will be next week before he works it out that it's all up with him and you all together. Anyway, this party has all the signs of becoming hell on earth before long. Let's retire with the child and you can mother him to ease your heart, so you can, so you can."

I was taken out of the hall and into the women's chamber. My last sight of Bert was of him placing plates and cups to show how his new church would be constructed, where the tower would be, here the altar (the salt-cellar), there the choir (two rows of walnuts), here the font for your lordship's babies to be baptised (a goblet), and here the front porch (Bert's hands spread into a span); on this side a chapel to the holy mother (a gnawed chicken carcase), and on this a chantry for the soul of your ancestors (a round of blood-pudding), somewhere in the middle your tomb (a loaf of bread).

As my father enthused over his design for the new church at Carlow, the chief of Athy remained on his knees at the bottom end of the hall, ignored.

IX

The women's chamber was a long, low room hung with painted blankets and tapestries torn from the walls of greater palaces and cut about to fit this unwindowed byre of a place, giving it a raffish luxury like a market-stall outside a prince's palace. With all the rich cladding on the walls it was airless and full of the odours of ancient fabrics. An enormous fireplace took up half of one long wall but there was no fire in it. The heat in the room was the left-over from the last one. As I played in the hearth I could feel the warmth of its stone as if a volcano had spewed it freshly out of the earth's inner chambers. The smell of women, old perfumes, food and flowers hung in the air like the smoke of the burning mountain, source of all stone as Bert had told me; the Evil God shoots it out of the world's carbuncle as matter.

Left on my own for a moment I played with a long grey cat that was coiled in a cushioned chair. Then two servants came in to lay the fire. They made a huge construction of twigs, branches and logs graded from sapling girth to full-blown beech boughs. I asked them why more heat was needed in the room as I was already sweating but they did not answer.

Belle d'Athy and Edna of the Thousand Children returned to me having changed out of their wedding robes. Both of them were wearing thin white shifts and their hair was let down loose. Behind them came more servants with a wooden tub which was set in front of the hearth. The fire was lit. The servants left and returned with pots of boiling water with which they filled the tub. As the fire leapt up and the servants withdrew Belle and Edna pulled their shifts over their heads and stood naked before me.

"I thought the bath might be for me," I managed to say, my throat getting tighter as I looked at them.

"It is, little one," Edna said softly, "but we must wait for the water to cool."

She bent over and put her elbow into the tub, withdrawing it swiftly with a sharp intake of her breath. In the upraised red flames of the fire I saw her black-nippled breasts crushed against the wooden staves of the tub and the incredibly rich curve of her rear. The iron band inside my neck was tightening on my throat, making it difficult for me to breathe. I thumbed my Adam's apple.

"Belle will cut your hair. She does it well," Edna said, turning to face me, her breasts trembling with the weight of those jet shields pointedly proud now, getting larger. My mouth watered and she knew it. "Lord Ranulf would never allow her to cut his hair in case she drove the scissors into his back while she was barbering him. But you can trust our Belle, I'm thinking, I'm thinking."

I had avoided looking directly at Belle having glanced at her once and caught an impression of strange colours and patches like tattoos all over her. Now she put herself right in front of me, threw the cat off the chair, picked me up and put me firmly on the cushion.

Her long white body was covered with bruises. The insides of her thighs were as though painted blue-black, each side matching the other. Her small breasts and narrow shoulders were covered with bite-marks. At the backs of her knees were thumb-sized roundels of purple.

"Ach, don't stare so," she murmured. "Didn't you know we Irish are always painting ourselves for battle?"

Taking a handful of my hair she pulled my head forward and pressed my temples into her bush. Above me I could hear the snip of scissors. There was a scent of musk and salt and I knew that I was weeping.

"There, there, get it all out," Edna said from the side, stroking my back. "Let's pity ourselves and each other for all the time we have. If you had a sweetheart then she'd want a lock of your hair, infested with nits though it is, it is."

Putting my arms around Belle's hips I clung to her and sobbed. All of the terror and unhappiness, all of the toughening and tension, all of the forced growth I had endured in my early years came pouring out in this blessed release. The women clucked and caressed. They kissed the tips of my ears, my fingers, the nape of my neck.

"Who's having a feast in Carlow today, us or them?" Edna chuckled. "There's a man under all that hair. There's a man under all those tears, be it known, be it known."

I was now entirely in their hands. Having shorn me, they took my clothes off and threw them in the fire. I stood on the chair and watched the sparks fly up the chimney.

"How old are you supposed to be," Belle whispered, her hand gently cradling my genitals.

"I think I'm supposed to be eight," I said in a voice that seemed to come from the hair that lay around my feet, "but I may have forgotten."

Edna screwed up her brilliant monkey-face and tugged the end of my foreskin.

"Ding dong. Time for church. We just wanted to have a good look at you before you grow up and get ruined. So sweet you are, sweeter than your father, I'll be bound, be bound."

The water was still too hot but I got in anyway. The attention that had been paid to my cock had made it stand and I was nearly crying with shame. Edna gave it a stinging flick with her finger and it subsided immediately.

"It's a waste of time a warrior standing to when there's no chance of a fight," Edna said with a snort. "You'll have to learn to control that. If you do, you'll be the first man in the world to manage it. My mother used to say, stay a virgin and die curious but I never had the heart for it, heart for it."

Belle rubbed me with soap that had grit in it. I winced and cried out but she kept on, scratching my skin.

"We have no better soap," she explained grimly as she worked. "Even the fat of our animals is rough."

Looking up out of the tub I saw the faces of the two women as they bent over me, their hair lank with the steam, their breasts gleaming with sweat. All the finery had gone, the scents, the robes, the glory of their uncoveredness. They were the two guardians of my two souls, plus and minus, creators of my life. Above the twisted roof of this barbarous place, above the tree-smoke and the sparks of my past journeys that must be up there, dancing in the darkness like fire-flies, were the Two Gods of my genius, male and female, the sexually divine duality. Which was good and which was bad would be the question of a lifetime.

When I was thoroughly clean they told me to climb from the tub, wrapped me in rough towels and left me for the servants to find by the fire, their interest in me going as fast as it had come.

I was taken to a dormitory where all the children of the fort slept. When I was put to bed all the other children were asleep. I lay and listened to the noise from the feast, trying to pick out Bert's shouts. Every time I heard furniture being broken or the clang of thrown vessels, I thought it was Bert, the ludicrous peacock who could make my heart turn with his sad, wild sounds. I had heard him come home many, many times; waiting like a wife to scold him. In those old days he would sit and talk to me, his head full of nonsense. Now things had changed. I thought Bert might never use me as his confessor again.

With this regret in my mind I fell asleep.

I awoke with a hand pressed over my mouth. My fear of the Carthusians came flooding back and I fought the man who held me. It took me a time to realise that it was Bert: too late to stop myself biting his hand. He cried out then slapped my face, pulling the bedclothes over my head.

"Hush, Hedric, calm down, it's me!" he hissed. "Keep quiet. Slowly he drew the bedclothes back and I stared up at him while he sucked his hand. "Trust you," he muttered. "Listen, I want no questions. We have to go. Lord Ranulf's having Belle, her brother and all the Athy followers killed tonight. He's letting me leave because I'm an artist . . . don't you dare laugh! He doesn't want the bloodletting to influence my design for the church. He's mad drunk downstairs and if I put a foot wrong he'll change his mind. So, whatever you do, keep your mouth shut."

We crept downstairs to the courtyard where Lord Ranulf waited, holding a saddled and loaded horse by the bridle. He was swaying and muttering to himself. My father gently took the bridle from his hand then began to lead the horse to the gates. Lord Ranulf wove his way in front of us, his bald head gleaming in the moonlight.

"I can stop you, Herbert Haroldson. I can stop you if I want to, but I won't. You keep my church safe in your mind and come back in a fortnight after we've cleaned up."

"I'll be back," Bert averred, "never doubt it, your lordship."

"But should I include my Belle in all this? I love her so. What d'you think? Ach, she'll make a gorgeous corpse and she can have my tomb you're making for me," Lord Ranulf said, smiling.

"Bert," I whispered as we walked through the gates, "what about the men off the barge?"

He did not reply. Lord Ranulf was holding the horse's tail and stumbling along behind us.

"A promise is a promise, mason. You swore an oath. God will strike you dead if you let me down," he shouted. "You must come back."

"I'll not let you down," Bert replied, "I gave you my word as a Christian, didn't I?"

Lord Ranulf let go of the horse's tail and came to stand at Bert's side by the stirrup. Bending over he cupped his hands for Bert's foot.

"I'd do this for no other man," he said.

"You honour me," Bert murmured as he mounted. "I'll see you shortly."

Bert clapped his heels into the horse's sides and we moved away towards the river at a slow walk. Lord Ranulf trotted along beside us for a while, his hand clutching Bert's.

"Love is a terrible thing," he whined. "I'd rather have all my teeth out than be in love again. But you, Herbert Haroldson, you put love in perspective. You bend it into arches and make it flower into spires. . . ."

"Farewell, Lord Ranulf!" Bert said firmly, stopping the horse and taking his hand away. "Do what you have to do, God help them all."

I held my breath as Bert urged the horse forward. Lord Ranulf kept silent until I could see him no more. Then, out of the shadows I heard him cry out as if in despair. Bert lashed the horse across the haunches with the rein and we galloped down through the dark streets.

"To the river, Dad!" I said in his ear. "To the barge!"

"No! Away, away!" he said grimly. "The only place for us is away. We must get back to England as fast as we can!"

"But the bargemen helped me. They're my friends!" I shrieked.

"We can't do anything for them. All the Athy clan will die tonight. It wouldn't be long before that maniac got round to us!"

As we tore through the maze of streets, the horse ploughing up showers of mud and refuse, I kept glimpsing the river further below. As we broke out of Carlow into the open road I saw the barge at its moorings by the chain, the Purbeck looming above the river reflections like an enormous tombstone over the grave of a giant. It had been my home and my saviour, a ship of revelations. Now it was a memorial to the lost.

There can never have been such a horse. Not Bucephalus, not Pegasus! It had no name or fame, but its Irish heart was tireless. Through the dawn, down the river-meadows of the Barrow to Ballybannon, slicing through cattle-herds and rolling swine, scattering the wool-packs of sheep to the wind, on, on, round Muire Beagh to Graiguenamanagh and Graig no Monach to Mount Garret:

"Where are we? Where are we?" Bert would roar at the folk as we flew past. "How far to the sea?"

You're at Ros Mhic Thrivin. You're leaving Priesthaggard behind. Here's where the Suir joins the Barrow. Sure you're not far from the sea, can't you smell it?

Such a horse.

Two days and a night after our flight from Carlow our steed charged into the waves at Waterford and stood in clouds of salt steam, its hocks bloody, its nostrils ringed with pink foam, its lungs whistling frantically.

We dismounted and stood by its sweat-lathered body, bathing it with our hands, the sea-weed caressing its trembling legs.

"I'm glad something good has come out of Lord Ranulf's fields," Bert said, his arm over the horse's neck. "May you find gentler journeys than that we've put you through."

We walked the rest of the way into Waterford. There were two ships in harbour, one English and one Spanish. Bert found us quarters in a widow's lodging-house that night and left me behind while he went to find the master of the English vessel. When he came back it was late but I had not fallen asleep, exhausted though I was with our ride.

"Will he take us?" I asked as Bert got into the bed beside me.

"He will," he grunted.

"How much?"

"A wind-broken horse," he said heavily.

A moment later he was asleep. I tried to follow his example but I could not. With my arms around him, my legs wrapped around his, I willed myself back into our old bond but it would not re-assert itself. Slowly I disengaged myself and lay as far as I could away in the bed. With that distance between us I sensed peace. Reaching out I laid my fingertips on his outflung hand. That was all the comfort I needed and I went to sleep looking forward to the morrow.

The vessel was a small merchantman that had brought a mixed trading cargo over from Dover, its home port. It was returning half-empty, its only load a consignment of greasy wool. As there were no passenger quarters we made ourselves a cabin out of bales which, although they stank, kept out the wind and some of the water. It need hardly be said that Saint George's Channel was unkind to us, it being the brother of the accursed Irish Sea, but after one day of turbulence the weather cleared up and the sun shone down from between fast-moving clouds. It was choppy but bearable, fair and blue and breezy. After some sickness I found my sea-legs and turned to my father for a full account of his adventures in Ireland.

He would not say anything about the time we were apart. Whether he had detected the change in my attitude towards him or not I could not tell. Our separation may have been a shaming chapter in his life, one that made him accuse himself of failure and neglect of my interests. What I found hard to understand was why he showed no enthusiasm for the chronicle of *my* doings during this time! When I attempted to tell him about the sufferings and dangers I had endured he made an excuse to leave my side and went to look at the sea.

So, the old days were truly over between us. No more confessions and soliloquies by candlelight. No more sharing of the great secrets soul to soul, the honest outlining of the agony. Yet some good came out of this reticence. Although he would not open himself up to me as he had once done, he now had a strong sense of duty as to my education. Suspecting the hideous nature of many of my perils — some of which I managed to touch on before he stumbled out of our wool-cabin in his walk-aways — he obviously felt that he had not prepared me sufficiently for a white cutter's itinerant life and all its vicissitudes.

Another benefit was the degree to which he would let me into the technical lore of our craft. Up until this time he had been willing to have me watch him work, even to ask a few childish questions, but there had been no true sense of apprenticeship to a mystery. This may have been because he was apprehensive about his own standing as a skilled man. I am convinced that Bert knew how bad much of his work was and this made him anxious about how qualified he was to teach me, but after Ireland there was no more hanging back on his part. He became determined to make me the best white cutter in the world, in which ambition he succeeded.

Without his tools, using only word-pictures and the planking for a drawing-board with a charcoal stick, Bert started to lay out the fundamental issues: how things stood in the air; how things fell to the ground; how one could lean on another; how a circle behaved when it was broken; how stone was as varied in nature as people are in temper; how nothing can be trusted not to break but the risks lessened by a knowledge of thrusts and stresses, the muscle-flexing of the Evil God.

"You will not master Him but you can channel His hate into places where good will come of it. He will support your work without knowing it. While He is bearing down on your building to crush it He will, without realising it, be holding it upright. This is not to say that some day He will not perceive how you have gulled Him and wreck the edifice in retribution for your impudence. That often happens. But it is a feature of the Evil God's mind that He is only intelligent in phases and flashes. He is not consistently thoughtful, being obsessed with His material empire . . ."

It was on this occasion that I asked a question that had a bearing on my father's silence about the period when he had deserted me: I pulled him up short in his lesson on forces and pointed out that up until this time he had always referred to the Evil God as It. Now it was Him.

"It was always Him," he answered me grimly. "Same as me."

X

We made no landfall until Dover, nor was the coast visible as we sailed up the Channel through summer haze. During the nights I sometimes saw a light to the north but it was only a pinpoint which soon passed. However, the land was there, we knew. It was a far way from the north — which we sometimes called home — but, after Ireland, the land-breezes were scented with security for us. As the ship came into harbour I realised how exhausted we both were, how much in need of a respite from wandering and danger. Dover's cliffs, castle and port had a solid, strengthening effect on us. They had stood for thousands of years in one form or another. My father and I felt the grave, settled mass of the site on our spirits. We knew it would be a good place to get our breaths back and make some plans.

Dover Castle was, at this time, still undergoing repairs to the damage caused by the French during King John's reign. Thirty years after the great siege there were still gaps in the defensive walls, including the breach made by Prince Louis's miners under the eastern tower. King Henry had ordered that the castle should be made impregnable again.

Upon our arrival Bert visited the lodge of the masons who were in the King's employment and requested that they consider him for a place in their number. They kept us waiting for a month while they took up Bert's references with the Church in the north, then told him they would have to test his skill. Bert was not too proud to submit to this examination. His only stipulation was that I should be allowed to be present. As the lodge was solidly of our religion all the members of it understood the need for a white cutter's son to view the rigorous disciplines of the craft. All of them had sons of their own who were under instruction as well.

Dover Castle has a very ancient heart. It goes back beyond the Conqueror to the Older English and the Romans. That hill overlooking the harbour has appealed to everyone who has had need to defend the part of England's south coast nearest to France. It is a sublime site, one I have always longed to build on myself, though more for the sake of extending the womanly lines of the hill than for purposes of defensive military strategy.

Bert's tests were held in the Roman lighthouse which was still in use. While a beacon fire burned overhead, its crackling and roaring clearly audible in the chamber where we had assembled, Bert was put through a trial of knowledge and skill. None of it was very hard and I was often tempted to give the answers for him but this I resisted as Bert would have found it humiliating.

One of the examiners was a Fleming. He was a small, swarthy man with deep clefts in his cheeks and darting, restless black eyes. He was about Bert's age but his hair had already gone white. He kept directing Bert's attention to the structure we were standing in — the lighthouse.

"What do you think of this?" he asked, waving his hand to include the walls and wooden ceiling.

Bert looked at the stonework for a moment, and the setting of the ceiling timbers. There were only two small windows which were no more than holes in the wall and one door which was nothing fancy in design.

"It is well built, what there is of it. It serves its purpose," he eventually replied. "I don't see why this room has to be as high as it is but then I wasn't here when it was built. It might have had a different function in those days."

I thought this was a good, reasonable answer and I could hardly stop myself nodding in agreement but the Fleming scowled and brushed Bert's response aside.

"It isn't designed at all!" he muttered in his guttural accent. "You can feel that no one took that trouble."

"The Romans were great builders," Bert ventured to say. "We have learnt most of our skill from them."

The Fleming stood close to Bert. My father was not a tall man but he had to look up to him. Such was the energy and restlessness of the littler man that it seemed as though he commanded all Bert's greater size, pulling him down.

"Slaves built this, mason," he said harshly. "Can't you see that?"

Bert laughed.

"Just from looking at it?"

The Fleming nodded.

"Who is this man?" Bert suddenly demanded, his cheeks reddening.

"Tell him!" the Fleming shouted and walked away into the shadows with an indignant stride. The other members of the examination board informed Bert that the Fleming was Hans Seersach, head of the Dover lodge, a great master who had worked on Bruges, Cluny, Maastricht, Rouen and Coutances, to name but a few.

Bert was silent for a while, thinking his way through this new turn of events. He needed to pass this test but the Fleming had irritated him.

"Was my answer wrong?" he asked, finally. "Or was it just not the one Master Seersach required for his argument?"

I was impressed by this tactic on Bert's part. What I had expected him to do was storm out after delivering a squall of abuse, telling the lodge elders to keep their job. But he was thinking, these days. Ireland had taught him diplomacy.

Hans Seersach came back into the group and touched Bert's sleeve; apologetically smiling up at him.

"You are right, brother. I was provoking you," he began.

He got no further. Bert hit him with a tremendous backhand blow across the face and all the Irish diplomacy was spent.

"Then you succeeded very well!" Bert bellowed as the Fleming staggered across the chamber and crashed into the wall. "I am provoked."

The other members of the examination board were amazed at Bert's effrontery in striking their leader. They stared at Bert as if he were a wild beast, holding up their hands to bid him keep still while they picked the Fleming up off the floor.

"You had better go, Herbert Haroldson," one of them said in a shaken voice. "But you will have to be punished for this."

"No, no, no . . ." Hans Seersach mumbled, passing his fingers over his bruised lips. "It was my fault."

The elders argued with him but he would have none of it. He kept looking across at Bert and holding up his bloodied fingers, grinning, while the old men fussed around him. When he had calmed them down he came across to where Bert had remained, feet apart, arms folded, his great no-necked head sunk into his shoulders like a boulder in a river-bed, and touched his sleeve again.

"I accept your reproof," he said with a nod.

"No!" the other masons chorused in disbelief.

"One should not play games with a man who needs work. If we all

90

stood up for ourselves as well as this man we would do better. But that was one blow, and against a brother. Would you strike as hard against a Cretin officer? I don't think so. I forgive you and you must forgive me. Shake hands."

Bert took the Fleming's hand. After they had shaken Bert found himself held in a mighty mason's grip which made him wince.

A white cutter standing at the door gave warning of the deputy constable's approach on his rounds. The other examining masons became agitated.

"Hans, leave it now," one said.

"I'll have no half-measures from him. If he can hit me he can obey me!" Seersach retorted, his eyes fixed on Bert's, their hands still locked. "The faith, the craft, are always first."

There was a clinking of armed men at the door and the bolt was tried. The Fleming released Bert's hand and went to the door and opened it as someone knocked.

"Sir," he said into the darkness where the party of soldiers stood in a circle of torchlight, "you cannot come in. We are having a lodge meeting."

The deputy constable came to the door and peered over Seersach's shoulder. He was a portly man wearing a grease-spotted sash over his belly as if he had been pulled out of a banquet. He rested a hand on Seersach's arm in a gesture of familiarity.

"Who is that?" he asked, nodding in Bert's direction.

"A man who has asked for work," Seersach replied evenly.

"Is he any good?"

"I think so. Do you like the look of him?"

The deputy constable laughed and stepped back.

"Don't ask for my opinion. You lads are a law unto yourselves, it strikes me. I can't keep track of your comings and goings. Here I am, supposed to hold this old place against the French and half the buggers you bring in are Frenchmen! Is he French?" The deputy constable came back to the door and jabbed a finger in Bert's direction. "Oi, you there! Are you French?"

"No sir," Bert replied.

"Thank God for that! Carry on, Hans."

With a good-natured chuckle the deputy constable walked off into the night to continue his rounds. Seersach shut the door.

"I will not come within striking distance, Herbert Haroldson, just in case you might think this another provocative question," he said with a lop-sided grin, "but do you know the deputy constable?"

"I have no reason to," Bert replied in a cautious tone, albeit friendly.

"Has anyone ever told you his name?" the Fleming persisted, remaining out of arm's-length.

"No," Bert stated flatly.

"He is Sir Henry de Montfort."

Hans Seersach moved away from the door and stood with the other senior masons as if rejoining their company. I was so taken aback by the identity of the deputy constable that I did not notice Bert's reaction. The name de Montfort is the most hated of all to anyone of our faith. It was the elder Simon de Montfort, the Butcher, who nearly annihilated the Albigenses of France and forced the remainder to flee into every corner of the world, my ancestors amongst them.

"So, the men of Dover lodge work for a de Montfort," Hans Seersach said sardonically. "We are actually paid by a descendant of the Butcher himself. Isn't that shameful? But answer me this: does our work look like the work of slaves?"

There was a long pause. Bert could not find a reply. He was obviously lost.

"You are in the south of England now, Herbert Haroldson," the Fleming said, "not the north. Here de Montforts and the Cretin kings are all-powerful, albeit in their customary confusion. We must live and to survive we must be cunning but, above all, marvellous in our work. It must never look like the work of a slave. And we must never be slaves in our minds. As you know, while the persecutions were actually taking place we were developing the First Style of Emergence. We are an inspired people. It seems that we thrive on pressure and pain but we must always use our wits to hold those forces in balance. We cannot afford to lash out. The way we will keep ourselves free in spirit is through the faith, and through the constant growth and change of our architecture which is our essence. Are you with me?

Bert nodded dumbly. Whether this meant he understood, I don't know, but I knew it meant that all the anger had gone out of him.

They sat in the Roman lighthouse with the beacon fire crackling on the roof until well into the night. I was forgotten about as they pulled the threads of our future together for my father. Bert had never met a thinker like Hans Seersach before. All of our brethren in the north had been content to get by, keeping themselves separate, discouraging debate for fear that disaffection might follow and renegades be created. They had good cause to prefer the quiet life. After all, the memory of the French crusade against our faith was still fresh in their minds and many were refugees from the Midi where we once were strongest.

"The French or Pointed Style was an Albigensian creation, as you must know," the Fleming said. "It was the original statement of our hidden, separate civilisation — our system of survival. Its inspiration was not entirely from our theological abstracts — too risky — but from Islam, a fellow victim of Christian persecution. Humiliating? Yes. But to the fathers of this new architecture it represented our truth as it thrust its way up through the Christian crust of lies. The Cretins took it because it is beautiful to them as it is to us. But they do not see the underlying truth, only the prettiness of the arrow-arch. Don't forget, those who adore beauty are not to be trusted unless they see the God behind it. What they worship is a harmony that they do not understand. The Pointed was the First Style of our Emergence as a great ulterior empire, but now we must have the Second!"

From where I was sitting I could see Bert's face. It was transformed. Herr Hans Seersach was taking the covers off all the thoughts that had been welling up in Bert's mind — thoughts he had used to articulate to me, believing that I was incapable of grasping them. Yet, in the delight there was a tussle going on. Bert did not like having to grant another man superiority of mind, or authority, if he could help it.

"What's this Second Style to be then?" he asked gruffly. "What other shapes are there left? You either have a round arch or a pointed arch or a triangle. There aren't that many choices."

"Ach, think outside the arch," Seersach said, "think about the true basis of all buildings. It is what they are filled with not what they are made of. Think of the shapes within light."

"We build with stone, not with light," Bert insisted doggedly.

"Then you think like the Cretins. You do not perceive that the truth works from its opposites. When you are fashioning stone are you not also fashioning light? Which is the purer? Which is the one worth worshipping? Stone? Dirt? Old sand and shit? Come, Herbert, have you spent your life with your eyes shut? What you should have been carving is the light!"

"I'll remember that next time I'm breaking my back over a lump of black granite," Bert rejoined.

"Do! It is the way to look at our work. It then becomes joyful not a slog. It becomes a profession of radiance. We are the mathematicians of the sun. We do not dwell on the dross."

It was nearly three o'clock before Bert's examination was over and his entry into the Dover lodge agreed. He was put on three months' probation but it was plain to me that Hans Seersach had taken a shine to my dad and had some hopes of making a lieutenant out of him. Bert's love of the tangle between death and life had come through in spite of his obstinacy and independence of mind. It may have been Ireland that had softened him up for a discipleship: such confusion can make a man desperate to learn. Hans Seersach was not only a rebel but a master as well; a man of piercing intellect and great manual skill. As Bert had begun to teach me in earnest it was good to know someone of even higher ability was teaching him in turn. Knowledge came through to me almost fresh from Hans before Bert had time to assimilate it. Often it was in conflict with other things my father had already taught me but I did not point this out. To humiliate my father would have jeopardised his apprenticeship to Hans as well as mine to him: for Bert could not admit his indebtedness to the Fleming. We were supposed to believe they were equals. It is a sign of the quality of Hans's spirit that he went along with this deception and always made it appear as though what he was revealing to my father was, in fact, emerging from Bert's mind under its own power.

The house where we lodged was one of the sweetest I have ever dwelt in. It was at the western end of the beach, away from the looming of the castle and closer to the ship traffic. We had a long walk to work each morning but it was worth it to live in such an agreeable place. Although there were mists and sea-frets to get used to — giving me many a cold and chesty cough — I loved the scent of the sea in the room where I slept, on my clothes, even in my food. All these years later, after many journeys across the salt, I can say that I would rather live by the sea than on it. I do not like my foundations to move.

Hans lodged at the same house and all three of us were cared for by Rosamund, the wife of a ship's master who worked out of Calais and the Flanders shore. He was away much of the time. From the familiarity and affection that developed between Hans and Rosamund and Bert and Rosamund I assumed that she was one of our faith. So much time was spent in intimate conference and passionate argument between these three. She was a big, fair woman with very light blue

94

eyes that opened wide as if in astonishment at the smallest day-to-day event. The way she kept her house was close to how she was in herself — clean, comfortable and tidy but with an aura of plenty and embracing warmth. She had five children, all of whom were older than I was, and I was tagged on to the end of this line as one of hers, unrecognisable from the rest in the manner in which she treated me.

She was also a woman of the most admirable patience. The amount of mason's mess which she tolerated in her house was amazing; after all, these men were only lodgers. Hans Seersach loved to make models of his designs and they littered the floors, tables, chairs and sills so we were surrounded by his masterpieces. We would have dinner with his apse at Aachen brooding over the meat and I have slept flanked by Cluny and Maastricht. Once he had finished with these models he would break them up, ignoring any request to have them preserved. It was a cause of disagreement between us as I wanted to keep them for myself as they were beautiful toys. But Hans knew my instincts and he refused to trivialise my future. "They are not toys, Hedric, or ornaments," he said to me as he crushed his model of the north door at Coutances under his heel in front of my eyes, "these models are tools. Once they have outlived their use we throw them away."

XI

The ordering of the southern lodges was much stricter than those in the north; demarcations in the craft were more rigorous, and the rewards for the top masons were great, but exposed to much envy. By the time that we were ensconced in Dover a halo of miraculousness had been spun over our work. Could ordinary men do what we had done at Salisbury and Chartres? We were being elevated, vaunted as the new hero in the ultimate battle, as the Cretins saw it: the Armageddon between the army of Human Prayer and the fortress of Christ's Indifference (sometimes called mercy). As we put up the great churches they took them as evidence of Man's penetration of the divine consciousness. The higher the church, the deeper it got into the core of the supreme being's *esprit*. So, more folk wished to become part of the masonic trade. It was a way out of serfdom if the novice could last at it for a year and a day. As the building hunger of abbots and princes became more acute our labour became more in demand. Wages improved. The result was an increased pressure by Cretins to join our ranks, until this time kept unpolluted by their noxious creed. It was this question of entry into our Dover brotherhood that precipitated the crisis I have mentioned.

Life being hard, people being what they are, it had not been difficult to persuade Cretins who had worked their way up through labouring and rough-quarrying to become *famuli* and then serve seven-year apprenticeships, that it was in their best interests to embrace our religion. Obviously this was a dangerous time for us as we were most vulnerable to betrayal. Everyone who worked in the building trade knew there were certain spiritual attachments and ideas which went with the mystery of the mason's skill. They were the subject of much folklore, gossip and speculation; but there was always a point when the aspiring novice had to find out what was expected of him.

At the stage where they were accepted as full members of our craft and our faith they were made to swear oaths of secrecy that were backed up by the severest penalties should these oaths ever be broken.

Knowing the Cretin appetite for the absurd and having things spelled out for them in pantomime, special rituals had been devised to reinforce in their minds just how seriously the whole hierarchy of European masonry viewed these declarations. We could not insist that they rejected their old religion entirely — being partly bound and dependent on it ourselves — but we demanded that our faith always be given precedence should a clash of conscience or loyalty ever develop. It was, of course, hypocrisy on the grand scale but these initiates were joining a fraternity that did everything at that level.

One Hogge Pollard, a Hampshire man from Odiham, was responsible for upsetting this apple-cart. He was forty by the time he had satisfied the lodge that he was suitable for acceptance, having spent many years supervising the conscripted labourers drafted in off the land by the King to repair his castle. This enforced employment had always been unpopular with the brotherhood because it created dissension and unhappiness amongst the workforce and kept the originating stratum of our craft, the humble hod-carrier and quarry-cracker, as a reservoir of serfdom. Hogge Pollard had worked double what other men had to teach himself the craft. To be an apprentice at his age was not easy, especially when he had to maintain his authority as a ganger into the bargain. Everyone at Dover respected him for his diligence and the energy with which he pursued his goal of self-improvement. No man deserved promotion more, it was said. Good luck to old Hogge Pollard.

Hans and Bert were the masons appointed to prepare this novice for the initiation ceremonies. To this end he visited Rosamund's house.

Hogge Pollard was a nondescript human being, already grey, his face pouched around the jowls and eyes, his bearing bowed and awkward. Only his voice contained any strength of character. It was harsh and hacking, made that way by his endless chivvying of the reluctant labourers, no doubt.

Rosamund would withdraw from her parlour whenever Hogge Pollard arrived for his lessons, leaving the three men together in comfort. I was dismissed as these ceremonies were not of the same nature as the practical tests that Bert had been forced to undergo in the lighthouse. Hogge Pollard was being prepared for mysteries beyond mere dexterity or adroitness. He was being shepherded towards our truth. Taxed with a temptation of this magnitude I could not forbear from listening through the thin walls. It was on the third visit that

Hans first broached the question of belief.

"I see you at mass, Hogge," he said. "The Lord means a lot to you."

"He is the Lord and I am his man," Hogge answered in his sharp Hampshire. "Mother Church is the only mother that I have ever known."

There was a pause, then Hans spoke again.

"It sounded to me as if you were anticipating something that I must say."

"I've been waiting for it."

"Waiting for what?" Hans demanded.

"Whatever it is you must ask of me."

"Ask? We don't *ask* anything. . . ."

"I'll say no more until you've finished your piece," Hogge said with sudden vehemence. "Let me hear what you expect."

Hans laughed but it was in a cold humour.

"You have your crucifix in your hands," he said.

"I do, and I may need it!"

Now a much longer pause. I heard chairs being scraped on the floor and boots on the boards.

"Tell us what you have heard, Hogge," my father demanded hotly. "If it is rumour we can discount it for you."

"No, you tell me what's on your mind, God's saints protect me!" Hogge squawked. "I can't answer questions that I'm not asked."

The last, longer pause. Then:

"Good night, Hogge," from Hans.

"Is that all?"

"For this lesson."

Three days later Hogge was killed in an accident at the East Tower workings. Two labourers carrying a barrow-load of waste stone stumbled while going up an incline. The stone tipped off the barrow into a deep ditch where Hogge Pollard was working. When his effects were collected from his lodgings the deputy constable's clerk found a note, priest-written it was thought, that had been intended for the King's justiciar. It was delivered to Sir Henry de Montfort instead.

Hans and Bert were summoned to the deputy constable's apartments several times that week. Each time they paid him a visit they would have to make a full report to the lodge. There was no coroner's inquiry and Hogge Pollard was buried quietly in an adjoining parish. Then masons began to leave: they gave various reasons but the result

98

was that only two senior men were left behind to conduct the lodge's business. Hans was one of them and a venerable man from Gloucester, John Blaunchespine, the other.

Work at the castle slowed down. Sir Henry de Montfort seemed to have Hans at the keep for consultations every day. Bert refused to let me know what was going on so all I had to go on was rumour, all of which led nowhere. At the same time as this was happening Hans and Bert began working far into the night on a model which I was never allowed to see. From the sound they made it was obviously one of complex surfaces requiring a large amount of planing, filing and rasping. In the mornings the air of my room would be full of misty sawdust and my hair stiff with the stuff. All my questions about the model were deflected. When I went into the room where they were working one night, my pretext being ear-ache, Bert threw me out but not before I had seen an odd rotund shape on stilts, gleaming with wax. Two nights later there was an argument between Hans and Bert and I heard the sound of breaking wood which I assumed to be the end of the model. Within an hour they were making something else.

Both men were beginning to look haggard through lack of sleep. Rosamund chided them for not looking after themselves properly but this had no effect. Now they worked with the door barred and even Rosamund was not allowed access to that part of her own house. Then, one morning, Bert and Hans announced that they were going on holiday. It was the Feast of Saint Dionysius the threefold Areopagite, an author who, though Christian, is held in some respect by white cutters. I hoped to be taken along with them but, to my disappointment, I was left behind with Rosamund.

On the morning of their departure they left before dawn but there was enough light for me to see them load a cart with a large parcel wrapped in canvas. They tied it down very carefully and stuffed grass between its edges and the side of the cart so it should not get damaged. When they left both men walked, one at the horse's head, leading it, and the other by the cart's side, his hand steadying the jolts.

Bert had told me that they would be away for three days but it was five before they returned. Both men looked miserable and arrived on one horse. When Rosamund saw them she turned away as if she could not bear whatever had disappointed them.

Upon their return to work at the castle both Hans and my father were fined for overstaying their leave and put on to the most uncongenial labour that could be found for them. They lost status in the eyes of the lodge also and were shunned by the other white cutters. This was very bewildering for me as I had no idea of the reason and when I asked for explanations neither Bert nor Hans would give me one. They merely looked grim and changed the subject. But the late-night working stopped. Indeed, both men became very inactive, doing only what was required. My learning suffered: requests for more teaching were rejected, often with bitterness. "Why should anyone want to learn from us?" Bert said on one occasion. "What do men like us know about anything?"

As the weeks went by Hans began to look like a different person. He lost his glow, the dart of his dark eyes. Once he had moved around the castle workings with the air of someone whose expertise was unquestionable and whose achievements were exemplary: now he shambled up and down the ditches, harassed, worried and dismal. One night at table he suddenly started weeping for no reason. When I asked Bert what was the matter with Hans he just shrugged and carried on eating his supper. I could see that their friendship was under a strain but they had become very careful not to talk in front of me or Rosamund. When they exchanged words they were deliberately mundane, studiously innocuous, to do with nothing of importance.

I came home in the middle of one day to get Bert a change of clothes after he'd been drenched working down a cistern. I found de Montfort's horse tethered at the gate. Such was my fear of him — genial though he was on the surface — that I could not go into the house on my business and I returned to the castle — which was a good long walk — and told my father why I had not successfully completed my errand for him. He went pale and said nothing, putting me back to work. Minutes later I saw him striding down the hill through the trees. I followed him but when he went into the house I remained outside, going to the window of the living-room. A scene hit my eye which I had never imagined possible: both Hans and my father on their knees in front of the deputy constable. I must say, de Montfort did not look comfortable in this position. He was receiving the supplications of both men with an air of acute embarrassment.

I could not catch what was being said as the shutter-hinge next to my ear was squeaking in the sea-wind and if I had stilled it I would have drawn attention to my presence. Words were not all that necessary to an understanding of the basic forces at work. My father and his friend were grovelling to a Cretin.

People tell a child very little once it can be seen that its mind is working on the raw elements of life, observing and absorbing. Parents are embarrassed that existence is so cruel. Perhaps I have treated my own children this way, though I hope this is not the case. As a child in my case I had to watch declines, odd comings and goings, sense dangerous atmospheres, be aware of tensions, smell trouble, all with no help. The more serious things became the less I was told.

But after the day of begging things improved. Hans found something of his old style in the way he conducted himself. He became close to my father again which was a relief to all of us as Rosamund's husband was home from sea. There were enough questions hanging over that house without those that are asked when good friends become bad enemies.

We lived more carefully, kept close to the rules and were as unobtrusive as possible: a difficult pose for men such as Hans and Bert who were inclined to swagger within their friendship and put themselves about a good deal. It was pitiful for me to know why so much of their steam had left them: their subjugation. But I had no idea of the reason for their craven behaviour.

Only once did I attempt to ascertain the truth behind what I knew. I caught Hans and Bert in a very good mood after they had been drinking down at the port with some of Hans's fellow-countrymen. Four of them had returned to Rosamund's house in order to continue their carousal. As the day went on it seemed as if all the dark clouds had lifted. In my stupidity I got caught up in their euphoria — which was from wine — and imagined all must be well at last.

"Has Sir Henry finally forgiven you?" I asked Hans who was sat beaming at the table, his dark eyes brighter than I had seen them for months. His mouth gaped and his eyes became horribly dead as he heard my question. Without attempting to answer it he got up and went to the window, gulping down fresh air.

My father was not a man of consistent mind. He had no time for the Ancients or the Schoolmen who might have provided him with a logical framework for his feelings. If there was a rational source for his thought it was in his resentments which were three-fold: first, that he had been born with a dram of talent and not a drenching: second, that he was at the mercy of his emotions; third, that his soul was incorporated into a scheme of such suffering — our faith. There were times when he admitted to a discreditable craving to become a Christian because in their teaching it is their god who has most of the suffering while Man has most of the guilt whereas with our doctrine it is vice-versa. We suffer because our Gods are guilty of the war of an unresolved creation, but we are the ones who must endure the great pain of what it produces. Without war in heaven there would be peace on earth but peace on earth cannot provide peace in heaven.

The last October of our time in Dover saw Bert subdued by an illness that nearly killed him. I had never seen him so poorly. Over our years together I had seen him plagued by only the minor malaises of our trade — headaches, colds, back-ache, heaviness of the lungs, spitting blood; but none of these bouts had ever prostrated him. As with all men who work in this craft he knew that there was a price to pay towards the end of life. The dust would start to reform into its original solidity within his body as it has with mine. I can feel it there: the dust of much magnificence, the dust of a hundred temples and a thousand triumphs, coalescing to make me into my own sarcophagus. When a white cutter dies there is no real need to bury him. His corpse can be put on a plinth or built into a wall for he is almost all stone by then.

My father's behaviour during his illness was in two phases: at first he refused to admit that he was sick at all and dragged himself to work — or made me drag him! — then, when he became incapable of movement, unable to eat or drink, he collapsed into panic. He lay in a small room facing the sea, his mounded body always half-uncovered, his red, sweating face as out of place on the pillow as an orange in a snowfield. He groaned, he shouted for Rosamund, he had the window open, he had it shut, he threw up his food, whined, grieved, complained, ground his teeth in his sleep, kept getting out of bed in the middle of the night with bad dreams and waking the whole household. In short he was not made for ailments, only for either being alive or being dead.

But some advantage did accrue to me from father's sick-bed. It is the practice for all good masons to make drawings of buildings they work on or observe to be unusual or new, and to make these available to lodges which they visit. The Dover lodge was at the port which controls most cross-Channel traffic and all the new work of France, Flanders, Germany, Italy and Spain was brought through and assiduously copied and passed around.

Contained within these designs were messages of unity and

optimism to be shared amongst us all. In the design of a choir or the intricate foliage of a chantry screen was a writing that only we could comprehend. In this manner was our political vitality maintained. No lodge went ahead too fast nor was allowed to drag its feet. Change flowed evenly through the network of lodges in a common language of curves and constants.

While Bert was under the sway of Hans Seersach he kept his sense of self intact by refusing to look at these. It was an act of typical perverseness on his part. Hans would bring rolls of vellum back to the house and spend his evening hours poring over them, inviting my father to join him. Bert would sit next to him and look in the direction of the plans but I could see that he was resisting the meanings that they conveyed. He would always ask Hans for his reading of the designs: were they possible? Was it known whether they had been completed? (Nine out of every ten buildings designed never get off the ground.) Were they too radical, too tame, too pompous, too florid, too foolish? . . . anything rather than attempt to comprehend them for himself. But I knew that was because Bert could not really read drawings: models, yes, he understood; stone on paper, unless it was his own scribble, he could not follow. When a French mason brought plans of Hans's work at Coutances to the lodge and Hans playfully slipped them in front of Bert as being the work of someone else, Bert could not recognise the stamp of his friend and master. Hans thought that it was sad for Bert to be so imperceptive. That was unfair: Bert was afflicted with a fundamental blindness to the art of drawing.

When he entered the worst trough of his illness Bert got Hans to bring all the rolls down to the house. He filled the room with them. They were in the bed, under the bed, all over the floor. He slopped food on them, sweated over them, lay under them as if they were going to be his winding-sheet. As I spent most of my evenings sitting with my father during his sickness I was surrounded by what had come to tempt and intrigue me most; learning and imagination, discipline and daring. In the piles of drawings was the best of my future, the race that was worth running. I began to look at them, unrolling them on to the floor and holding the corners down with four of Rosamund's pleating irons. At first Bert would mock me when he woke to find me lying on the floor reading these hugely intricate plans by candlelight; then it would infuriate him that I was making the effort; then he got to the stage where he would have the plans laid out for me when I came in, his head cocked to one side, his smile in place as if to say: conquer this one, son.

In those drawings I found the theology of our faith and its true meaning: that our existence is held in tension between creation and destruction; in the energy between good and evil which, under pressure, makes a bending line, indicating the supple power of nature. It has no recognition in the Cretin creed which abjures the curve. Christ is served with straight lines and darkness: the tree rising in the wood, the star over the stable. It was not only the fig-tree that Christ withered for not bearing fruit, it was all the arches in its branches.

As I pored over the plans I was always aware of my father suffering his malady by my side. His life was held in the same tension as those great buildings and those great forces.

There were days during this illness when we were all prepared for his death. He went into such pitches of fever and convulsions that it seemed impossible that any human frame could survive such a racking. As we have no priesthood it was up to Hans and myself to minister to him. In the crucial moments of one bout of fever when Bert was so shaken that he looked like a man who had been seized by the throat and his head used to knock Christ's nails in, Hans offered him the final Consolamentum. Bert pushed him away with a fierce, fretful moan and told me to shut the window.

Again I had to close off his sight of the sea and the southern sky. That window tormented him, accused him pitilessly when there were clouds rolling past in thousands of architectural shapes and sizes. All light, Bert would babble, all light. And when the air was clear he would lapse even deeper into gloom and say he felt unworthy of the day's pureness.

This was a battle in heaven that was lost by the Good God: His failure was echoed in my father's weakness. Bert's inability to grasp Hans Seersach's novel architectural principles and the reason for the beauty created within them, was the source of his severe sickness. He could not see that light, so it was that light which offended Bert. It hurt his eyes and abused his mind. He never succeeded in assimilating clouds or clarity into his vision of the potential of matter. To force material to be the servant of light has been my function, just as the Good God has continued His campaign to make the Evil God capitulate. It could be said that there are more monuments to my success than His, but let that be said softly.

XII

We left Dover shortly before Christmas in 1250; our going bitter and recriminatory in the wake of a raging argument between Bert and Hans. Ostensibly it was over Rosamund but I knew better. Once my father had recovered from his illness he had discovered that Hans had made a new model without his help and behind his back, and had sent it over to Flanders in secret. He had done this while Bert was prostrate and it made my father suspicious that some part of the design was his. He had not hesitated to claim so, but Hans had laughed in his face, with justice I should think. Although he loved my father as a friend he could not help but realise he was a disciple rather than an equal. He knew as well as I that with Bert it was the question and the pain of the question which came first. My father was scared of all full and complete answers and resolutions. He could not soar, only skim.

This realisation had come as a slow and painful disappointment to me — a mere apprentice of eleven who had filled his head with the splendours of his people's uncredited genius. So I passed Bert at this point and dreamed my dreams with Hans, sharing his strong ambition to bring our faith into the open. I had been able to see the full extent of our influence. We were the builders of a new civilisation! It occupied the heights, exceeding all the vaunted achievements of the Cretins. From our towers and spires we lorded it over the age: with our secret knowledge and skill we ran an empire. We had no army — except it was an army of artists — we had no authority — except it was the power of shaped stone.

When I shared these thoughts with Bert he hardly had the patience to answer me. "We are underlings!" he roared at me once when I accused him of defeatism.

At the lodge's farewell to Bert I sat apart, consumed by scorn. Other apprentices sat with me, their conversation full of vulgarity and trivia. I was far too grand to join in. They had not seen the future as I had. Their knowledge of what it meant to be a mason was meagre; their comprehension of our potential prestige as the unifiers of matter and spirit, the dead and the living, the good and the bad, was non-existent. They were just *boys*. Boys! I had been brought on so fast and hard by my trials and adventures that I had entered into an extreme precociousness which imperilled my sanity: for whatever the spirit may desire it will depend on the body's fortitude and stamina for the strength to find that goal. The will is wedged into the flesh's clefts and corners. I can remember the fierce feeling shaking me during that farewell party. Above all I wanted to talk aloud to them all, to shoot up a foot in height, deepen my voice, hammer the table, demand their attention. In fact I sat by the wall with an untouched plate on my lap and fidgeted. Not wanting to be what I was did its work of demolition: self-disgust! to be uninformed and ignorant! Yet Hans had failed: Bert had failed. All of these fools had failed. When Sir Henry de Montfort popped in to share some wine and bid farewell the room went cold and quiet. I could stand it no longer. I went out and stood on the walls, watching the beacon on the Roman lighthouse flare out its ancient warning: come amongst us and you may founder.

The next morning we set out for London.

It was Bert's wish to find employment at Westminster or Windsor, thus remaining in the King's pay. The lodge furnished him with introductions but warned him that jobs on the abbey and the Windsor chapel were few. It was now winter and the working day had shortened. Bad weather would set in before long and make outside operations difficult. Less men would be needed until spring. It was their opinion that Bert would stand a better chance of white cutter's work at Canterbury where, although the great cloister had been finished, there was talk of a large undertaking connected with the shrine of Thomas à Becket which might be due to start before Christmas. This was to be a screen carved in marble depicting all the miracles of the saint.

Bert was not keen on the idea but he had a curiosity to see Canterbury and the road from Dover to London took us through that town anyway. Supplied with some horses by the lodge we were in sight of the tower by four o'clock that afternoon. I had tried to get my father to talk about the choir of William of Sens, the drawings for which I had studied in the lodge library: but he was not in the mood for chatting about other men's architecture.

"Two things about the Cretins I hate most — that turn my stomach, boy — martyrs and miracles," he grumbled as we came in sight of the cathedral towering over the town's roofs. "They wouldn't know a martyr if they fell over one in the street and any miracle belittles the power that performs it. We have no miracles. We have never asked for any and don't expect any."

"Is that why you don't want to work on the screen, Dad?" I asked. "Screens are hard, aren't they?"

"Thomas à Becket had no love for us. If he had lived then he would have ridden stirrup to stirrup with de Montfort. He was killed by a gang of drunks for sport."

Urging his horse forward Bert put himself out of earshot until we entered the southern gate. We found the lodge on the High Street, well away from the walls of the great church: usually a sign of old dissensions. We were received by a crowd of masons who had obviously been idle for months. The warmth of our welcome was more of a demonstration of their relief at seeing a new face with a chance for some fresh entertainment than any genuinely hospitable reaction. There was to be no new screen, we were told: there had been no new commissions of note for twelve years. The lodge had been through thin times. Many of the members who had welcomed us were local men who had been driven to London through lack of work and had come back to Canterbury for Christmas with the pilgrim bands. They told us what opportunities were to be had in London and it was hopeful news: apart from King Henry's work on Westminster Abbey there was the new church of Saint Paul which was having its chancel extended and improved in the latest style. Saint Paul's was already a wonder, but when this further work was completed it would be one of the greatest churches in Europe, the pride of London whose citizens were building it with their own cash rather than that of the King, Church or monastic orders. A competent white cutter could reasonably expect to get work on Saint Paul's but entry into the Westminster lodge was tightly controlled. So Bert concentrated on the Saint Paul's men whom he met. They were real southerners. Bert's bluster and odd northern speech put them on their guard but once they had found him to be so amiable and well-travelled, so close to great talents like Hans Seersach and . . . Brendan O'Toole of Offaly (who? they should have asked but didn't!) they began to look kindly on him — so kindly, indeed, that Bert decided it was in our best interests to spend Christmas-tide in Canterbury and reinforce our fellowship with them. He became a generous-hearted comrade, spending his money on wise wine. After his long stretch of regular work in Dover his purse was full. He had not been spendthrift, nor had he been in love; a common cause of liberality in Bert. We found ourselves a room in the Burgate and settled in for the festival.

Canterbury was packed with pilgrims, many of them from faraway countries. The popularity of Becket's shrine was great during any Christmas as he had been killed only four days after the feast, but this year was unusually well attended as it was the eightieth anniversary of the martyrdom. Our lodgings were rowdy at night, the air full of queer languages wrought into prayers and songs. In every corner, in the street, on the stairs, were pilgrims asserting their right to set up church and publicly perform their outlandish rites of penance. It smacked of strange madness; a feverish appetite for guilt. However, they received respect.

While Bert haunted the lodge and his new friends I was left to instruct or amuse myself. There was the great church to study and many smaller town churches, some very ancient. I used to get up with the Prime bells and take my breakfast with me in order to get ahead of the hordes of pilgrims eddying around the town from dawn till dusk. Even so I never found a time when I could be alone to make drawings. Before I had been at work for five minutes someone would start looking over my shoulder. A discussion would begin. Should this boy be allowed to copy these divine dimensions? Is he not being disrespectful? You've left out that window. Where's the top of that pillar? No, it's not like that at all! It's like this! My worst moment was when a Benedictine monk found me eating my breakfast as I was sketching the eastern bays of the crypt. The man was so incensed that a boy should bring his own bread into God's eating-house that he drove me out with blows from his knotted girdle.

The cathedral was still only half rebuilt after the great fire which did great damage four years after Becket's death. This inferno had had a most august author, so it was said. The arson was attributed to Christ himself! Lanfranc's old pile is not magnificent enough for our Tom, said the Lord. Away with this heavy heap! The Benedictines saw the destruction of the old church as an advantage as it coincided with the need to build new premises for their pilgrimage business. The new church could be designed with the martyr's shrine in mind; ambulatories, corridors, channels and gutters for the human rain.

Much as this legend amused me I knew different. The burning of stylistically obsolete churches to make way for new work is a practice within our brotherhood I have always deplored but less so then. To a child there is something deeply attractive in the wanton wreckage of beauty, even to such a child as I was. I had heard from Hans and stories circulating around Dover that the old cathedral had been burnt because Rome was jealous of its eminence and had paid Canterbury lodge to bring it down. This either demonstrates the gullibility of masons or the insane hypocrisy of the Christian pharaohs of Rome.

If we have been guilty — and I am afraid I believe that we have — then I say that such acts of arson are wasteful and dangerous. If a new building is needed on an old site then let us take down the existing structure stone by stone. Make the children do it to satisfy but discipline their need to destroy what inspired devotion in their forefathers. But let it be done carefully and cleanly and respectfully. The past is precious, even in parts.

So I spent my days with the pilgrims who milled about in the burnt choir, moving from place to place to keep the drips from the canvas roof off my drawings. I deliberately starved myself of the wonderful new work that had been done in the chancel during the last seventy years. Two of our brothers, William of Sens and William the Englishman, had made beauty out of ash. I focused that beauty down into the doorway of the screen which kept the vulgar eye from the elevated mysteries. It was only a hole I wanted to look through, an eye-hole, a squint at their achievements. While the huge herd lowed around the shrine as if it were a water-trough I remained outside, drinking from the sight-lines. Many of my drawings from this period are indecipherable to me now. I cannot fathom what I was trying to do in terms of perspective or self-instruction. Nearly all my sketches were scaled down into tiny spaces as if the magnitude of other men's intelligence and vision alarmed me. Sometimes I wrote notes alongside my sketches. There is one of the Trinity chapel and corona viewed through a circle. My note reads: "This is a bull's-eye. Could Bert do better?" As if acknowledging the answer I had then drawn a swan swimming beside a duck with its wing around its neck! Strange are the minds of children.

One morning I was at work in the new cloister copying the ribbed fretting of the roof and its bosses. I had already been chased by a couple of surly old monks who had tripped over me as they came out of Lady mass and I was drawing with one eye looking over my shoulder. It was a hard, cold, blue day and I was shivering so much that it was affecting my line. Stopping to chafe my hands I caught a glimpse of a bowed blonde head in the opposite diagonal corner. As it moved and the face came into view I realised that it was a girl and she was doing what I was doing — drawing!

Glad of an excuse to break from my neck-aching task I got to my feet and sauntered around the cloister until I was standing behind her.

As I peered over her shoulder she unhurriedly folded the drawing over so that I could not see it.

"Why are you drawing this bit? There's nothing of interest in this corner," I said. "You want to have a look over where I am."

"I like places where there is nothing of interest," she replied, turning her face towards me. Her eyes were blue and slightly slanted as if her skin were being drawn tight around her ears. It was, I noticed, an architecturally distinguished nose, tending towards a heavily sculpted finish. Having my father's constant example to compare with I had become a collector of smiles: this one was a fine specimen, when it came.

Her name was Anne and her father was a French white cutter from Bourges who had been living in England for twenty years. He was staying with a friend in Canterbury, a master-carpenter who had worked with him at Salisbury. He did not frequent the lodge as he was a private man, something of a recluse. His wife, who was from Bristol, had died when Anne was born. So, Anne's history was not unlike my own, except her drawings were not part of any apprentice-ship studies but done solely out of duty to her father who used her as his draughtsman. They were not well executed. Not knowing much about girls of fifteen I told her so. She was very insulted.

It did not occur to me that I was of no use to a woman, no matter how warmly I felt about it all. I suppose my courting of this girl must have appeared comical because I clearly remember how she was always laughing. I did many of her sketches for her and I was able to estimate the degree of her father's need for them by the fact that he never noticed. I doubt if it was anything more than a device for getting her out of the house. What he knew about girls was probably as much as I did, or Bert knew about boys. What she did give me was a sense of exciting purity — not chastity — a wholeness, separate, beautiful and strange.

The snow came flying out of the east. The canvas flapped on the roof of the nave. There were ceremonies and fights and much abasement of the spirit and idolisation of the flesh. I often thought that Canterbury was going mad, so intense and abandoned were the scenes we had to witness. What we shared was the unique security of being the children of masons. Our background was stone. All the human strangeness and disorder we came across was no more than a butterfly beating its wings against a mountain.

She sat with me as I sketched. I became adept at drawing one-handed while I held hers with the other. She laughed at me even more. I spent so much time with her that even Bert became aware of my absence from our lodgings. It was cold in Canterbury and he did not know how I was keeping warm.

On the morning of New Year's Eve we were sitting under William the Englishman's corona while I sketched a detail. The area around the shrine was unusually empty. I was ready to move, having finished what I could manage in the bitter cold. Anne was with me, her body wrapped in an old fur cloak of her father's.

As we stood up to go four monks came up to us. I knew their faces as every one of them had harassed me at some time or other. But now they were smiling. They bowed to us and asked for my name. I told them, expecting their masks of geniality to be dropped at any moment. Instead they all got down on their knees and beat their foreheads on the pavement.

"Regis pastor Hedricus!" they cried.

Having seen me about the cathedral for so long, the monks were conversant with my ambitions; all worthless, absurd and pretentious in their eyes, and had elected me to be the Fool's Bishop at the Feast of the Ass. I had no choice in the matter and when I protested I was manhandled into the monastery cellar to be dressed for my part. When I had been made ready in a paint-streaked robe and tattered straw mitre, I was hustled to the refectory where all the monks, canons, priests and lay-brothers of Canterbury were waiting. They had all been drinking hard since dawn, having just been released from Christmas fasts and frugalities. I was put into a chair which had been set up on top of the abbot's table and told this was my throne.

As I sat up there holding back my tears they launched into a spurious ceremony they had devised for my enthronement. It was of ancient origin, they assured me, and was used for Saint Augustine when he was crowned by King Cunt.

Details of this fatuous ritual are of no fascination: a lot of sham Latin, bowing and scraping, kissing of my toe, showering me with water from a holly branch, pouring wine down my neck, pulling my hair, poking me, knocking my hat off, grabbing my genitals, spitting plum-stones at me, all great fun. As the monks had seen me hanging around the cathedral doing my drawings for so long, they had a second identity for their bishop — I was not only Pastor Hedricus but the Puerile Penman, king of the hated scriptorium where they laboured in boredom. Books were brought to me and interpretations of the scriptures demanded: mock manuscripts were unrolled before my eyes and then burnt at candle-clusters. Monks made themselves into archways, chancels and naves and demanded to be drawn. Come on, reduce us to lines and figures, ink-drinker! They stood on their heads against the walls as flying-buttresses holding up the hall, their robes around their ears and their lower parts exposed. Draw this! they yelled. And get the angle right!

As they taunted me I realised how much my passion for architecture had irritated them. To them the abbey building was a cold, gloomy tomb in which their lives had corrupted. It had no beauty but plenty of power; power that oppressed their spirits and broke their hearts. To see me copying the forms of their prison with such intense respect was a great provocation, hence this unleashing of mad antagonism against my apprentice studies.

I survived without any flow of tears for the first hour; often I was close to blubbing but I held it back. Some of the monks saw my discomfort and distress and attempted covert acts of kindness but they were always howled down. The Ass-Bishop must submit to the authority of his flock. The Arse-Episcopus must preach a sermon on the cathedral drains — which I had drawn, no doubt: as I drew everything so *brilliantly*, they said.

It was true. I had plotted the positions of the sewers, lavatories, jakes and drains that lay beneath the church and the monastic buildings. Willing to join in their fun if it meant that they would stop tormenting me I, somewhat hesitantly, began a discourse on the sanitation of the minster. Before I had got far the monks went berserk, some of them shitting on the floor and smearing it over the walls, others wiping themselves off with spoiled illuminated manuscripts from their workshops; unfolding the face of their god in order to smear it with excrement. It was then that I wept openly and struggled to get out of my chair but they grimly held me down, not to be gainsaid.

There were brothers who held back from these excesses; men too old or sick to be so crazed with carnival. They sat together and feigned revulsion at the madnesses of their brothers, tutting and clucking with reproval, then grinning indulgently. Although the intemperances were wild enough to give the impression of spontaneity it was obvious they were rehearsed and organised. When I appealed to the most aged and sober monk present to stop the grosser acts of vandalism he lectured me, saying tolerance is something any mason's apprentice should learn as it helps to build character. This sally was greeted with loud hosannahs as a paradigm of ecclesiastical wit and I was battered around the head with pigs' bladders and told to keep quiet until I had something equally sagacious to say.

Gradually I was able to raise myself above the chaos they had created. Not that they discontinued their humiliations but that I belonged to a superior philosophy which did not derange itself for evil's sake. The joy of this feast to all Christians is the opposite of the joy their religion promises them. It is a reprieve from hypocrisy and inconsistency. For one day they can scream out loud that their faith *does not work*! They can use their common sense and their common urges to recognise the way things truly are in this world.

We Albigensians have no Feast of the Fool because we do not need one: the licensed disorder of that day is incorporated into our dogma because we always give the Evil God His due: one half of the Creation and the power that moves it. The horrible thought has subsequently come to me that the Feast of the Fool is the one day when all Christians are really Albigensians. However, at the end of what is an ephemeral revelation they retreat into blindness again: they crawl home and sleep it off, waking next morning with their satan sour in their mouths and good sense banished for another year.

Thus I wrestled up there on my throne in my wretched costume: trying to keep the dignity of my beliefs out of touch of my tears or the trembling of my hands. I did not completely succeed. That was of no great importance to my tormentors who crowned me and recrowned me and crowned me again with riot, mayhem and mortification, the quintessence of which came with cups of hot wine which they poured down my throat.

At first I felt sick as the wine filled my empty stomach but then it did its work and I felt stronger. As the monks whirled, I whirled in my head. As they mocked me I began to mock them, finding a new courage. This was exactly what they wanted. They begged me to abuse them so I did, foully. Hammering on the tables they declared that at last this brat was a proper bishop. I had been sent down by the holy ghost for this day of dichotomies. Damn us, they cried as they shook my hand, patted me on the head and embraced me. Put us in purgatory if you like, Pastor Ass!

So I damned them. I sent them to the pit to suffer, gave them thousands of years of pain and they loved it. More, more, they yelled, give us more!

So my punishments rose to millions of years: years beyond numbers, beyond infinity. They would never get out of purgatory! Even so, they bellowed, give us more, O glorious Pastor Hedricus! Just as their god might consider himself demeaned by such disrespect for his chastisements, so did I. The Ass-Bishop lost his temper and cursed his flock. He said that there was not one of them worth condemning. No one was trying. How about some *real* blasphemies!

Now they were my slaves! My devoted disciples! Each one strove to be the most depraved and despicable, searching their memories for the ultimate in sacrilegiousness. But I was already well ahead of them, delving into our repertoire of salty anti-Christian jokes and songs. I made cracks about sex within the Trinity that made them groan and cover their ears; I sang ballads of such disgusting filth about the Virgin that they were incredulous. Where can he have learnt them? they said. He must be the Pope's bastard. So, by the time that I was hoisted on to their shoulders and carried out into the nave I was a devil of a fellow.

And I might just as well have been for I was transported into a veritable hell.

The great nave was packed with people. Snow that sagged down the leaking canvas roof caused showers of water which hissed into bonfires. There were lovers, fighters, dancers and drunkards everywhere. Vendors shoved their way through the crowd screaming out their incomprehensible cries. Overhead the bells tolled out in an arbitrary time as if swung on by apes. To be carried high into this heaving chaos was no honour but never in my life have I made such an entrance or been received with such a roar of approval. My juvenile heart could not help but beat faster, nor my mouth refrain from smiling. Many women and not a few men have said of me that I must have flattery — not mild affirmation of my talents but full-blooded, uncritical adulation. I have consistently rejected this charge. This has been made easy by the vindictiveness and jealousy of those who have accused me of vanity. But, in my soul, there is a response to that hurrah in the hall. It is nothing to do with me as Hedric Herbertson or the Pastor Ass but me as a man set apart from the crowd. If I see another person given such acclaim it brings a lump to my throat. It is an old, old need, I say, a vestige of our individual creation before being put out to suffer in the human commonalty.

Now, the bacchanalian Benedictines struck up an obscene chant about the virility of the Ass. I was adorned with a huge wooden pizzle and supplicated to wave it and bray. As I hee-hawed I thought the burnt, old walls would burst asunder, so loud was the applause. This was too much for a child who loved to shine. I repeated it so often that the people told me to be quiet and demanded new tricks. Blessings I gave backwards; holy water I made from my own urine: buttocks I kissed; loaves of bad bread I addressed as god and broke into the foul puddles. More wine, more madness. The din was terrible. The only worse sound I have heard was at the sack of the city of Philippopolis when the rebel Ivailo was made King of the Bulgars in 1277. Then the screaming and shouting was in Tartar, Magyar Greek and Church Slavonic, but this was as bad a Babel.

We Albigensians do not desire the end of the world as the Christians do. Our faith is not finite, nor does it worship the destruction of the Creation. To us the Creation is unfinished and will always be so. Our task is to aid the Gods in their handiwork, not plead for its ruin. It is the desire of the Cretins for this apocalypse that makes them unfit for the art of architecture. To build beautifully one must believe in the permanence of life. If we masons took the Christian view and always had our eye on the heavens for the storm of fire we would never put stone on stone. What would be the point? Who dreams of rubble when he builds?

That, I say, is why the Feast of the Ass was so hectic at Canterbury — it was its venue, a damaged beauty, that inspired such abandon. Judgement Day was Fool's Day. The promise of the world's end was writ upon the walls.

I do not remember the end of the feast, nor all the parts that I played in it. My last memory was of a tall, gaunt man standing beside me with a napkin tied round his waist. He had his arms spread out wide and he was pretending to be the tree on which Christ was nailed. "Am I beech or am I oak, did you hear the wheelwright spoke?" he chanted over and over.

The end of my reign as Regis pastor Hedricus came when I passed out after too much wine. I was put in a corner to sleep it off until my father came with Anne to find me. There was an uproar, I understand, as Bert had been at a Feast of the Ass of his own somewhere and was as drunk as the monks himself.

XIII

As a result of my notorious behaviour as Pastor Ass, Anne's father forbade her to have anything more to do with me: not that he believed that we were lovers but even a maternal or friendly interest was discouraged. I had disgraced myself in front of the whole town and brought the lodge into disrepute.

This did not stop our meetings, however, and I was happy to have someone to talk to as I was shunned by all and sundry for weeks after the event. Our stay in Canterbury was protracted by the bad weather coming from the east, bottling up the pilgrims who should, by now, have been on their ways home. Great falls of snow blocked the town streets and made the roads impassable in all directions so we sat and stewed. To be unpopular in such an atmosphere of frustration is hard; you are the first target when folk want to release their impatience. And although Bert did make an effort to forgive me for my public ridicule, and slyly encouraged me to see Anne against her father's wishes, if his prospects for work in London dimmed I tended to take the brunt of it. Not that he ever said it was my fault, or that he had lost face because the Pastor Ass had been his son, but because when he got home in a bad mood my backside was the only one available to kick.

I continued my studies, concentrating on Canterbury's smaller churches and chapels where I stood less chance of being recognised. This did me good because it adjusted and developed my values of size and scope. Many small spaces, in their exquisiteness, are more suggestive of the concentrated power of line. My work in the tiny cathedrals and churches of Muscovy, Greece and the Balkans was much influenced by those days in Canterbury. I suppose I felt that architecture was a place to hide my shame: it took on the dimensions of a den, a private lair where the Gods knew I was hiding but could be confident that I was not strutting about with pride.

But I could not always avoid the Cretin clergy. During my sketching expeditions I had many encounters, some of them with great prelates. The monks took delight in showing me off, sticking my drawings under the noses of their masters as if my talent were something ludicrous. Some brushed my work aside, others stared and exclaimed. Whatever happened, I always ended up being kicked out of the building with a flea in my ear.

There is a small church that was built in the reign of King Edgar on the banks of the Stour just outside the town walls. It is dedicated to Saint Adrian, the African who became Archbishop of Canterbury five hundred years ago. His feast-day falls early in January. It is no longer a great event but the canons who control the church still hold a series of masses for the saint's soul during that day and many church dignitaries attend. As the weather was so cold and many of these senior ecclesiastics so far gone in years, four big fires were lit inside the church. Anne and I visited the building at six o'clock in the evening, unaware of the feast-day, and found it empty, all the ceremonies being completed, but with the fires still burning.

We sat in the warm church and I drew, expecting someone to come and throw us out at any moment. No one came. When I had finished sketching an embrasure and piscina I turned to Anne and found her asleep beside me. After a day tramping around the freezing streets or sitting in churches chilled to the bone, the heat in Saint Adrian's had lulled her into slumber.

I had never kissed a woman as a man kisses. If there was part of Anne that I had come to adore it was her mouth. It was not full, or thin, but — as far as I was concerned — perfect and pure. So, taking a deep breath, I leant across and kissed her.

Her lips were warm and they moved under mine. I pulled back, interpreting this as a rejection — which was what I expected. But I found her hand on the back of my neck pulling me down to kiss her again.

Kissing is an art and one I did not know. As long as it lasted I was all right but I did not have any idea how to end it without being discourteous. Why should I want to take my lips off hers? So it went on and on, both of us breathing through our noses. Eventually she took the decision to break and I was grateful as the kiss was in danger of having no imaginable end.

Up to this point we had said nothing. The four fires were burning red and the wind was howling outside. There was no reason for us to leave. I wanted to speak, to tell her that I loved her but I knew that was comical. All I could think of to do was kiss her again, so I did.

We rolled on to the rushes on the floor, still joined. Now I knew that there were things that I should do, and would! Fumbling with her long scarf and coat I tried to find a way in to her breasts.

She shook her head so violently that our teeth clashed together. I sat up, holding my mouth. For a while I looked away from her, anticipating a rebuke. None came. When I had found the courage to look at her again I found her lying as I had left her, smiling.

My only course to follow was the next kiss. This was by far the longest to date. During it I heard the squeal of the weathercock on the tower as the wind changed direction; the soft tones of the bells as the clappers nudged the sides in the gale; the sounds of the wood falling in the fires; and my own heart-beat which was now as clear and rhythmical as a choir of baritones singing tactus tempo. It was not manhood, maybe, but it was near enough.

I cannot pretend to have counted beyond the fourth. All we had were kisses and they went on until we silently agreed we could take no more. I was exhausted. As we picked ourselves up from the floor my lips were so numbed from kissing that it was hard to frame a reply to the first words she had spoken since our marathon began.

"Are you hungry?" she said.

Hungry? I thought. My only hunger at the moment is to grow up. I felt dismal with failure, cursed with immaturity, so angry with my body that I stood in a corner and rapped my head against the wall. Anne left me in the shadows for a while and when I returned to her she was squatting close to the fire at the left of the altar eating the food that she had brought out from home.

She always had the same: hard-boiled eggs, cold beans, flat bread and fruit. This time she had some small onions which she was peeling with a knife. Anne's father was a strict member of our faith. He accepted the teaching that all flesh contains elements of the spirit which will transmigrate into the consumer. It was not until Bert and I arrived in the south of England that I discovered we were supposed to be vegetarians. Bert loved meat and when I taxed him with our omission he told me he had never said he was Perfect.

I did not know, until Dover, who the Perfect are: it was a condition Bert held in awe or disrespect depending on his mood but the Perfect are not a state of mind but an élite abiding by the ancient principles that have come down to us from the earliest worship. They are so pure, so scornful of material things, they will not have children and their greatest privilege is to starve themselves to death in order to avoid the contamination of matter.

This is certainly a long way from Bert. As with most Albigensians, he was a mere believer, adhering as best he could to our credenda but repeatedly acknowledging his imperfection. Anne's father had become one of the Perfect after her mother's death and he lived a life of absolute austerity though I do not know whether he ever took the final step. The other member of the Perfect whom I had met by this time was old Blaunchespine at the Dover lodge. He always looked as though he was on the edge of the grave. It may be unkind to record this criticism of two such pious men but, from my remembrance, one part of the material world that they had difficulty in unsticking their hands from was money.

We left Canterbury in mid-February during a bout of brilliant weather: the air was warm, blue skies lapped the frost-faded fields in oat and indigo hues, and the hedgerows were full of birds. We rode up to London with a huge swarm of pilgrims who had been held back by the snows: their businesses, their lives had been frozen by the winter and now the future had thawed out fine. There was a lightness in everyone's step and we approached the great city as if it were close to its celestial counterpart. It was a short, exciting journey that I remember as a flawless flow of optimism: we would do well, in London, I believed. Bert was going to become a top white cutter, a crack craftsman who could pick and choose. The Saint Paul's job seemed to be in his pocket and that would be just a start. After a few months whetting his edge there, he would re-enter King Henry's service and shine right under the monarch's nose. These were spring thoughts: a mite early, as were the frolicking birds.

I have entered many cities with joy. To complete a great pilgrimage is to experience a triumph that exhilarates the heart. The blood lifts like a freshened fountain; all poison and sadness is put to flight. To be with the London pilgrims on their return home was like this — as if their pilgrimage to Canterbury had been reversed and London was the shrine they had sought and suffered for. When I compare it to my arrivals at Santiago de Compostella, Rome and Jerusalem it has the same nature: unbridled happiness. That is what swept us through Southwark to the Thames and that bestriding colossus of a bridge. I have never been so awed by the thickness of folk. They streamed over it both ways, so many of them I thought it must break. If there is a bridge from this world into the next it can never be as full as that which buckles London to the South. It was good for me to enter the city over such a phenomenon; the pilgrims singing the praises of their home louder than they would for a saint. If I had crept in with my father in foul weather, seeing only the dirt and confusion of those crooked streets and forelock-tangled houses, it would have been even harder than it turned out to be. At least we had a good start and that is always worth a lot.

My first sight of the new Saint Paul's was from well south of Southwark. The buttresses of the great church are visible from a distance, knotty as knuckles; the tower outstrips in height every building on the north bank of the river. It is an immense structure, perhaps *too* big if the truth were told. Before the day was out I was inside this giant and sketching, my pen trembling with the excitement of it all. Such size! Such multitudinous, multifarious work! I followed Bert around as he went on a visit to inspect the recent work and the new projects. There was so much to do! It is laid out in an immensely long cruciform: twelve bays to the chancel and twelve to the nave plus five to each transept. When I was there they were talking about a tower and spire that would be the highest in the world: four hundred and fifty feet! easily putting the one being built at Salisbury in its shade. By then my interest in height had become schooled to the interior. As far as exteriors were concerned it was length impressed me, that laying out of the argument upon the earth for the Gods to read. Great height does not awe the divine. How much of it is visible to them from above? Height is for prayer-makers inside the church. Length is for the lordly powers as they pass by, our praise taken in at a glance.

I expressed my reservations about the proposed spire to Bert as we ate dinner that night at an inn. He chewed on his mouthful long enough to indicate that he didn't want to talk about it. He was too excited by the city. Not wanting to own up to this, he feigned nonchalance, trying to appear as if he had been a Londoner all his life. I watched his eyes drinking everything in, every detail, every passer-by, every gesture. Something must happen, he was thinking. I have made my way to the centre of the world. I am here! Let me get going! Will I be lucky and shoot to the top? It's all there for the taking.

"Surely a spire that tall is not a good idea in the middle of a crowded city or on high ground with exposure to strong winds? What do you think, Dad? Do you like spires? I don't. I prefer towers myself," I said, chattering on though I knew that it was wicked to intrude on his dream. "I find spires arrogant in essence. They're weapons, not pointers. Nor do I think that they truly extend the concept of the pointed arch. They're too linear, too geometrical."

"Shut up and eat your dinner," Bert muttered, his eyes on the black and gold bizarre finery of a fellow who had just come in off the street, his face sparkling with pleasure, a tall, pretty woman on his arm. "Do you want to put me out of a job? If it's a big spire they want then it's a big spire we'll give 'em. It will be ten years' work for us all."

"Yes, but ten years' bad work can last for five hundred," I protested. "And think of the cost!"

"But I won't last for five hundred years and neither will you. Mop up your gravy," he said curtly, then his manner softened. "Will you look at the way that woman has dressed her hair? Did you ever see anything like it in your life?"

Sliding a piece of bread on to my plate I slopped it round as I pretended to sulk. The delights of this inn had not escaped me and I was as taken with its atmosphere of richness and knowingness as he was; yet I liked to keep my father on the hop. It had become my self-appointed task always to hold his art up to his face. That way he might improve and stand a chance of greatness. But as another jug of wine came to our table, I knew that aesthetics had lost out. Bert was in an enchanted land with the smell of sweet living strong in his nostrils.

That night I went back to our lodgings alone, leaving Bert deep in conversation with a gaudy tart whose eyes were ringed with sleepless-ness. My father probably thought she had painted this shadow on for him, so far sunk in the bottle he'd gone by the time she gained access to our table. By leaving them together I hoped to avoid the unpleasantness of having to share my sleeping-quarters with Bert and one of his whores — a not unusual imposition for me in the old days in the north.

I got into bed and listened to the street-noises until they died down. Through my window I could see the space that would be occupied by the great spire when it was built. In my mind I sketched its outline on the stars, sliding my mental pen from sparkle to sparkle, holding the complex framework together in flowing memory. Tomorrow morn-ing comes, I reasoned, great bells will shake this room and wake an artist such as I will be: that is the way for a mason to come out of sleep, called by his Gods to dress them.

I woke to the great bells. My only complaint against my awakening in the capital was that I had to rise alone: dear Bert had stayed out all night and did not return until the middle of the afternoon.

XIV

Our enforced stay in Canterbury had eaten up the most part of my father's savings from Dover. He had spent a lot of money on his new friends in hope of work in London; we had had to live for nearly three months without Bert having any income and that included Christmas, a feast not famed for frugality. By the time we arrived at the Saint Paul's lodge we were altogether stripped of cash. The lodgings Bert had accepted were far too expensive for us and the life of pleasure he then embarked upon was similarly beyond his means. However, the lodge treasurer gave us credit for up to three marks with a promise that this limit could be extended if Bert landed a white cutter's job on the Saint Paul's site. As Bert considered this to be virtually in the bag, and he could anticipate getting in on the white cutters' piece-work as well as being on a high daily rate, he spent freely, buying himself new clothes, eating out every night, consorting with people wealthier than himself, and chancing his arm at dice.

My father rapidly became a victim of London's alluring fantasy of success. Because it stirred him he believed himself to be in touch with its harsh inner laws; in fact that feeling of excitement was sure proof he did not understand the requirements for daily survival in the city whatsoever. As he waited for the summons from the lodge to present himself at Saint Paul's I explored the rest of the metropolis and discovered that the north bank of the Thames was a builder's yard. There were great houses and palaces, churches and chapels, law courts and hospitals going up everywhere. There was work in abundance and good white cutters were in short supply. When I reported this to my father he took no interest in the news, telling me he was already fixed up with his friends and, besides, he needed some time to get his bearings before he started work.

After one month he was still getting his bearings and we had run through our three marks of credit: a vast sum for people such as ourselves with no pretensions to luxury. I was already an unpopular figure on the building-sites because I had, in panic, actually secured jobs for Bert on a casual basis to get cash and he had refused to go and do them!

It became obvious to me that there was something wrong in Bert's approach to either the lodge or his friends. They were either messing him about deliberately or he was not interpreting their true needs or demands. It was difficult for me to ascertain wherein lay his negligence. I could hardly go up to a senior mason and say, "My dad is a bit slow on the uptake. Tell me what you want and I'll sort it out," but that is what I felt like doing. What emerged from his confused wrestling with the Saint Paul's lodge labour-brokers was that they expected him to make an initial payment to secure the job, then a second payment to get into the piece-work ring controlling the bonuses. That was what the advance of three marks was designed to cover but Bert had not realised this and had spent it on whores, dinners and dice. The brokers remained coy and refused to make this arrangement clear to Bert, trusting that any mason who was seeking such top-flight employment in London would have taken the trouble to find out the proper way of going about his business. When I finally got the information I needed to set Bert right on this delicate matter its source was another apprentice. This boy told me that my father had become a figure of fun because he appeared to be incapable of recognising the system without having it spelled out. Other white cutters were calling him The Rock of the North.

Manoeuvring my father into a position where I could sit him down and tell him how to organise his working life was not easy. He was depending on company and contacts to save him: drinking mates, alehouse bluffers and fraudsmen, but not one of them would lift a finger, I knew that. The secret religious bonds of the lodge were supposed to guarantee mutual assistance, basic respect and fair treatment to all members and Bert believed this, but now I knew better. I would have to destroy this myth before he could get a job at Saint Paul's. He would have to learn from me that London has its own laws in everything.

How can a boy tell his father a thing like this, especially when he must, as his apprentice, call him master? It was an impossible proposition. I knew Bert would not take it from me. So I had to find a third party who would undertake this work. It could not be anyone in the trade as they might pass the details of our private business around as gossip and my father might hear of it. When I examined Bert's habits I arrived at the conclusion that the only people I could sensibly ask to help me were either whores or gamblers. Both of these prided themselves on knowing everything there was to know about the unspeakable, the unattributable and the unrecognisable. They could claim inside knowledge of the ins and outs of the masonic world without turning a hair and no one, especially Bert, would ever doubt that they had come by the information in any way but the most untraceable and mysterious. Clients, they would say, we got it from clients.

A wide choice of confederates was open to me. If all I needed was one of Bert's whores or gambling colleagues then I had plenty of choice. All of them were unreliable, of course, and I would have to fix it so it would never be in their interest to reveal that I had arranged this part of my father's education.

Bert had got into the routine of leaving me to look after myself in the evenings. Before going he would provide my dinner and he always set me tasks of study. I had my own library of drawings by now and I was already designing my own buildings. The expense of keeping me in ink, pens, instruments, parchment and vellum was high but he did not shirk it. Also he found an old priest who came in to our lodgings twice a week to teach me to read and write Latin and started paying a widowed housekeeper in kind to watch over me. So, each night he went out with an easier conscience: I had things to do and someone to be on call if I needed help. He never asked how I had fared the previous night when I encountered him in the mornings. Mornings were not his best times in those days. All he might do is glance at what I had drawn the previous night and check my writing exercises, then shamble off in search of his breakfast.

In fact I had got into a nocturnal routine of my own which ran parallel with Bert's. True, I ate alone in our room, and I did my drawings or sat with Father Horace until our hour was up, but then I went out into the city. The streets were full of children, mostly of the poor, but no one was surprised to find a boy of my age flitting around in the darkness. The citizens always assumed that I was up to no good, a thief or a brothel's runner, and I could never stay in one place for long, but I was none of these things: I was out in the night because it suited me to walk through the city when it was in the hands of the Evil God. Nothing of good was at work, certainly. The pious were safely locked up in their homes: only the uncaring and the sinful remained at play with doors open to welcome the dark. It was a difficult place once the light had left the sky and I was enchanted with it. That said something about myself, of course. I could see how I was my father's son and not cut out to be one of the Perfect. But, at least, I knew that I had a taste for the world whose shape I would change.

In order to recruit a helper in my campaign to put Bert wise I had to follow him one night. The housekeeper was ill and in bed early, sleeping like the dead so getting past her room was easy even though her door was still left ajar for Bert, whether she be sick or no. Having completed two sets of drawings the previous evening and hidden one of them to show Bert as the work for the following day, I put my dinner in a bag and set out after Bert as soon as he left the house at half-past six, his usual hour of exit. There were still plenty of people in the streets and it was not difficult to stay hidden in the crowd and keep him in sight at the same time. I had expected to go north towards Clerkenwell and its stews and gaming-parlours but, instead, he went east towards Bishops-gate, walking so fast that I had to trot to keep up with him.

It was a clear, frosty night. The weather had not broken since our arrival in London and the ground was very dry. Above us a moon was rising. It looked to be twice its usual size. Through the chimney-smoke it was as yellow as a piece of fat cheese with dark teeth-marks where the rats might have been at it. I saw the star Venus and the rusty nail-head of Mars as I jogged along, the crisp air clipping at my lungs. With a start I realised I was only too happy literally following in my father's footsteps no matter where they went. I did not want his journey to end — especially in the sort of squalid den I was certain he was headed for. My old unquestioning love of my father came pouring back and I wanted to gallop up behind him and jump on his back for a ride: but I did not.

There was a duty I had to perform. It implied an enfeeblement of my father's authority over me but it was his fault. Bert had never really grown up! The urge to scrap my plan was immense. I would much rather have left the man to his silly pleasures and paid part of the cost, as I always had to, but a nagging voice told me to persist and see the shameful business through. If London broke Bert then the rest of his life would be one long regret. It was the centre of our white cutter's world and once we acknowledged that we could not handle work there then we would have to spend the rest of our time on the periphery, mourning our innocence and incompetence.

Now we were out in the fields. Bert was threading his way through a meadow towards a battery of lights. As we approached it I saw that it was a building under construction illuminated by huge torches. People worked on scaffolding, wheeled barrows, carried stone, mixed cement, all by the light of wind-blown flames. Bert entered a hut and emerged a few minutes later with a bag of tools not his and went over to a pile of stone where white cutters were working. He joined them, opened his bag, selected his tools, then started dressing what looked like a window-ledge.

I crouched behind a hedge well out of the torchlight, my mind spinning. What was all this about? I ran through all the possibilities of what Bert might be up to. This was a private house for someone, a domestic dwelling. Whoever was having it built wanted it finished in a hurry, probably taking advantage of the good weather. So, my father was earning money — good money if he was working in this haste under these conditions — but he had not seen fit to tell me about it. Why? What was going on? There was a moment when I nearly left my hiding-place and went over to confront him with it but I resisted the temptation.

Retreating into the darkness I left the glowing building-site at my back with its calls and sounds and made my way home. I did not go out on my explorations again that night but went to bed and tried to fathom out what my father was playing at. I felt cheated and excluded. To make things worse I still had the same problem I had set out with but it was now more complicated: Bert was working but he was not working in a way he wanted to. There was a reason for this and I knew I had to discover it.

I stayed awake all that night, waiting for my father to come home. It was after five o'clock before he came in and got into bed beside me. I pretended to be asleep as I had often done before and relied on the sounds he made and the smells he brought in with him for clues as to his night-time activities. Up until this moment I had read these clues wrongly, it seemed. What I had always taken for perfume was the cold smell of mortar and stone-dust. The whistle of his breath was not due to wine but to hard work. I knew the smell of my father's sweat as well as I know the scent of dandelions and I had thought I could distinguish between the sweat of his labour and the sweat of his pleasures: but I had been deluding myself. All my skill and knowledge in father-craft had fallen into disrepute. I didn't know Bert at all.

He was asleep within a minute. I lay and harked to his breathing for a long time, listening for the long, rhythmic sound of deep sleep. By seven o'clock I could wait no longer and I got up, dressed and went out to see the building Bert had been working on, this time in the light of day.

There was a mist over the fields as I retraced my steps along the path and I was at the site before I knew it. In spite of the poor visibility work was in full progress with a new shift having taken over. They did everything at double-speed in the manner of men who have an inducement to work fast and there was a foreman who seemed to be everywhere at once, chivvying and criticising, directing and damning. I kept well out of the way as it was obvious that trying to prevail on someone to give me a moment of spare time was pointless: none of them had any. However, I could not conceal myself from the foreman's sharp eye. While I was watching operations from the hedge he suddenly appeared beside me.

"What do you want, boy?" he demanded.

"Work," I replied without hesitation.

"What kind of work can you do?"

"Rough-hewing for the white cutters, helping the layers and setters, anything, really. I've just come from Dover. They know me at the lodge. . . ."

The foreman frowned and poked the hedge with a stick.

"I don't want to know anything about the lodge. Any lodge. This isn't a lodge site. D'you understand?"

"I thought all sites had to be lodge sites," I said carefully, watching his face.

"Well, you thought wrong. I've got labouring work here at the moment if you want it. A penny a day. You'll work the first day for nothing until I can see what you're made of. Well?"

It had not been my intention to take a job on the site but I quickly calculated that during my one probationary day — which I could foul up deliberately in order to bring the episode to a close — I could find out all I needed to know.

"I'll take it," I said stoutly. "You won't regret it. I'll give good service."

"That remains to be seen. Come with me."

I followed the foreman through the mist to the site. As I got to the edge of the foundations I asked him what the building was going to be.

"A summer residence," he replied. "All this land around will be laid out in a garden, right down to the stream over there."

"Ah, I see why he's having it built in February and in such haste,"

I said knowingly. "It's for *this* summer."

The foreman took me into his hut and asked for my name. I told him that it was Ivo of Sparkford which brought a smile to his face. As he took me out to allocate my work to me I asked him whose house it would be when it was finished.

"No one you'd know, boy. What does it matter to you? I pay your wages, not her."

"Could I see the design? I'm very interested in houses of this size especially if they're intended for leisure. I see that she's going to have a courtyard . . ."

I babbled on as I crossed the ditches and diggings, hoping to intrigue the foreman with my percipient questions to the point where he would divulge the name of the woman for whom Bert worked night-shift in secret.

"Who is she?" I asked, finally, as I was directed to the bottom of a ditch dug in clay where five ragged men were plying picks in puddles of water. "Please tell me her name."

The foreman watched me as I climbed down the hurdle ladder to start work with my fellows. As I stepped into the icy-cold water he smirked.

"I don't want you thinking about ladies down there," he said, mockingly. "This has to be up to the end wall by sunset. And don't relieve yourself in the bottom but that's the only reason I want to see you climbing out for, boy. Those lads will tell you all you need to know about architecture."

And that is how I spent the day: in total misery with men who had never known any better. They were good-natured enough and did not torment me too much but we had little to say to each other as we worked. Certainly, they had no idea whose drains they were digging, nor did they care one way or the other. When I emerged from the ditch at sunset I was so covered in mud the foreman did not recognise me as the bright Ivo of Sparkford who had taxed him with questions that morning. All he did was to confirm that I had passed my probation and could work again tomorrow, starting six o'clock in the morning. As his clerk checked my name on the list of labourers he did not bother to hide the other rolls lying on his table, not thinking it possible that a labourer should be able to read. One of them was partly open and I was able to discern the first few lines. It was all Latin but in the forms we know in the building trade. It was an order for payment delivered to the private exchequer of Simon de Montfort, Earl of Leicester, thirdborn son of the Butcher himself.

XV

There is an age to be disappointed in one's father. If the revulsion comes in good time it can be very useful: but I was well in advance of it. With most sons it happens at fifteen or so, and they must suffer in silence while they are beaten and bullied into the shapes of men and not asked for their opinions on anything, let alone for their views on the paternal performance.

That Bert had been forced into collusion of some kind with the de Montforts was very clear. Whether this included being used as a spy on his own people, I trembled to think. With the variety of work available to him in London, for my father to *choose* employment with a de Montfort woman, whoever she was, must mean the Butcher's kin had a hold over him. Bert's faith was shaky, I knew that. He was not at all consistent. In him Albigensianism was little more than a tortured Epicureanism. But his weakness with money, his waywardness and failure to concentrate upon the essentials of his craft, his craving for drink and women, all these were garlands when compared to the thought that he might be a traitor. The intertwining of mutual aid, influence and skill is the form of the masonic knot and we tie it around the neck of anyone who will serve, or employ us. We have lived with our destroyers for a long, long time, and made them proud of the beauty of the new world we have built for them on the sky-lines of their cities: but we do not put ourselves out for anyone but our brethren. And working nights in the middle of a frost-bound field in February on a fornicatorium for a de Montfort whore was going well beyond these limits.

I walked back towards Saint Paul's, my mind teeming with poisoned thoughts: contemplation of Bert's endearing frailties not amongst them; they were redeemable. But not this! I had to recognise his evil; his shabby, raffish peccability. That I should not have seen this in him until now! That I should have been so deceived! Bert had been bought in Dover. He had spied on Hans Seersach, on the lodge, on all the connections we had with the continental lodges. He had betrayed the entire network. Even now the kings of England, France, Spain and Italy were in consultation with the Holy Roman Emperor and the Pope preparing to switch their crusade from the war against Islam to a war against us. The terrible twenty years of our suffering would return and our craft, our genius, our works, our faith and our blood would die at the hands of the Butcher's son.

"What have you been up to? Where the hell have you been? Why are you covered in mud? What are you crying about? Why haven't you been back at the digs since before breakfast?"

It was Bert on his way to the building-site. He was furious with me and gripped my elbows with tremendous force, lifting me off the ground. I looked into his raging eyes and started to blabber something about going out on the Moor for the day. Bert softened and put me down. For a moment I thought that he was going to come back with me, see me bathed and fed and settled down. This was not to be. If he had abandoned his clandestine labours for that one day my suspicions might have cooled. But his anger with me was plainly caused by his impatience to be away.

"You get yourself straight back and stay there till I come home. Don't wait up. I'll be late," he said coldly, then stalked away, leaving me red-eyed and shaking in the street. I walked the rest of the way back to our quarters in a daze of misery.

I did not return to our room. My unhappiness drew me towards the great church. I went inside to be swallowed up by the bustling, coloured darkness. The hordes of folk swarmed in the candlelights, their voices as monotonous as bees. What do any of them truly believe? I asked myself as they brushed against me. It is all words and incense and money. High above me the masons were working on the clerestory of the choir, their banging and tinkling as clouded as pigeons' wings in the huge space. What impact did the work of such tight-fisted, mercenary men have upon any supreme lord of light? How could he tolerate such mean beginnings for his beauty? Why send it to the earth through such a twisted medium as Man? Every one of the little figures crawling about in the roof-lines was a spider-sign of my scuttling father. He would spin out his web of stone until he died and catch nothing but shame. Oh, how I cursed him!

You must not forget that I had seen the foul face of Cretin power by then; and that Bert had always professed to have the mastery of its many masks and disguises. His attitude was he would obey another man only as far as it was necessary to live. No matter who it was — Christian or Albigensian — he would never give more of himself to servitude than he could afford. Cunning had to be part of his armoury. Some politeness, agreeableness, even bonhomie, he could manage when the need arose and it was worth it. But within himself, at the wild core of his being, he was free on his own chain, shackled to life at one end and death at the other. And there was always the ultimate liberty of choice, such as the Perfect made when they had reached the point of total contempt for the material world: to be a pure spirit freed to hold hands with the Two Gods and question them. This, I thought, was a valid attitude; indeed, a noble one. It precluded any form of slavery and reduced the onerousness of service to a bearable burden. All my life I had considered my father to be a free man, which is a glorious thing — even now I think it is glorious after forty-eight years of my own foolishness on this earth. I had never been proud of my father's skill at his work — but I had been proud of his employment and of his stand against the world's monstrous unkindness. He had always been a brave man to me and I had preferred that to having him as a cowardly, creeping genius: the genius I would provide, but I wanted it to be blended with his courageous independence. Now my teacher had traded his liberty for . . . what? Why had Bert done this?

If I had had a mother I think this is the time I would have run to her. She would have understood my anxiety to find fault. In her own knowledge of the man she would have found cause to doubt my accusations. What a woman knows of a man she has lived with for a long time is not only Aphrodite- and Eve-learning, but the wisdom of common suffering. She would have said: "Hedric, your father will have his reasons. Trust him!" It was with this expectation of sage advice that I squatted in the buzzing, brawling nave, my head as frantic and fluttering as the sparrows that had come in from the cold London skies. Help me, I asked the gloom and the flames, help me. Within the thick hum of human prayers and negotiations and the twittering of tired sparrows, my plea did no more than squeak.

There and then I decided to abandon my apprenticeship and reject my faith. Somewhere there was a simpler life for me to lead. This one was too hard and too embittering. If I remained wedded to it I would be destroyed. This meant I would have to leave Bert because he was that life: it existed within his control of me. As I crouched against the wall and the folk washed up and down the giant nave I worked out what I would do. I could not spy upon my own father any more. He had disgraced himself and broken our mutual trust. All I could offer him was an alternative: give up the trade, the de Montforts, the life, and we will make a fresh start. Find a tenancy, a small farm, sheep, a cottage. . . . What with? We had no money. Go back up north then. Fishing. We could take a part-share in a boat . . . soldiering . . . suicide. . . .

My mind drifted hither and thither, unable to fix on a plan. Numb with sadness I left Saint Paul's and crept back to our lodgings to be scolded by the housekeeper for trailing mud into her house. All evening I lay on top of the bed in my dirty clothes. When Father Horace came for my lesson I refused to let him in, shouting through the door that I was giving up my classes. By the time Bert got home in the early hours I was drained of reason, hysterical, filthy with tears and grime (and I am a clean person by nature), and mad. When I heard him coming I got into the bed and pulled the sheets up to my chin, feigning sleep. He got in beside me.

Suddenly I went mad: I battered at his ribs with my fists and kicked his shins, making him double up so that he cracked his head on mine and I yelled out with pain.

"Hey, hey, what's all this about?" he remonstrated with me, holding me down and trapping my legs with his. "Are you sick?"

"No, I am not!" I said, hissing. "Leave me alone!"

"Oi! That will be enough!" Bert snapped, sitting upright. "Don't you talk to me like that or you'll get my belt across your back right here and now!"

I heaved the covers off the bed and pulled my shirt up.

"Go on then!" I said. "Do it. See if I care."

"You will if I get going, son," Bert said warningly. "You're trying me. What's the matter?"

He pulled the covers back over me and lay down, one arm remaining on my side of the bed, its weight across my shoulders. I remained face-down, my mouth pressed against the pillow.

Bert sighed and patted me.

"Fed-up, are you? You're right. I've neglected you lately. I'm never with you . . . you're left on your own too much . . . ah, this bloody place. . . ."

He sighed again. This time it was deeper and harder and it touched an underlying despair.

133

"Why are you doing that job?" I asked.

"What?" he demanded, twisting my head round off the pillow. "Talk so I can hear you!"

His hands were cold and rough on my cheeks. In the darkness of the room his eyes drew all the starlight and blazed.

"Say what you just said!"

"It doesn't matter, Dad . . ." I muttered, trying to turn away.

"Doesn't matter? I'll say whether it matters or not. You're all I've got, my only friend. There's not a single mate of mine in this damned city . . . Hedric, what did you say?"

I sat up, hoping he would take his hands away. I was afraid that when I repeated the question he would break my neck. Taking hold of his wrists I braced myself.

"Why are you doing that job you're doing?"

My father let go of my head and sank back on to the pillow, his arm across his eyes.

"How did you find out?" he asked in a low, miserable tone.

"I followed you."

He laughed quietly and took his arm away. In the tangle of his black hair and beard I saw the glitter of his eyes.

"Ah," he sighed, "so you know."

"Yes, I do!" I said, seething. "Why didn't you tell me?"

"I would have done . . . in time. . . ."

It was as if my arms had minds of their own. While I remained deeply furious with him for his weakness I could not help embracing his great, mad head and weeping with him.

"Don't worry, Dad, we'll sort it out," I heard myself say.

"Ha!" Bert snorted. "Not this one. I've outsmarted myself this time."

I was about to ask him to tell me what had happened but I stopped. If he was going to confess that he had become an informer I would rather not hear that news with my arms round his neck. Before he could start to speak I snatched them away and retreated to my side of the bed.

"What d'you do that for?" he asked.

"My arm had gone to sleep," I answered, rubbing it.

Bert propped himself up on one elbow. The silvery light from the window made a spiky halo out of his hair and beard. When his lips moved starry flashes came from his teeth. I was in bed with Moses or

John the Baptist; a huge stone figure that had flown down from the tower and through the window to tell me the grim story of human wrongfulness, to lie on the pillow beside me, a god on a cloud remorselessly enumerating the sad sins of men in a voice tired from grieving. I was not alone in this sense of ancient rigmarole; from my father's intonation I could tell that he was feeling it as well. The head-count of the rough figures he had carved to adorn the temples of the Cretins was high: into each of them he had put part of his own acquired knowledge of our weary way with truth. It had guided his chisel, axe and saw — now it guided his tongue through his confession.

"There are things you do not know," he said. "Even now I would rather keep them from you. You are too young by half but you are all I have so I must share the weight with you. Forgive me for that."

I could not say the words so I nodded. In that nod I managed to express my acceptance and my reservations. If Bert had taken more care of me then I would not have been deprived of my childhood. To this date I have a strong awareness that I have lived a very long time. There is no doubt in my mind that this is because my adulthood had to be anticipated. True childhood will never be mine. Maybe in old age I will slip into that time but I will never recognise it, or enjoy the full sense of the completed cycle before death. My life has been a spear thrown before the leaves could be stripped from its shaft.

We must go back to Dover: that is where the deception had begun.

There are two realities for a child: the one it faces on its own as a solitary creature created to suffer on this earth: and the other that it must pretend to recognise in order to appease its parents. The second reality is a false one but it is the world it must appear to inhabit if it is to have any peace. The result? Two natures, two ways of looking at the world, two appetites — one for truth, one for lies — a duality in every soul. It occurs to me that this may be the work of the Two Gods themselves so each will have its territory marked out in the child.

My suspicions were both founded and unfounded. He had betrayed the lodge but in a manner that was only selfish and short-sighted. The real blame for his lapse was not his, but Hans Seersach's.

While at Dover Hans had become impatient with the older and more conservative masons who had got into the habits of comfortable survival. Although they admired his fire and energy they did not share his aggressive and challenging instincts — nor did they think much of his obsession with the Second Style of Emergence. Most of them were still struggling with the First!

Bert had become his disciple (apprentice, I would say), and together they had worked on a scale model from Hans's original concept of the new style. Hans had persuaded my father that it would be pointless to show it to the members of the Dover lodge whose minds were numbed with earthworks and buttress-building. He wanted the model to be first seen by King Henry in Westminster; the best friend that an innovative architect would have in England as he saw buildings as the highest art. The model had been carted up to London and, through the influence of Sir Henry de Montfort via his uncle Simon, the King had examined it. It had caused a lot of disquiet in his mind. Being a pious Christian he had shown it to his bishops and councillors. They had been horrified.

"Tell me what the model was like!" I asked him. "Please!"

"Oh, very new," Bert muttered, "very new."

"Give me an idea . . . draw me something. . . ."

"Not now. I'll do you a sketch in the morning," he said, countering my request with a grimace. "They were Hans's ideas more than mine."

"I'd guessed that."

"Oh, had you?" Bert murmured, a flash of malignancy in his face. "Perhaps you've guessed it was all to do with pebbles?"

I suddenly remembered the summers. The beach at Dover. Pebbles. The waves rolling them up and down, up and down. Hans sitting with his feet apart, his hands plunged into the skimming surf. Pebbles in pockets. Pebbles on window-sills. Pebbles piled in the grass, in the garden, on the roadside. Games with pebbles. Jacks on the back of the hand, falling through the fingers.

"Didn't you do any drawings?" I asked.

"They were all burned."

"Burned?" I gasped. "Oh, no! Why?"

"By order of the King."

I felt hot panic rising in my throat. I could almost see this model! That all evidence of it should have been destroyed was impossible.

"But you can remember it, roughly . . . approximately . . . a bit . . . can't you, Dad?"

Bert shifted on his elbow. He looked down and twitched the covers.

136

"We were told never to reproduce the design again upon pain of death," he said ashamedly. "I've tried to forget what it looked like."

"Pain of death! Don't talk to me about pain of death! This is everything that Hans was working for. You might have made a mistake by sending it to the King but it doesn't mean that the idea has to be forgotten."

"Oh, it won't be, knowing him. He'll find a patron somewhere. He went to try and get an audience with Frederick, the German emperor, when he left. You know, the one who's just died; the one who the Pope said was Anti-Christ and Lucifer and in league with the Tartars. Hans said he sounded just the right man to get behind the Second Style. Perhaps it was the shock of seeing it that killed the poor old bugger."

Bert chuckled ironically and smoothed out the pillow. He waited to see if I was going to press him about remembering the design. He regarded me with a lonely, dog-like anxiety, head lowered. Wanting to hear the rest of his explanation I kept my hunger to know the details of the Second Style at bay. There was always tomorrow and a piece of parchment waiting to be drawn upon.

"Is this why we left Dover?" I asked.

"Yes. The King wanted us away from his royal fortifications. At one time he wanted us in prison. The Inquisition was mentioned but Sir Henry headed it off. He was good to us. He spoke up and made excuses for our . . . how did he put it? . . . exaggerated ambition to please."

Laughing softly Bert lay back and put his arms behind his head.

"I had to swear an oath that I would never reproduce the Second Style in any manner whatsoever. So did Hans."

"But you'll do it for me, won't you?" I demanded urgently. "Hans did it for the Emperor."

"I don't know that he did, finally. He just said he'd try."

We paused as if by agreement. There was more and it was obvious that Bert was not looking forward to revealing it. After a while I nudged him.

"Might as well get it all out in the clear, Dad. It's not so bad as I thought it was: not so far, anyway."

"You can imagine something worse for your own father to do? Something more stupid? That tells me a lot about what you must think of me."

This time I did not nudge him but rested my hand on the round muscle of his bent arm. Beneath my fingers it tensed; then he got up and lit a candle from the dying fire.

"Hans is a marvellous mason, Dad. He taught you things that no one else had ever done. You weren't stupid," I said with as much reassurance as I could muster. "One day you'll have the chance to put his ideas to work."

"Ha!"

"You will, somewhere. The style can't stand still. It never does. We'll find a gap and push something through. It will be your masterpiece . . ."

My voice trailed off as I caught Bert's glance. It was savage. He knew, as I did, that he would never be given the position of magistro cementariorum for a completely new building where fresh principles of design could flower. He would always be extending the old ones, painfully drawing them out into a slightly modified form. If we had been given Salisbury to do — ah, that would have been perfect. An empty space to fill. No old structure to accuse the new. Every serious mason in England had envied Elias of Dereham this opportunity to build from clean beginnings. He had chosen to create from within the centre of his age's urge. It was a prudent, pruned efflorescence of his mind. But then, in the Midi of France the persecution of our faith was still going on as Salisbury rose from its foundations. Elias had to be cautious. The lodges did not want King Philip's thirst for the blood of heretics passed on to the English monarch. King Henry, as lord of Poitou, was already half-guilty of complicity in the massacres of our people during those terrible times. He had aided two French kings by giving permission for "crusades" to cross his territory to get at us. He had abetted two vicious popes, Innocent and Honorius, to campaign against our truth. Now the French king was a crusader of the proper Jerusalem sort. He saw the enemy as Mahomet, not us. By the time Salisbury was finished we were safe again but the style remained as a monument to our apprehension: beautiful but not bold: poised and nervous rather than sublime.

"Did you know that you were going to have to work on that summer place before we came to London?" I asked carefully.

My father tightened his lips and stirred. He did not answer for a while. I could see the vein in his temple throbbing as he thought it out: what shall I tell this whelp? What do I have to tell him? I prayed hard

138

that he would see fit to take me completely into his confidence and not retreat into evasion.

"Yes," he said finally.

"So all the talk about getting a job on Saint Paul's was a lie?"

"No! Don't call me a liar, you little snooper!"

Bert sat up, his eyes staring. I thought he was going to hit me and got ready to slide out of the bed beyond his reach. As my toes touched the floor he sank back with a grunt of defeat.

"I'm not allowed to work on any church building or royal palace, any castle or fortress, any harbour, anything of use. . . ."

"Does the lodge know that you're working for de Montfort?"

Bert groaned and turned away from me.

"Boy, is there anything you don't know?" he whispered.

I got it out of him during the next hour as the dawn rose. The words streamed out of him like the sparrows coming out of Saint Paul's into the new morning. Sir Henry had been given charge of Hans and my father and made responsible for their good behaviour. Hans had agreed to leave the country but Bert needed employment. As a favour, because he liked him (Bert's words), Sir Henry had fixed up a job for him on a love-nest built for Leicester's chief concubine.

"You never thought of taking me to work on it with you," I said, interrupting him. "After all, I am your apprentice as well as your son."

"They didn't want boys working on night-shift," Bert muttered. "Not with the scum you get on sites like that."

"Oh, I thought *you* might have been protecting me, Dad."

"There's nothing for you to learn there. It isn't a straightforward job. Nothing is with the de Montforts. They know how to nail you down."

"But they never suspected that you and Hans were Albis? What about the Inquisition? Why did they mention it?"

"The design was outrageous. It went against all the rules of existing masonic practice. No one ever thought that we were heretics. They thought we'd been possessed by the Devil!"

Here Bert brought himself to smile in his brilliant, beguiling way: full of excitement and pleasure. It hurt me to think of what that model must have looked like. I yearned to see it. What a waste! To be crushed by the ignorance of barbarian lords and lame-brained bishops! What Hans had created must have been as fragrantly novel as a new rose in a freshly-created colour.

139

"What did you say to satisfy them?" I asked, my voice as purged of interrogation as I could make it. "If you're possessed by the Devil you're dangerous."

"Hans told them he had got the idea from his travels in Asia Minor. Some old Greek cities somewhere, cave-dwellers . . . what was the name? I can't remember. One of the bishops had heard of the place. It is mentioned in the Dream of Saint John. Hans said that he had been there while returning from Constantinople where he had been studying the dome of Saint Sophia. This was a good point to make to our lord king. We have borrowed a lot from overseas. But this idea was one that was better left behind, the King said."

"And you agreed with him?" I asked.

"We had to. They said we had spawned a new evil; a prodigious monster. All I could see was a little model made of bits of wood, but they were afraid of it."

He rambled on, always skirting around the part of his story I was desperate to hear — what was the Second Style? — but I did not interrupt him again. We would return to that later on. Meanwhile we had the love-nest to deal with: how, when he had started work he had discovered that his recruitment was for a special purpose. Simon de Montfort, the Earl himself, had drawn up the design of the house. It was to be a double storey built around a courtyard with a maze of cellars below. Bert's task was to construct a passage from a small freeholder's farmstead eighty yards away into the cellarage. This passage had to be drained and lined with stone and well ventilated. Bert had to go on shift each night, work one hour on ordinary tasks, then take his two labourers to the farmstead — now vacated as the property had been bought by de Montfort — and drive the passage to the house so that when the whole work was completed they could break through unseen. Bert had been forced to take a second oath to keep the matter secret. As it was made upon the Christian scriptures it was invalid but if caught breaking it he could expect the severest reprisal. So, he had not told the lodge exactly what he was doing. The members were surprised my father had not taken the day-work that had long been available to him on Saint Paul's — payments made, of course — while he continued working nights.

"It's clay, son. Sopping wet. When I get back here I'm done for. If I got up on scaffolding straight after doing ten hours on that passage, I'd fall off," he told me. "Some greedy sods might try it but I know my limitations now. Between the King and the clay they've got me well bogged down."

That was the last thing he said before he fell asleep. There was more for me to find out but I did not try to wake him. To go from working on the King's most important castle to making a back entrance for a Frenchman's whore is hard enough: but to suffer the humiliation for the sake of sublimely provocative architecture? . . . Well!

As I watched him slumber I realised I could not keep my mind on the dangers: the King's displeasure, the Earl's notorious cruelty, the scent of heresy the prelates had inhaled as they looked at Hans's model: no, all I could think of was pebbles.

XVI

I awoke at noon, my head pressed against my father's side. Moving carefully so as not to wake him I got out of bed. The sensation of being up and about was very different to what it had ever been before. I could not determine what made me feel like this until I recalled the events of the previous day.

The Second Style was in existence. It had broken through. I had not seen it but I had heard of it. One day I would actually *touch* it! It was a transforming power that was loose in the land.

London was oddly silent. From our room I could hear neither wheel nor hoof on the street below. Voices from the host of church-goers to Saint Paul's were as familiar to us as birdsong but this morning I could hear nothing. When I looked out of the window I saw why.

It had snowed heavily during the morning. While we had slept a foot had fallen, deadening the city. As I surveyed Saint Paul's in its white robe I began to feel the cold. It had frozen hard outside and the breath of our sleep was rime on the inside of the window, spangled with geometrically perfect plans.

I got back into bed and lay shivering. Then I returned to Bert's side and warmed myself. He was in a very deep sleep, his breath rattling and whistling right down in his chest. I could not stop myself thinking that inside his living body was the most precious knowledge: a vision! He had received a revelation. It had terrified a king but I knew I would adore it, given the chance. What could it be like, this undermining, seditious, blasphemous beauty?

My drawing materials were at the side of the bed. I took some parchment and my pens. The ink in my bottle was carrying a thin topping of black ice which I broke. First, I drew the rough roundness of my father's head sunk in the pillow; then I surrounded it with pebble-shaped chapels as if his skull served as an apse. Dissatisfied with that, I filled his head with more small pebble-shapes until the whole drawing took on the character of a honey-comb. Was it a church full of very small rooms? A room for each soul? Was each

142

pebble a cell and the meditating mind of its occupant another cell within that cell? Had Hans seen the prayer rising from this cell within a cell as a pebble thrown at the Evil God just as David slung his stone at Goliath? Was the Second Style merely a change of weaponry — from the spear-pointed arch to the parabolas of flung pebbles?

I put the parchment away, disappointed with my efforts. It looked like nothing at all: eggs in a basket! When Bert awoke I would tease the information out of him. I knew there would be no point in talking to him for the first hour as he was a slow starter once he had wakened. However, as soon as he stirred and turned I had my drawing under his nose.

"Is the Second Style anything like that?"

Bert blinked at what I had drawn. His eyes were only half-open. Cautiously he wet his dried lips with the tip of his tongue.

"Hedric," he whispered.

"Yes, Dad?"

"Shut up and leave me alone."

I rolled the parchment up and held it to my chest, lying in silence while Bert laboriously put his thoughts together. I had observed, over the years, that it took him half-an-hour to re-assemble the pattern of the previous day's events in order to work out what he must do to survive in this one. But I could not wait. He was as slow as an ox!

"Was it perfect circles or parabolas?" I said, my lips spouting mist into the air. "Or was it an oval mode?"

Bert snarled to himself and got out of bed, lurching over to the bowl for a wash.

"I'll never tell you anything again," he muttered as he tipped the jug.

Ice tinkled into the bowl. He looked at it, then through the window. Stumbling across to it he rubbed away the rime and stared out.

"Oh, no, no!" he groaned.

It had not occurred to me that the heavy fall of snow would halt work on the summer-palace. To me this might have been a cause for rejoicing but one look at Bert's face was enough to dispel any thought he might share it.

"Where's all this come from?" he grumbled bitterly. "Don't say it hasn't been sent. I saw no warnings of this. Talk has done this. I should have kept my mouth shut. If I hadn't told you what had happened this snow would still be up in the sky! You're bad luck, Hedric! Another month and I'd be free of that job — free to work where I liked. But I can't find new work until that passage is finished."

"Why don't we run for it? We could go and find Hans," I suggested as I watched him lumber about in the snow-light, dragging on his coat.

"And be an exile for the rest of my life? The lodge would be told — never allow that man to work in England again! Never mind England! King Henry can put the block on me working in any country in Christendom. He can stop me anywhere, anytime. So what do I do then? Change my name? Change my face? Jump in the river and drown?"

He got his boots on and stamped his feet down in them until the floor shook.

"You brought down this snow on my poor head, you little ape! Don't get me talking again, ever! It does no good. You're not old enough to understand. Here! Get yourself some breakfast and keep out of my way."

He threw a silver penny down on the bed and left the room, crashing down the stairs, still muttering to himself. I hauled my clothes on and ran after him. I knew where he would be going for his breakfast. I did not care what I suffered for it — how many clouts round the ears, how many kicks and curses — I would have the Second Style out of Bert or perish.

I saw him go into the shop. Knowing it was his habit to sit there for a full hour over his breakfast I decided to give him time to cool down before I tackled him again. As I was too excited to eat I decided to go into Cheapside to buy more parchment with my penny. The rows of narrow shops were aflame with colour against the snow, their frontages as speckled and strewn with reds, blues and yellows as the banners of barons. The shopkeepers had brought everything out into the pulsing snow-light now the fall had eased off and the sky was showing blue. But no one was out purchasing goods. I was the only one making footprints.

The stationer from whom I had been buying my materials since arriving in London was standing in front of his shop leaning on a shovel. He had been clearing snow and his fair, round face was flushed from his labours. He watched me coming up the street through the virgin fall.

"Thank God for someone," he called out. "I thought everyone had died. Is it less deep where you've come from?"

"No," I replied, staring at his blue, pouched eyes and the roundness of his belly under his apron. "It's the same."

From the River Holborn end of the street came a speeding sledge drawn by a huge black horse. It tore through the snow, hooves thumping, its tail hanging high, nostrils spouting. All the purity in the street was ripped apart as it came towards me, the faces of befurred men gleaming in the packed sledge. I had to step out of its way.

"Bad news from Gascony," the stationer said, ushering me into his tiny crib of premises. "That was the Lord Mayor."

"What bad news?" I asked, fingering a length of lamb's vellum which was faintly marked with whorls. "Is something up?"

"Oh, it's always bad news from Gascony. Ask the Earl of Leicester. Bad news is foreign news. More money from the city for French pockets. They'll break us yet."

The Great Tom bell of Saint Paul's began to sound over the city. People emerged from their houses and filled the streets and alleys in seconds. All the whiteness was trampled underfoot as the crowds streamed westwards. I bought my parchment and waited for the stationer to shut up his shop. He was trembling with anger.

"More money. It will be another tax for Gascony. I won't pay it. A quarter of my last year's income was taken off me for this French frolic. Oh, it makes me wonder. Is our lord king a baby? Will he ever get wiser while there is a hole in his arse? If Earl Simon couldn't master the Gascon lords then I say no one can. Let it go. Give it back!"

We hurried along to Saint Paul's Cross. The sledge was standing close and the befurred men crowded the steps, looking out over the crowd. Above us Great Tom was still beating out its summons over the glittering rooftops. As we joined the fringes of the crowd I remembered Bert at his breakfast. My curiosity was divided: Gascony or the Second Style? There was no doubt as to which was more important so I moved round the outside of the crowd towards Paternoster Row and the aleshop where Bert would be breakfasting. He was standing in the doorway, a cup in his hand, looking across at the Lord Mayor who was standing on the topmost step of the cross waiting for the bell to stop. Some of the children in the crowd started throwing snowballs at the aldermen but this was not in the general humour of the crowd. The offenders were roughly handled and thrust to the back.

"It's about Gascony," I said to Bert.

145

"Oh?" Bert answered with a tight smile. "You're an intimate of the Lord Mayor?"

"They're saying the King is a fool."

The Lord Mayor began to shout up at the bell-ringers, waving his arms. Whoever it was tolling Great Tom was overdoing his job. After another minute the bell stopped. Bert left the doorway and strolled over to hear what was to be said.

It was a strange performance by the Lord Mayor. He was obviously full of rage but he was bottling it up. From the way he spoke it was plain he was carrying out a duty which he found almost intolerable. He called out his news over the heads of the crowd in a strained monotone.

"King Henry III of England, Lord of Ireland, Duke of Normandy and Aquitaine, Count of Anjou, to the archbishops, bishops, abbots, earls, barons, justiciars, foresters, sheriffs, stewards, servants, bailiffs, liege subjects and citizens of London, know that on this third day of the month of March in this year of Our Lord one thousand two hundred and fifty we have taken the Cross."

The Lord Mayor paused to see the effect of his announcement. There was no immediate reaction. A few snowballs lazed heavily through the air towards him and broke on the steps.

"When's he leaving?" someone shouted out from the back, "Has anyone told him where Jerusalem is?"

The Lord Mayor pursed his lips and beat his gloved knuckles together. The muscles of his jaw were knotted in teeth-grinding.

"My lord king has promised the Pope that he will set out on his crusade on the twenty-fourth day of June. . . ."

Loud jeers came from the crowd.

"The twenty-fourth day of June one thousand two hundred and fifty-six!" the Lord Mayor went on, his eyebrows raised. "That is, over six years hence."

"What's he waiting for?" someone shouted. "Doomsday?"

The Lord Mayor smiled grimly and held up his hands. He did not have to tell the people the purpose of the meeting.

"Our lord king must raise a tax to pay for his part in the crusade. . . ."

"In six years' time we'll pay it!" a man called out. The crowd roared its appreciation.

"Our lord king wants the money *now!*"

The Lord Mayor's hand slammed down on to the stonework as the Londoners burst into cat-calls and jeers. I looked up at Bert who was looking thoughtful.

"What does Earl Simon say? Is he going to allow this?" he mused to me. "Or is he pushing Henry out of the country for a while?"

The tumult was getting out of hand. The Lord Mayor and aldermen were pelted with snowballs as they piled into the sledge and drove the black horse through the crowd towards the Guildhall. There would have to be more meetings to decide what the response of the monied citizens would be to this new demand. In the ale-shop to which we retreated a man suggested, with impunity, that the tax be approved if it meant that the King might get himself killed overseas. Others were quieter but deeper malcontents. They gave the opinion that the money was not for Jerusalem but for another lost campaign in Gascony. The Pope had provided the King with a cover for the true reason for the tax. But whatever opinion was expressed everyone knew who the defender of London's interest would be: Simon de Montfort, Earl of Leicester, the King's brother-in-law. He had taken the Cross ten years ago! He would know this was a ploy. Instead of spending the money he had gathered for the crusade on that great enterprise the King had made him spend it on the attempted subjugation of Gascony; the King's ungovernable folly, a savage country, a madhouse. Earl Simon had told Henry — get out of Gascony! Leave them to it! Waste no more money. Thus the talk went, round and round, with one pivot: the reputation of our Simon, a warrior whose sword had been kept sharp by common sense, not battering at mountains.

"See how they like him?" Bert said with a grimace. "What chance do we have? Do you know what the King's crusade will turn into? He will never leave these shores. The cross he's taken up will be turned against us somehow. They know we're here, they know all right."

I sat dumbfounded, all thoughts of the Second Style hounded out of my head.

"But you said that they didn't suspect you . . . that they thought it was just . . . excess . . ."

"They're watching me. They know. When de Montfort thinks the time is right he will raise the hue and cry. We will be blamed for everything. King Henry will protest: he adores his architecture: he loves his masons, his builders. Do you think he will stand by and see us slaughtered? We will be used as the excuse for Earl Simon to usurp the throne as the champion of Christ. He's the Butcher's son, the bloody dog, and these Cretins follow him!"

Bert glared at the packed customers as they babbled out their rumours and gossip. Contempt glowed in his eyes and his colour was high. He was in a mood to pick a fight with anyone who looked at him sideways.

"Finished your breakfast, Dad?" I said. "Let's go. It's too crowded in here."

He looked down at me, his scarred hands balled. He would have *loved* to start something. Perhaps he could see the fear in my eyes for he suddenly ruffled my hair and picked me up, barging his way to the door using me as a battering-ram.

"Make way, make way!" he shouted. "Dying child! Dying child!"

That evening I took my lesson with Father Horace. He had returned in the hope he would be able to earn his fee, being a poor half-deaf priest in need of the money. Bert had gone out to Bishopsgate to find out what the builder intended to do now the site was under a foot of snow. When I wanted to accompany Bert he refused to let me, arguing that I would profit more by staying at home.

When Father Horace arrived I apologised for my bad behaviour of the previous day. He was a dithery, benign old man who was never quite sure which pupil he was teaching and often mixed me up with other boys. We sat in our coats by a small fire and I could see he was half-asleep with the cold gnawing at him and little food inside his old body. He was so fatigued the book kept falling out of his hands into the hearth. After I had fished it out for the third time I kept it and allowed him to doze for a while before I took my stool over to his side.

"Father, what is an Albigensian?" I whispered into his large, hairy ear.

He did not move or acknowledge my question. Thinking that he was asleep I stirred his foot with mine.

"Have you ever heard of a Cathar?"

Father Horace sighed and rubbed his stubbly jaw. Reaching round he retrieved the book from my lap.

"What have you learnt?" he said.

"Not very much."

"There are some things that are not worth learning. Not all

knowledge is good. What I am trying to teach you is good. What you are asking me is bad."

I had been forbidden ever to mention the faith in the presence of Christians, even to disparage it for the purposes of disguise. This prohibition was laid upon all Albigensians for their own protection but also to prevent them confessing under torture. To do what I was doing was a heinous crime: but it was not looseness on my part. I suddenly had to know how the world looked at me: why an entire nation could be stirred up to destroy me: how a pebble became an offence against a stone-making god.

"Is an Albigensian a kind of Christian?" I asked softly. "Or is it a Saracen?"

"Boy, curb these questions. Make me some letters."

Father Horace bent down and picked up my box with all my drawing and writing materials in it. The piece of parchment with all my doodled guesses at the Second Style fell out. Father Horace looked at it, his rheumy eyes blank.

"I see that you are a wasteful child," he muttered. "If I had scribbled over my work that way I would have been beaten black and blue."

I rolled the offending parchment up and put it away.

"Father, I have an uncle who married the widow of a man who went to Carcassonne with Earl Simon's father. He has a head which he keeps in a jar in the chimney. Every Easter he brings it out and hangs it in his porch. He calls it his Albigensian. Then he calls it his Cathar. Sometimes he puts flowers in its mouth. Other people have Turk's heads, or Tartar's heads, or Saracen's heads for trophies from the Crusades. But my uncle has this. I would like to know what it is."

Father Horace shuddered and stuffed his hands far up his sleeves.

"Ask your uncle," he croaked. "He should be ashamed to have such rubbish in his house."

Not a word of what I had said was true, of course. However, the repugnance the old priest felt for my people was very obvious. He had expressed no sympathy for the owner of the head (the *original* owner!) in my story. No mention had been made of a proper burial, or honour for one's enemy.

"My uncle has said that when he dies I am to have the Albigensian head. He has written it into his will. What would you advise me to do with it?"

I was taken aback by the relish with which I embroidered my

horrible tale. It was an extension of my nature, an odd nook I had not explored before.

"Burn it!" Father Horace said passionately. "Then throw the ashes into the cess-pit!"

"Why?" I demanded, his heat clearing away the fogs in my mind, pushing my calculations forward. I was beginning to see what had always enraged Bert so much. The fury of this old man's hatred of our faith was actually breathing new life into him! I had resurrected what few scraps of spirit he had left.

"Beware of the Manichees. I will say no more. Even to put that word in my mouth is a sin. But, because you are a boy and know nothing I will do penance for it."

He got to his feet and headed towards the door.

"Is a Manichee an Albigensian and a Cathar?"

"They are all the same thing: the accusers of God!" Father Horace said with shaking jowls. "Those who condemn the Creator!"

"They made my uncle rich. He says they made Earl Simon's father a great man with their lands. When my uncle is in a cheerful mood he kisses the head of his enemy. Without him nothing would have been achieved, he says."

Father Horace covered his eyes and leant against the door-jamb. I could see I had gone too far. The poor old priest was about to faint.

"I will not be coming back to teach you any more, Hedric," he mumbled with a bitter weariness. "My soul is not strong enough."

Then he was gone, flapping flat-footed down the stairs like an old black bat anxious to get back to its cave.

XVII

My father did not come home the next morning. I waited for him until nine o'clock, listening for his tread on the stairs. During the night more snow had fallen and the city lay muffled and gagged beneath it like a corpse wrapped in a shroud. More snow was waiting to fall from heavy, iron-grey clouds which lumbered over London from the east. As yet the wind was light but there were warning gusts making the weathercocks creak. From our window I watched the pious flounder through the snow to Lady mass. The thought that these folk would pray for my destruction if encouraged increased the chill in my bones. When I could stand the cold no longer I put on every piece of clothing I had and took Bert's staff and bad-weather broad-brimmed hat. Before I left I laid the fire with what few bits of wood we had remaining. I told myself Bert had been forced to work in spite of the conditions and that he would finally get home perished. This was my hope. What I truly believed had happened was of a much more frightening character.

It took me three hours to walk to Bishopsgate. I followed carts when I could as they cleared a way through the snow but there were not many of them about. By the time I reached the city walls the east wind had got up and it was drifting the snow. Clouds of biting, blinding frost poured through Bishopsgate off the Moor. My route lay directly into the mouth of the wind as it blew across the meadows. Feeling my way forward with the staff I followed the hedges that were rapidly being covered. When I paused for breath and looked back my footprints had disappeared and the city with them. I was in a white, whirling world.

Before I got to the site of the summer-place I knew no one could possibly be working on it. Before the second fall of snow and the wind had arrived then it might have been possible to press ahead with the underground passage which would be sheltered. Now that access and exit to the site had gone and the drifting was so bad then a halt must have been called. There was a chance Bert had holed up there, unable to get back. I looked ahead into the blizzard, hoping to see or smell fire-smoke.

The site was deserted. It was almost invisible under the drifts, humps and bumps with only a few sections of scaffolded wall visible. I skirted the edge of it, knowing the pit-falls and ditches that were there from my day's labouring, and ploughed through the drifts to the farmstead where Bert's tunnel began. When I got there I found three military mounts and a mule-cart standing in the lee of a small wooden barn. The horses wore the saddle-cloths of de Montfort.

I could not stand in the freezing wind. Already I was losing my strength and a distinct numbness was crawling up my legs. From our days in the northern winters I knew I must find shelter. Slipping past the animals, using their hoof-prints to mask my marks in the snow, I entered the barn.

It was dark. Only slits of snow-light between the wall-boards gave any illumination. I found a pile of hay and sank down into it, hugging myself for warmth.

As my eyes got used to the poor light I looked around me. There were sacks hanging from the rafters. Free from the glare of the snow my vision took time to adjust. The edges of things were indistinct. It took at least ten minutes for me to realise that the sacks were men.

There were two of them hanging there. I could see faces now, their hands, their feet. I could not bring myself to stand up. It must not be my father. It must not. Not a death like this. Not my Bert.

All control went from my limbs. My teeth chattered like a baby's rattle. The bodies turned in the slips of wind coming from the gaps between the boards. I saw masses of hair, the glisten of eyes and teeth. *Both* of them were Bert! He was hanging alongside his own soul!

The doors of the barn were hauled open. It was too late for me to move and, besides, I could not get action into my limbs. Even with the danger I could not take my eyes off the faces of the hanged men. In the extra light I saw that neither of them was my father. Sinking back into the hay I thanked both Gods for this wonderful deliverance. Meanwhile the mule-cart was being backed right over my head. Whoever was controlling the animal had not seen me. I watched the man's legs from beneath the axle. He left the mule then went outside and brought in all three saddle-horses, tethering them side by side at a manger, which he filled. Then he climbed up on the cart and I heard two dull, heavy thumps over my head which made the cart shake. He had cut down the two dead men so that they had fallen into it. His work finished, the man left the barn and shut the doors after him.

I could not move at first. My frozen body had seized up in my terror. It was only when the fluids liberated by death in the corpses above began to drip through the bottom of the cart that I hurriedly dragged myself from under it. But I could not stand. Each time I got to my feet my knees buckled and I collapsed back into the hay. Finally I crawled across to the horses and hauled myself up on a stirrup, then pressed my body against the beast for warmth. It snickered as it felt the stranger at its side but the gale outside cloaked the sound.

Standing by the horse, holding on to the saddle, I felt the contents of a bag tied to the bow. I undid it and groped around inside. It was bread, cheese, meat and a bottle of wine: a full meal for someone. My immediate thought was that the owner would be back to collect it before long. Searching the other saddle-bags I found identical rations. These men had been sent out on a job that someone had estimated could take some time. My temptation was to eat and drink in order to regain my strength for whatever lay ahead; but I tried to resist it. If the men-at-arms found that their cheese had been nibbled I would have given away my intrusion into the farmstead. But I was so cold and weak I decided that I must sustain myself: so I took a bite from each bit, a sip at every bottle. No mouse has ever been so fair-minded.

I needed that new energy for my next task. The identity of the two dead men was important to me. They were poorly clad, rough fellows but both were strongly built. Reaching over the sides of the cart I felt their hands. They were hard and calloused as are those of all men employed in our trade. Their clothes were muddy and wet and they smelled of lime.

They were building-labourers, and, if I was not mistaken, they had probably been employed with Bert on the making of the passage. I searched their clothes for anything which could identify them but they had been cleaned out by their killers. There was nothing left. Two entire existences had dwindled down into these cold carcases, nameless and homeless. I respectfully pulled their clothes back into place. As I drew up the waistband of one corpse my hand snagged on something. It was a small silver disc hung on a cord loosely tied around the man's scrotum. I cut the cord and took the disc to the light by the door. It was stamped with the letters BHM.

Bonhomme.

The man had been one of the governors of our faith: a priest insofar as we have such things. I went to the other corpse and searched it in the same place. There I found an identical disc.

Bert had been working with two of our bonshommes: men who would not have been common building labourers by occupation. They had been senior members of our faith, leaders charged with the care of our bodies and souls.

Before I went to look for Bert I pulled the mule-cart forward into a column of shafts of light so the faces of the dead men were bathed in that holy medium. I prayed over them, asking the Two Gods to give them safe passage into the universe of the spirit up the ladder of this swaying snow-light. I knew that whatever the horror of their deaths, their spirits were now in full flight as they soared off on their greatest adventures: and they were mine, and brave men, and I wanted to act as family and friend rather than leave it to the mule, horses and hay.

I tied the two silver discs around my own scrotum but they kept falling off as I had nothing to keep them in place. Finally I put the cords around my neck and hid the silver discs beneath my shirt. With these badges of office against my skin I felt more courageous and they seemed to slow down my heart which was pounding with apprehension. Once I left the barn and went into the farmstead I knew I might find my father was dead. If he was then I wanted to join him. If these butchers refused to murder me because I was a child then I would show them the badges of the bonshommes, the best of men, and demand execution. If a heretic has any rights it is to his death.

These were mad thoughts at a mad time. I was well beyond intelligent reasoning. To expose our whole brotherhood for the sake of one man's suffering would have been a colossal sin but I would have done it if the circumstances had worked out that way.

The snow in the courtyard was now knee-high. The tracks of the man-at-arms who had come over to the barn were almost obliterated. Using them as stepping-stones I hopped from the barn door to the farmstead entrance then slipped along the wall to a pig-sty which abutted the side of the house. It was empty of swine. Climbing up on to the roof of it I got under the eaves of the thatch and slithered along until I found a gap which I could slip through into the pitch of the roof. The rafters were open, there being no ceiling to the empty room below. I swung myself down, alighting carefully so as not to shake the floorboards: then I stood very still and listened.

I heard sounds below me. They were muffled and indistinct: clanks, dragging, voices interspersed with long silences.

Moving soundlessly from room to room of the first floor I found the staircase and looked down into the hall of the house. The floor was covered with clay and the white walls were streaked with it. There had been a lot of barrowing of spoil out of the entrance. Creeping down the stairs I followed the trail of clay down to the door of the main living-room of the farmstead which was pegged open. Several hand-barrows were stacked on the floor. Beyond was the kitchen. That door was also pegged open and I could hear the noises more clearly now, coming to me from that direction. I entered the kitchen and saw a fire and a door which was open to steps leading down to a large larder below ground level. As I stood by the door I heard the scrape of a trowel.

But only one sound did I hope to hear. It had all the music of my world in it. If the instrument was broken then I was broken too. Speak, Dad, I prayed, my fingers touching the badges of the bonshommes. Let me hear you.

There was a voice. It was not Bert's. It rumbled, grumbled, stopped. The scrape of the trowel and the slap of wet mortar on stone followed. Someone laughed. It was not Bert. I clutched the door-jamb, repressing the urge to call out, "Are you down there, Dad?" then run away when I heard his blessed answer. "Yes, boy, I'm here. Help me if you can."

I did not want to see him. I knew that he would be with the de Montfort men: the trained myrmidons of the Butcher's son who had reproduced the massacres of the Midi in horrible miniature on our bonshommes. The terrible twenty years had been repeated for me, a child's lesson. I had never seen a martyred brother before: they had looked different to other dead men — the wind in their eyes as if they were in haste to be away from such a wicked, wicked world.

"Will that do you?"

It was Bert booming down in the larder. I heard the trowel thrown down, the clap of his hands, the expulsion of his breath, all the sounds he made when the job was over. I chewed my hand to stop the tears starting. Oh, I will never think ill of you again, Herbert Haroldson. No matter what you have done! I vowed. You are alive and that is all that I will ever ask of you again.

"Clean up after you," one of the men-at-arms said down in the larder.

"That would take a day's work," Bert replied hotly. "This place will have to be scrubbed out by ten women if you want it to look as though no one's been doing any building down here."

"We were told to leave it clean," the man-at-arms insisted. "Get on with it!"

I heard Bert start to ply his spade.

"Why don't you lend a hand?" Bert demanded. "I'm no sweeper-up!" Then I heard the spade being thrown down. "I'm a craftsman! Do you understand? A skilled man!"

"Clean up or I'll beat your head in," he was warned. "We're skilled men too, remember."

I had seen the mess that Bert would have to clear up. It would take an age to complete. The pride in the killer's voice as he boasted of his bloody art acted as a provocation to me to find an art of my own on this day. Building was not going to save my father. There was a note in his voice I had only heard at the gallows when the condemned try to speak.

Bert had told me the stories of the great cremations of our folk in the south of France: of the bonfires of women and children. For them the fire had been a sea of light on which they had sailed into the joys of the spirit. It had freed them but only through dreadful agony. From those days onwards fire had become the ally of the Albigensians: our friend and our ferry-boat. With it we erased old work, cauterised our wounds, purified our place of suffering.

With great care I took the hand-barrows and stacked them against the door to the next room. There was lard on the shelves and I smeared it over the wood and the door. Then, brand by brand, I moved the fire until it was close but not touching the hand-barrows. At the end of my preparations I opened a side window and admitted the wind.

It blew across the room and raised the flames. I went to the fire and pushed it into the middle of the hand-barrows. New fire hurled itself up the door. The interior wall was only wattle and daub and soon caught. When my inferno started to roar I climbed out of the window into the snow and waited.

I was up to my waist in snow, pressed against the wall, listening. It seemed to be a long time before I heard shouts of alarm. By then the fire had taken hold of the first floor ceiling above the kitchen.

What I did that day was ill-advised. The risk was too great. I was banking on Bert's wits and the mortal fear of hardened soldiers, men who have to be familiar with danger. One sword-thrust and my father

156

might have died. We will never know what orders those men-at-arms were operating under; whether Bert had to be killed once he had finished bricking up the passage or whether de Montfort had other plans for him. Certainly it was later claimed that there had never been any intention to murder Bert but I have my doubts. The deaths of the two bonshommes speak against it.

The first of the men-at-arms came out of the window and then ran out into the snow. He was followed by Bert, then the other two men-at-arms. They stood in the snow looking at the burning farmstead. Not one of them looked at me as I stood frozen against the wall, my mad scheme swirling up in useless confusion with the smoke.

Before they had time to notice me I sank into the snow and hid there cursing my stupidity. I had given my advantage away. For nothing. Oh, so much of what I had done had been for nothing! The men-at-arms had to realise someone had built that fire — or else believe in walking fires.

Over my head the farmstead groaned as the flames gripped its centre. I peeped over the snow and saw the barn door being hauled open and Bert ushered inside.

Now he was truly in a cell of execution, companioned by the dead. I had forced the issue. What I will do, I said to myself in my lunatic urge to act and not wait for the adult world to bring about its conclusion, is push it all further. I will face them. Say I am a passer-by who saw the fire. I dragged open the barn door and stepped inside. A floating, wild crimson shone on the faces of the three men-at-arms who were standing by the horses. Bert was sitting cross-legged in the hay, his face turned up towards me. He could not see who I was with the flames behind me and it was difficult to get my voice above the frantic neighing of the horses and the terrified honking of the mule.

"Hello! Hello!" I shouted. "Do you know there's a fire? Sparks are flying. You'll need to get out of here."

"Close that door!" one of the men-at-arms roared as the horse he was holding broke from his grip. The animal crashed into the next horse and made it rear up and fall across the back of the cart, forcing the shafts up so the mule was choked in the harness. All three horses went berserk as flames were sucked into the courtyard by the swirling wind, lashing the sides of the barn, searing through the snow. I was knocked flat by the mule as it regained its grip on the barn floor and heaved the cart out of the door. The wheels went over my legs but I was saved from injury by the drift I had been knocked into. As I lay there the three horses bolted out into the snow and made off, floundering madly. I got up and looked inside the barn. Bert was still sitting in the hay, his eyes raised. Beside him lay two of the men-at-arms. The third hung on to a wall-manger hugging his ribs.

I grabbed Bert's arm and shrieked into his face. He did not recognise me, or look at me. His eyes were on the two lengths of rope still hanging from the rafters.

"Dad!" I shouted into his ear.

He shook his head.

"Are those bastards dead?"

"I don't know. Come on, we can get away."

"Are those bastards dead?"

"What does it matter?"

"They were spying on me!"

I could get no sense out of this. I pulled a sword from one of the fallen men-at-arms and thrust it into Bert's hand.

"Get up, Dad!"

"Spying on me, on me . . ." he cried. "What for? Wouldn't I always do my best for the faith, given half a chance?"

I managed to get him to his feet. Pushing him out into the snow I guided him along the ruts left by the cart until we came upon the mule standing with its head lowered against the wind. Bert was still gabbling about being spied upon, trailing the sword in the snow like a broken rudder on a wreck. I heaved him against the cart and begged him to climb up.

"No, not with them in there," he said, spitting on the bodies of the bonshommes. "I'll not go near those treacherous swine."

As I argued with him I heard a muffled beat. A rider on a heavy horse hung with side drums emerged from the blizzard, striking his rhythm with one hand, sweeping snow off his instruments with the other. Behind him a cavalcade appeared, guided and kept together by the drum sounding over the wind. They all ignored us and spurred their mounts forward as they approached the fire then tumbled from their saddles and stood as close to the flames as possible, swaying with exhaustion. I looked questioningly at Bert who was grinning grimly.

"I hope when the snow melts from their shields we don't find they're the Earl of Leicester's men," he said.

★

158

There is no hell. The imagination of the Creators cannot exceed the pain of this world. Purgatory, eternal punishment, are jokes to the lumpen mass. What have they done? Did any man or woman ask to be born into this tribulation? How can they be blamed for the flesh which cries out for comfort and warmth? Christianity exists only because the Jews had become desperate for the Messiah — anything! anything! they said, that will stop this grief and pain. Let it be a boy from Bethlehem. Let it be a preaching lizard if you like. But get us out of this, O Lord!

But hell on earth is limited. All horrors and agonies may be finite; they can be alleviated. It was not the retinue of Simon de Montfort that came upon us that day on the Moor but Queen Eleanor's, King Henry's French wife. With her we watched the inferno: the Queen from between the curtains of her wagon and we from the daze of our recent experiences. It seemed hours we stood there, numbed by shock and cold, while the retinue milled around us getting more and more lively as they thawed out after their gruelling progress down the snow-covered Great North Road.

While the Queen's men dragged beams and other timbers together to keep the fire burning on a big scale, the blizzard abated and blue sky appeared overhead. No one had taken any notice of us as we stood in the lee of the cart. In their enthusiasm the Queen's men came over and unhitched the mule then dragged the cart over to the huge bonfire they had made. They did not bother to look under the snow that had fallen into the back. I watched them tip the cart sideways on to the fire. Steam rose from the snow as it melted, then smoke of a different colour. I think some of the men noticed what they had thrown into the flames — the corpses of the bonshommes — but they raised no alarm. They were too numbed and frozen to care a fig for another dead man here or there. It had to be shrugged off. More timber was stacked around the place where the bodies were being consumed. The men held out their hands to warm at the very flames. By the time Bert and I joined them there was nothing left to see of the bonshommes.

As the sky cleared we saw that it was a vast party. They had been caught by the blizzard as they came down from Waltham Abbey, having travelled for a week in a journey from Lincoln via Newark and Peterborough. Queen Eleanor was with her four Poitevin uncles, her three Lusignan half-brothers and the Bishop of Winchester, another Frenchman. They had been to Lincoln to court Robert Grosseteste, bishop of that see, and make him more a friend of the King than a servant of the Pope.

This I learnt from the chatter of the men-at-arms as they warmed themselves. That they hated the Queen was evident. The way Grosseteste had spurned her embassy had delighted them and made the bishop a hero in their eyes. If it had to be a choice between the French relatives of Queen Eleanor and the Romans then they were decided. Anything was better than the French and their relentless rapaciousness. "Old Grosseteste saw the bitch off," one of them averred, ice-crystals melting in his beard. "He told her straight what he thought of her fucking brothers and sons. I wished he'd cut their fucking throats but he's an Oxford man and more subtle than me. When King Harry the Hopeless married that French cow he did none of us poor fuckers a favour . . ." And so on and so on in this criticising vein.

Tucking ourselves in behind the Queen's wagons as they made a wide road through the snow towards the city walls we stumbled back along the way I had come only that morning, too exhausted to speak, even to congratulate ourselves on our survival. It was a short but strange journey for I felt as close as I ever have to stone: I was as cold and lifeless as a walking statue with the marks of my making all over me.

When we got back to our room I was surprised to see how unchanged it was. If I had opened the door to find wall-paintings daubed by a madman and a bed made of iron spikes I would not have been surprised. But it was as we had left it: quiet, comprehensible, comfortable. All of the change and chaos I had anticipated to be reflected there was locked inside myself, crying out for calm.

I lit the fire which I had laid for my father's home-coming. Together we sat in silence and watched it take hold. I had no doubt that Bert saw what I saw in that hearth: a second fire behind the first:

A blazing farm, and its stream of red-streaked smoke was the banner of the Butcher's boy lazing over England.

XVIII

We were summoned to attend the masters of the Saint Paul's lodge by a message delivered to the door that afternoon. Ten minutes later Bert tried to go out and found a couple of men sitting on the stairs outside our room. They had a message countermanding the first; ordering my father to be at the Westminster lodge fully packed for travel at six o'clock that evening. When Bert queried the instruction he was told the order was backed by a royal writ. When Bert retorted that no lodge summons needed any further authority than that of the lodge itself the men made no answer but looked at him pityingly.

"You're in a lot of trouble, Herbert Haroldson," one of them said finally. "Don't make it any worse for yourself."

"What kind of trouble? Who's making the trouble? What have I done?" Bert jabbered suddenly, his face white. "I won't come unless you give me good reason!"

"You've been busy out at Bishopsgate. There have been losses, too many to ignore. Is this your boy?"

The man looked hard at me. From his way of examining my face with an edge in his eyes I could tell he was a white cutter himself.

"I'm his son, and his apprentice," I said sternly. "And wherever he goes, I go."

"I shouldn't be too quick to say that if I were you, youngling. Your father may be headed for some strange places this winter."

I looked at Bert. Fear had exhausted him. I knew his mind was just not keeping up with events so I spoke for him.

"Does the Westminster lodge know he has a son who must necessarily travel with him?" I asked.

"No son was mentioned. Can you prove that you're his son? You could be anybody: his boy-friend for all we know," one of them replied. "If you're his apprentice you should have an indented document to prove it."

161

"Look at me!" I said. "I could be no other man's son!"

Without a word Bert went to his box and took out my indentures. He unrolled the parchment in front of them.

"I've done my bit for the trade one way and another. I'm loyal and I'm on the level. How about letting me know where they're sending me?" he pleaded.

"Sending *us*!" I insisted. "Wherever it is, I'm going too."

The men returned my indentures to Bert and left us in the room while they went out on to the staircase. When they returned they told us that we would have to wait for a second message which would say whether I could accompany Bert or not. Until that time we must not leave the house. Food and drink would be sent in.

Bert begged them to tell him what was going on. They refused to add to what they had already communicated.

"Come on, come on!" Bert fumed, his temper rising as his fear got cooler and he began to think. "We must all help each other. In our common faith, brothers, there is room for a little mercy. Tell me what you know."

"You will learn everything from Master Henry de Reyns tonight," Bert was told grudgingly. "If you will take good advice — be obedient."

"The King's mason? To see me? Why?" Bert expostulated.

The men went to the door. We heard them going down the stairs. I went over to shut the door and saw two new men climbing the stairs with a basket. They handed it to me, pulled the door to, then I heard them settle down on the landing, swords clinking.

Bert and I sat with the basket in front of us for a while. It bulged with food and wine. We could not touch it because it was part of a dream. A few minutes later there was a tap on the door and a third man entered with a pile of wood. He made up our dwindling fire with great care, blew the embers up into flame, then went out again without a word. A quarter of an hour later a fourth man appeared with a whole set of new clothes for Bert — from linen shirt and drawers to breeches, jacket, cloak, boots and hat. He was followed by a fifth who bore a beautiful leather bag of new tools, each chisel sharpened to the point where a man might shave with it.

"Hedric," my father whispered, "I'm going mad. I must go out."

"They said for us not to, Dad," I warned him, stroking the tools. "This looks good. These are gifts."

"I don't want gifts!" Bert sighed, banging his temples with the heels of his hands. "I want to get out of this mess! Get out of London!"

An hour later the second message arrived with permission for me to accompany Bert. It was followed by a second hamper of food and drink — a little bit smaller — then more fire-wood, then my suit of clothes. I waited within this dream for the best gift. To Bert it was a nightmare, the room stuffed with things he could not afford: were they bribes? pay-offs? farewell presents? Some tribes give a dying man full provisions for the journey of death.

My tools arrived.

I took them out of the beautiful leather bag. They were a full set, like Bert's, but, as I laid them side by side on the floor, I realised they were even better than his.

I got so excited I forgot our situation.

"You haven't got one of these, or these!" I said, showing Bert. "I wonder why?"

He stared at me accusingly then deliberately put on his old shoes, kicking the new garb aside as he went to the door. When he opened it he looked down at three men huddled on the landing, their faces pinched with cold.

"Where d'you think you're going?" one of them said. "Get back in there by the fire, you lucky man."

Bert paused, looked across at the baskets of good things, the warm clothes, me with my new riches spread out at my feet. Out came the brilliant, effulgent smile, the inspirational flow of friendly, warming sunshine. Where he summoned it from so suddenly I simply don't know.

"Lads," he said kindly, "while we're waiting why don't we have a do? No talking shop, no side, no nothing. Share with us."

And so we did. By the time we started out for Westminster to meet Master Henry de Reyns we were all mates together without a care in the world. It was only when we climbed into the covered sledge with our baggage heavy on our knees that the dark weight of London re-descended on us and our spirits sank.

We had expected to be driven west along Fleet Street but the sledge headed east across Friday Street and down to the Vintry. We ended up on a snow-laden jetty at the mouth of the Walbrook near Dowgate. A barge was waiting at the bottom of green-slimed ladders and we

163

climbed down, smelling the brine of the timbers uncovered by low tide. Our baggage was lowered down after us by rope and we sat in the stern, our backs to the river-wind, all our questions stifled by the blackness of the winter night. There were no stars, only the pinpricks of light on the belt of London Bridge. Below us the Thomas flowed as black as liquid coal.

Our drunken comrades and turnkeys left us at the jetty. All their good-nature evaporated as we disappeared into the well of the barge. I took note they cried out no farewells into the darkness but pulled their hoods up and disappeared as if they had just buried an enemy.

The barge's sail was unfurled as an east wind began to blow up the river. Six oarsmen stayed in their places, dipping their blades in a languid way as the wind was fierce and drove the barge along at a good pace. We did not try to talk to these men or the master who kept himself in the bow to be free of any conversation with us. The lights of Queenhithe and Bishop's Wharf slipped by like the jewelly eyes of mice. We passed the mouth of the Fleet and the marsh. All was dark in the Temple. Now we were tearing along with the incoming tide, the pale sail stretched full-bellied above us, hawsers thrumming, oars raised because they could not be plied fast enough to assist the wind. Heeling over to the north bank the barge plunged into the darkness.

"We'll not be free men by the end of tonight," Bert muttered, holding me close to his cloak. "Better than being dead perhaps, but not better than what we've had in the old days."

"They're going to give you work at Westminster, I think," I said hopefully. "That's what will happen."

"As a reward for burning down the Earl of Leicester's property?" Bert said with a sailor's sniff at the wind. "I don't know what they want with me but it won't be to say thanks."

"They don't know it was us," I protested without conviction.

"In this town a flea doesn't fart without it being registered by some clerk somewhere. They let us loose, they watch us, they write it down. We don't know the hundredth of what goes on. It's nothing to do with building, Hedric, but it's everything to do with the nature of lords and their knowledge of the land. We live on it, we build on it, but we don't know it because we don't own it. This river is rushing up and down daily. It stops for no one. You would think that it is free to do what it likes. But it is property. The keel of this boat is on water that is land."

"Yes, Dad," I said, unwilling to confess to my confusion. "You've got a point there."

"Let me do all the talking, remember."

Bert gripped my shoulder as he said this. The barge's sail was being lowered and the oarsmen were helping to bring us round to a wharf. A group of men stood at the top of the ladders, torches in their hands. The master of the barge went up first then beckoned us to follow. Our baggage was hoisted after us and the torchmen picked it up and conducted us through the darkness.

We had arrived at the palace of Westminster.

Since our arrival in London I had walked out to Westminster several times to see the dismantling of the old Benedictine abbey and the new building King Henry had ordered. It was an enormous enterprise which many estimated would take fifty to a hundred years to complete but the King was determined to see it all done before he died. As he was now forty-three this did not give much time for the masons. Master Henry de Reyns had been under the whip for nearly five years, pressing ahead with one section of rebuilding while, adjacent to it, the old fabric was still being pulled down. It was dangerous work and the Saint Paul's lodge had been full of stories about accidents caused by haste and poor management at Westminster. The other scandal had been the King's insistence on the French style: everything had to be copied from Rheims, or Amiens, or Beauvais or Paris, and the English masons had been given precious little chance to show their paces. In many wanderings about the site I had picked up a lot of gossip about the King's mason.

Master Henry de Reyns was a shadowy figure, delegating much of his authority to men in the rank immediately below him. He was not popular with the work-force although the men respected his ability as a draughtsman and philosopher. He did not have the common touch and served his master the King too well at the expense of the lower orders. To be going to meet him in the night with the huge, broken hulk of the abbey all around us was somehow fitting. I had always imagined him this way: a man who juggled with forces in darkness, knocking down the Confessor's tower with one hand, building up the Chapter House with the other — and all of this upwards and downwards, inwards and outwards, done at top speed as if the world were to end tomorrow. No wonder he tended to hide himself away and let his subordinates take the brunt of the workmen's complaints! And in this weather, with progress impossible because of the snow and ice on the fabric, he would be doubly difficult to track down; for I had no doubt that King Henry would still be chasing him to keep things moving. At the same time Master Henry knew he must satisfy the requirements of the abbot of the Benedictines, Richard de Crokesley, who had been made directly responsible to the Pope for the abbey's administration. Thus Master Henry de Reyns had two masters. It was also rumoured that there was a third: the King of France, the crusader Louis who was now a prisoner of the Saracens in Egypt. Louis had been a friend and supporter of our king from the early part of Henry's reign when he was fresh on the throne and suffering from the weaknesses caused by the troubled years of his minority. Whether the saintly King Louis was locked up in Egypt or lording it in Paris did not affect his hold over the English king. Henry was forever in his debt: some said in the palm of his hand. So, who was really building Westminster? To many people it was no more than a giant symbol of French and papal power designed to threaten London, and, therefore, no favourite with the citizens.

We were not conducted to the lodge, where I had expected us to go, but to the gatehouse at the southern entrance of the monastery, close to the Sanctuary Tower which was full of noisy fugitives evading the King's justice. The marshland around Westminster was riddled with thieves and whores as the royal court offered rich pickings and the Sanctuary was conveniently close if they were pursued by officers of the law. The din from the tower was terrible: singing, shouting, swearing, blaspheming. I had stood and listened to the foul language, learning a few things for when I might need them in street encounters. Even now, in darkness, the noise was great.

We were admitted to the gatehouse by an armed porter who looked as though he had not had a good night's sleep for a year. He locked the door behind us and took us through two small chambers where men sat on benches, slumped against the walls, waiting. I assumed they were petitioners or men looking for work. Some of them, however, had insignia to wear. As we passed through they gave us the tired, heavy-eyed looks of envious dislike those who wait give to those who have immediate entrée. Some protested, getting to their feet like sick men from a bed, swaying as if unused to standing. They were brushed aside by the porter who was in no mood for explanations.

We had to wait ourselves beyond the second chamber. There was a low passage with no seating so we leant against the cold wall. Servants went in and out of the third chamber with dishes and we had to press ourselves against the stone to let them pass. Eventually the porter returned and, with a sigh of distracted relief, commanded us to follow him through right away.

It was a room of modest proportions, not high, with one end taken up by an old carved fireplace. A table was set close to the fire and one man sat at it, his napkin thrust into the collar of his tunic, a knife in his hand. He was fat in the most extraordinary way: with no suggestion of softness even though his belly was enormous and his jowls rolled down to join his chest. A man's eyes are shadowed in fire- and candlelight and I had learnt to withhold judgement about a human face until I could view it in daylight: but Master Henry de Reyns's eyes transcended the soft disguises of flame. They were thickly hooded and prominent, the lids very coarse like those of a lizard. The pupils of his eyes were always half-covered by the lids and the bottom semicircle did not touch the lower lid but floated free giving him an insecure stare that was also oddly sympathetic to the object or person he held in his glance. It would be wrong to say these were eyes that gave any impression of weakness or indecision: in fact they were bold and tended to make one look away after a while: but they did convey vulnerability and openness and intelligence in unusually large amounts. At first I thought — ah, women! — either he had suffered because of them or he had much of their nature in his — but I later decided that Master Henry de Reyns was neither victim nor devotee of the female. What he was hopelessly in love with was his own mind.

My first acquaintance with that face was an initiation. Until then I had taken little real interest in the features of humankind. Even my own father's physiognomy did not stir me — except for the smile. There is no style, no reaching out, no true architecture in a face, no logic that removes it from its details. It is always just a couple of eye-holes above a couple of nose-holes above a slit — until the feelings transform the animal mundaneness and we recognise a fellow, a friend, a lover, an enemy, or no one.

There was no architecture in the face of Master Henry de Reyns either. His slash of a mouth, his massive cheeks as broad as a piece of pink parchment, his thick-lobed ears and black, curled hair around his bull-neck, his thin thatch and great rumpled forehead looming over his sleek, thin eyebrows, were all out of proportion and seemed to belong to different heads. He was a conglomerate man, rolled together in this hardened putty of a body. All this leapt into my brain before the King's mason had had time to open his mouth and speak.

Oh, his voice! His voice. It boomed. It buzzed. It shook the warm air. All the music I had heard in the tones of the lords and their women in London was played by the tongue of this man. It was effortless for him. He knew he was charming us and that he would win. I cannot remember the first things he said because I was so instantly enchanted. With my eyes fixed on his mouth and the gleam of his tongue in the firelight I put myself into a chair when he beckoned us to sit.

His hand was small and pale with one ring on the little finger. It showed a sun bursting through clouds. I calculated that it must be two inches across the diameter, lying across the third finger when his fist was made: an odd ornament for a practical man who must keep his hands free of impediments.

"There is fish soup which you will enjoy. I have had it for three days now. Each day it matures. My advice is to take toasted bread, pepper it, dip into this garlic sauce, then into the soup, put a sprig of parsley over the top, then munch. The salmon comes through wonderfully. This wine, the golden one, I already have in my mouth when I pop the lot in. It complements fish. Do it. From the Loire, this golden wine. A river, you see? They know their fish on the Loire and they make wines for what they know."

Drugged by his voice and the delicate gestures of his hands I obeyed his instructions. I took the toasted bread, shook a cloud of pepper over it, plunged it into the garlic sauce so all the pepper came off, drowned it in the fish soup so all the sauce disengaged from the bread and floated away, plastered a bit of parsley on the soggy stump, took a mouthful of wine, put the mess in my mouth and the wine streamed out over my chest.

Master Henry de Reyns looked at me with his beautiful lizard's eyes, his splendid mouth lifted in a gentle smile.

"Take time to learn: a little goes further than a lot. What do you say, Herbert Haroldson? Does a little go further than a lot? You have never had a lot to go far with, have you?"

"I have not," Bert replied with rough dignity, "but what I have I have earned."

"And what have you? What is the most precious thing in this world to you?" Master Henry persisted. "Come, tell me. Eat as you talk. Don't let this go cold. It is all for you. I have dined but I may just have a little to keep you company."

"My most precious thing is my freedom . . ." Bert began.

"No. That is not a good answer. Freedom is not a thing. I said a thing, Herbert. What thing?"

Bert was silent. He stirred his soup without taking any.

"I have had many things sent to you, Herbert. Those gifts are now your property. Before I sent them you had very little. Are my gifts the most precious things that you have? Answer me, man. It is a fair question."

Bert's mouth assumed a sullen, twisted line. He lowered his mouth to the soup bowl and drank.

"So, you will not talk to me. Perhaps your son will. Well, boy? Ready for another go at the toast?" Master Henry said with a flick of his finger. "Try again."

Now I was fascinated. As the King's mason's visage was the first ever to conquer my attention above all other distractions (and do not forget I was in a building new to me) I had convinced myself that I was able to read it correctly. All the qualities of the man appeared in his face — or so I had thought! Now here was a cold, playful cruelty at work. I had not spied that in my reading of him. Here was a petty wilfulness which did not go with his grandeur at all.

"You would do well to remind me that I am of your faith and must serve you," Master Henry said with sudden urgency. "Do not allow me to treat you with such contempt. Answer my questions proudly. You are one of the Purified. Your Catharsis is beginning. Tell me — what is the most precious thing in the world to you?"

Bert's mouth hung agape. Soup dribbled over his chin, making him look very foolish.

"What does it matter if I find a thing precious?" he snarled suddenly. "Who am I?"

"Because you must swear an oath on it. We do not swear oaths lightly, we Albigensians. You know that. We have no scriptures, no books, no relics, nothing that we can call our own. Our churches we must share with the Cretins. So, there is the inner light of a man's value. What can you tell me?"

Bert shook his head violently.

"No more oaths. I've done with swearing oaths!" he said passionately. "I'll never swear another!"

"The tools I gave you? Your fine new clothes? The food in your
belly? The wine? Tell me what you can swear on, Herbert Haroldson.
I must have an oath from you."

Bert got out of his chair. He was very agitated and stood gripping
his thighs, bent over as if in pain.

"The boy," he whispered. "I will swear on the boy if I must."

Master Henry de Reyns smiled. It was the equal of Bert's best.

"I trust that reply. Sit down. Eat your dinner and I will talk. Do not
interrupt me. I am the King's mason, that much is true, but before that
I am your brother."

"We'll see about that," Bert muttered.

"Oh, I am, I am. Do not doubt me. Do you want the boy to stay
while I talk? He is nearly a man. His future is tied up in what I have to
say. But you are his father."

I looked at Bert. He refused to meet my eyes. I was willing him to
agree but he shook his head and my heart sank.

"I don't care," he said quietly.

"You should. He looks to be a good prospect. I think he should stay
and hear it all. The oath will bind him as well so he might as well know
what he is in for. Come, eat while everything is hot, and listen."

The enchantment Master Henry had exercised over me at first sight
was resumed as soon as he forced my father to admit me into the
future with total knowledge. It was an act of supernal wisdom and
generosity as far as I was concerned. Later on I came to realise Master
Henry had been quite cunning in his recruitment of me as an ally.
Within Bert's oath would be a mechanism to determine how
absolutely it must be kept.

"What is your name, boy?" Master Henry asked, his small, sculpted
nose raised so the firelight shone red along its delicate shaft.

"Hedric, sir," I replied.

"Yes, I know. Your name is already familiar to many of us. And I
often ask unnecessary questions for fun. Has anyone tried to persuade
you that life is simple?"

"No, sir."

"If anyone ever does then take him for a liar. It is all deception. The
learning we lean on is all deception. If I were to choose a life for myself
it would be as brief as this flutter-by's."

170

Out of his sleeve he produced a tortoiseshell in a stupor. It had its markings intact but they were dull, no longer incandescent with summer.

"I found it in my bedroom this afternoon. It cannot fly. What is it waiting for, this insect? Why did it not die with its fellows at the end of September? It crawled away to live off nothing — nothing! What keeps it going? Do you believe in signs? This is an Albigensian flutter-by, boy. It is you, me, your father, all our brethren hiding in the chamber, waiting for another summer which Nature says it cannot have. But look at it! It opens its wings. It staggers about. It believes in a long life. Do you know, it cannot feed. I have tried it with all sorts. Its only sustenance is light. That is why it is happy here. That is why we Albigensians are happy here in spite of the hindrances and hamperings, the hatred and persecution: the light feeds us as it feeds this slip of gossamer."

Master Henry kept the flutter-by on the end of his finger. It swayed drunkenly in the candlelight, the fragile veins in its wings showing through where the powder had rubbed off. It did not leave its perch for the entire time we were in the room. As Master Henry spoke, his lovely, rich voice flowing, rolling along, he would occasionally raise the flutter-by to his lips and softly puff its wings apart. As I listened to his effortless speech my mind opened up to him with equal lack of resistance.

XIX

"Do not leave the lamb until last. It is good hot. It is good cold. In-between it is pointless. Eat heartily. Don't worry about the mess. A fair mason's motto, I'd say. Herbert Haroldson, you are my guest. It is not proper I should insult or criticise you. When I do so, please remember it is an essential part of what I am saying and I take no pleasure in it. We are all fools at one time or another. What matters is when that time crops up. With some of us we are fools when we are asleep: with you, you are a fool at crucial moments. To have made a bid for the King's eye with your model of Seersach's Second Style of Emergence was ill-advised. You by-passed me, for a start. Not a wise move. I saw the model, of course. I was consulted. I did not reel back, appalled, like the lords and the bishops. Nor did I scratch my head and look stupid. My opinion, expressed to the King in a brief missive, was that the design seemed rootless. It came from nowhere. No principles passed down to us from the Ancients were visible in it. The harmonious proportions of divine arithmetic were missing. It was brutal, unrefined and belonged to an alien intellect. An aberration, was my succinct verdict. The Fleming and his acolyte have been temporarily seduced by the architecture of Nature, I said. Forgive them for they know not what they do.

"Furious glances from you, Herbert. First I call you an acolyte when you believe yourself to be a creator of equal standing with a genius — for Seersach is no less and his Second Style is magnificent — and secondly I admit to begging for you to be forgiven. Intolerable! As intolerable as your silly ambition. You are not a white cutter of the first class. It is ten years since you did any work of quality. Most of the stuff you have been employed on has either been aborted before completion or never even got started. A hack is the best description of you. It is the best description of nine-tenths of our profession. Do not be too ashamed. Save some of your shame for later on. You will need it.

"But why should a hack, even in the company of a genius, give more respect than he naturally has to the Roman Vitruvius, the Greek Pythius, to anonymous Egyptians and their pyramids, even to numbers themselves? History is there to be consumed, not imitated. Why should we copy old forms when the world teems with shapes we can permutate? This thing I am building here — what am I seeking with it? To please? To salute? Is there something in the air dictating to me the ratios of height and width? When I look at it I do not see a lucid geometry. I see a feckless jumble, a jelly. Often I hope it will fall down so I can start again. So does my lord king. He would like the state of England to fall down so he can start again. Both of us will never have our dreams realised. We must persist with the jelly. Hans Seersach would not, Gods give him bliss. Did you know he'd drowned in a cattle-trough at the back of Maastricht market-place a few weeks ago? Yes, spare him a tear. He had a wonderful imagination, that Fleming. If he had got to the Holy Roman Emperor Frederick (a man neither holy nor Roman) before that superb heretic died then the Second Style might have flowered somewhere — perhaps in an adapted form for military usages — but his new model fell into the hands of the Emperor's architects, our fellow Albigensians, and they contrived his death in order to preserve their positions. Hans Seersach was a dangerously brilliant man. I have written him a verse. If you should wish to weep while eating keep away from the small bones in the chicken or you may choke.

> Some are born for storm,
> some are born for sorrow,
> some are born ahead of their time
> and should have been born tomorrow.

"Boy, when I see eyes like yours brimming with tears I want to run out and tear everything I have ever built down to its foundations. No edifice can be so eloquent as the grief of the young. The future is spoiled for you, I know. In your heart you cherished the thought that this world is changing to fit your requirements. Tears are acceptance. You accept the demise of great talent. So do I. I am not fit to be the King's mason. I am not a fraction of the man your hero was. But I know the jelly, and the forms that swim, unrealised, inside it. Do not hold me in too much contempt. Do not hate our German brothers who destroyed your friend in Maastricht. We do not accept the world

173

as it is. To build is not an act of acceptance. It is an act of change. But we will only change what is within the miasma, not something that stands too concretely outside it. Hans Seersach drew his lines too boldly, too hard, too defiantly, his pen went through the fragile fabric of our faith. Genius, you will need to remember, Hedric, is always in the minority.

"Try the goose. It is a good goose. It has walked all the way from Norfolk and it has seen the world. Suck its brains out and you might see better. If you could leave me some of the crisp skin for when I have stopped talking? It oils the jaws.

"To build in any style is a brave act. We masons are to be admired. What other art demands so much time and material, so much unity of purpose? We cement an age together! And we must bear in mind that the Christians are braver than we are in one sense. They do not believe in permanence. Their world is always ripe for destruction. That is why they do not make good architects; because their hearts and souls cannot be in it. So, they are brave with their purses. They pay for an illusion of permanence that we more fortunate sons of the Creators can provide. Our predicament is permanent. We know there is no Doomsday, only more of the same and more of the same. Our buildings are as capable of infinite existence as the material universe. Once our form has been imposed upon it and the beauty created then it belongs to the Two Gods as part of their essential natures for ever. And that is where Hans Seersach went wrong.

"His Second Style of Emergence went backwards. It echoed the state of natural evil within which all material exists. He drew his inspiration from the failure of the Creators. Geometry and arithmetic are divine tools given to us to re-work the world in order to improve it: they do not emerge from Nature without our intelligence and perception being applied to it.

"Can any Albigensian go backwards? We were never heretics, never. We held Christ but in our own religion, as a struggling man corrupted by this creation. Our only hope for bliss is in the new conflicts and what sparks may be struck.

"The white beans in oil and vinegar are good. Make a boat out of a cabbage leaf from near the heart, put the beans in the boat, a sliver of sharp cheese on top, a touch of rosemary . . . ah! If I could only join you instead of wasting my mouth's motions on words.

"It is my duty to conduct both of you through to an enlightenment

174

that may affect your appetites. Do not falter too much in your trenching. On the mind's palate paradox is piquant.

"You are from the lower levels of our craft. The family which you stem from has never been of senior rank in our faith. There is not a bonhomme to be found in your genealogy. Although we can say, in safety, that you are the backbone of Albigensianism, you are not the brain. Before, there was no reason to tell you what now you are about to learn.

"In the year 1231 of the Christian reckoning a privy concordat was reached between the elders of our faith and Pope Gregory IX, the Inquisitor. We were granted freedom from persecution, toleration, the right to our own religion and its practice, provided that our existence and the agreement were kept concealed from common view. Below the rank of baron or bishop no one was to know that a compromise had been concluded with a major and ineradicable heresy. The Church had admitted defeat. Christianity had admitted defeat. The cost to us was the subterfuge we must play on our own people: to keep them anxious, to keep them in a perpetual minority. For we had to agree further never to evangelise our faith but only replace ourselves one for one as death wasted us. The trade of mason was allotted to us but that was only a recognition of our domination of the craft, our exclusive ownership of this mystery.

"You were never told because you fall below the rank in masonry privileged to know. The only way it affected you, Herbert Haroldson, was you were commanded by your northern lodge to breed at least one son and train him up in the craft.

"You have overlooked that dish of stuffed cabbage. I admit that it does not look appetising but be assured, it tastes delicious. I recommend a little butter. There is pepper in the stuffing and a pinch of cummin. Go for the heart, is the stuffer's maxim. And over there you have the heart in a cheese sauce.

"Yes, you may well stare at your father, Hedric. He did have you born because it was his religious duty. For once, he did as he was told. And we must be grateful.

"Now you will swear your oath, Herbert Haroldson. Put your wine down. Leave your knife on your plate. Stand up. Roll your breeches up to your right knee. Oh, don't carp, man. Do it for fun. Put one hand on your son's head, the other on . . . let's see, put the string from that roll of pork round your neck and make a noose . . .

175

hold the end. Now, my muse, visit me! An oath for a white cutter who knows more than he should.

"Repeat after me. . . . Are you ready?

"I, Herbert Haroldson, swear by the genius of my son, Hedric. . . . Don't gape, man! Get on with it!

"I'm waiting. Yes, I said the genius . . . didn't you know?

"The Benedictines at Canterbury took one look at his drawings and knew immediately. Hedric's oratory as Pastor Ass convinced them further. Many senior churchmen went down to see for themselves.

"I am losing patience. Two bonshommes are dead because of you. Some members of Council voted for your death but I spoke strongly against it. The boy needs you. He will flower less readily as an orphan. . . .

"Stand still, Hedric. Your father has come round to my point of view. He knows that his life depends upon your talent. What is trembling? Your head or his hand?

". . . by the genius of my son, Hedric, never to divulge what I have learnt of the inner order of High Albigensian Masonry from Master Henry de Reyns in the gatehouse of the Abbey of Westminster . . .

". . . on pain of torture and death.

"Excellent.

"Silly business, swearing. If we had a Bible it would be so much easier but nothing can be written down. When our best minds amongst the Martyrs of the Midi were arguing with Saint Dominic and beating his case with sheer intellectual superiority they were constantly frustrated. The cunning saint kept producing books, scripture, learned commentaries, piling them up in front of our Perfect professors. What have you to put against this? the scornful saint said. Where are your authorities?

"Is a civilisation where nothing is written down a civilisation at all? Is our faith as barbarous as the Holy Roman Emperor was? It is as ancient as the stars themselves and has never been refined in public. That is what we need, Hedric. A mind so supple it can sophisticate our faith undetectably within Christian schooling. You will be a great mason and a great secret scholar which is why I am sending you to the University of Paris.

"Oh, don't be frightened of the French. They are not so cruel as once they were. What the Inquisition is persecuting these days is Christian deviation, not other strong-minded religions. Even the crusading spirit has been turned in on itself. Most of the warriors are spying on each other for minor theological offences while dining with the Saracens and bedding their splendidly perfumed concubines. What do you think King Louis is doing during his captivity in Egypt? Worrying himself about heresy?

"In Paris, Hedric, you will study with the nation of English scholars. You will do Arts which is the Trivium: Grammar, Rhetoric and Dialectic; and the Quadrivium: Music, Arithmetic, Geometry and Astronomy. After many years you will put all this trivia behind you and concentrate on Theology which is all the Cretins really care about. Theology is a sign of their anxiety about truth. And they have cause.

"You are being groomed, Hedric. But show your paces quietly. One day you could refute Christ for us, in words and design. And what about you, father? Oh, no. Paris would be too much of a temptation for you. You will stay in England where I can keep an eye on you. No, you will not be working on the Westminster fabric. You are going somewhere restful and pleasant. Hedric will go with you until October then I will take him to France myself.

"You must try the pudding! If I had my way there would be one dinner a week that is entirely puddings — every course! To begin with I would have something sharp — gooseberry pie — then there would be grades of sweetness until the final plate would be so crammed with nectar that one spoonful would suffice. I would simultaneously challenge my tongue with the nectar wines of Hungary. Such dreams I get from sweetness. Rampant, rearing dreams of coloured chapels sculpted in stiff candy, pillared with liquorice, roofed with raspberry flan. When we go to Paris, Hedric, I will take you to a pastry-shop that will amaze you more than Aristotle can.

"Ah, I am glad to find you have a sweet tooth, Hedric. I do not trust anyone who is entirely savoury. However, you should not abjure things like watercress. Watercress is a swift cleanser of the palate. I admit it looks as though it is only food fit for a sheep but I have a dish every morning to freshen my mouth. Another excellent sharpener of the tongue is the radish. Both watercress and radish purify the blood if you should ever need to care about your health. For myself, I have forgotten what a sense of total well-being must feel like. Later life is so packed with aches and pains I have decided to look upon them as entertainments. Indeed, I have come to believe that one can be too

177

healthy as supreme fitness is a brake upon the mind whereas a little indigestion is a useful spur.

"Hedric, I fear your father is getting impatient. Does he always grind his teeth this way? The jaw is an instrument of speech or mastication, Herbert Haroldson, not an engine of war. Stop being so absurd. You object because I love your son's talent? I even have a little talent myself. Talent, you will find, Hedric, is what keeps us close to the Creators. Your father has been a poor Albigensian because he has so little. If his gifts were of a higher order he might perceive more truth than he does. As it is, I must deal with him as I find him.

"Without my intervention your father would now be lying in a ditch somewhere with his throat cut and you alongside him. The lodge, my lord King, the Earl of Leicester, all desired his death: not out of vengeance, you must understand, but because he had become trapped between two planes of being like a bluebottle. He was buzzing, buzzing and being a nuisance. So, I argued that he should be pulled up from the lower to the higher plane: not that he deserved it in his own right but because of your talent, something I could prove from your drawings and doodlings. Nonetheless, only the future will tell, eh? Father Horace thinks that you have the potential to do great things in Paris. We need a champion of our own if we are to resist the intellectual temptations of Dominicans and Franciscans, oh brilliant, bad men, who reject our argument that architecture is a form of intellectual proof. Whereas they must write, we merely build our reasons. It is an advantage to be able to point at Amiens or Lincoln and say, 'There stands our dialectic! Argue with that, if you dare!' but since the concordat and the founding of the Office of the Inquisition the Cretins have refused to recognise our philosophy as expressed in stone. We must dispute with them in airy metaphysics. That is the basis of the concordat. If we can prove our case, point by point, they will continue to respect our right to exist, albeit clandestinely. If by the end of this century we have failed to assemble a body of demonstrable evidence in support of our faith the Vatican will instigate a new persecution that will set out to destroy us root and branch.

"Herbert? Something to say? Why are you squirming in your seat? You are huffing and puffing. I see disbelief in your eyes. Ah, you know your son too well. How can we expect this imperfect child to be our saviour? When I look at a plot of ground I see a shape that will fill

178

it. There is nothing there — a few blades of grass, a tree, a cow perhaps — but I see a powerful structure that brings out the best from the land. Hedric is a plot. Paris will be his time of construction. When you and I are dead and in our graves, he will be roofed and buttressed, towered and spired. I wish that I had a son for whom such hopes could be had. Be glad! Rejoice for the boy. It will not be a simple matter for him and he will need your help and support.

"Of course you need time to think about it. Not that you have any choice, I would remind you. Hedric, fill your pockets with sweetmeats when you go. They will break your journey. The Portsmouth road is a hard one and the snow will make it even harder.

"No, take what you want now. I have other friends who are waiting to clear the table. Put the wine to one side. They are not allowed to have the wine. Is that all you want to take? Bert? Nothing for you? Here, take this beef in a napkin for breakfast, and this egg custard. Do you love those colours? The yolk-yellow, the dusting of cinnamon, the burnt aureole like an ox's eye!

"Enter!"

Master Henry de Reyns pushed back his chair as the door opened and fifty boys filed into the room in their sleeping-clothes. They carried bags and boxes. Within a minute all the food on the table had been taken. Then the boys lined up against the wall, their plunder clutched to their chests.

"Hedric, these boys are scholars here at Westminster. They are devoted to learning and to eating. Every one of them will be eminent in one field or the other.

"What will it be, boys? How will you pay me?"

The semi-dormant scholars glanced at a short, freckled boy who was standing nearest the fire hugging a duck's carcase. He raised an inky finger and beat time as they sang:

> Lovely it is while summer lasts
> with the birds singing,
> But now the howling wind comes on
> with the snowflakes flinging,
> Alas! how long the nights are now
> with the dawn bringing
> darkness.

The song over, the boys trooped out, ushered by Master Henry who was patting his beautiful hands together in applause. As he shut the door on them he turned and stared closely at Bert.

"That music did not touch your heart. I saw you scowling! Oh, you are a stupid man, not worth preserving. If I have any more trouble from you I will not have to tell the Earl of Leicester he has my permission to make you suffer. I will make you suffer myself. To jeopardise our faith as you have done — out of witless ambition and petty arrogance — is unforgivable. You are not a good mason. You never will be anything but a stone-bully, but this boy . . . this boy . . . oh, I get angry which upsets my stomach. You see! You have spoiled my dinner, you offensive dog."

"Who are you calling a dog?" Bert muttered wrathfully.

"You're no greyhound, that's certain. You couldn't catch a rabbit if its legs were tied together. Don't make a face at me, Herbert Haroldson. Yours is ugly enough to me as it is. You are the child here: an unformed, petulant pest!"

Master Henry de Reyns sat down again and put his pink jowls in his hands so they spread out like the ruff of a great bird. His reptilian eyes were protruding and the pupils had expanded into dark discs of fury.

"Perhaps I should just keep Hedric. Many boys lose their fathers and are happier for it. You have been of little use to him since his birth. The number of times that he has nearly been lost! You don't deserve to be such a boy's father."

"I'm his father, all right," Bert replied with a coolness that surprised me. "And if he is a genius then it is because I have made him one. It is my blood that has given him all he is or ever shall be. If you had a son of your own you would know what that means."

Master Henry nodded so his jowls pulsed. He sighed and held out his hand.

"Forgive me, brother. I am a lazy man. I hate people to make my life difficult or take up too much of my time. I am building an abbey for the King of England, after all. And you are going to Guildford."

"Guildford? Why Guildford?" Bert demanded. "Why not Wells or Salisbury, somewhere I can do work that's worth-while!"

"Oh, you're not good enough for those: besides, they are not under my control. No, you'll enjoy Guildford. It's very quiet. Our lord King has a small establishment there: a very comfortable little place by the river. He has been repairing it and spends much time there. It is only a day's ride from Westminster so he makes up his mind to come or go on the spur of the moment. Guildford is the town for you right now, a modest town best remembered for a great act of betrayal. Every house, every tree, every stone of the castle, is impregnated with this ancient treachery. Even the river is full of it, and the willows, and the willow-warblers, and the worms that the willow-warblers eat . . . I'll tell you about it. . . ."

"Stop!" Bert roared, leaping out of his chair.

"How dare you spoil my story!" Master Henry said reprovingly. "Sit down!"

Bert folded his arms and stood by the fireplace, his shoulders hunched.

"I did not betray my faith," he whispered, "I did not. You have, all of you. The Cretins own you lock, stock and barrel. If Hans and I made a mistake it was out of ignorance. We did not know how hand-in-glove you lot were with everyone. We believed, we trusted . . . fools that we were."

"You have always worn your faith very lightly," Master Henry said evenly. "What you have taught this boy about our truth and principles is undoubtedly erroneous. It will take years to unpick it. Out of charity we have assumed that your heresies arose out of wrong-headedness rather than any perverse desire for intellectual eminence; something common sense must have cautioned you not to aspire to. We say that Christ can be proved wrong by thought, not rebellion. But even your thought is no use to us. It is too wild, too formless. You are a ball of rage, not reason."

"You want to stop me thinking? Cut my head off then! I don't care."

"No," Master Henry said with an amiable look, "we will not cut your head off. We will use what few brains you have in Guildford. The building stones down there are soft — limestone and chalk — there is flint, a few Roman tiles, for stiffening the fabric — but it is a messy structure made of rotten stone, a weak fortress which is always threatening to fall down, which is why King Henry loves it. Strength disgusts him as it betokens a state of mind too firmly set. He likes to have things in flux, our King. Apart from its vulnerability, the other reason he likes Guildford is it reminds him of a famous diplomatic coup which he admires. Two hundred years ago Earl Godwin of Wessex invited Alfred, son of King Ethelred the Redeless, to Guildford to claim the throne after his father's death. During the night he slaughtered the entire company of six hundred men, blinded Alfred and delivered him to King Harold Harefoot trussed up like a chicken. King Henry lies in his bedchamber and imagines himself producing similar master-strokes of statecraft but the man lacks decision. Have you any idea how often he has altered my design for the chapel of Saint Edward the Confessor? Perhaps your son should have a go at it for me?"

"To mock me in front of my own child does you no credit," Bert said sourly, taking his seat again. "And just because the brat can draw and doodle doesn't make him a genius."

Master Henry sat back in his chair, his gorgeous jowls sinking down to the line of his shoulders.

"Do not be jealous of your own son's ability," he counselled carefully. "There has never been a law to protect fathers from eclipse. Love him for his superior mind, my man. Adore the fact that he is better than you are. He will fulfil all your dreams. Hedric is part of your eternal life."

"The death of me, you mean?" Bert growled.

Master Henry laughed out loud and held up his hands. The clean, pale palms were uncalloused and the skin so tight that the lines did not show. They were the hands of a saint in an altar-painting.

"Herbert Haroldson, I am already less displeased with you. As I thought, you are merely mad, not malign. But you do not know this boy's worth. My own father, for all his wisdom, did not understand me either. He always thought of me as a gluttonous libertine, a fat owl, he used to call me — a bird that catches mice by moonlight. And now I must sleep. And you must go to Guildford."

Before we left the room Master Henry pressed upon us a bottle of his sweet Hungarian wine and two cups, then ushered us out into the passage. We stood there for a while and then sat down with our backs against the wall. It was well past midnight and we could hear the shouts and cries of the fugitives in the Sanctuary Tower of the abbey nearby. I was glad of the noise because my father refused to speak to me, keeping his back turned. At one point we heard the sound of a woman's screams and sobbings coming from the tower and the shouts of the King's guards who watched over the entrance to the Sanctuary. There were stories in those sad cries; pain and despair, escape, futility, irredeemable crime and weakness. Yet they did not touch me as I sat on the cold stone floor of the passage waiting for my father to thank me for saving his life. He never did, nor did I thank him for having me born.

182

XX

We spent the night in the abbey guest-quarters to be roused at dawn, given breakfast, then taken to the King's Hall where we joined a detachment of court officers formed up by the ferry. Our baggage was already loaded on to a pack-horse and we were put at the end of the convoy. As the weak sun filtered through the marsh-mists of Westminster the convoy boarded the wide ferry platform and we were rowed into the rising tide. I looked back at the broken abbey, its unfinished condition giving it a stark, sad guise in the mist. Workmen were already moving around in the stone-stock, loading ox-sledges. I was glad not to be one of those who would have to clamber up ice-coated scaffolding that morning.

Bert kept his eyes on the approaching Lambeth bank. No one had welcomed us to the convoy but we were conscious of some attention from the senior officer, a tall, melancholy-looking man who kept examining lists and walking round the horses checking their loads. He passed us several times, put his hand on our baggage, then moved on with a shrug as if we were of no consequence. Before the ferrymen had got us across the current to the southern shore Bert had managed to catch his eye and discover that we had been attached to a party detailed to carry currency from the Mint to Guildford. Bert laughed when the senior officer told him this.

"It amuses you to see me landed with all this worry?" the doleful officer said reprovingly. "I should have fifty men to protect this treasure but they have given me ten."

His name was Maurice Welbilove and he was a fellow-countryman of ours, coming from Preston. He had been injured in the Gascon wars and was now working in the royal household on transport duties. He spent most of his time carrying goods for the Exchequer or the Wardrobe or the courts — mainly books and pipe-rolls of parchment for clerks — articles of no interest to the criminal brotherhood of the forests. With a tongue loosened by boredom and indignation he told Bert that if anyone knew we were carrying blanks of gold for the

King's crazy scheme of introducing a coin of that metal into the currency of the kingdom, we would be easy meat.

"We wouldn't stand a chance. I would have to give up my life, of course, but these others would scatter. So would you. Why shouldn't you? It's not your responsibility. I said to them this morning — you send me out into all this snow with forty pounds in gold? You're mad. I could get caught in bad weather and have to spend it all on keeping us warm. We could drink the lot. You would join me, mason. I know you builders. Always dry-throated, always moaning, always proud. I don't know how you get away with it."

Bert tried to smile at the man's sardonic affableness, but he could not. It was clear he knew all about us and had his orders. From the way he moved and the used look of his weapons it was obvious he was tougher than he pretended to be. His men treated him with a firm respect, refusing to be drawn on by his self-derogation and pessimism. We later learnt that Maurice Welbilove had only ten men because they were all he needed.

The blizzard of the previous day had not been as severe south of the river but, nevertheless, it took us two hours to get from the ferry to the junction with the Winchester road. We had to walk alongside our pack-horse, it being too heavily loaded with Master Henry's gifts for either of us to ride. We were soon soaked and, by noon, very tired.

No halt was called. We went past inn after inn. None of the soldiers grumbled. Eventually Bert gave me the reins of our horse and strode up to Maurice Welbilove to demand we stop for a rest. He refused, explaining why there could be no break in the journey. In spite of the conditions Guildford had to be reached that night. That was a regulation governing the movement of the King's treasure. Guildford was one day's journey and had to be reached before dark. Winchester was two days' journey and had to be reached before dark. The regulations applied as far as Auch, the capital of Gascony, in the south; Galway in Ireland to the west; Carlisle in the north and King's Lynn in the east, each journey laid out to a strict schedule.

And Maurice Welbilove was as good as his word. We did not cease journeying all the way through Richmond, Kingston, Esher, Weybridge, Cobham and the forest of Surrey. There was no traffic on the good Roman road, all other travellers having had the sense to stay at home. When we were attacked near Ripley I was too exhausted to have much awareness of what was going on. Bert thrust me under the

184

horse's belly and took out a crowbar to defend us, but he had no need. The men who swarmed out of the trees were a ragged lot, badly armed with old pikes and weak bows. When their arrows struck they did not penetrate. Maurice Welbilove had his men organised very quickly around the King's treasure. When the first of the beggarly thieves encountered the soldiers they only struck a few blows before they realised that the mettle of the opposition was too much for them. They broke and fled back into the forest, screaming and shouting abuse. One of them was left behind, badly wounded in the snow. He was obviously not going to survive his injuries and his cries were terrible. Maurice Welbilove killed him with one swift stroke then had him buried in a shallow grave on the roadside, the spot marked for the sheriff.

As the column got under way again Maurice Welbilove rode up to us and dismounted, beckoning Bert to take his place.

"Take my horse," he said, "I feel like a walk." Then he picked me up and put me behind Bert. I felt the steel in his grip. "Two hours and we will be in," he said. "Keep to the rear of the party. Did you loosen any stones with your jemmy, Herbert Haroldson?"

"It would have been bad for us if they had seen we were not your greatest concern," Bert rejoined, ungratefully. "You would do better to give me a weapon."

"I can't do that. You are half a criminal yourself. Ride that horse carefully. I've had him for five years."

With that Maurice Welbilove strode back to the head of the convoy and took his place at its head. As we reached the banks of a swollen stream he drew his sword and scanned the bridge. It was a strong timber structure with the spate water surging under it in a broad, brown torrent. The surrounding water-meadows were flooded and the road was not visible beneath the water.

"This is a bad place, mason," he said as he reclaimed his horse. "A lot of poor folk wait here for pickings. Keep very close while we cross the river valley."

"Do they know what you're carrying?" Bert asked as we got down into the icy water.

Maurice nodded, cradling his sword's blade in the crook of his arm.

"They know me. They approach us only to warm themselves at the King's wealth. None of them have ever got a penny from us. I come from people like that myself and, no doubt, when our lord King has finished with me, I will have to go back to them. Then the King's treasure should look out for itself."

We crossed both stream and flood without being attacked. There were people in the wood though, pale faces peering out of the gloom. Maurice Welbilove saluted them right and left as he splashed along at the head of the convoy.

"Forty pounds in gold I've got for our lord King. Come and count it!" he bellowed over the inundated fields. "All squirrels are welcome!"

An hour and a half later we followed the horses down the High Street into the gatehouse of Guildford Castle. The sun was holding on to the horizon by its fingertips as Maurice Welbilove handed over his charge to the King's lieutenant.

We were given quarters in a timber dwelling within the bailey of the castle, close to the great hall. The house was run by the King's Exchequer for visiting officers and guests. For the first time in my life I was given a room of my own and not expected to share with my father. There was a large table, twenty candle-holders, a huge supply of candle-ends, a good window, and a bed that would fit ten of me. Bert objected to my having the room because it was superior to his own. I at once offered to swap but the housekeeper, a small, dark widow of some worn beauty who came from Provence and was named Lucy, refused. She said Master Henry de Reyns had chosen my room and instructed her that I was to keep it against every parental protest. This enraged Bert even more as it was obvious Master Henry had not only anticipated but prepared for the trouble this might cause. Bert immediately moved out of the house and into an inn at the end of the street. Within two hours he was conducted back to the house by an officer and told he had no choice in the matter of accommodation and must stay where he was put.

Bert stayed in his room that evening and refused to open the door to me. I ate a meal with Lucy, which was very well cooked, and she talked to me for a while. Her husband had been a bailiff on the King's service in Herefordshire. He had been killed in an accident on a fish-weir. After ten different jobs up and down the country she had ended up in Guildford. Her cooking was a guarantee of employment for her. On three occasions she had prepared food for King Henry himself and been complimented.

Upon returning to my room I set up the table by the window and laid out four candles. In a chest by the bed I discovered a store of parchment and vellum. Ink and pens were in a box on the window-sill. One wall cupboard was locked. As I was sitting at my table in the candlelight there was a knock at the door. I thought it must be my father who had come out of his sulks. When I opened it I found Master Henry de Reyns and Maurice Welbilove arm-in-arm, both of them beaming.

"Did Dame Lucy feed you well, Hedric?" Master Henry enquired jovially. "She is known for her tripe pie. Did you have that? Let me see your room. Maurice, be a friend, go and drag that recalcitrant white cutter out of his pit so we can take him on a spree. Your father likes sprees, I believe."

Maurice went down the passage and started hammering on my father's door. Master Henry stood by the wall cupboard and took a key out of his belt. When he opened the door and held his torch up I saw that the cupboard was full of books and rolls.

"These are worth a great deal of money, Hedric. They will be checked every day by Father Horace who has kindly come down from London to continue your education. Do not spill things on these volumes, or tear them, or lose them. They belong to me and my friends. One or two even belong to our lord King himself and I have borrowed them for your sake. I want you to have read every one of these works by October when I take you to Paris. Before we go you will be examined on them. There."

He put the key down on the table and sat in my chair. Beneath his full, dark cloak he was dressed in peacock-blue with a golden collar and pearl buttons. His wonderful face gleamed with oversized good health and intelligent merriment.

"Don't misplace the key. If we have to break down doors for education it will teach us to be barbarous," he said with a sly smile on his firm, perfectly shaped lips that went so strangely with his cold-flamed cock's jowls.

My father opened his door after Maurice had nearly kicked it down and appeared in the passage.

"What do you want?" he muttered churlishly. "I have had a long journey today and I would like to sleep in peace."

"I have made the same journey," Master Henry said lightly, "and with a call on friends for lunch. What is a day's ride? Get your coat and hat. You're coming out for a drink."

"I drink when I want to, not when I'm ordered," Bert replied, moving back towards his room. Maurice Welbilove barred his way, black gauntlets held high, sad eyes shining.

"To be taken on the High Street Run by the King's mason is no small honour. I would find a thirst if I were you," he said. "Come with us. If you pass up this chance you will curse yourself in later days."

Bert surrendered without further quarrel. I was prepared to be left behind but Master Henry told me I must accompany them as the spree was part of my education.

"Before we start, I have a question for you, Hedric," Master Henry said, his lizard's eyes mobile with merriment. "It is simple enough. Who rules this land?"

Bert pulled his hat down over his eyes and leant against the wall, allowing Master Henry to hear his sigh of exasperation.

"Your father has no idea who rules. If I shook him for a while he might answer what you might answer, Hedric. Who rules?"

Putting his beautiful hand to his chin Master Henry smiled at me. A line of silver rings went from finger to finger, each one differently wrought. As he surveyed my face Master Henry bent his knuckles and kissed them.

"It's not us, is it?" he whispered. "We are all servants of one thing or another. Give me the answer the humblest would give — just for the sake of the argument."

"The King, sir," I said.

"Thank you, Hedric. Yes, the King. Now — and you listen Herbert — by the end of this spree I will have shown you *sans doute* who is lord of all. No words! All we will talk tonight is nonsense but if you keep your eyes open you will see the King who rules Guildford."

We went out into Quarry Street and walked to the Older English church which I had noticed as we entered the town. A steep hill rose from the bridge over the river and we plodded up it, Master Henry at our head, his breath surprisingly steady as he hauled his bulk along. As he walked he talked the nonsense he had promised us, he sang, he danced with his fingers, he whistled. By the time we arrived at the top of the High Street and entered the first inn he was already drunk, having drunk nothing at all. He had achieved this by sheer exhilaration of mind.

"Now the landlord of the Woolpack does a very spicy dilled lamb ball. We will have a plate with our wine," he said as we sat down by the fire. "Notice the smell in here. Observe the look of the customers. The wine we will drink must be the Vernaccia from Tuscany, ignoble but good with him who rules. Ah, Hedric's wits are intrigued with my case!"

So we had the dilled lamb balls with Vernaccia at the Woolpack. Bert demanded to drink ale with the shepherds off the downs who crowded the place in their greasy garments but Master Henry forbade it.

From there we walked barely twenty paces to the Fleece where we drank a sweet Cretan wine with farced mutton roll. The place was packed with red-faced, bow-legged farmers and their half-wild sheepdogs fighting round the table legs.

Another step down the icy hill and we were in the Sheepshearers which was a low, stinking establishment. Here Master Henry ordered sheep's garbage pie garnished with parsley and roast turnips, a surprisingly tasty dish from such a foul kitchen. With this we drank an English wine called Whippet. When we entered this inn Bert was still surly and uncommunicative but by the time we came back out into the street again he had warmed to his drinking companions. What had conquered his heart had been a duet sung by Master Henry and Maurice Welbilove to the girl who had served our food. She was a short, dumpy, freckled creature with large ears and an upturned nose who had nearly fainted with shyness as they sang:

> A woman's worth is no thing light,
> She serves a man both day and night,
> Into her work goes all her might,
> And yet they give her care and woe,
> Care and woe,
> And yet they give her care and woe-oe-oe.

By the time we had ducked into the Ram and Hurdle four doors down the three men were feeling the effects of fine wine and frosty air and much mad talk and they had become kindred spirits, with me trailing forlornly behind, quite forgotten. I crept into the room behind them and watched as they consumed smoked lamb's tongue salad in pastry, Rhine wine, and told each other riddles for which they had mostly forgotten the answers.

In the Lamb and Flag all the customers were of many colours as they worked in a cloth-dyer's in a yard behind. They had a primitive, wild look in their reds and blues but Master Henry was held in esteem there and he managed to squeeze out of the rainbow-splashed kitchen some spiced sheep's sweetbreads in sauce and a bottle of a mysterious wine called Theologicum made by clerks in Capernicum.

A moon had risen and hung over us as we rushed down the slippery hill to the Leg of Mutton, the three men sliding over the packed snow like children, their cloaks flying. This was an inn for wealthy patrons and Master Henry had ordered a booth by the fire. We were served by quiet, austere old men who might have been more at home in a monastery. It was the favourite hostel of clerics who came to Guildford on court business. A party of Dominicans from Hull was in residence.

There my companions ate lamb's livers raw and drank Torrentyne of Ebdrew and sang lewd and filthy ballads.

Our final call was the Sheep's Head in Quarry Street itself, adjacent to the castle. Here all Maurice Welbilove's friends in the soldiery were gathered. However, they paid more attention to Master Henry who was clearly a man whom they held in some awe. We were given the best table and I was made to sit on Master Henry's right hand. He put an arm around my shoulder as the gingered ewe's udders in milk and Muscadelle were ceremoniously served by captains of the castle guard.

"Now, Hedric, in front of these warriors, these protectors of the royal dignity, who rules in Guildford?" he asked. "Tell us."

I hesitated, not afraid of the answer but that I should frame it right. With Master Henry's passion for doing things properly I did not want to botch it up.

"Why, sheep it seems."

Master Henry hugged me hard and gazed warmly at Bert.

"What a boy. Yes, sheep rule England, and may they always keep you warm. Tomorrow we may do the other side of the High Street: the Two Weavers, the Fullers, the Tanners, the Fold, the Spinners Arms, Ewe and Compass . . . God save the King, and I mean mutton. Baa! Baa!"

Everyone in the room started to bleat. I was amazed that the King's men could be so disrespectful. Many of them were of senior rank with their inferiors around them but these were the loudest of all.

"To the sheep of Provence, to the sheep of Lusignan, to French sheep everywhere. May we learn how to steal pastures as they do, with impunity!" Maurice Welbilove roared above the bleating. "To the hunger of English sheep!"

I saw Bert's brilliant smile fly to his face. He sensed, as I did, that the unpopularity of the King was an advantage to us here in Guildford. If the King's mason and his officers were able to speak out so savagely a few yards from the royal castle gate our own predicament could only be less severe. These men considered King Henry to be a poor joke: their obedience was poisoned. Within the disintegration caused by this lack of respect was the maze where wended Master Henry and my future.

Spring came to Guildford early that year. Warm weather broke the buds in early April. My father worked in the quarry and on the castle outer wall alongside a small band of rough-hewers, mortarers and setters who accepted him as the senior man in their lodge as there was no other white cutter working on the fabric. Master Henry did not busy himself in the local lodge's affairs and seemed happy to give Bert some authority in order to offset his recent humiliations. Bert's work was not interesting, it being mainly composed of wall repairs with a bit of simple carving in the Queen's chapel for which he was well paid. The keep is an ugly, ungainly structure made up of chalk, sandstone, flint, tiles and any old rubbish the original builder had to hand. It was no wonder to me it had fallen to the French so quickly in John's time; being no more than a pile of mortar with lumps in it. But inside? That is a different matter. There the King had richly lined his nest. As it was a favourite resort of his son, the lord Edward, our present King, I would be surprised if it were now not even more magnificent. But I do not think that great soldier will think more of it as a defensive fortress than his less military father. Guildford is a place to relax, not fight.

Father Horace came down and lived in a small friary guest-house while he taught me. He would arrive at seven in the morning and have his breakfast with me in my room. In time he became friendly with Lucy and she joined us for my Latin lessons for she had a good mind going to waste with too much cooking and cleaning. Before long I knew Bert had started sleeping with her as I could never find him in his own room in the mornings. This was his way with housekeepers, but Lucy did not fall in love with him which pleased me. It meant she and I could handle his outbursts together rather than it being left to me to commiserate with her and control him. All in all these were happy times and a harmony developed between the four of us that was most unusual. By the time summer brought the valley of the Wey into full green and the lambs were strong my father and I had chosen to submerge our London days in our memories and put aside all thoughts of the changes my going to Paris would bring. Master Henry de Reyns did not visit us again but we saw Maurice Welbilove occasionally who brought us news of his friend and the progress of the building at Westminster.

I enjoyed this time of peace and study. Father Horace had forgiven (or been paid to forgive!) my forwardness and insolence and we made fast progress together, avoiding all reference to Albigensian heads, uncles or suchlike. He knew I was already dreaming of Paris, of the Abbey of Saint Denis, of university and freedom, and of being with Master Henry on a great journey, so he used this promise of a vastly enriched life as a carpet to tempt me on. Whenever I failed, or was idle (which was not often) he would threaten to stop me going.

"You will be put to work on the walls like your father if you're not careful. Do you want to be a drudge like him? Idleness is the curse of any generation. That is the truth the Ancients have left us with. If you have talent it is your responsibility to use it to its full. God knows I have not the vision to imagine the world that you may make — if you are let loose upon it. But without Cicero you will get nowhere. Learn that passage again or, in October, you will be left to rot in ignorance instead of going to Paris which is only for great minds which appreciate other great minds!"

These may sound harsh words but they were not cruel. I had the capacity to do all the scholarship that was set me. Master Henry's laudations of my genius were a constant inducement to work hard. I could absorb anything the wider world could tell me of its secrets. No discipline could hide its essence from me: perception upon perception rolled in. Arithmetic unravelled itself in my sleep and I wrote down long answers in the dark as they woke me. While other boys were down at the mill-race or out with the drovers in the sun I stayed with Father Horace, trying to keep up with the appetite of my own mind which sometimes took my body beyond what it could bear. Many times I woke to find myself at my table with my head on the books and the candles guttered at my side. A wiser person would take the flesh's hint and go to bed at this proof of fatigue but I seldom did. I would relight the candles and continue until all the knowledge that I needed was within me, such was my passion for learning.

Then we learnt that the King was coming to Guildford in the second week of July on his way to celebrate the Feast of Saint Swithin at Winchester with his brother, the new bishop.

XXI

A week before the King was due to arrive in Guildford I received a message from Master Henry. It was an extract from a book, not of his authorship he assured me, that he wished me to learn by heart before the Court collected at the castle. It was very long and difficult and Father Horace did not recognise it. Upon studying it and starting to commit it to memory I became frightened. It was the first piece of writing I had ever seen that was Albigensian in terms of character and content and I should not have shown it to Father Horace. Fortunately, the old priest was incapable of penetrating the reasoning and he was not at all suspicious. As I became word-perfect in it he listened to my recitations as if I were chanting something from Saint Augustine and not a proof of an heretical principle.

As I worked on the extract it occurred to me that Master Henry was probably preparing me for Paris. He had already mentioned the beauties Abbot Suger had created at Saint Denis and promised to teach me the arithmetical and geometrical basis of the French arch: a secret that was widely used by copying but not through understanding. This architectural shape was a servant to the principle of light, a central truth of our faith, for light is immediate, daily visitation by the Good Creator. Master Henry had suggested to me that Abbot Suger — whose name had rung through Christendom as a great innovator in building — was not the man to whom the credit of the First Style of Emergence belonged, but the brotherhood of Albigenses had allowed him the plaudits for its own political purposes.

On the day I finally mastered both the words and the logic of the piece, Father Horace asked me what I thought would be its use to me. To be able to recite it for Master Henry, in obedience to his desires, was enough and I said so. Father Horace differed with my opinion. He thought that the King's mason would have asked for it to be set to music if it were only for his private pleasure.

"Be prepared for a great occasion," he advised me. "I think you may have to show off to prove Master Henry's faith in you. This work is

193

the product of a wasteful, over-convoluted mind, the kind of stuff people listen to without understanding. It is all sparkle and no substance. If I were you I would start thinking about what costume I should wear."

The evening of the King's arrival was warm and blue with the sun still a presence in the river long after it had sunk beyond the downs. I stood by the bridge with my father and waited for the cavalcade to come down the London road, my eyes on the herons standing as patiently as we, waiting for food. Out of the gentle swell of birdsong came a deeper, angrier note. The forest to the north-east was filled with a strange, raging sound which disturbed the large crowd which was waiting with us. They recoiled from the ferocity of the noise as it approached, its source still invisible. My herons stirred, retracted their long necks and took off, their huge wings beating slowly in a doleful farewell. Somewhere was a quieter water.

I had seen the Court in parts, and in motion, but always in London. Within those streets and great buildings it had a certain naturalness: it belonged to what it had helped to create. But here, in the dusky peace of the wooded valley, it came down the High Street, a dragon, horned and clawed, breathing a fire of rage and recrimination. As the mass of it poured down the hill towards us we could not see the King, only the jockeying, barging, bumping horsemen trying to wedge themselves close to a turbulent focus, their voices high and indignant, their hats raised.

I found myself moving closer to my father to keep a buffer between myself and such a hornet's nest. When the King actually went past I could not see him for the agitation and pushing between the courtiers. It was so cruel and desperate a scene I felt sorry for everyone in it; King Henry most of all.

Pressed against the parapet of the bridge we waited until everyone had gone past. I was uncertain as to whether Master Henry de Reyns had been amongst them, the crowd having been so great. We did not follow the Court up to the gatehouse but waited in the dust, enjoying the returning silence as the castle swallowed the Court and its hideous din.

Then I saw a spot of brilliant colour slipping through the trees on the southern part of the road. Someone had made a detour, fording the Wey lower down, thus avoiding the congestion. As the cloak flew among the purpling trees and the horseman spurred towards us I saw from the size of him and the gigantic stature of his mount that it was Master Henry. He was dressed in a suit of clothes embroidered as stonework from top to toe, the lines of mortar stitched in silver thread. His hat was a spire with a wonderful golden weathercock on top and his boots were painted to be green grass. On his chest he wore an altar so cunningly sewn the flames of the candles seemed to be alight. It was an outfit only a man of supreme style and inner beauty could wear, and Master Henry carried it off as if such apparel were everyday garb to him.

He reined in his horse at the bridge and looked down at me through the fine summer dust he had raised from the road.

"Do you know the piece I sent you to learn?" he asked, orbed eyes gleaming in his red cheeks like gems in a casket.

"I do, sir," I replied. "By heart."

He dismounted and led his horse down to the Wey to drink. The animal plunged in up to its knees and buried its nose in the cool waters, grateful for the refreshment after bearing such a magnificent load so far. Master Henry then sat down on the bank and patted the grass beside him.

"Let me hear it now," he said, lying back and resting his weight on his elbows. "Has your father heard it yet?"

"You did not instruct me to tell him, so I didn't," I answered.

"Would he understand it?"

"Father Horace doesn't."

Master Henry looked up at Bert who was regarding him with ill-disguised dislike. The imaginative, carnival clothes were not designed to appeal to men like my father. When he decided to be ostentatious it was always in a conventional manner rather than with any flair.

"I want you to listen to what your son has to say, Herbert. Tonight he must perform in front of his king. He will need all your support."

I gasped at this news. It was not through fear of the event itself but because the meaning of what I must recite was so evidently from an unChristian source. I mentioned my misgivings to Master Henry who laughed a little.

"Oh, don't worry. Compared to the Arab philosophers this will be almost orthodox. To most of the Court it might just as well be Chinese. Did I tell you that it must be translated out of Latin into English as you recite it?"

"Who by?" I squawked. "Who can do that fast enough? Not Father Horace, for sure."

195

"You will do it. By now a simultaneous translation should be within your capabilities. So, first you remember the line in Latin, thinking in Latin, then you transfer it to English, speaking in English. I have boasted to our lord King that you can do all this without thinking about it."

I felt giddy. The horse splashed out of the river and wandered down the bank. Master Henry whistled for it to come back, giving me a moment to recover from the shock of what he expected of me.

"Who is the author of the piece?" I asked, still trying to control the panic in my breath. "We could not work it out. We were under the impression no one in our faith is supposed to write down any form of testimony to our truth, that it must all be held in the mind and passed on by word of mouth. I admit things have changed since you saw us at Westminster and we are still trying to catch up, but isn't this going too far — to stand up and chant heresy in the King's face? He found out Hans Seersach and my father by what he saw. May he not be able to find me out by what he hears?"

Master Henry got to his feet and prepared to mount his horse which had unwillingly returned from its wanderings.

"Give me your hand, mason," Master Henry commanded. "No, not to my hand, you ox, to my boot!"

Bert went very pale, staring in indignant astonishment at the King's mason who was standing with one foot raised.

"Your work is behind. I have reports that you arrive late and leave early. There are things we will have to talk about!" Master Henry said coldly. "I am not pleased."

My father bent forward and cupped his hands. Master Henry drove his boot into the palms and hoisted himself into the saddle with a splendid, arrogant grunt.

"Thank you, Herbert Haroldson. Put your best clothes on for tonight. I want you to bring your son to the hall at half-past nine and I want both of you sober. Do not fail me. There are worse jobs in the world than walling."

Then he turned his horse's head towards the bridge, his spired hat nodding. I ran alongside him, holding on to his painted boot.

"You haven't told me who is the author of the piece? Is it Plato? I don't think so, from what it says. It must be one of the Ancients, well before Christ. Democritus? No, no, he is not that complicated . . .

please tell me . . . it's not one of the Arabs is it? You were only joking . . ."

The King's mason bent down and fondly ruffled my hair.

"No, Hedric, he's not an Arab. The man who wrote what you have learnt by heart is Robert Grosseteste, the Bishop of Lincoln; and he will be there to hear you."

My fingers gripped his heel in a seizure of fright as I heard these words. He shook his foot to free himself then galloped over the bridge, leaving me numb with shock. Bert looked at me contemptuously.

"Now we see whose slave you have become. I have to stand and watch my blood cant Cretin," he said bitterly.

"Are you my father or my tormentor?" I shrieked suddenly into his envy-filled face. "What have you done to help me? You're stupid, and you're proud of being stupid! You're not in the same class as Master Henry at all!"

Bert did not hesitate. He struck me fiercely across the cheek with the back of his hand so that I fell to my knees. When I looked up from nursing my face, anxious only if I should be marred by a bruise for my performance, my father had gone. I saw him striding over the bridge without giving a backward glance to see if I had recovered.

In my room I rehearsed the piece for all the intervening hours between the arrival of the Court and the time we had been summoned to appear. To translate it and convey the full sense of what it was saying at the same time was difficult and I was concerned at the amount of time it took to deliver. When I had dressed myself in all my best clothes I went to Lucy to have my hair brushed. Bert was sitting in a chair in her kitchen wearing the new clothes Master Henry had sent us in London. Lucy had already brushed his hair and tied several ribbons in his hair and beard. When I arrived she was passing a big, horn comb through the hair on the top of his head and crooning to him. I stood in the doorway until she saw me.

"My husband liked me to do this," she said with an apologetic smile. "It is reckoned to order and tidy the mind."

"Hedric knows how I need that," Bert added. "Come in, son."

He stood up, his eyes bright with amiability, and embraced me strongly. I caught the whiff of perfume.

"We will show them who we are and not be afraid," he murmured. "Together we are a match for anyone."

197

"Why, what is it that you have to do tonight?" I asked him, immediately regretting my insolence for the man was trying to make up to me without using the word sorry.

Bert laughed and chucked me under the chin with enough force to rattle my teeth.

"Whatever you suffer, I will suffer," he declared. "Whatever you achieve, I will achieve."

This was sufficient grace from him for peace to be made and we set out for the hall arm in arm after one cup of wine between us. The night was clear and there were many stars above as we left our quarters and stood in the warm summer evening air. I could hear music and the hum of the Court coming from the great hall nearby: people stood in the twilight, talking before going in, women floated by with high winged coiffures; huge, scented moths. Master Henry was waiting outside the entrance. He was dressed in a toga-styled pink and black striped silk gown with swirling designs and a broad bronze-buckled belt of black otter-fur. On his feet he wore matching bronze sandals.

"Are you ready, Hedric?" Master Henry enquired softly. "I will introduce you to your King. Have you ever laid eyes on him before?"

"Only from a distance," I whispered, "and then I wasn't sure who was who."

Master Henry nodded, then looked at my father.

"Don't leave my side, Herbert. Stay close. The Earl of Leicester, and his wife, the King's sister, and his concubine, are here. Sir Henry de Montfort from Dover is here. All the bishops who hated your model are here. Everyone who is anyone is here. Do not talk out of turn. Do not drink too much. Do not applaud your son too much. All I want you to do is listen and marvel that you should have produced such progeny."

Bert looked at his feet and gripped his gloved hands together.

"Look at me when I'm speaking to you, mason! This is a moment I have been waiting for. Your son, the son of our faith, will dazzle the Cretins with *words*. Spoil it for me at your peril."

Bert raised his head, wrestled with the gaze of Master Henry's beautiful snake's eyes, then nodded in submission.

"Good. Without more ado, young Hedric, let us confuse our enemies!"

So saying, Master Henry opened the door and shoved me in ahead of him. Once in the hall the uproar was tremendous, as was the strange high stench of excitement, scents, sweats and stirrings. The dancing had freed the animal odours from beneath the silks and velvets and all the faces of the men and women gleamed in the heat. The people seemed to be stacked up to the ceiling, so many of them there were. As I went forward I could not help treading on feet and the hems of garments but no one seemed to take offence as they milled about, colliding with each other, worming through gaps, waving to friends, shouting over heads. After several minutes of forcing my way through the crowd ahead of Master Henry he pulled me to a halt in front of a tall, fair man with a bald head and fluffy curls above his ears that tumbled into his beard. His expression was sweet but out of true. As I stared into his eyes I could feel Master Henry's hand on my shoulder forcing me to my knees. As I sank down I noticed what it was that put the man's countenance on such a tilt. His left eyelid drooped giving him the look of one who is drunk and fatigued.

"The boy Hedric Herbertson, sire," Master Henry shouted above the din. "Will you hear him now?"

King Henry smiled at me. His other eye was lively with interest.

"Will they listen?" he shouted in an odd yaw-yawing voice as if he were loath to finish off each word. The languor of his speech was in keeping with the drooping eyelid and the stylish French laziness of his gestures.

"We will make them listen, sire. This pure English boy is a prodigy. He is better than the best of France. I challenge any of those present to come up with his equal. Sire, he is the future mind, what will define our past, our achievements and our failures."

"By the saints then, I have cause to be scared of him," King Henry replied, rubbing his long nose thoughtfully. "He looks to be a perfectly ordinary boy to me. I do not want to shame him in front of this pleasure-loving crowd. Are they in the mood for intellectual matters?"

"You promised you would hear him, sire," Master Henry said with a touch of impatience. "I have got him ready to amaze you."

"Then we had better get silence," King Henry said, tugging at the sleeve of an old man who was standing with his forehead pressed to a silver-plated staff. "Bang for quiet, old fellow."

The officer drew his head back and glared at the crowd, drawing his lips back from his teeth in a snarl. He hammered his staff on the floor with great force, keeping the noise going long after everyone in the hall had fallen quiet.

199

Eventually he stopped and resumed his stance, eyes closed, brow touching the staff.

"Announce this boy," King Henry said with a soft breath. "His name is. . . ?"

"Hedric, sire. He is an apprentice white cutter of humble birth, from the north," Master Henry said with a rush. "He will give a proof of supernatural intelligence before the Court."

"You all heard that? This child is one of my subjects and Master Henry de Reyns is of the opinion he can already outthink you all. That remains to be seen. But the boy is brave. He is not shaking as I have seen all of you shake when the mind is put to the test. Most of you would rather stand in the battle-line than in the schoolroom. That must change, as Master Henry here insists, and he is right."

King Henry turned to me, his drooping eyelid comically twisted as he raised his eyebrows.

"They are yours for the taking," he said with a little smile of encouragement. "Go to it."

As I heard the silence I became aware I had not taken an important decision during my rehearsals: where to put my hands. Suddenly they were all of me, hanging by my sides like useless fins. I did not seem able to speak until I knew where they would best be kept while I spoke. I put them behind my back: I put them in front, clasped over my groin. In a long, terrifying moment that was all sweat and palms I heard every breath, every small sound of boredom, every tut and titter. I made my final choice and hooked my thumbs under my belt. Later on Master Henry commented that it was the most impudent and disrespectful posture I could possibly have selected.

As everyone saw what decision I had taken with regard to my hands they mockingly applauded. I looked around and bowed. A second thought had come into my head: which one was Robert Grosseteste, the Bishop of Lincoln? Was he tolerant? Severe? Light-hearted? How would he react when he heard his unconventional ideas expounded by a mere boy? Would he get into trouble as a result of all this? Was this mischief on Master Henry's part? I put these thoughts aside and spoke:

"This proof was written in Latin, which is not my native tongue, nor is French, I may say." (There was an immediate buzz from the more embroidered and sumptuously-dressed courtiers.) "First, I will give you the sentence in Latin, then I will give it you in English to understand, it being a suppler tongue, and a better language for philosophy."

There were a few cries of "Non" and "Ordure" from the French folk there which brought a frown to King Henry's brow but he did not gainsay me. Sticking out my chest I made a stiff bow and began, the words reverberating in the bones of my head: another person could have been speaking, so little real control I had over them. It was my mind and memory producing the language but it now belonged to someone else within me, a second self who was much older and braver:

The primary material form which some call materialness is, in my opinion, light. Light, of its very nature spreads in every direction in such a way that a point of light of any size will immediately create a sphere of light unless some substance impervious to light stands in its path. Now the extension of material in three dimensions is a necessary appurtenance of material existence, and this in spite of the fact that both material and materialness are themselves simple substances lacking all dimension as concepts . . .

Here I paused to check that they were all keeping up with the argument. Many nodded and fingered their chins. Some of the women were staring at me by now as if I had vaulted out of a cot with my brain in flames.

. . . But a form that is in itself simple and without dimension could not introduce dimension in every direction into material, which is likewise simple and without dimension, except by multiplying itself and spreading itself immediately in all directions and thus extending material in its own diffusion. For the form cannot desert material, because it is inseparable from it, and material cannot have form withdrawn from it. However, I have already proposed that it is light which possesses in its essential nature the function of multiplying itself and spreading instantly in all directions. Whatever performs this function is either light or some other agent that acts in virtue . . .

King Henry held up a hand for me to stop. Taking a ring from his little finger he stepped over, taking my right thumb from my belt, and slipped the ring over it.

"Marvellous," he said benignly. "Absolutely marvellous."

"But I haven't finished yet, sire," I said, nearly in tears, "there are pages more!"

"I can't wait to read them, my son," he replied. "Don't ever sell that ring. Wear it in Paris for me so they will know that I appreciate the English genius. And now, a song! A song!

Lutes thrummed and drums thundered from somewhere deep in the crowd. Several high voices began to sing in a nasal French. "Li joliz temps d'estey, que je voi revenir . . ."

I sat on the floor and wept.

When I had got past the point where my tears were just for myself I felt the need for support, but none was forthcoming. I stopped crying and struggled to my feet through the legs and skirts of the dancers; once up I was pushed and jostled again so I staggered from place to place looking for somewhere safe. I searched for Henry de Reyns but could not see him: while doing so I saw Bert. Far from worrying about me he was dancing with a lynx-eyed woman in a green gown, his most winning smile plastered all over his face. When I arrived by his side and poked him in the ribs he bent down and hissed, "Not now son, not now!" and danced on.

Blundering about through the crowd I found a corner I could squeeze into and squatted there, trying to get my thoughts together as the huge mass of perfumed people milled past. I was still holding my hand protectively over the ring on my thumb, so hard indeed that the gem's facets had dinted my palm. Peering through my fingers I examined the jewel: it was a lozenge-shaped agate, not a very precious stone but of unusual colour, richly fox-red, set in twisted silver. As I peered at it the realisation that it was a gift from the King, a reward for my performance, began to creep up on me. Although I had not finished my piece I had done enough to win his approval. To be truthful, I imagined I would be able to hold the Court's attention for a good hour — which was as long as my rehearsals had taken — but five minutes had been sufficient to astonish everyone.

Master Henry de Reyns intruded upon my increasing satisfaction with myself. He hooked a fat finger into mine so our rings clinked together and hauled me to my feet.

"Well done, Hedric," he said with a beaming smile. "I am very pleased with you."

"Did anyone take any notice?" I asked.

"A few. Not many people here are capable of following that kind of thing. But they could see you are an extraordinary boy," he replied assuringly, taking my arm. "Come with me. There is someone whom I want you to meet."

Master Henry led me by the hand through the mêlée, barging his way forward with no regard for those unfortunate enough to encounter his bulk. This seemed to arouse no offence as it was the same for all — no one cared about collisions at Court. It was how one moved about.

We got through the crowd to the entrance of a narrow staircase, bringing us out on to a gallery overlooking the great hall. Leaning over the balcony was a mass of furs, propped up by four young clerks. As we got closer I could see they were grouped around a high-backed chair, their heads bent towards its occupant who was invisible except for one hand which protruded from the furs. It was long and pale, the skin papery and blotched, devoid of jewellery. I noticed the nails: absolutely clean and perfectly manicured, each finger a tapering, elegant stem.

Master Henry pushed aside the clerks on our side of the chair and squeezed himself between it and the balcony railing, looking down into the depths of the furs.

"Can you hear me, Robert?" he roared above the din which poured up from below. "I have brought the boy to meet you!"

There was a hoarse, whistling whisper from down in the furs and Master Henry leant forward, pulling me roughly to his side so I should be able to see to whom he was talking.

A very, very old man, thin and wasted in cheek and throat, glared up at me with eyes that could have belonged to a baby. His few white hairs, thin, wet mouth; pinched, hairy nostrils and rotten fangs, all belied the green intensity of his gaze: even his eyelids and brows were of another man, an ancient creature who had somehow collected around those eyes.

"Hedric," Master Henry bellowed, "this is your author!"

I stared into the emeralds of the old man's eyes. They did not change their glitter.

Master Henry took the hand I had not yet seen out of the furs and put it into mine. The owner did not resist but allowed it to lie there passively. A large fretted gold and ruby ring hung loose on one finger.

203

"You should kiss the ring, Hedric," Master Henry whispered. "This is His Grace, Robert Grosseteste, the venerable Bishop of Lincoln, and today is his birthday."

I obediently bent over the hand and kissed the ring. As I did so my lips brushed the dry, pale skin and the old man stirred, drawing his hand back into the furs.

"Your recitation from his treatise 'On Light and the Beginning of Forms' was my birthday present to my old friend," Master Henry went on, a twinkle in his eye. "You enjoyed it very much, didn't you, Robert?"

There was no response, only a pressing together of the lips and a slow closing of those verdant eyes.

"Did he hear any of it at all?" I asked in a low voice close to Master Henry's ear. "I think he may be a bit deaf."

He laughed and ruffled my hair.

"He is eighty-one today. There is nothing Robert has not heard in this noisy world. Tomorrow we will get him going and he will tell us something of it all. Meanwhile, we will let him enjoy his disapproval of all this nonsense down there. We will come to you for mass in the morning, Robert."

Master Henry made me bow then pushed his way back past the young clerks who had not listened to a word we had said, their eyes and ears being only for the dance below.

When we reached the chamber Master Henry took me straight over to Bert who was leaning against the wall, without the lynx-eyed woman. He told Bert to take me home and put me to bed, this having been enough excitement for any boy for one night. Bert grumbled all the way back and I have no doubt he tried to get back into the proceedings once he had seen me to my room; but I did not spare him a thought. As I lay in bed with the outline of the great tower visible through my window I could only think of the old man, his thoughts about light, and his eyes which were so much further from heaven than the rest of him.

XXII

Master Henry de Reyns came to my room with the dawn. When I awoke he was standing by my bed, prodding me with his finger. He was in a very genial mood, still drunk, I suspected, from the revels, having never been to bed. He sat at my table while I dressed, his eyes on the huge whitewashed tower and the King's standard flying from the top of it.

"Wear your ring, Hedric," he said quietly. "I want old Robert to look at it. He will know its provenance."

"I expect the King has hundreds of rings," I replied, breathless in my haste to be ready and away, pulling my shirt over my head.

"So he does, Hedric, and they all come from someone or somewhere, and they all have a meaning. Everything has a meaning. Come on, hurry up! I don't want your father waking before we can get clear."

We left my room and tiptoed past Bert's but the door was ajar. As we got to Lucy's room we could hear Bert's deep masonic snore, stone-dust in perpetual motion, coming from inside. Master Henry made a disapproving face and ushered me on.

We had to rouse the gatehouse guard to get out, then we walked down to the bridge and along the banks of the River Wey to the west. The sun was rising over the Surrey downs and the willow-warblers were already in full song. As we walked along the narrow footpath I could see hundreds of figures in the mist by the river. At first I had thought they were trees or fence-posts but they were people, men and women from the great hall who had danced and talked all night and were now wandering silently in the calm air by the river, cooling down.

"Where are we going?" I asked, eventually, having, until then, trusted that we were on a journey of importance, not following a drunken whim.

Master Henry paused and watched the rising rings of a fish in the smooth surface of the river.

"Robert will not stay in the vicinity of the Court; he despises it so much. He is quartered in a chapel not far from here. He is sick of the wasteful and ceremonious ways of the great. They nauseate him."

"Are we really going to mass?" I asked.

Master Henry looked at me, his protruding eyes pink and tired with all the drink he had taken. He blinked a few times as if to give himself time to remember.

"You know how to follow a mass, surely," he said with a confidential smile. "Even half a mason can follow a mass."

"Of course."

When we reached a place where the rich orange-brown sands of the hills had broken through the soil cover and spilled down to the river's edge, Master Henry led me up a steep path through a wood to the top of a knoll overlooking the valley. It was crowned with a small chapel surrounded by horses and wagons. Smoke rose from several fires and servants were already preparing to make breakfast.

We were admitted to the chapel which had been turned into an apartment for the aged bishop. Clothes, furniture and baskets were littered all over the floor: priests, monks and clerks roamed everywhere. The altar was a simple wooden table raised up on stones. A phalanx of people stood packed in front of it as though the mass had started. Master Henry pushed his way over and got to the front. I followed him, wondering what stage in the ceremony the Cretins had reached so I could have the correct response ready.

Peering round the side of Master Henry's pink and black striped bulk I saw no priest making mass. The people were gathered around an open coffin in which Robert Grosseteste lay wrapped in a winding-sheet, his beads in his hands, kept folded on his breast. He was talking in a very low voice.

Everyone was leaning forward to catch his words. In the company I recognised the King, his eyelid drooping more severely than when I had seen him last.

Under the old bishop's head was a pillow; beside the coffin a green and gold blanket lay tossed aside. Judging by his pained expression, the bishop had spent all night in the coffin.

Master Henry straightened up and shooed all the spectators away, leaving only myself and the King close to the bishop. The clerks, priests and monks watched us with dog-like fixity from a distance, their ears pricked.

"I smell something," old Robert whispered.

206

"It could be me," Master Henry said with a laugh. "I have been dancing most of the night, much over-heated."

"Wild garlic!" Robert groaned. "I can't stand it."

"Ah, yes, the woods were teeming with it," Master Henry said, putting his huge, rubicund face close to the pale, dried-up head in the coffin. "I have brought the boy."

"Which boy?" Robert demanded querulously. "Who said I wanted a boy?"

"The boy who will be the fusion . . . we hope."

Master Henry leant back, one eye on the King who had now closed both his, clearly exhausted.

"The King does not want to listen!" Robert suddenly shouted, sitting up. "He never does! Why should I speak to him when I have better things to do? He comes here drunk. You come here drunk. Is there anyone in a serious frame of mind but me?"

Robert moaned and showed the whites of his eyes then sank on to his pillow, his beautiful fingers passing his beads along the string with manic speed.

"Curse you all for destroying the peace of the creation and the unity of all living things," he breathed. "It is one world and I will die knowing it has been divided by ignorance. What use will Paradise be to me? I will never rest, leaving such imperfection, such weakness . . . aah, I cannot face God with that on my mind . . . We must find a way to impose His divine integrity on every spirit . . ."

There was a long silence. All the priests and monks had crowded closer as the ancient ecclesiastic began his cry from the soul. Irritably, Master Henry shooed them away again. They retreated, frowning with frustration.

"It is unlike you to despair, Robert," Master Henry said, massaging his own neck and sinking down on to a stool. "Please remember the boy. You will have great influence over him. If he is to do the work we want of him he will need encouragement."

Robert sighed and twisted his head away, touching the rough timber of the coffin with the end of his sharp nose.

"A boy to do a man's job," he whispered. "We have spoiled our chances. Chaos will reclaim it all, then what?"

King Henry sighed and sat back, holding his temples with the tips of his fingers. He obviously had a bad headache and was struggling with his temper.

"We agreed on the experiment," he said with a hint of rebuke. "However small, we said, we must have something to go on."

"What can I say to a boy?" old Robert grumbled on. "I have held this kingdom together by strengthening the spirits of men, not children. They promised me I would die on my birthday. I have been cheated again. Now it will be next year."

"Spend it on the boy," Master Henry whispered. "Supervise him."

"A heretic's child!" Robert moaned softly, his fingers gripping his beads convulsively. "Is there no one better?"

"A heresy you have some sympathy for yourself," Master Henry pointed out with wry good humour. "That word has come to mean nothing. Trust his innocence. He is the perfect subject."

Innocent? Me? After all I had seen and heard in my short life? As I pieced together the reason for my preferment I became astonished: that grown men should have forgotten the state of being of a twelve-year-old boy! Innocence indeed! Ignorance, perhaps. And what was I doing at the feet of my teachers? Learning as much old knowledge and error as possible. I was tempted to join in the debate but I caught a warning glance from Master Henry telling me to shut up.

"De Montfort will not stand for it. He has said so," Robert sighed quaveringly. "He refuses to compromise. Once we have made the experiment and seen what the boy comes up with he will simply destroy it."

"Simon has more sense than that," the king averred. "Don't worry about him. I can control the Earl of Leicester."

"Ha!" Robert snorted, sitting up again and putting one unbelievably thin leg over the side of the coffin in preparation for getting out. "He is totally of this world, that man, and you are not — which is your one virtue. All right, I will spend some time with the boy, but I want him to meet Simon and be promised his protection, otherwise nothing will be achieved."

Priests edged forward and helped the bishop to his feet where he stood swaying while they unwrapped the winding-sheet from around him. As the cloth was pulled gently from his body he turned slowly to assist the process. His cadaver — for I can call it nothing else — was exposed part by part as the old man slowly pirouetted; flesh almost translucent in its thinness; bones and sinews standing out so much I could not believe they belonged to a living person. The only parts of this withered and gaunt creature that had life were his terrible, green-eyed head and his genitals, the latter seeming to belong to another beast, not of humankind, so gross and grey they were, hanging from his wasted loins.

Yet I could not help but feel tenderly towards all this ugliness: and I was not the only one. There were tears in the eyes of Master Henry and the King as they looked on Robert's nakedness, and all the priests and monks were openly weeping. As they dressed him they began to set up a cry, "He is up! He is up!" which was carried to those outside the chapel.

When he was fully dressed in his white and green vestments Robert walked to the door and out into the open air.

"We all know he will be made into a saint," Master Henry whispered to me as we followed along, his eyes impudently on the bishop's back. "A great man, the old devil!"

When I reached the door and followed Master Henry out on to the grass I saw the whole hill was covered with folk. All the men and women who had been down in the water-meadows had climbed up and were on their knees in the grass; weavers and spinners, dyers with Guildford Blue on their hands, shepherds with their dogs, soldiers, even the poor people who haunted the woods too afraid to live in open space, were there, all of them crying out "He is up! He is up!" as the fierce-faced old cleric gave them his benediction.

With the skylarks rising and the herons beating their leisurely way up and down the curving river, Robert barked out a mass which was as brief and to the point as a workman's breakfast. Not all of the people heard it and many were so intoxicated with wine or love or the times or fatigue that the points of the mystery did not register: but they were with great Grosseteste, ignorant of his indignation, basking in his sacerdotal radiance, already awed by his imminent eternal fame.

My only thought was: if I am to learn anything from him I will have to be quick!

After the open-air mass the bishop's servants brought out breakfast for his retinue and visitors. King Henry sat next to Robert and both men were careful to eat very little, watching each other's plates for any sign of impious gorging. Master Henry and I were not held back by any such affectations and we ate well, sitting with our backs to the chapel's eastward-facing wall close to the King's table. In the three hours we sat there I saw old Robert eat one pancake with butter and drink a quart of wine. Remembering the sight of him gleaming like a bottle in his translucent nakedness I imagined the red wine visible as it went down his gullet into his belly and thence to his bladder, for he was always having to piss in a bucket the priests brought to him and thrust under his robes. Each time the crowd saw this they called out to the priests to bring them some of the bishop's urine for their ills but the old man had forbidden such idolatry and it was always poured away into the sod.

"Fools," he grumbled sourly. "They see the cure for their ills in as foul a place as you see the solution to your problems. Modern politics is the art of collective waste."

The King smiled tiredly, one hand propping up his cheek beneath the drooping eyelid and distorting his small mouth.

"Robert, do try to be kind to me," he said with an attempt at a laugh. "You're being very hard. I do admire you so much."

"And I do not admire you when you threaten and bully the Benedictines at Winchester into accepting your idiot uterine brother as their bishop. If I had been in England then, instead of wasting my time at the Roman Curia . . . oh, what I would have said!"

"Robert, you should not talk to me this way. . . ."

"Cut off my head, if you please," the old bishop replied grimly. "At least that would keep me quiet and you would be doing me a favour. Is it any wonder I despair? We have got nothing right, Henry, nothing. Our religion denies our state and our state denies our religion. They contradict each other and always will. I can see no answer. After Christ there was never an answer . . . except light and that is too universal to mean anything. It is all a mess, a confusion. . . ."

"We know that, Robert," Master Henry interrupted. "That is something, at least. If we can create an insight within this boy then we may be able to deduce how to resolve the most pernicious paradoxes. There must be a new way: as a man of science you must believe that."

Robert made a sardonic sound under his breath and licked his lips. He stared at the King with a hopeless expression in his green eyes.

"That we are reduced to this is a great castigation of our time together — all those pointless arguments, the squabbles and quibbles — you would never listen," he said bitterly, dabbing at his lips with a handkerchief. "Why should this boy listen? If you are to talk to him, and Earl Simon is to talk to him, and Master Henry here, then all the teachers of Paris, why, he will be the most confused boy in the world."

"That is not how his mind works," Master Henry assured him. "The boy always seeks out the essence. That is his natural talent. We know that he will express this in architecture but if we train him intelligently then he may be able to express it in other forms — words, ideas, the tools of government and faith."

"So you say, so you say," Robert muttered.

"We agreed to give it a chance. There is nothing to lose. If things go on as they are there will be war on all the points of dispute," King Henry said with a surge of vehemence. "The Church cannot rule a creation it affects to despise. I cannot rule a people who are taught to despise my authority. Let the boy try to find the form . . . anything! Anything is better than what we have now!"

"I suppose we agree on that much," Robert replied sourly. "But I would not like to be in this boy's shoes. I will not have him hurt, or penalised if this experiment should fail. Science can lead us astray, as Aristotle knew, as I know. Earl Simon must swear never to harm him, or his father, again."

"He will," the King replied. "I will see to that."

"Have you understood a word we have been saying?" Robert suddenly asked me as if noticing my real presence for the first time. "At twelve years Jesus taught in the Temple."

I looked straight into his fierce green eyes and put down the piece of bread and butter I had been chewing.

Before I could compose any reply — and to *that* question I might have been forgiven for taking my time! — Robert got to his feet and started to take frantic deep breaths.

"Oh, it's coming, it's coming," he panted. "A day late, that's all."

Without more ado he set off walking over the field as if he were trying to escape from something within himself, shaking his head, snapping his elbows to his sides. His acolytes followed him at a distance but when the people began to run up and touch him they ran ahead and fended them off. For quarter of an hour Robert wandered around the top of the hill, doing a full circuit of the chapel and the place where we sat. The King watched him disconsolately and played with his short beard.

"It is a difficult way to get to Heaven," he said eventually to Master Henry de Reyns. "Sometimes I lose all interest in the idea."

So, at last, all was revealed to me. I was to be part of the new Science, the subject of an experiment in education. What I could have said to Robert Grosseteste before he flapped away that morning was that their assumptions about me were dangerously incorrect: I was not in a state of original innocence and had lived a quarter of my anticipated life already, which had left its mark — Christ in the Temple preaching out of *his* innocence or no! What I already knew was, in some quarter-measure, what I would know: but I dared to think I could find that universal truth they dreamt of: that truest truth — a dazzling, sensible, luminous form of meaning that could be the basis of all design in thought and matter. They trusted to an instinct they had noticed in me on very little evidence and, I suspected, they had been talked into the experiment by Master Henry, the King's mason who had the interests of our brotherhood more in mind than those of either Church or state in England. I was not so much of a fool to imagine that if the experiment went wrong I would not be disposed of like a piece of disappointing apparatus. However, there was one advantage I had: I knew there was a form in existence that terrified them in its implications and the power of its novelty: the Second Style of Emergence. This was the outer limit of their experiment: they had seen it and understood my blood-connection to it through my father. Within his scientific understanding old Robert knew the authority of inherited ability. It is a talent prophesied.

When Robert returned to the table he was exhausted with his troubled tour of the meadow and immediately demanded to be left alone in order to rest. Master Henry asked for permission to accompany the King back to the castle and we returned along the river. I heard them mention de Montfort many times so I was not surprised when Master Henry took time to warn me I must prepare to meet the Butcher's son at some time during the day.

The opportunity was not long in presenting itself. As we rounded the high ground which runs down to the River Wey opposite the south-western limits of the castle walls, we came upon the entire Court bathing from a broad sand-bank. There was a general air of slightly mad gaiety about their antics, most of them floundering about in the shallows in their finery, chasing each other with much thrusting of heads under the water in fun. It was a good way to get rid of the after-effects of the night's excesses and it made a light-hearted scene for the King to enjoy after his sobering interview with the Bishop of Lincoln.

I suspected word had already been brought back by some of the onlookers that King Henry had been given a severe roasting by old Robert for allowing the Court to become so frivolous and French and now their design was to demonstrate just how frivolous and French they could be when they tried!

There came a great uproar as the King was sighted walking along the bank with Master Henry and myself. A crowd of men rushed out of the water and ran over to us, whooping and hallooing. I could see the battle-scars drawn on their chests and arms as they charged us, the wine livid in the old lesions. A short, hard-muscled man of about forty with grey in his beard winked at Henry as he came up then put an arm around his shoulder and invited him to bathe with them. The Court, waiting in the water, roared out their enthusiasm for the idea. When King Henry shook his head the four warriors picked him up, carried him to the river where the Court was now screaming with delight, and threw him in. When the King came up he pretended to be amused but I could see he was not: but he stayed and swam for a while, his cloak floating out behind him in the slow current, the four warriors circling him like water-spaniels with a wounded fowl.

I looked at Master Henry for advice on what I should do next but he was already half-undressed. I followed suit but we were too late. The four warriors rushed out of the water again and the short, grizzled man confronted us when our garb was only partially discarded.

"If the Earl of Leicester will give me a moment," Master Henry said, puffing as he tried to get his beautiful linen shirt over his head. "I will be ready."

"Ever helpful, as is your custom," the man said with a jeer. "For God's sake don't tear your chemise, Henry."

"This is the boy, Hedric, by the way. You will remember I told you about him. . . ."

"Yes, I know who he is," the Butcher's son said.

His voice was harsh and unmusical even with its strong French accent. When he looked at me I could not meet his eyes which were dark-coloured and hostile, belying his wide, gap-toothed grin. His gums were very red.

"This is he, Simon," Master Henry began to say but he got no further. I was given the same treatment as the King but, being smaller, I flew higher into the air and into a deeper part of the river. The Court were even more delighted and applauded. When I surfaced no one saw

213

how angry I was: their eyes were on the next victim, Master Henry, and the four warriors were having a harder time with him and his great size for he had decided to resist — for the fun, no doubt.

But I was incensed. To have been seized and insulted by the enemy of my people, the would-murderer of my father, knocked all common sense out of my head. I swam out of the river and charged up the bank to where de Montfort fought with Master Henry then hurled myself into the fray, swinging punches and kicking hard. A moment later I was in the air again, higher this time, and I fell awkwardly on my belly: but the rage did not go away. As soon as I could get back to the bank I assaulted the Earl of Leicester again and the four of them threw me back in again. This happened five times in all until Master Henry's ducking was a forgotten prospect and the attention of the King and the Court was solely upon me and my solitary campaign of revenge.

After the fifth time I had been thrown in I swam down into the depths and did not surface until I had got a good twenty yards downstream to frighten them. When I came up there was a huge shout of approval but that did not comfort me as much as the sight of Master Henry actually running down the bank, his belly shaking under his shirt, to help me.

"What a temper you have, Hedric!" he said as he pulled me out of the water. "Yet, it might have proved useful. I think the Earl of Leicester has decided you may be worth encouraging."

Master Henry put a protective arm around my shoulders and led me back along the bank to where the Court still frolicked around the King. With humble grandeur of manner we picked up the clothes Master Henry had discarded, then, abjuring the bridge, forded the river, bowing and nodding to all and sundry with the calmest coolness and dignity. Simon de Montfort watched our exit from his place by the King, his eyes thoughtful and his hands spread over his scarred shoulders like a maiden. If the look he gave me was one prompted by liking then I have never encountered one similar. To me it was subtle, humorous but calculating. However, it had more mock-paternal tenderness in it than I received from the eyes of the man who stood on the opposite bank, his body crouched like a baited bear's tugging at its chain.

My father was not pleased, not pleased at all.

XXIII

It was not above three hours before I saw Earl Simon in a different light altogether; as a man of stern, austere religiousness who could compete with old Robert Grosseteste in this arena. The King had summoned his great nobles and bishops to the church of Saint Mary outside the castle bailey walls to witness his reading of the Great Charter, the famous document signed by his father, King John, at Runnymede.

It was a curious ceremony. The cramped church with its three overbuilt aisles stuffed with people all craning their heads for a glimpse of the King merely reading to himself, poring over the charter with his drooping eyelid much in evidence. It gave him the appearance of a man who was not really interested in what he was doing.

Beside him knelt Earl Simon in full armour, his unsheathed sword serving to support his lowered head. Not once in the ceremony did he stir. Kneeling alongside him was old Robert, swaying with weakness but refusing to be outdone. The King kept them like that for two hours while he followed the words on the parchment with his fingernail one by one, pausing in reflection, occasionally looking up at the ceiling as a man does when his mind is straining to comprehend a difficult piece of another person's reasoning.

My view of the King's reading was through a squint on the upper part of the northern aisle. I sat between the knees of Master Henry, fresh from a bath and a stand-up row with Bert who had followed us back to the guest-quarters, raging about my showing-off and getting him into trouble by drawing unwanted attention to myself. Master Henry dealt with him sharply and sent him away, warning him not to interfere in what was being done in my interests. Now Bert was back on the far south-western wall, working alone on this King's holiday by order of Master Henry. But I had no thought for him as I watched the strange, silent charade visible through the squint.

"What does it say?" I whispered, turning in order to speak very closely into Master Henry's ear.

"That the King may not do as he pleases with those who have the power to stop him," Master Henry whispered. "King John's son is King John's son. We must never forget that."

"But wasn't King John an Albigensian like us?" I whispered. Master Henry's response was to dig me hurtfully in the ribs to be silent.

Obediently I paused but the sight of the King held in this weird paralysis within the stone forced me to go on: was he confirming his father's weakness? Making a gesture?

"Is the King a true Christian?" I whispered in as light a way as I could, my lips brushing Master Henry's ear. "If he is the son of an Albigensian he would have been brought up in his father's faith, surely. . . ?"

Before I could receive another rebuking dig in the ribs old Robert Grosseteste moaned and pitched forward off his knees, cracking his head on the altar steps. There was a flurry of movement as his acolytes swept forward and picked him up, bringing him to a space they cleared against the chancel arch. The King did not look up from his reading of the charter nor did Earl Simon waver in his vigil. After a few minutes of moaning and rubbing, the indomitable old Bishop of Lincoln was back alongside the indefatigable Earl of Leicester, a big bruise on his pale forehead and his eyes rheumy, but still determined to remain in public prayer.

"I appeal to the glorious Saint Veronica on this, her day, to put an impression of the true meaning of this charter on the King's memory in the same way as she took a faithful impression of Our Lord's face on her handkerchief as she wiped His sweat away on the road to Calvary. Blessed be the diligent memory of all who serve God's will," he said in a shaky voice that was firmness itself in its intensity, "and blessed be the son who keeps the word of his father sacred."

"Amen to that!" Earl Simon growled, still refusing to budge an inch though he must have been in agony after such a long time kneeling in full armour.

King Henry made no sign he had heard what had been said. He merely put his face a little closer to the document spread out in front of him and thoughtfully touched his lips with one finger. There were no further interruptions until he finished and rolled up the charter, rubbing his eyes. It did not go unnoticed that he allowed it to roll on to the floor from the table and made no attempt to pick it up, even brushing it aside with his jewelled slippers as he walked on his way out of the church.

I could feel Master Henry shaking with suppressed laughter behind me.

I was summoned to Earl Simon's quarters in the late part of that afternoon. A squire came to my room where I had been taken straight after the reading by Master Henry and given a copy of the Great Charter to examine for myself. The youth was very jocular with me as if I amused him for some reason and it took me some time to recall the events of the morning at the river, my mind being full of what I had found in the charter and the strong sense of foreboding it had created within me. The scene at Saint Mary's kept coming back to me: what was going on in the minds of the three chief actors and how they wished to influence each other, and how they had failed as far as the King was concerned. The power remained his, charter or no charter. He might just as well have torn it up for all it mattered to him. Then again, it was a reminder of the sufferings of his father. As for the liberties it attempted to lay out, they were foreign to someone like me whose liberties had always existed (or not) at two levels because of our Albigensian faith. The conflict between public and secret existence does not create a strong sense of rights but merely a yearning for the favour of being left alone. In my case, however, this was to change but in a manner never conceived by King John at Runnymede as being the ambition of any of his subjects.

Earl Simon was quartered in the great whitewashed keep that is the strongpoint of Guildford Castle, and a badly-built strongpoint it is too, as I have said before. I had to climb up through the gatehouse which is on piles over the ditch on the western side. There were soldiers on guard at every corner wearing de Montfort's livery, stirring up violent memories for me from that day at the farm during the snowstorm. Each time I saw it my stomach knotted under my belt and my legs went cold. With the King held in such contempt he was unlikely ever to remonstrate with his greatest adversary over the disappearance of a boy, a slight loss.

With thoughts like these buzzing in my head I was not prepared for the welcome I received, nor the presence of the other guests in the earl's chamber and the warm atmosphere of ease. The King was there, lolling on a couch with his hands behind his head: old Robert sat close to him in a wooden chair with arm-rests, very bright and alert; and Master Henry, now dressed in a simple sandstone-coloured robe with a collar of enamelled cherries. When I was brought in they all turned to look at me. It was Earl Simon himself who gave me his seat and made me take it while he sent the squire away and closed the door fast behind him.

"You are among friends, Hedric," Master Henry said soothingly. "Now, don't be afraid."

"We are the ones who should be afraid!" Earl Simon said as he found himself another seat. "If his intellect and his temper go hand in hand then I feel sorry for his teachers. Can you handle him, Robert?"

"I have taught *you* a few things," the old bishop replied with an indulgent but distant smile, "but first I had to convince you of your ignorance. Humility is essential."

"Then you did not do a good job on Simon," the King drawled softly, "for he is always defying me, as you are."

"That is because you need it, Henry, not because I want to," old Robert said with a quick cackle. "Oh, come on. You try to get away with murder, as does Simon."

Master Henry looked up to see how this exchange affected me. He rightly suspected I would be bewildered. There was only the animosity companions pretend here, yet I knew it was a most serious business; one that had shaken the country from end to end during the anarchy of John. He winked at me as if to say: "Bide your time, they will show themselves as they are if you wait."

There was a pause as Earl Simon made a point of pondering. It was his turn and he was obviously formulating his best reply. He rubbed his long nose; he tugged at his lip. Old Robert waited with the shadow of a little grin on his lips. Eventually Earl Simon sighed and nonchalantly crossed his short legs.

"The trouble with you, Robert, is that you are so ancient. We, the King and Master Henry and myself, are in the years when our little knowledge comes into its own. What we want is of this world which is where the Creator means us to flourish."

"Nonsense!" expostulated the bishop. "How deluded you are! All you do is give your avarice the dignity of form. Can one justify earthly ambitions by merely owning up to them? One's desires cannot be trusted. They stem from our incompleteness before the Creator. The ambitious man must accept that he is the slave of sin. As for you, Simon, you are a camel trying to lever its way through the eye of the needle, with a sword."

There was a deal of good-natured laughter at this and Old Robert sat back in his chair, satisfied. Earl Simon stroked his throat for a while, casting glances at the King as if to encourage him to join in. After a while the earl chuckled to himself.

"My ambitions, as you call them," he murmured. "Shall I tell you what they are? Simply to hold what I have."

"That's a lot of ambition," Master Henry replied with a grunt, "when one has as much as you."

"Oh, no, no," King Henry chipped in, "there is more for the earl to covet: all my sorrow, for instance. Simon would like to have my throne and, oh, how I would love to give it to him. But, as a friend, I must protect him from disappointment. He would get so bored."

"Talk to me of sorrow when you have fought six years in a hole like Gascony for a king who says he is forced to deny you support and money, who favours the opinions of rebels above yours," Earl Simon responded with a shrug. "If I were king — and thank God I am not — much shame would be my sorrow."

"Let us talk about this boy," the King said as wearily as he could beneath his apprehension, "and get it over with, as you would get Gascony over with."

"You like to move on from a point before it can be answered, Henry," Earl Simon said bitterly. "If you keep saying I want your throne often enough people will believe it. They don't know how it is a standing joke between us."

"Har-har," the King said under his breath, then straightened himself out and sat upright on the couch, all readiness. "Something dear to all our hearts! Our gamble! Our experiment! What is his name again?"

"Tell His Majesty," Master Henry said encouragingly. "I'm not doing your talking for you."

"I am called Hedric," I announced in a voice a fraction too confident and a mite too loud.

"Haven't I seen you before somewhere?"

I looked at the King in disbelief: it was impossible he should have forgotten my recitation of Bishop Grosseteste's theory of light so soon! And I had spent the morning with him. Ah, another joke! I decided, and smiled though it was not easily achieved.

"What are you smiling at, boy?" the King asked with a touch of irritation. "Do you find me funny?"

Master Henry caught my eye and held up his hand and tapped one of his rings. Clutching at this straw I thrust my hand forward and showed the King the ring that he had given me.

"Do you want me to kiss your hand?" he said in surprise.

This was the best joke so far and everyone laughed out loud. Master Henry then explained the mistake and more laughter followed. I had no doubt in my mind King Henry had no recollection at all of the events of the previous evening concerning me. Would he remember any other arrangements regarding my future welfare? I wondered.

"Sire, we are involving this child in an important matter. It is time to be serious," old Robert reminded him. "Perdition is not a state a young mind can easily grasp in concept: to be of his tender years is to stand at the entrance of the maze, not to be lost in the middle, as you three are, or unable to find the exit, as I am. Either we help him to understand now, or I will insist he is excluded from the experiment."

"All right, Robert," the King replied with some acerbity. "Don't take every opportunity you find to preach. If I talk to the boy will he understand?"

"He understood the entire text he recited in front of you last night," Master Henry said. "I doubt if there were ten people present who could keep up with him."

"Ah, yes . . . I remember . . . the Latin was very good . . ." the King murmured reflectively. "And I gave you a ring, didn't I? It used to belong to a ward of mine, a girl from Luton or somewhere. . . . Yes! We're lost! Have you got that?"

The infusion of enthusiasm and emphasis was so sudden that I jumped. The King's drooping eyelid was raised and a different character emerged from behind it like an actor from a curtain.

"Will you help us?"

Now he was gentle and winning, standing in front of me with his hands on my shoulders. I could not look up but remained with my eyes fixed on his chest, inhaling his flowery scent. When he went down on his haunches and took my hands in his I nearly started to cry but caught sight of Master Henry's stern gaze.

"We are on the threshold of either madness or changes so marvellous we may die without comprehending them," the King explained to me in a charming sing-song, taking me on to his knee as he sat down. "We have all gone wrong in our ways, we four: as king, cleric, captain and craftsman. This is something we recognise. It is a joke between us but there are times when it is hard to laugh. Our one virtue is we are open to revelation. All of us are too old and too battered about to receive a vision that is pure in its meaning but you . . . Hedric . . . it has been put to me that you . . . half-Christian, half-heretic, half-man, half-woman . . ."

I stiffened and tried to stand up.

"I am no woman," I muttered.

"Don't be vexed . . . sit down and I will explain . . ." the King said soothingly. "You draw with the inner eye of a woman's world. That is all I am saying. Master Henry will make that clear to you. But no, you will be a man shortly! Maybe you are one already. Can you make seed yet?"

I struggled to get off his knee and found a place for myself nearer old Robert who was watching me carefully.

"Answer the King's question, boy," old Robert said with a nod of encouragement. "We need to know what passions you have, that is all. It will affect the way you think and that is what we are interested in."

I felt like throwing myself out of the window. The question was one that tormented me above all others as I waited, night after night, but I covered my blushes with anger.

Old Robert read my thoughts and shook himself as though to dispose of the unpleasantness.

"We are not prying. There is no need for shame. We have to talk frankly with you if our experiment is to have any value. You are an open soul, we believe, barely written upon. If we put you in the way of the highest learning and the richest experiences . . . who knows? As friends we have agreed that it is possible . . . while we are friends."

"Let us leave the question of his coming aside for the moment," Earl Simon said roughly. "Master Henry has already said there is no evidence of it from his bed-linen. What we must know is his willingness. It must not arise from fear—and I speak as one who has made him afraid in the past—but out of a sense of privilege, of being chosen . . . Hedric!"

His commanding bark had me straightening up like a soldier. I glanced fearfully at him.

"Will you risk your peace of mind for us?"

It was such a plain, humble question, said without any suggestion of challenge or authority, that it took me off-guard. It seemed to come from a less fearsome soul than the one who inhabited that grizzled, thrusting head with its stern brows and livid helmet-abrasions.

"I can only grow, sir," I said after some hesitation.

My reply hushed them. Master Henry made a pout of approval to me and nodded. Old Robert used his sleeve to wipe his eyes and I thought I heard him murmuring to himself: "Such faith, such faith."

It was a long time before I made the effort to speak again. Meantime, the King had gone back to lolling on the couch and Earl Simon had walked up and down cracking his finger-joints. As I opened my mouth to follow up the good impression I felt sure I had made, the King held up a lazy hand to stop me.

"Say no more. Your precociousness has exhausted me," he said crossly. "Even so, I still feel guilty about what we are expecting of you."

"As long as you do not punish me if I fail . . ." I began to say but King Henry cut me short with a sharp action of his mouth, something between a snarl and a yawn.

"Oh, I can do no more of this today. Edward, you are a tiring person . . . failure is always punished. Look at me. These three men are my closest friends but they do not hold back from hurting me whenever I displease them."

"My name is Hedric, sire, not Edward," I corrected him.

The King's eyes went dim and cold and his cheeks coloured. I hung my head, knowing I had gone too far.

"Forgive me, sire," I said quickly. "I will be called Edward if it will help you to remember not to punish me."

There was enough wit in what I said to mollify him but only just. Shortly afterwards I was dismissed, having been curtly told that Old Robert would be helping me to prepare for Paris. As some point in the next month I would have to go to Lincoln to be with him a while. To this day I can remember the squeeze Master Henry gave me on my arm as he ushered me out of the chamber. It was his signal that we had succeeded very well so far; that I had made the right kind of impression; that the suspicion under which Earl Simon had held me by dint of Bert's involvement with Hans Seersach and the Second Style of Emergence had been reduced; and, finally, I had shared a room with the four men who ruled England and not been overawed. "I can hold my own with any man, be he pope, emperor or monarch," I said to myself as I climbed down the steep steps of the keep's gatehouse into the dry ditch and followed the beaten path over the sward. "I will never be afraid again."

"Never speak too soon" is a good motto provided it does not make one always speak too late. When I got back to my room I found Lucy waiting for me. She was pale and red-eyed from weeping. She told me that my father had fled the castle, leaving me a letter. He had made her promise to have me read it in front of her then supervise its destruction.

We sat together at my work-table and spread Bert's letter out. In the late afternoon light I read what had obviously taken him days to compose for he wrote labouredly. It was a small scrap of parchment and he had crammed as much as possible into the space. As Lucy could not read herself she watched my face for my reactions. It was not long before she had cause to resume her crying though not all for sadness's sake.

She laughed as I had to laugh: she frowned as I had to frown. As I read the letter Bert began to come back to me and I realised we had not really shared a common thought since Christmas. In spite of it being a letter of farewell this was also a message of redemption: he was lost but as I wept I knew that I would find him again, some day when all had been fulfilled.

There was no urge to run out and find him. If he had been still packing in his room I would have left him to it. The letter told me what I needed to know: that Bert was still mine and I was his son. It was better this should be so in freedom rather than in what was, for him, a painful and humiliating predicament.

Before I burned the letter in Lucy's kitchen, I committed it to memory. Ever since that day, it has served me as an antidote to arrogance. Here is what he wrote:

To my liege lord, Hedricus, Pastor Ass, king of the seven fat kine (and thereby their servant!), greetings from his loyal bondsman, his dad and progenitor and protector, now cast aside. No more will I tax you with my paternal attentions, there being so many to take my place: namely those who have seen fit to try and murder me within this last half-year. All I have taught you I leave in your care: if it is all undone by schoolmen and philosophers then that is your loss. As for me, my dear son, I go to better myself with more learning and practice of my skill amongst my own where my allegiances are not so twisted as to have to be in question. You may become a better talker but I will wager a year's money that it will not make you a better mason. He who is silent is not asleep, as the saying goes. When you are hanged in Paris for not having all the right answers, remember me.

What you should think on is not my failure but your own. When we discovered that our faith was compromised at high levels and encroached upon by the Christian powers, did we have to accept it like slaves?

223

do our brothers who hold the faith in every land maintain their strength by abject surrender? I taught you some forms of cunning in order to combat Christian deceit: now, when the Christian shows his cunning, and his conquest of our leaders by that cunning, you adopt their deceit. That is not the way of our forefathers. The King's mason is wrong in what he has done in England and the elders who agreed the concordat with Rome on our part have acted evilly. It is not how we wish to live, nor shall any good man have to if he will resist.

There is a great deal you have yet to know. Your ability is not as extraordinary as others have claimed. It is my opinion that you are being used, through your vanity (for which I blame myself in not chastising you often enough for it), and nothing but shame and defeat will accrue on your part. This will fall on stony ground with you but I am bound by our shared blood to say it.

I have remained at Guildford for so long only to decide what danger my escape would put you in should you accompany me; or whether you would be better left behind because it appears to be your wish not to be separated from those who praise and cosset you so far beyond your needs. My decision will speak for itself but it was not easily made. I do not trust the King's mason, nor do I believe the Earl of Leicester intends anything but harm. All that gives me comfort in leaving you with them is that you are such a thorn in anyone's side that one day they will want to pluck you out: by that time you may (and for this I ardently hope!) have come to your senses and forestalled them by fleeing as I do now. When you do then look for me in the north but do not be wearing the King's coat. Where I am going is a place which is proof against all potentates where a simple man like myself, though a prey to the odd confusion of mind, need not be a traitor.

I would wish you good luck but I fear where you are headed is not famous for luck, only for greed and disgrace. You are no longer too young to be without a father and there are those who can try to do my work in your upbringing, if there is any work left to be done. My worst thought is you may be made in your final form already. If that is so, prepare for a hard life.

This letter must be destroyed in order to protect those who have helped me. It is my hope you will not suffer too much by my going. Most sons will miss their fathers, given a chance; but you are not most sons, Hedric.

May your later years make all this clear to you (if you have any). May whichever gods you give the privilege of your notice look after you. May you get together enough wisdom from somewhere to give you a true idea of your worth in this world.

The Second Style is dead. Long live the Third.

XXIV

The King left for Winchester on the first day of a stupendous heat. It had been a good summer so far but there had always been a breeze to cool us: now, in the middle of July, the air went still, the birds stopped singing, and the sun rose up like a furnace spewing heat. I sat in my room expecting Master Henry to come in full of rebukes about Bert. I tried to work, keeping my attention from the window and the assembling cavalcade. Men and horses milled about in confusion for most of the morning, getting more ill-tempered as the heat increased and the dust rose. The King was late — as always — and the Court buzzed angrier and angrier as noon approached. By the time King Henry joined them I had still not received a visit from Master Henry. I watched the mass of riders, wagons and walkers slowly pour out of the south-west gatehouse in a great cloud of dust just as Lucy called me to my food. She came into my room and leant over my work-table with me, watching them all go.

"I did not see the Earl of Leicester out there," I said to her. "Is he still with us?"

Lucy tucked her curls which were damp from the heat further under her linen cap and wiped her face with a cloth.

"He left early this morning. Earl Simon will not wait for any man," she answered. "Now we will have some peace."

"Master Henry will be round, I expect," I muttered, pretending to be busy putting away my inks. "He will want to question me about Bert's running away."

Lucy put her hands to her waist and leant back from the window. She grimaced and sighed, then stood up straight.

"Master Henry has just left," she declared.

"I didn't see him!" I cried, going back to the window.

"He was with the rest but keeping his head down," she said as she smoothed out my bed and started to tidy my table; something she did that exasperated me as I was always mislaying things afterwards. Although I appeared to work in confusion there was an

225

underlying order there which I understood. I always knew where everything was.

"Please don't do that," I pleaded with her. "I won't be able to find anything when I need it."

"Your father . . ." she began to say, then tore the top blanket off my bed with a single, savage movement. "You won't be wanting this in such heat!"

She walked swiftly out of my room, the blanket trailing behind her. I could hear her choking back her sobs all the way down the passage to the stairs. But when I went down for my dinner a few minutes later she had composed herself.

Winchester is not far away from Guildford. As the burning days went by I sat at my work-table by the window and watched the gatehouses and the daily traffic in and out, watching for Master Henry. Other guests came into the house and Bert's room was taken by a treasury official who was as lecherous as he was light-fingered. He was determined to have Lucy but she would have none of him, remaining quiet and morose while the fellow turned himself inside-out trying to tempt her. In the heat I found my thoughts sinking time and again to Earl Simon's question about my making seed. It was late. Someone of my age should be able by now. The importance of it grew until I found it deflecting every item of knowledge and skill that I was struggling to learn: there was always this ache, this yearning; even in Mathematics, more so in Music . . . oh, those bad, bronze afternoons full of delicious dreams that were empty because I was, as yet, empty. Father Horace became impatient as I frustrated all his attempts to drive me on to higher levels: in fact my ability in Latin slipped backwards as I dawdled listlessly in my imaginary Elysiums. The heat was a severe punishment for him as he was unable to sweat. One morning he came into my room so silently — for he had to move so slowly — and found me caressing my erect cock. I do not know how long he stood there watching me as I had my eyes closed but when I opened them he had sat himself down and was praying, his elbows on his knees and his face in his hands. That was what brought me back to earth; the sound of his despairing orison:

"Forgive him, Father, for he knows not what he does."

My dream collapsed and my cock with it. It was a challenge: what to say? What face to put on it? Father Horace could not look at me as I broke out in a sweat that was enough for both of us.

I pulled on my drawers and started to recite some Cicero he had set me.

It was never mentioned but from that time on Father Horace always knocked long and hard on my door before he came in.

Bert's doubts about my intellectual prowess did have an effect on me even though I knew they arose from envy rather than impartial observation. It did appear to me that The Four were taking much for granted in terms of my potential. Between us, Bert and I had created very little (except trouble!) and whereas I was his disciple in some ways, Bert was only a mouthpiece for Hans Seersach. If the truth were known both of us rode on the back of the Fleming's genius and it would be some time before my native talent flourished.

But that late, late summer, those dreams, the delay, the waiting . . . I needed all the self-esteem I could muster to offset the fear that my mind had outgrown my body. Had I arrested my natural progress towards potency by too much study? by too much hammering away at my cock? My days became filled with these terrors. As the town heated up and the river dried out to a trickle, I burned like a flake of glowing ash about to go out. Death and waste oppressed me and I suffered from many nightmares, some of them so horrible my cries brought Lucy and the other guests running to my room in the middle of the night. I took to wandering the countryside in the darkness, trying to keep cool and away from my bed and my own hand. There was never a cloud to shut out the moon and stars so I could always see my way. I wandered for miles in all directions, oblivious of the dangers as those within myself were ten times worse. Eventually I fell ill. I could feel it coming but could not resist. When the sickness took hold of me it was almost a relief from the madness I had been enduring. I could not go out and listen to the parched sheep bleating in the darkness. I could not mooch about the stinking streets with the rats frolicking in the night-heat. I was flattened, all my energy pressed out of me. My endeavours had to cease while a fever and a livid rash worked their ways through my flesh.

Lucy nursed me through all this. She bathed me every hour in my bed and fed me with a spoon because I was so weak, holding my head to her bosom. When I could take more solid food she fed me with her fingers. Gradually the rash died away but she did not reduce the number of washings she gave me. As she applied the sponge her lips always moved and I heard the beat of her breath. Sometimes she blew on my skin and smiled. By the end of my illness I knew the waiting would soon be over.

I had been afraid my returning strength would manifest itself in the vice which had mortified Father Horace. As Lucy continued to bathe me long after I could do it myself, I found a way of gripping my cock from between my legs and drawing it down to prevent it rising. Lucy never commented on the effect this created as if she had come to believe that all men adopt this defence when they are out of sorts.

On the afternoon of the twenty-eighth of August — the Feast of Saint Augustine of Hippo (as Father Horace had informed me that morning while we pored over the ablative case of source, agency and action in Latin nouns), as Lucy was washing me I felt a sudden sharp pain in the upper arm of the hand holding the erection down. I released my grip and my terrible cock was flung up like the arm of a released catapult. Putting the needle she had pricked me with into her bodice, Lucy threw one leg over me, took the head of my cock and eased it into herself with one skilled motion. Helplessly enraptured I lay beneath her while she rode me, praying to come as a man comes. I did, and that was my first time, thanks to her.

She was not my dream, and I was not hers, but where she took me that day was as close to heaven as mortal men can go on earth. I was a man at last. If I could put it into words, I would: if I could put it into stone, I would: but no eloquence or art is up to that challenge. Love's feeling is our bond with the original moment of creation in all its imperfection: it is our share of the great generative orgasm of the Gods.

It was Maurice Welbilove who, with Lucy, had helped my father get away from Guildford. He returned to the castle on his way back to London from the West Country in the middle of September of that year, 1251. He sought me out in my room and gave me news that Bert was safely in the north. Bert wanted to know how I had been treated in the interim. Had the father's sins been visited upon the son? I had to say they had not.

"Has there been no sign of displeasure?" Maurice asked, sitting on the end of my bed for he had come visiting at a late hour and I had turned in for the night, my books spread all around me.

"No one has mentioned it," I replied, my hands behind my head as I leant back on the pillow.

"That will be difficult to tell your father."

I sat upright, scattering rolls of drawings and calculations off the bed.

"Do you know where he is?"

Maurice shook his head.

"I don't know where to find him but he knows where to find me," he said. "I am a King's officer, on oath, and I cannot aid fugitives."

"But you helped Bert to escape," I said, insisting.

"He was not a fugitive then, nor was he a prisoner, as far as I had been told. He was a white cutter who wanted to borrow a horse, and that was that."

I had to laugh. Maurice had a style of self-presentation full of ingenuousness; as if he were made unhappy by the slowness of his wits; but I had seen him with his melancholy stripped away. If Bert needed allies within the King's service he would not find better than this lugubrious Lancastrian.

With sudden interest he leant forward and pinched my shoulder.

"You're filling out. Is Lucy feeding you well?" he said with a flicker of fun. "She's a good mother."

I blushed hotly and ransacked my brain for something else to talk about. Maurice gave a swift, knowing look.

"She is a kind and generous woman. Bert owes her a great deal which should be paid somehow. Hasn't it been hot?" he went on without pause, picking up a page of Euclidean area geometry. "What's all this?"

"I am trying to find a method of calculating the thrust of a dome downwards and outwards," I explained. "Domes are my favourite."

Maurice fingered the parchment.

"Then you are your father's son. One thing he did ask me to convey to you when we said goodbye: he hates Master Henry de Reyns and takes him to be a sodomite, no less. He demands that you never allow yourself to be polluted by that kind of thing."

Maurice looked at me hard, his tousled eyebrows raised as high as a hare's ears. In his eyes there was no embarrassment; in fact there may have been some accusation, but I could not be sure.

"Master Henry is not a sodomite," I replied, looking down and fiddling with my books. "He has never touched me."

"Never goes near a woman," Maurice reminded me. "Surrounds himself with boys."

"Now you have polluted *him!*" I cried angrily. "How will I be able to speak to him again with that in my mind?"

Maurice held his gauntleted hands open and shrugged.

"It was your father's wish I should put it to you. Also, I have to say, amongst those who work close to him, and by general reputation, he is held to be what your father suspects."

"That means nothing," I protested, now up on my knees on the bed, so violent was my indignation. "Gossip and rumour! Who would be guided by that? Only a fool!"

Maurice got up off the bed.

"If you get into serious trouble, tell Lucy to get in touch with me," he said as he opened the door. "She knows how I like her cooking as well as you do. And respect your father, Hedric. There is no one he cares for more than you."

Then he was gone, whistling.

I listened to his boots going down the passage. They faltered and nearly halted outside Lucy's room but then continued more swiftly than before.

In a manner I could not completely fathom, my comprehension and memory welled up into a fresh dimension in anticipation of my journey to Paris. Ideas that had evaded me came smoothly into my understanding and a host of detailed processes of calculation and reasoning were made my servants. My day started earlier and earlier as the drought went on and I found it more congenial to think intensely without the sun glaring into my room. By ten o'clock the haze and dust were so thick inside the bailey walls I had to take refuge in the woods with my books to get better shade. Cattle and sheep were my companions there, keeping close to the river. A large amount of livestock had already died through thirst and the castle wells were in daily use by water-wagons helping to sustain the outlying farms.

Yet nothing would stop me being back in my quarters for dinner. The furniture was covered with dust, even the food itself was gritty with the stuff, but it could not dispel the allure of those afternoons. They seem to have gone on for more than the waking day. As the castle slept in the sun's blaze Lucy taught me how to play Love's game, not cruelly, or with cheating, but fairly. It was upsetting for me at first when she would doze off and wake with my father's name on her lips, but I made myself get used to that. I was, after all, his son and of his blood: if that could comfort her then she was welcome.

It did not rain until the second day of October. We were lying on my bed asleep when the thunder came rolling from the west with a strong, fresh wind following. We knelt up and saw the huge plum-coloured clouds towering up towards the sun. When the first shadow came the birds began to sing again after more than two months of silence.

It began to rain at seven o'clock that evening and did not stop until dawn. There was no sleep for me that night. The break in the weather had wrought a violent change in Lucy who, until then, had seemed to me to be a creature of habit. There was little of the matron left in her with the rain beating down and the earth breathing strange scents: she was moved by older passions I did not, as yet, understand; as if she could sense the end of things and wanted to take as much from life as she could before it was all snatched away.

Two days later I received my summons to Lincoln from Robert Grosseteste and the news that Paris was in the thrall of a pestilence. I would have to wait until word was received telling us the city was free before I could take up my scholarship.

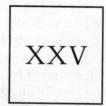

XXV

The Bishop of Lincoln had sent me a text to contemplate on my journey. I was to travel from Guildford to Oxford during the last week in October, starting out on the Feast of Saint Felix of Carthage. Before I reached Oxford I was enjoined to have penetrated the true meaning of what Aristotle says in Book Five of the Physics, namely: "Nature always takes the shortest way." From the day of my arrival in Oxford I was to remain eight more then travel to Lincoln via Leicester and Nottingham with a party of students and scholars. During my stay in Oxford I was to be in the care of the Franciscans. Between Oxford and Lincoln I was to contemplate a text to be imparted to me by someone in that order of friars, provided I had given satisfactory proof of an understanding of "Nature operates in the shortest way possible." (Which Old Robert obviously didn't!)

As an ancillary to this syllabus I was exhorted to examine the life of Saint Felix himself, upon whose feast-day I was commanded to set out upon my journey. This research did not take me long but its message was clear. Felix was a bishop at the city of Carthage in North Africa when the Roman Emperor Diocletian began his persecution of the Cretins. Felix was ordered by the authorities to hand in all his books for burning. He refused, declaring in front of the proconsul it were better that he, Felix, be destroyed himself than sacred knowledge should suffer. The proconsul immediately obliged him by having his head struck off, then burned the books at his leisure.

Whatever instructions I had received from Old Robert did not allay the concern then closest to me — my dear Lucy. When she learnt of my forthcoming departure her strange, autumnal desperation increased. By the time I was to leave there was hardly enough strength in me to climb up on the horse. She did not cry, only gripped me by the hand as a man will do, and smiled stoically. As our small party rode across the green towards the gatehouse she walked alongside my horse, her arms folded over her breast and her head bent. I held back my horse to allow the others through and be last, making time for a farewell kiss. As I bent down to her she turned away and hurried back, her woman's shape one among the many as servants, maids, washerwomen and all the assorted workfolk of the castle crossed each other's paths in the morning bustle, each one indistinguishable from the next. Soon she was lost to my sight, not that my vision was unimpeded, my eyes being full of tears.

Ours was a mixed party that morning: my travelling companions were three Dominicans, one of whom was part-paralysed and kept sliding off his horse; two old brothers, officers of the King's household, off on leave to their family home in Gloucestershire; five cattle-drovers from the Welsh marches who had asked to join us for protection; a choir-boy from the King's chapel in Windsor on his way to Oxford with his mother (he had to ride at the head of the party so he would not get dust in his throat); our armed guard of six men, and me. On the north-western edge of the town we were joined by a solitary rider who let us go by then tagged along behind us. He was of middle age, very sharp in the eye, with a long nose and jutting chin. When our sergeant saw him following he stopped the column and waited for him to catch up. The man halted and wrapped his broad blue cloak around him as if he had not noticed our presence at all and was merely about his private business. One of the soldiers galloped back and spoke to the man then grabbed his rein and pulled the horse along to make the man face our sergeant.

"Can't get any sense out of him," the soldier reported. "I think he's mad."

"What's the matter?" the sergeant asked the man. "You can't ride with us."

"I don't want to ride with you. I want to ride behind you," the stranger replied in a harsh, high voice.

"That won't do," the sergeant replied. "This party is the King's responsibility. We want no one shadowing us before or behind, if you please. You'll have to wait an hour if you want to use this road."

"Then that is what I will do," the man said with a tight grin, working his jaws as if his promise troubled him.

A little way further on there was a small hill. I asked permission from the sergeant to ride ahead and look back over the town. So much had happened to me there I would never truly leave it: the boy I had been was buried within the castle walls. Around the bailey and on both sides of the High Street, the yards and yards of Guildford Blue were hung out by the dyers to dry. From where I was looking it seemed as if part of the sky had fallen down.

I heard the sergeant calling and turned my horse's head. No more looking back, I said to myself as I spurred over to rejoin the column before it disappeared between the trees.

In my life I have found that walking induces thought but riding induces nothing but discomfort. Try as I might I could not get my mind to apply itself to Aristotle's dictum: "Nature always takes the shortest way," while mounted on a jolting hack that strayed from one side of the road to the other, shook itself every minute, farted frequently, and obviously resented my presence on its back. Is this horse intrinsically natural? I asked myself. Or is it an essence of horsiness? It is a difficult, uncomfortable creature subject to a difficult, uncomfortable force, Nature. May we assume the force and the horse are synonymous and coincident, in *nuda veritas*, identical? This was not Aristotle's case at all but by the time we had reached Reading it was certainly the case of my poor arse. After all the months in Guildford I was no longer travel-hardened. One forgets how motion affects the mind, disturbing its mechanisms. For every ache of the body there is an equal pain in the intellect, making coherent thought arduous. No matter how many books Old Robert had written I guessed none of them were put together on horseback. My examination of the Stagyrite's dictum would have to wait until I had regained a modicum of *stasis*.

That night we were housed at the royal castle at Reading and the Dominicans decided to take their afflicted brother to touch the right hand of Saint James at the old Cluniac abbey. More for the purpose of enlisting me as a carrier than as companion, they invited me to go along with them. As I wished to study the building, then over a hundred years old and the first of the new black monk structures from that time, I went along and took my share of the burden.

We borrowed one of the castle hand-carts and put Brother Bartholomew in it, preferring to take him in this style rather than have to get back on our horses and re-awaken our sores. As we pushed him out of the main gate we came face to face with the man in the blue cloak who had tried to follow us that morning. He was standing beneath a tree with his horse's reins in his hands. We passed him without pausing, hurrying on as all of us thought he must be mad. A moment later I looked over my shoulder and he was following, leading his horse, a short sword over his shoulder.

As we were off the King's highway and in the borough there were no prohibitions we could invoke so we ran, Brother Bartholomew hanging on to the sides of the cart and complaining that this was as bad as being in the saddle. The man mounted and galloped ahead of us, barring the way.

We stopped the cart and stood breathing hard, looking up at him.

"Are you taking him to the rubbish-pit?" he asked with a fleck of foam on his lips.

"What do you want?" one of the Dominicans demanded in a quavering, wheedling tone. "We have nothing of value. Do not obstruct us, dear soul."

The man put his sword away, wrinkling his long nose at the friar's pusillanimousness. He suddenly shot a finger forward, pointing straight at me.

"Where are you taking this fellow?"

"Who is it wants to know?" I replied with some haughtiness, aware that the madman was encouraged by cowardice.

"I am the Earl of Leicester's man and I have orders to watch over you. There is nothing I have been told that says I must trust these brothers with you. There is nothing I have been told that says they may not be abducting your person at this very moment. Go back to the castle and go to bed."

I stared up at him in astonishment. The Dominicans murmured in protest at the calumny but when I tried to insist I accompany them to the abbey they shrank away, not wanting the trouble.

"I wish to see the abbey as part of my studies," I said to the man. "I am an architect."

"Ha! These brothers will not have invited you along for that purpose. They hate education as they hate work," he replied with his sharp eyes boring into mine. "Get up behind me and I'll take you there myself."

I could not refuse, it being obvious that the Dominicans were anxious to see the back of me. Behind the madman, my sore bum jolting on the edge of his saddle, I went to the abbey and sketched for an hour with the madman always by my side. As we left and rode back to the castle he pointed out that the Dominicans had not turned up to give Brother Bartholomew the benefit of the famous relic's curative powers.

Nor were they with us when we resumed our journey to Oxford the following morning.

The madman was called Nicholas Hawsley and he was, in truth, mad in a certain manner. Returning with him that evening through the dusky streets of Reading I made an effort to find out how and why he had been sent to look after me when I was already in the King's care. His response was to unleash a vituperative attack on the King's competence, saying that no man, woman or child in England was safe; that the laws were flouted with impunity, especially by the King and his officers; and that he was the principal victim of this anarchy, as had been his father before him and his father before him. Three kings had wrecked and dispossessed three generations of his family, once yeomen in Hathersage, Derbyshire, now a scattered clan of mercenary soldiers.

"It has turned my mind," he confessed over his shoulder, "which is why you might find me a mite peculiar."

I held my tongue, aware of the hardness of his body under my hand. Mad or not, peculiar or not, I had no wish to be on the wrong side of him.

From then on until we got to Oxford he allowed me to forget him though I was always conscious of him somewhere over my shoulder.

We reached Oxford by nightfall of the second day, having pressed on when we discovered we had made such good time. The sergeant's decision to do this was against his orders and it was a sign of the laxness of the King's administration that our company was put at risk by travelling in the dark. Sure enough, when we were within five miles of Oxford itself we were attacked. Our guard immediately fell apart and we had to scatter, meeting up on the road further on after an hour of blundering around in the woods. The sergeant apologised, counted us all and expressed himself satisfied — why I don't know as there were two of us missing, a drover and one of the Gloucestershire brothers — then insulted us by asking the choir-boy to sing for the rest of the journey to keep our spirits up. His mother, still in a state of nerves, struck the sergeant on the head with her stick which did for us all as we were disgusted by the timidity of our protectors, perhaps a demonstration of Nature's short ways when survival is in question.

Having come into the town so late we were not able to see it clearly, except it was a populous place with many mean buildings packed together. The streets were full of mud from the recent rain. We dismounted beneath the walls of the priory church of Saint Frideswide and I was heartened by the vastness of its tower and spire looming over the damp street. The yard of the church was full of stone and timber and a masons' lodge stood close to the north wall but I found it empty when I went over and knocked on the door. Its presence was a comfort, however, and I made my mind up to visit them when the opportunity arose.

Having disbanded the party, the sergeant took me to the royal castle. The dark streets were sporadically lit by moving torches as gangs of youths paraded past, jeering at the guard in their livery, calling out "A Montfort! A Montfort!" and thrusting their torches under our horses' noses to make them rear. The sergeant swore under his breath but did not retaliate. It was only when we were within a hundred yards of the castle gates that this open provocation ceased but even then I heard stones landing around us in the darkness, thrown by our tormentors.

At the castle gatehouse we came upon the cattle-drover and the brother from Gloucestershire whom we had lost in the forest. They were unhurt, having been saved by the madman, as they called him. He had brought both in and left them where he knew they would meet up with the guard. After giving the sergeant a good tongue-lashing for his haste and negligence the two men went to find lodging for the night while I, in thoughtful mood, entered the King's stronghold wondering whose side anyone was on in this strange country any more.

I was not in the castle long, more is the pity. Waiting for me there was the lay master of the Franciscan house, a tall, prematurely white-headed man in his prime who had huge, sad brown eyes. When I met him he did not say a word but ran his fingers over my coat, shaking his head disapprovingly. When he saw my baggage he held his head and sighed. As I lugged it along behind him — he offered no help — I could not resist asking him if I had done anything wrong.

"The Franciscans are a poor community," he said in a nasal West Country drone. "They value anyone's poverty."

And he was not lying. The house I was conducted to was bare, cold and draughty, badly constructed and ill-kept. My room was no more than a cupboard, having no window, and the jakes so

237

squalid and unseemly I preferred to go out in the rain to relieve myself.

As I was preparing to settle down for the night, tired and sore from my travels, drained by our adventures, the master returned and sat himself cross-legged by my bed, a candle between us. He rubbed his bush of springy, white hair, put his small chin in his hands and started to drone.

"You can't go to sleep yet, student. Order your mind to keep working a while. We must make a start on Book Five of the Physics. There is not much time. You have had two days to think about it. What does the dictum mean in our terms, today? Does it have a relevance? Before we start must we not have some idea of what Aristotle meant by Nature?"

He paused, oblivious to my reaction which was one of helpless annoyance. My eyelids could scarcely remain open. No food had been given me. Although this man was my senior and I knew it was necessary for me to please him I could not resist showing a flash of temper.

"Is it going to bother Aristotle after fifteen centuries if I do not work on him until the morning?"

The master laughed and left the room. Shortly afterwards he returned with a tray of hot bread, stewed apples and beer. While I ate he washed my feet, chuckling all the while.

"A week will not be enough," he said, his great eyes shining. "You and I will need longer than that to sort out the universe. My name is Roger Bacon, a master here but still a student. I have come up with no answers to amaze you or the Bishop of Lincoln, whose protégés we are, for our pains. The students call me Ham, their humour not being as developed as yours. Good night. Sleep well. I will call you at a decent hour."

With a final flourish of the towel he got to his feet and carried the bowl out, leaving me the candle. I could not sleep, the food churning in my belly and my brain fired by the identity of the man who had been in my room. After Grosseteste he was the most advanced philosopher in England, Father Horace had said: equal of Albertus Magnus and all the Dominicans put together. How was I to survive with such a man, coming from my antecedents? Our oppressed Albigensian faith had no scholarship. It was so pure and ancient it did not need any. We did not have to care about reconciling Aristotle's thought with our creed, in fact to do so would be an act of pollution as Aristotle's passion is man in the material world which we hold to be evil. Our leaders had succumbed to this hunger, this mad search for intellectual consistency: this implied a joining of forces, a co-operation between Christian and Albigensian thinkers in order to agree on the ground of the great dispute. The intertwining of our history with the Cretins' had got that far and now I was a crucial point in it, pressed by both sides.

Suddenly I had to escape from the tiny, airless room which had become as oppressive as my concerns. I went out on to a landing and looked out of a window into the street. Students were still about, cavorting with their torches in the rain, fresh from drinking-houses somewhere. They were singing a fierce song I was to learn later, shouting and stamping in the mud:

> I am a wandering scholar lad,
> Oppressed by toil and sadness;
> Aristotle drives me mad
> But doubt's as bad as madness.

In an open field opposite, sheltering beneath his horse's belly, I saw my madman, Nicholas Hawsley. Who better to watch over me in this circumstance? I thought.

Returning to my bed I resigned myself to sleep, hoping for inspiration in the hours of my unconsciousness. Why, why must we bow to Aristotle all the time? He wasn't a Christian, he wasn't a Jew, he wasn't an Albigensian, I said to myself, butting my pillow. Then I paused.

Or was he?

XXVI

Ham (what else could I call him after he had let that slip?) was at my door with the dawn. He took me out into the garden where I washed in a stone trough. Other students were at their ablutions and they gazed at me with curiosity but I had no opportunity to introduce myself: Ham would not stop talking long enough to offer one. He seemed to be very nervous of me now, his good humour of the previous night put away.

"Your protector, the man Hawsley, gave me a message after I had left you last night. It was an instruction from King Henry, counter-signed by the Earl of Leicester, the Bishop of Lincoln and Master Henry de Reyns, the King's mason, that I was to treat you as an equal. Now, I am prepared to do this because I am not a proud man — but you are some twenty-five years younger than I and there is the question of knowledge and experience. You cannot be expected to be capable of the same feats of mind as a man who has had more time to study the world. Have you any comment so far?"

We were walking across a large vegetable garden at the back of the Franciscan house. It was full of weeds and the slugs had had the best of every crop. Two novices were leaning on their hoes, talking. As Ham and I approached they did not swing into action with their tools but merely opened their conversation to us once we had come level with them.

"We were saying, Roger, that it is difficult to define all the possible functions of the *primum mobile*, without knowing the source of its original power . . ." one of them said while making the lightest of scratches at the earth with his hoe.

"Get on with your work!" Ham admonished him sternly. "Think about carrots if you must think about anything." Then he moved on, beckoning me not to get ambushed.

"Science is worse than wine in an empty head," he said with a sigh. "Getting them to do anything but chatter is impossible. Contempla-tion is such a wonderful excuse for doing nothing. Have you ever thought of the amount of time that has been wasted in thought? Add up the sum, my friend. Thousands upon thousands of intelligent and capable men sitting around for centuries, the slaves of inertia: for what? To answer questions that may be unanswerable, and, even if they are not, will certainly prove inedible — unlike the humble carrot."

We had reached the banks of the river. There was a narrow wooden bridge made of poles. Ham picked up a large stone and walked to the centre of the bridge, then held the stone over the water.

"Watch, student! Nature taking the shortest way!"

He dropped the stone and laughed as it splashed into the water below him. Hurrying on over the bridge he strode into the quadrangle of a student hostel which was of recent construction. The quadrangle had been planted out with grass and flowers. Some effort had been made to keep it pretty but the students had taken short-cuts and worn a pattern of paths taking them from any given point to another in the briefest possible distance.

Ham pointed these out, beaming as if they pleased him.

"Nature taking the shortest possible way again!" he shouted over his shoulder. "Do you wish to dispute this now or later? We have all morning."

Whether I did or not was never uppermost in his mind for he marched on out of the quadrangle into a field of old corn stubble. Snapping off a stalk he waited for me to catch up then thrust it under my nose.

"Straight! From root to ear!" he exclaimed. "Are you with me yet? No opposing arguments rearing up inside my equal?"

A bumble bee was gathering pollen from a late red poppy near my feet. I tipped the flower with my toe and the insect flew off on a wavering course. I pointed to it, silently.

"Ha! Very good. We can hardly claim that the bee is carrying out its most urgent function, that of escape, in the shortest possible way. Let us ask why does the bee zig-zag? From observation we know it was gathering pollen: from observation we know it carries that pollen on its legs. May we not surmise it has an erratic and indirect mode of flight because it is carrying more pollen on one side of its body than the other?"

"Therefore all bees must carry more pollen on one side than the other, that following on from the observation that all bees fly in this manner; unless you have seen an unloaded bee flying in a straight line?" I said with bravado.

"I have not. Nor do trees grow straight to accomplish their purposes. Nor do men think straight in order to be saved. Nor do all flowers show their secrets."

He sat down in the corn and cradled the poppy in his hands, staring into the beautiful soot-black centre of its crimson petals: then he snapped the stem and sniffed its milky juice. "A narcotic. The bee was under its influence."

From other flowers the bumbles droned in harmony with his West Country burr. I sat cross-legged beside him as he extemporised about opiates, the effects of the moon on sleep, the alchemic values of algebra, and magic in the Scriptures.

"I do not mean to be disrespectful of those who are my mentors," I said while he was taking a pause for breath, "but it is pointless for them to imagine I am already your equal. Your learning is much deeper than mine."

"Nonsense!" he murmured. "If we are to go to Paris together it must be as brothers. All I've just said is froth."

"Am I to go there with you?" I asked cautiously.

"That is the scheme as far as I know it. I am old enough to be your father but we must go as brothers. One thing you must learn. Don't quote authorities at me. It is only a means of hiding the fact that you have nothing to say of your own. Avoid being overawed by the Ancients. Anything they said can be improved upon. Remember, one individual has more reality than all the universals joined together. Never allow yourself to be crushed by learning."

This was refreshing to me. It was to the credit of The Four that they had asked Ham, in particular, to treat me as a brother. It showed they were anxious to help me grow.

"Let us deal with this rusty old dictum of Aristotle's now," he said briskly. "We must revise your idea of what he meant, or rather what I say he meant and he is not here to contradict me . . . 'that which necessitates the answering of a minimum of questions from a perfect demonstration can be said to be the shortest way as it requires fewer circumstances'. That is what I say he said."

We sat in the cornfield for seven hours while the bumble bees droned round us, swerving in and out of the poppies as Ham meandered through his sequence of proofs, most of which he disclaimed at one point or another. When I could not follow him he knew without being told and retraced his steps, patiently leading me forward again when I was ready. By the time the sun was overhead I knew what Aristotle had said in Book Five of the Physics. It struck me that the Stagyrite could have been clearer about it in the first place, and I said so.

"Ah, you would take the pleasure out of all philosophy if it were made immediately accessible," Ham said, getting to his feet and rubbing his legs. "The best thoughts are directed at future generations, safely beyond the reach of your own. I expect to be fully comprehended after the elapse of another thousand years. Then my wait in eternity will be worth it. What I will do after that for amusement, God knows: maybe I will spend the remainder of the time in refuting myself."

It had been a fine morning but as we returned to the house the rain came back. While we were crossing the vegetable gardens novices were hurrying away with their implements, leaving the weeds to thrive. Ham held out his hands and looked up at the overcast sky.

"To live in this country you must learn to love the rain, Hedric. Is that not so? Is architecture any more than the disciplining of rain? The Stagyrite has little to say on the subject. He lived in a dry country. What do they care about keeping the rain off Greece? Nothing. But we English are different: the rain is part of the air. It is in every thought and action we take. Whatever you design for us in your maturity, remember to invite and coax the rain: make it go where you want, supplicate the rain! Make it your embellishment, not your enemy. To see a wet roof shining is more of a pleasure to me than to see it drab and dry. . . ."

In this vein he continued all through dinner (which was a dire diet, best forgotten), and his cat-nap afterwards, during which I had to sit by his bed and listen while he rambled on about the four causes of ignorance (poignant stuff for me!), indulging in much quotation of authorities in spite of his previous warnings. We had Seneca and Cicero; Averroes and Avicenna, the Arabs; Adelard of Bath and many others before he actually fell asleep.

I looked around his room. It was sparsely furnished, being mostly taken up by a big table littered with writing materials. The head of his bed was under the overhanging edge of the table and I could see texts pinned up on the underside, enabling him to read them while lying down in bed. Craning my neck I encountered columns of mixed letters and figures indecipherable to me. Wavering lines connected different groups of symbols implanted in the columns: these symbols were of a character I had never seen before. As I peered at them I leant on the bed to get closer. Suddenly I heard a chuckle and glanced to my right: Ham was smiling at me, his huge eyes blinking.

"It will never mean anything to you no matter how hard you try," he said with a smirk. "What I have up here is my own language. There is no better protection against the long noses." Raising a hand he stroked the cyphers, levering himself up on his other elbow until the top of his bush of white hair was touching the table.

"Most of my best work has been written in this way," he said in a confiding whisper. "It is a guarantee of anonymity. I have a strong aversion to fame."

That afternoon he took me to one of his classes in Mathematics. My training so far had been mainly in Euclidean geometry and Arithmetic and I frequently got lost in his discourse which seemed to rely heavily on Arabs — Alfarabi and Albumazar among others — and be concerned to demonstrate that Mathematics, whether it be taken from the heathen or not, was the key to the Creation and had to be the only true source of divine wisdom. Many of the other students were as perplexed as I was and some of them protested against the emphasis and weight Ham gave to Mathematics. There was even a suggestion his views inclined towards, if not heresy, a revision of the Church's teaching on the nature of God. Ham shrugged and referred his accusers back to the various proofs he had demonstrated.

"There are two authorities Man cannot argue with," he said blandly, "God and Mathematics. If they are not one and the same thing then whoever holds that opinion is admitting a second supreme authority in the universe, and *that* is heresy."

The older students — some of whom were men in their thirties — were those who disagreed with him most. Ham had a greater popularity with the younger ones. When the tutorial was over many of these stayed behind to talk further. I had much to think about so I asked Ham's permission to visit the church of Saint Frideswide where I would be able to meet the masons — practical men with their feet on the ground who employed Mathematics in a less abstruse usage.

"This is Hedric who is an extra-mural student in architecture,"

Ham explained. "He requires applied proofs, and rightly so, *operae pretium est*! Yes, get a demonstration out of your stonemasons. They may do better than we philosophers. Don't be surprised if they throw you off the site. They don't like students."

It took me no more than twenty minutes to walk from where the tutorial had been held to Saint Frideswide's. The streets were full of students running through the rain between classes, their bags held under their shirts to keep them dry. It occurred to me I was the only one on my particular course; my university extending far beyond these muddy streets and half-erected buildings. The mass of these young men were being fitted into an existing structure in order to sustain and strengthen it against change; but the power at the heart of that same structure was preparing to alter it and, in so doing, make all prior education defunct. These students were racing to classes I would make obsolete within the decade if I found the Third Style of Emergence and the New Way. Yet I wanted to hasten with them, to be one of their company, sharing their aspirations and ideas even though it was my task to make them futile. Made solitary by these thoughts I slouched on through the rain.

"Where are you going?"

It was Nicholas Hawsley, his blue cloak held over my head as he walked along by my side. "You look as though you have a lot on your mind."

"I'm going to the masons' lodge at Saint Frideswide's," I answered as casually as I could.

"What for?"

"They are doing work that interests me."

"I will have to come along," he said, wrapping the cloak closer around my head. "Something might fall on you."

There was no one in the lodge when we called so we entered the church. I admired the odd Corinthian columns and the double arches they supported, finding it all very reminiscent of drawings I had seen of the basilicas of Rome. Someone had worked and saved money all his life to make a journey to that city and had brought back the idea for this design in his head.

Beyond the nave, to the west of the choir aisle, we could hear the sounds of men working. Slowly I paced up, stopping to examine the richly carved capitals of each pillar. My madman kept behind me and I could sense his insane eyes darting from side to side, roaming over the upper levels of the triforium and clerestory. When I had reached the last column before the rood screen there was a loud shout. Hawsley threw himself in front of me, his hand on the hilt of his sword.

"Oi! What do you think you're doing," the owner of the voice bellowed. "You can only come in here for mass. If you're a pilgrim you've had it because the shrine's shut."

A short, stout, balding man waddled out from between the pillars on the north side. His mouth was as big as his voice, something akin to a frog's in its shape. He was wearing a leather apron with a pocket full of tools.

"We were only looking," I said over Hawsley's shoulder, who was growling softly. "I'm an apprentice white cutter."

"From where? What name? Let me see your indentures," the mason demanded. "You should have sent word. This isn't the way to do things, you should know that."

"I'm staying at the Franciscan house . . ." I began to say.

"You're a student?" he roared back at me, his mouth gaping in disbelief. "You're a student and you don't know better than to just walk in here while we're working? Out you get, and your monkey with you!"

Hawsley snapped his sword back into his scabbard.

"Don't worry, he's all wind," he said. "This is a man who will listen to reason without having to have his throat cut. Talk to him."

The mason paused, his eyes looking into Hawsley's which were unpleasantly bright and threatening. I walked to one side, hoping the mason would follow me. After trying to stare Hawsley out, and failing, he came over.

"So? What do you want?" he grumbled.

"Master Henry de Reyns, the King's mason, is in charge of my apprenticeship now," I said to him. "Before that I was with my father. I doubt if you have heard of him."

The mason frowned and thrust his hands into the pocket of his apron in disgust.

"Obscure or not, your father will have given you a name at some time, or perhaps you've taken Master Henry's?" he said surlily.

I told him my name and was gratified to see it meant something to him.

"Come with me," he said after a moment's thought, "but your bully has to wait here."

246

Hawsley sank to his knees on the cold floor, his long chin raised to the roof.

"At last, an opportunity to say my prayers," he said with an odd snort of laughter. "God has missed my voice lately. Mason, do not harm that boy or you will answer to me and the Earl of Leicester."

Without responding to this, the mason led me through to where he had been working. They were building a Lady Chapel in the Second Style, laying it alongside the choir which was done in a dying flourish of the First. As I passed from one to the other I felt the jolt of that change, then the inertia of what my brothers were building. Although it was new it was already frozen into the past, a reproduction of something fulfilled and exhausted. Even the bodily motions of those working on the chapel seemed slow and unwilling, as if they did not wish to participate further in such a waste. We were standing in a half-constructed hiatus.

"You don't need protection from us if you are on the level," the mason said, grumbling. "There's no one here who wants trouble. Do you need anything from us? Master Henry did send word of your coming though he didn't ask for us to do anything in particular."

"No, I just wanted to be with my own folk," I said alarmed by the feeling that took hold of me. "It's been a long time since I was with a working lodge." Now I was close to tears and the mason was looking at me enquiringly. "Let me watch, or even do something if there is a job within my abilities," I muttered, turning away, defeated by my tears.

The mason was mollified by my humility. He stuck his chest out and swaggered up and down between the piles of cut limestone, looking about him, his frog's mouth snapping.

"Well, I'm not sure what there is for a friend of the King's mason and an intimate of Earl Simon but I should be able to find something to keep you occupied for a few hours. No pay, mind you. Strictly educational. Ever tried a flower? We had one broken on a spandrel yesterday, see up there, at the springing . . . by the stiff-leaf. . . . Want to try it? Or is it beyond you? Are you freestone yet? Or is it basic white cutting you've been on? No matter. Give it a try, son."

He laughed as he rooted around in his apron pocket and produced a handful of small, fine chisels, which he gave me, then led me to a bench where he put a small block of medium-grade half-marble into a vice. The other workers watched all this from up on the scaffolding, curious to know what an intruder was doing at such a sacred workplace as the head mason's own bench.

For the remainder of that day I worked on my minor item of repair. It was to be no more than five inches across and mortared into the damaged stiff-leaf pattern, it being not in a prominent place that would be noticed by anyone passing. When I asked the head mason what sort of flower he wanted he made a joke of it:

"Whatever you like, but we favour those that are identifiable," he said. "No flowers that are meant to stand for all flowers, if you know what I mean. A flower you can look at and say, ah, that's a . . . whatever it is."

So I did him a poppy, that being still fresh in my mind. I would have liked to add the philosopher's nose but my freedom of choice did not extend that far. When I had finished I called the head mason over. He carefully examined my handiwork, running his fingertips over it.

"That will do well," he said, "though it could do with a little more sanding."

"Do you recognise the flower?" I asked him.

"It's what I expected: a rose. Every boy your age will do a rose. Let's hope it did you some good. Now, be on your way while we pack up."

I left the Lady Chapel and went to find Hawsley, not wanting to leave him in the church in case further antagonisms developed. He was exactly where I had left him, his back against a pillar, his legs thrust out. Black Augustinian canons stepped politely over him on their ways to their Opus Dei in the choir, assuming him to be asleep; but I could see the gleam of his eyes in cat-slits he had left open. He thrust himself against the pillar and shoved his body up with his legs.

"That's the longest I've ever prayed in my life," he said thoughtfully. "I got into the right rhythm after the first hour: the things I saw in my mind! the thinking I did! There's a world I've wasted." Then he smacked his cheek and started striding towards the west doors. "Truth won't be found here, Hedric, my lad," he shouted, waving at the massive Corinthian columns. "We've spent the afternoon in a whorehouse for angels."

XXVII

The remainder of my time in Oxford was spent encountering men of widely different opinion, though all professed to hold common ideas and beliefs within their respective disciplines. The Ancients were respected but undermined: the heathen and alien were closely examined and anything of use lauded far above its real value. That Ham was deliberately bringing me face to face with as many diverse interpretations of the universe as possible was obvious to me; nor did he shrink from pointing out that every one of the proponents of these views claimed to be a devout member of the Church. It did not need saying that they could not all be right, nor that all these unorthodox ideas would be immediately abandoned should the Church contest them. The situation amused my tutor.

"The best students are always the best heretics," he said as we sat drinking ale after a protracted discussion on the essence of music with eight youths from Northumbria. "Every mind of quality has two levels of religious thought: one conforms in keeping with the natural need to survive within the law; the second is the more penetrating, knowing faith, based on observation and inductive reasoning. It is on this second level we encounter God. I believe all men of true sense see the same God once they have scrutinised the creation: the Pope, the King, the bagpipe-player, all end up in the same Church, but it is not Mother Church: nor is it your church."

"Then how have these churches arisen if there is one perception of the truth?" I asked.

"Because men of sense have not controlled the affairs of men. If I rack my brains for a time when a man of sense had influence over earthly power I would have to go back to the first five years of Nero's reign when the playwright Seneca ruled the Roman Empire for him: then he fell, and what a falling off there was to follow him!"

I looked across the room to where Hawsley was sitting, a pot in his hand, his mad eyes fixed on the wall. Around him brawled a crowd of grimy students who were mocking their own studies in medicine, spitting down each other's ears, feeling each other's balls and so on. He sighed frequently.

"For true religion who must we turn to?" I asked Ham, my eyes still on Hawsley. "When we are lost, or sick, how do we find the men of sense?"

Ham grinned and clutched two handfuls of his springy white hair as if in despair.

"Ah, there you have it," he said with a little scream, "once they know someone is after them, they hide. God never meant the men of sense to rule but only to be a thorn in the side. Religion cannot be agreed upon, only imposed. For those without sense — the majority — religious truth must be created by force, not revelation."

"Perhaps we had better just stick to music," I replied with a groan as the medical students started probing each other for piles. "It is a lot less confusing."

"Which music?" Ham responded wickedly. "Have you heard Saracen music? Indian music? The music of the Khans? The question is, Hedric, is there one original music that was played during the Creation? And have we distorted it merely by *listening* to it? Or was it imperfectly composed to begin with? Does God have a good human ear?"

I stared at Ham in surprise. He met my eye for a moment, then buried his nose in his ale. As I was waiting for him to give me back his attention Hawsley became so disgusted with the medical students and their antics he booted one of them. A fracas began and we were forced to leave.

"Do they realise some of us ordinary people actually have piles?" Hawsley roared once out in the street. "When I pay for treatment, is that the kind of man I'm giving my hard-earned money to?"

"A far more important question than any we have spent our time discussing," Ham murmured to me as we hurried back to the Franciscan house. "Come on, I want to show you an experiment I'm conducting. You'll find it useful as well as interesting. . . ."

The end of his sentence was drowned out by another huge shout from Hawsley who shadowed us from across the street.

"Whom can I trust?" he bellowed. "Who deserves my respect?"

"When I say *show* you an experiment, that is not truly accurate," Ham said as we went down the cellar steps of the Franciscan house. "All I can really do is take you into the presence of it."

Unlocking a small door set in the furthermost, darkest corner he crouched down, beckoning me to do likewise.

"Beyond this point we will be in absolute darkness. Keep hold of the hem of my shirt," he said, his eyes bigger than ever in the poor light. "And do not speak, only listen."

He blew out the candle. I reached forward and took hold of the tail of his shirt and followed him as he carefully moved forward through the door.

"Pull it close behind you," Ham whispered.

I did so. As the door shut Ham started moving again and I lost my grip on his shirt. I cried out in the blackness. Almost immediately I was gripped by the neck.

"Ssh! I'm here! Don't use your voice. The subject mustn't hear any other voice than mine."

I was full of questions as I stumbled along behind Ham. We travelled for at least thirty yards, a foetid stench getting stronger as we progressed. Then Ham stopped and pulled me close to him, putting his hand over my mouth to caution me.

"Are you there Gregory?" he called out.

There was an instant reply: a mixture between a groan and a grunt as if someone were waking up.

"Are you well?" Ham asked in a peculiar sing-song.

There was another, more complex reply in which there were words but they were so slurred and malformed I could not make them out.

"Good, good," Ham replied soothingly. "I will be back to talk to you tonight."

Suddenly there was a terrifying outburst of screaming and a sound of a body crashing into a wall. The rattle of chains and bars accompanied this horrible din. I felt Ham tugging at me to follow him and quickly found the tail of his shirt. My heart was thumping wildly and I felt nauseous as I crept along through the darkness, running away from the poor mortal cooped up in that disgusting place. It was not until we were safely through the outer door and had it shut behind us that the screams stopped. Ham strode off through the cellar and up the steps into the sunlight, leaving me to tag along as best I could. I found myself shaking and unable to walk in a straight line. When I got out of the cellar I ran to the garden and was sick.

Ham made no attempt to comfort me and it was not until an hour later that he bothered to speak to me. By then I was indignant about the fate of the prisoner. For a place of learning to be used as a penitentiary struck me as a wicked travesty, and I did not hesitate to say so.

251

"It is not what it seems," Ham assured me. "Gregory is a prisoner by choice. If he were not here, giving me valuable assistance with my researches, he would be dead."

"He might as well be dead!" I said hotly. "Why should anyone choose an existence like that?"

"Gregory was a priest, once. He committed murder, killing a King's officer. The Bishop of Lincoln, our patron, refused to allow him to be tried except in the church court and there was a serious disagreement with the King. Gregory was found guilty," Ham paused, looking at me to see if I could work the rest out for myself.

"What was his choice then?" I demanded. "He was found guilty and imprisoned. But why here? Why not in one of the church prisons?"

Ham gave me an annoyed glance.

"He is not a prisoner in the full sense of the word. He was approached by the bishop and asked if he would rather help us in our experiments on the effects of the deprivation of light on the human soul, spirit and physique or go to the gallows."

"You call that a choice?" I said, my bile rising again.

"It was a very savage murder he did. His motive was greed and self-interest. No man has been more contrite than Gregory. When we bring him out at the December equinox and give him a full examination he will, I hope, feel that some part of his crime has been forgiven."

"But the man is mad. His speech has gone which means his mind has gone also . . ." I argued passionately. "Anyone with common sense can tell you what will happen if you lock a man, or even an animal, up in total darkness."

"Guesswork. For instance, Hedric, would you say that Gregory will, of necessity, have lost his faith by the time we bring him out? When faced with the hangman he was afraid of Hell."

"Having been in Hell I doubt whether that terrifies him any more," I retorted, "and if you offered him death or his imprisonment again, providing he has enough of his wits left to judge sensibly, I'd say he'd choose the gallows."

"An assumption you cannot make," Ham said with a grin. "His moods change. Today he was in despair but I have spent hours with him when he has been calm, lucid and amiable. After all, his state is only a copy of that of the desert fathers, the hermits and anchorites; they lived in a not dissimilar fashion, with one exception. And what was that?"

"They had light," I said grudgingly and with a sigh to signify my objection.

"True, so, perhaps light is the *most essential* element of our vitality? Certainly our Gregory does not often behave like the desert fathers, but he can be serene when he feels like it."

"He didn't feel like it just now, did he?" I said boldly. "This experiment is the gallows in disguise. It may take longer but the result will be the same. He'll die."

"Ah, but the result is the same for all of us," Ham replied. "What is important is the process. Gregory is going through an uncommonly intense experience, I agree, but it only means a result will be provided sooner than Nature can manage."

That night there was uproar in Oxford. I heard it as I lay in my bed, gloomily working out The Four's plans for me. I was no more than Gregory to them; a subject in a desperate experiment made by men driven half-mad by unknowing. All the old certainties had gone from under their feet. Christ looked down at them with a foreign face and he could not speak their language any more. The world was too much for their understanding: in mine it was still the botched work of the Evil God, brother of the Good, and to this sense I clung as sleep withdrew me from all philosophy into dreams.

The next morning I went to Ham's room but he was out. From other residents of the Franciscan house I discovered all the masters had been called to an urgent meeting at the castle. The uproar I had heard during the night had been a running battle between the northern and southern students; people had been killed; also properties had been set alight and much destruction done in the town. Ham did not return until noon. He had no time to talk except to forbid me to go into the streets which were, he said, still dangerous. After he had gone back out again I tried to read some Seneca but the temptation to see what was happening was too strong. I went out and headed for the centre of the town. Within a minute Hawsley was by my side.

"You missed the best of it last night," he said with a breathless chuckle. "What a time we had. Blood was shed for both sides of the Trent."

He walked with difficulty, half doubled up. There was a contusion on his right temple and his hair had been singed. When he saw I had noticed his injuries he straightened up.

253

"The medical students?" I asked.

"Oh, no, the King's students, the northern students, the students of Christ, but not the medical students. They were still staring up each other's arses when I saw them last." He put an arm across and stopped me. "No further. It's not over yet. They're playing tag with hatchets. The northern nation holds the town."

Further down the street I could see smoke too great for any chimney to emit. Figures ran across the spaces between the houses shouting shrilly.

"We will have to go earlier than was planned," Hawsley said as he pulled me into a doorway. "These lads are after southern blood. I swore to them that I hated the King. I swore an oath I was Earl Simon's man. It made no difference, they beat me anyway. Maybe I said the wrong thing, or I'm too old to be treated kindly. We must pack your things and be gone before they get to the Franciscan house. The northern nation hates the Franciscans because they're as poor as them."

A mob appeared at the end of the street. Before they could see us Hawsley pulled me round the side of the building and down an alley which led towards the river. We ran through the meadows until we were back at the Franciscan house. It was already deserted. Hawsley bounded up the stairs to my room, hurled my books and clothes into my bag, then led me to his horse which was tethered in the vegetable gardens. As we galloped out on to the road we could see the mob already half-way up the street. I clung to Hawsley's back and turned my face away. It was a strange time to think the thought but all that would come into my mind as we pelted along the dusty road to the north was the memory of Gregory's stench and the sound of his screams in the darkness of the cellar.

Hawsley did not arrest our headlong flight until we were several miles out of Oxford. By then the horse was beginning to feel the pace under its double burden. Hawsley made me dismount then got off himself, giving me the reins to lead the animal. We walked along in silence for an hour. Now and then I heard Hawsley take his breath in sharply.

"An education cut short can be worse than no education at all," he said as we came to the top of a rise and looked down at a village between the trees. "If you know nothing it can be better than half of something. I'll have to sit down for a while. They kicked me in the belly and I'm bleeding into my mouth."

He went to sit down in the grass by the roadside but pitched forward before he could get there. I rolled him over on to his back and put my bag under his head. As I did so he belched out blood and came round.

"Cured before nightfall," he muttered. "Whoever did it broke their toe on my bowels."

Leaving him by the roadside I mounted the horse and galloped down the hill into the village. The first person I saw was Ham who was standing by a cart full of books and rolls, ticking them off against a list.

"Ah, so Hawsley found you. Good," he said absently. "I managed to save most of what I need this time but there are invaluable pieces left behind, irreplaceable. . . . So hot, isn't it? Must keep them in the shade or they deteriorate. Have you got any linen I could borrow? That is best for keeping books cool."

"Hawsley is badly hurt," I said stiffly, outraged by his lack of concern for me, or my arrival. "We need your cart to bring him in."

"Can't he ride, or walk?" Ham enquired blandly.

"He can't stand up and he's bleeding internally," I replied, snapping at him.

"Is he indeed?" Ham said with a smile, looking over my shoulder and raising one white eyebrow.

I followed his gaze and there was Hawsley leaning on a thick branch which he had cut. Blood was running down his chin but it did not stop him laughing.

"Give it an hour and it will heal," he said, seating himself on the tail of the cart. "The good thing about inside wounds is the flies can't get at them."

We found a bed for him in Beckley, which was the village we were in. He was given several infusions to stop the bleeding, all of which he spewed up. We stayed that night by his bedside, sure he was about to die. Ham thought it fit to pray for him and offered to find a priest when a fever broke out. Hawsley snorted with contempt and fanned himself with his hand.

"No priest can help me," he said, gasping. "What I need is a tailor to stitch up my maggoty entrails. Bring me a needle not the Cross."

At dawn he fell asleep. At first we believed it to be death, his breath was so light. Ham felt his forehead and listened to his heart.

"He has survived the ordeal of an Oxford education. Let us hope you are similarly strong. Now, before all the saints and the Stagyrite himself, let us settle this question of Nature's ways. Are they so transparent after all?"

255

With Hawsley lying between us, his pale face gleaming in the window, a fixed grin on his lips, I could finally open up my heart. If there had been a priest with us that night it was Nature: if there had been a doctor it was Nature: if there had been a murderer within the mob it was Nature. I poured out my opinions in a long, strenuous passion of criticism while Ham nodded and poised his finger-tips together, glancing at Hawsley's long nose and paper-thin eyelids under which the orbs moved ceaselessly as if searching for the villain who had struck him down.

When I had finished Ham stood up.

"Those are your feelings; but are they your views? They can be quite separate, especially in the young."

"That is what I *think*!" I almost shouted.

"Then your gods have gone if you will but admit it and you are at the beginning of knowledge if you will allow it," he said quietly. "Your faith is destroyed. You are no longer an Albigensian. You are not a Christian. Before the painful truths of this existence you are what all men of sense are: lost."

"No, I'm not!" I protested. "If I were allowed the full exercise of my beliefs with the help and support of my own people I could . . . I might. . . ."

"Refute your own convictions?" Ham said gently, his hand now on my shoulder for I was in tears. "To be found one must first be lost. After you have lived your life fully and seen all there is to see and thought about it, maybe you will return to the faith of your fathers. But as from now you must accept your new status as a seeker. That is what The Four hoped you would achieve. If they had the choice and were free from their responsibilities in this world, they might be seekers also. They hope that you will do this for them, however, by proxy."

He paused, a quizzical but sympathetic smile on his long face.

"So, was Aristotle right? Does Nature always take the shortest way? After your own life, even at such a young age, can you agree?"

Hawsley laughed in his sleep; blackbirds started to sing sweetly in the trees outside the window. I began to feel hungry as I wiped away my tears on my sleeve.

"Short or long is hardly the way to measure it!" I said indignantly. "Who can calculate anything in Chaos?"

"Exactly!" Ham cried joyfully as he gave me an embrace. "Now you are truly one of us."

XXVIII

We remained at Beckley for another day. Hawsley accepted this as time for recuperation but only because it had been the intention for us to leave Oxford for Lincoln later than the riot had precipitated. The house where we stayed was comfortable enough and Ham was well known to the owner, having come there with his books many times as a refugee from the university's turmoils.

Before we left, Ham took the cart and went off with the owner of the house to hide the library in a place he had used on previous occasions. It had not been in The Four's orders that Ham should accompany me to Lincoln but as the university was in such disorder and Ham had matters to discuss with his patron, Old Robert, he decided to come along. Hawsley protested as it would double his custodial responsibilities. Even from his bed in the cart where Ham insisted he ride, the old soldier continued to complain. He lay bound up in a sheet that had been wrapped round his abdomen, very hot in the late autumn sun, constantly drinking his cold infusions from a jug clutched to his chest. He was still haggard with pain and often lapsed into chattering deliriums which interested Ham so much he would stop the cart to listen, then write notes.

"He's dying," he whispered as we resumed our journey after one such halt. "That is his soul speaking."

"No, I'm not," Hawsley called out from behind, "and my soul talks Persian, if you please."

"You do not know yourself too well, Hawsley," Ham said over his shoulder. "A man of your character, having not long to live, should set his thoughts in order."

"They are in order. I've been mortally wounded twenty-three times, left for dead on nine great battlefields, condemned before five judges and never died once. Can't that horse go faster?"

Ham shook his head and slapped the reins across the animal's rump. We rode on in silence through the orchards of Merton until Bicester was in sight, the tower of its church showing grey against the turning leaves. When I turned to tell Hawsley I found he had got astride his horse which we had tied to the back of the cart. His face was grey and he sat bolt upright, the sheet's tightness holding him together.

"Bister!" he shouted. "That will do for today."

Ham stopped the cart and I helped him to get Hawsley down off the horse and back on to the bed we had made for him. His flesh was raging hot and streaming with sweat.

"If I lie down, I'm lost," he said weakly. "Let me sit my horse and the poison will pool into my boots. There is a struggle going on inside me, Master Bacon, but I will win. Let me drive the cart. . . ."

Ham pressed him down by the shoulders and put a finger to his lips.

"Think on your creator," he whispered, "on the beginning and the end."

We drove into Bicester as quickly as we could. Once in the high street I jumped down to find a place for us to stay. Having done so I returned to find no sign of the cart. Upon asking passers-by I discovered Ham had driven on through the village and taken a lane to the mill. It was not far outside the town and I was there within ten minutes. When I arrived I found Ham having speech with the miller looking down at Hawsley who was stretched out on the pan of big weighing-scales, his feet and arms hanging over the sides as the pan swung in the air, balanced against a pile of iron weights.

"What are you doing to him?" I demanded angrily. "I've got a room for us back in the village."

"Shush, Hedric," Ham said irritably. "I may not get the chance to weigh a soul again."

"That's cruel and shameful!" I stuttered with indignation. "Hawsley needs to be comfortable. You are treating him like . . . like . . . a carcase. . . ."

"Not at all," Ham replied soothingly. "You may find the rigours of experimental science shocking, Hedric, but you must accept that the surgeon has to cut, the hunter must move swiftly, and so on. We cannot allow knowledge to remain hidden because we are too choosy about our feelings. Hawsley, do try to lie still, if you can!"

I walked away and put my face in my hands. I was very tired; my spirits were low; all my enthusiasm for my new life had suddenly drained away in the face of this callous behaviour. At other such moments of fatigued disillusionment I had gone to my father for comfort, knowing that within his angry sufferings there was room for understanding of my own, crude and rough though his sympathy might be. Ham was not capable of offering that kind of consolation. He had no special concern for the tenderness of youth. A boy's ignorance was to be confronted and destroyed, not gently eased aside.

"The nature of the soul is, with the nature of God, the most pressing question we have to answer," Ham said as he held Hawsley's feet still. "Some advance has been made of late with regard to the nature of God. I believe between them, Alexander of Hales, Bonaventure and Albertus Magnus, along with my mentor Grosseteste, have done sterling work in that direction though they have committed many basic errors of supposition and speculation. You cannot make a statement of truth then simply marshal selected facts to prove it; you must look at all the facts and see what pattern they form, if any. . . ." He gripped Hawsley's ankles tighter and beckoned me to take his hands, which I declined to do. "Oh, do stop being so fastidious, boy. If I were dying myself do you think I would not treat the experience as relevant to my studies? This is for the future generations, Hedric, not merely to satisfy my curiosity. Miller, have you no smaller weights that will register the loss of a very light mass?"

The miller was as upset and confused as I was. He looked dumbfounded but I saw his fist was tightly clenched around a coin. He swore to Ham that he had no smaller weights, then crossed himself several times.

"Well, I will have to be satisfied with a crude calculation. If, when he dies, the point of balance shifts with the departure of his soul, then, at least we will know the soul has a positive weight and mass, though any accuracy in the matter will be difficult. Of course, the soul may weigh a hundredweight or a pennyweight. Who knows?"

The miller could not stand the sight of Hawsley any more and went into his mill. I was so horrified at the coldness of heart of my tutor that I thought of taking Hawsley's sword from the cart and killing him. This poor madman was a companion of sorts, a fellow-sufferer on this cruel earth! Ham read my thoughts. Kneeling down, he stroked Hawsley's forehead, who opened his eyes and smiled.

"I love my brother as I love knowledge, Hedric," Ham said. "We must not waste our chances to learn. What enlightenment comes of this will be sacredly kept and respectfully valued. If I could die in such a useful manner I would rejoice."

"I am satisfied," Hawsley sighed, "but let us not waste any

opportunity to help science. Prepare yourself, doctor. I feel a great fart building up. Let us weigh that first, if you please, then compare it with the heaviness of my soul."

Ham gnawed at his bottom lip, his eyes on the point of the scales. It was swinging violently as Hawsley waved his feet.

"Gently, gently," Ham said in a croon.

"You do not want the fart?" Hawsley asked.

"Address your soul to your creator," Ham instructed him. "This is no day for levity."

We stood there for all the hours of the evening sun during which time Hawsley fell asleep. The miller took his family away into the town to prevent them witnessing the iniquities being practised on his property: I watered the horses and groomed them, washed Hawsley's spare clothes and my own, doing anything to make it unnecessary for me to talk to Ham. As Ham saw the night approaching he became impatient and examined Hawsley frequently for signs of deterioration, but my poor protector was sleeping tranquilly, each breath moving the great iron pan of the scales very slightly. When the stars came out and a cold breeze began to come off the river I was able to speak without cursing.

"Are you going to wait here all night?" I asked.

"I am. For me to lack diligence now would be a sin against my profession. Who else will have such perfect experimental conditions presented to him? Aristotle did not think of this: it never occurred to Galen or the Arabs. You go to sleep."

I reminded him that we had not yet eaten.

"I could not get food past my lips while this man suffers," Ham replied, his huge eyes roaming over the pinched, honed nose of Hawsley as the nostrils flared with each breath. "But you feed yourself."

I went down to the river and took some pears from the miller's garden, eating them with bread we had brought from Beckley. As I was throwing the last core into the mill-race I heard Ham calling out. I ran round to the side of the mill and found him on his knees beside Hawsley who was still on the scales.

"It weighed nothing, O Lord," Ham was whispering, "nothing at all."

We buried Hawsley in the graveyard at Bicester church though I could not help feeling it did not suit his mad, soldierly spirit. Putting him in the earth was a dangerous piece of planting. As yet we had not heard from the Earl of Leicester on the subject of the loss of his sworn man. Somewhere in Oxford was the culprit who had given Hawsley his fatal blow and de Montfort would want to know who it was; we could not tell him and I could not imagine such intelligence coming out of Oxford's present confusion.

Hawsley's death saddened me so much Ham became impatient with me. He rode ahead when we resumed our journey north, stopping to make notes as his thoughts struck him. When this happened I passed without look or question. Our journey to Northampton went by in this manner, then up to Market Harborough. When a giant, thick-set man with sloping shoulders and a short red beard was waiting at the door of the Franciscan house in Leicester as we came out next day, I was not over-surprised to learn he had been sent as Hawsley's replacement. His name was Angel, the only item strange about him: otherwise he was a hale, bluff, simple soul, about thirty years old, long in the earl's service. He had known his predecessor but had found Hawsley hard to get close to: nonetheless he had been glad to learn that those responsible for his death had suffered the same fate at Oxford within twenty-four hours of our exodus, condemned on Hawsley's written, lodged testimony. He had known all along how damaging the blow had been.

"The earl allows no man to go unavenged," Angel affirmed, cracking the bones of his short, freckled fingers. "He looks after those who will look after him and do their duty. I watch over you and he watches over me and Christ watches over him. That's how it works."

Ham glared at Angel and I saw the desperation fill his big eyes. This was the terrible framework in which he, as a philosopher, was attempting to find operating truths. Loyalties like these superseded any ethics; without the protection of great men Ham could not unravel this world. His books were buried; his university in flames, so he had to shelter behind the strength of the earl and the bishop even though that strength imperilled every virtue he had perceived to be of lasting value. Whatever revelations he produced might just as well be incorporated in the armorial bearings of the mighty as scribed in any book.

With these grey thoughts going through my mind I rode between Ham and Angel towards Lincoln, feeling I was more the servant of

261

anarchy than any apprentice to sense. If there was to be a way forward which all men might share it could never be as spurious and arbitrary as the whims of kings or the dreams of saints. Within architecture I had seen all the resolutions of injustice and confusion and that is where I knew I must keep looking. Our craft had provided the statements of real harmony for every civilisation and they were still dotted all over the earth as a witness to the mason's powers of vision, a humble workman who toiled within simple things. Halting my horse I dismounted and picked up a pebble from the roadside, putting it into my pocket and holding it there in my mind. It served to remind me of my father, of the value of simple things, and of the risks of life: and it inspired my hopes, encouraging me to work for the future The Four believed possible. But it was not to earn their plaudits I would struggle, or for the fame and wealth they could offer me. My ambition now was to astonish, to shake, by one great step to bestride all old learning, then men would forget their fears and welcome a redemptive newness. A little, water-worn stone would do it.

When we were just south of Willoughby-on-the-Wolds on the Fosse Way we entered a holly wood. Angel rode ahead to scout. We heard his horse scream and spurred to catch him up. We found him hanging on to the beast's back as it charged around a glade with a dozen arrows sticking out of its head.

XXIX

Our captors emerged from the trees as we galloped up. They cut the wounded horse's throat and stripped off saddle and baggage all in one practised motion. There were at least a hundred of them; dirty, wild-looking fellows clad in threadbare, green-mouldy apparel. When Angel offered token resistance they simply swarmed all over him until he was subdued. While this was going on all three of us shouted and yelled questions at our attackers: Who were they? What did they want? and so on, but not one of them spoke. After Ham and Angel were tied up and blindfolded and I was placed firmly between two outriders, they moved off in a column to the east. We must have travelled twenty miles in complete silence, passing through settlements where the people ran indoors and the dogs slunk to their kennels at our approach. All my attempts to talk to the men surrounding my horse were ignored, and I was kept well to the rear of Ham and Angel in order to prevent any communication between us; but I was not tied or blindfolded. Indeed, I was conscious of a certain gentleness in the way they treated me.

As the shock of our capture faded I was able to make a guess at the identity of our captors in spite of their silence. I had heard rumours in London concerning a band of lawless men which kept a separate state in Sherwood Forest, living by pillage and common robbery under the leadership of one Hude or Hood. When captured we had been on the south-eastern edge of their bruited territory, fifty miles square of forest between Nottingham and Barnsdale: and they had ruled this since the death of the old King Henry sixty years ago. Hood still lived, it was said, a man of great cunning who had frustrated the efforts of three kings to catch him. No officer of law, Church or military dared to enter Hood's domain, the royal forest having been removed in its entirety from the King's jurisdiction. It was said that no greater encouragement to disobedience existed than Hood's rule in Sherwood. It undermined all royal authority and made government a mockery when it pleased. The rebellions of barons or common men were blamed on it; the intransigence of abbots; even the truculence of foreign potentates. All the eyes of the world came to rest on Sherwood when there was a contest to be fought with the English throne: it was the glaring weakness, the shame, the living proof of royal inadequacy.

There was a half-moon. Its occasional appearances through the canopy of leaves gave me some orientation as we plunged deeper and deeper into the forest. We were going north and west but not directly; our route meandered and our large party was constantly breaking up and re-forming as the narrowness of the path dictated. Several streams were crossed and one sizeable river, all flowing east by my reckoning. But, although I have always had a strong sense of direction, within an hour of entering the forest proper I could not remember the line of our march. When the column halted at the foot of a cliff of ghostly limestone the position of the moon indicated to me we were now headed west and the stream running alongside the base of the rock was a tributary of one we had frequently encountered during the last half-hour. Nevertheless, I could not connect my observations back far enough to estimate our whereabouts. We were on the edge of higher country and more broken ground with the thickest forest behind us. There were no domesticated animals along the way, or beaten tracks.

My horse was led to the head of the column where Ham and Angel were being untied. As their blindfolds were taken off Ham swayed and had to be held up.

"Steady!" I shouted.

It was the first word anyone had spoken since our capture. One of the hooded men hissed and raised his bow to silence me but thought better of it. I slipped under Ham's armpit to support him, smelling the fear in his sweat. He was mumbling incoherently to himself. As I gripped him round the waist I realised he was rushing through a prayer.

"Eripe me Domine ab homino malo," he whispered more clearly. *Deliver me, O Lord, from the evil man.*

Suddenly I was torn away from Ham and crushed in a terrible embrace that knocked all the breath out of me. I cried out, clawing to free myself but was swung into the air and spun round.

"Hedric, my son, my son!" I heard close to my ear. "At last you're here!"

To meet my father in the dark like this was a maddening thing: he was hooded like the rest with no face to scrutinise for signs of change or wear, no eyes to examine for tears. All we had was our touch, which is a harsh medium for the feelings of the reunited. We stood there running our hands over each other's faces, choking back our shouts of joy, giving our names and greetings back and forth in a kind of delirium, straining to see each other clearly in the fretted moonlight. Between my cries of rejoicing I hissed quick questions at him, only to be told to wait until tomorrow. Meanwhile, we continued our reunion by touch, Bert's hard finger-tips scraping on my skin; my own probing his nose and beard and ears until he clutched them.

"You've not been doing much white cutter's work," he said with a laugh. "Your hands are as soft as a churchman's."

"I'm a student," I replied with as much dignity as I could. "But I have kept up with my practical work. I did a bit with the Oxford lodge. . . ."

"I know, son, I know," Bert said, kissing me on the forehead, "not a bad rose, so I heard."

Ham came over and thrust himself in front of Bert, his white hair standing up on his head.

"Who is this man?" he asked me. "Have you some influence with him?"

"This is my dad," I replied.

Ham paused. He had the sense not to ask what my father was doing with a pack of outlaws but I could see the question in his eyes.

"Sir," he said, "I beg you, if you know the minds of these men, tell me what they want with a poor scholar like me."

"Oh, never fear. This is a better university than the one you've left, Master Bacon. Any thinking man is welcome here," Bert replied, his intention obviously to obfuscate rather than explain.

The company of hooded men moved forward into the valley of the stream that opened up beyond the cliff. Bert led my horse with one hand and me by the other while Ham walked behind us.

"What did you mean by that?" I asked my father.

"I was just pulling his leg."

"My friend is terrified," I whispered. "Has he got anything to be afraid of?"

"No more than any of us."

"I am right, aren't I? This is Hood's country."

"Could be," was all he would say, and I could get no more out of him.

We had climbed up a rise where the plateau ended and gazed down over a vast further spread of forest brightened by the moon. From where we stood it had the appearance of a frozen sea with swells of silver and shadow extending to the horizon, a storm caught in mid-motion. Our company halted on the edge of the escarpment where the ground was even and a low ridge of exposed limestone provided shelter. Bert tethered my horse to a rowan tree which was in full berry but in this light they were clusters of bronze over my head as we lay down to sleep. Ham saw to it that he was close by. As I was enfolded in my father's arms, all my questions faltering on my tongue, I took a last look over his shoulder down the declivitous ground to the moon-tossed forest. It was as silent as the hooded men had been silent. What tomorrow will bring can only be good, I thought to myself as I drifted off, exhausted by twenty hours of travel, fear and joy. There was no dream could rival the day of my reunion with my beloved father, even with all the mystery that remained to be explained.

I slept as one who is blessed, in nirvana as the Buddhist monks of the Red Sect at Sam-ya monastery in Tibet described it to me when I worked on their temple in 1277: a state of unison with the eternal powers when the soul is in bliss, enfolded within the supreme spirit.

I was awakened, in the most pleasant way possible, by a sound filling the dreamless trance of my sleep with delightful song: thousands upon thousands of birds were singing in the forest below, a surging sea of music which echoed the moonlit vision of my first sight of this part of Sherwood. No one could sleep long within earshot of it and soon we were assembled on the lip of the ridge, ready to move off. Going towards the rear of the column I saw Angel. He was chatting easily with a group of bowmen who stuck close to him as if he were still under escort, but he was not bound or hindered. During the night all the bowmen had removed their hoods and wore them folded at their necks. With so many new faces to look at I hardly noticed when we began to move forward, descending the slope to the forest. My attention was brought back to our progress when someone ahead of us blew a horn.

I was startled and looked across at Bert.

"Who is that?" I asked.

"Not King Henry's foresters," Bert answered with a tight smile, one hand playing with his wilder, bushier beard in which new streaks of grey had appeared since he left me in Guildford.

This was not the only change I could see in him now we were in daylight: his eyes were deeper, darker and set within patterns of grave wrinkles. It created a different impression of the man: now, he was someone more serious about himself, more self-critical than critical of others. It was not a monkish pose. From my knowledge of him I could see that it went deep.

"What's happened to you, Dad?" I asked him carefully. "You seem different, somehow."

He laughed curtly, snorting softly through his nose.

"That I am."

"Have you been suffering?"

"Not so you'd notice."

This obtuseness and evasion was starting to anger me. We had been separated for months! He had run off and left me to the mercies of men he didn't trust, and now, when I was on my way to sit at the feet of a great teacher in Lincoln, he had had me kidnapped.

"I didn't want to come here, you know," I said aloofly, "I have managed perfectly well on my own."

"Oh, have you?" Bert replied with a shadow of a sneer. "That's not what I heard."

"Was it you who arranged for me to be brought here?"

"Perhaps."

"Oh, stop being so stupid!" I raged at him. "You're ruining my future, everything I've worked for. . . ."

"You're better off here, with me. . . ." Bert said hesitantly, his eyes averted.

"Tell me why! How can I carry on my studies in the middle of a forest? I need teachers, books. . . ."

"There's plenty to learn here. . . ."

"From you? When have I ever learnt anything from you?"

I immediately regretted what I had said but my father made it impossible for me to be anything but cruel. Intoxicated by the pain I had brought to his face I pressed on.

"Can't you understand how much I've grown away from you? You've been an obstacle to my education in the past. Once you'd run off and left me it all became easier for me. Things fell into place, I could think clearer. I don't know how you did it but, somehow, you have always contrived to mess up my mind. What is it you want out of me? Have you any idea? If all you wish to pass on is your own puzzlement then I'm not interested. . . ."

Some of the bowmen closest to us stared at me then moved away, clearly indignant at the way I was behaving towards my father. Bert looked up to the sky, trying hard to control his reaction. Oh, what was I doing? I hadn't been back with him a day and already I was tormenting him! The realisation of how cruel I had become astonished me.

"I'm sorry," I mumbled, "but you should have sent for me sooner. I thought you were dead. . . ."

"It wasn't in my power to send for you!" Bert snapped back, then his eyes bulged and his hair seemed to stand out from his head in anger. "I would never have sent for you, left to my own devices! What, to take you away from such good fortune? Would I do such a thing to my own blood? Never!" He stormed ahead, his arms flailing as if he were beating away the rage from around his head. "Oh, Hedric, Hedric, I swore that we would never fight again. I took an oath to myself and already you've made me break it!"

The bowmen left a space for me to walk in as we left the slope and entered the forest. Bert stumbled ahead and joined his companions, not looking back at me once before he disappeared. Ham hung back, not wishing to be contaminated by my unpopularity. I became aware of myself in a new way; not as a prodigy but as an outcast.

"If you knew how your father has missed you, boy," shouted a fat, stubble-headed man from beside me, "you wouldn't be so mean-spirited. You deserve to be whipped scarlet and rubbed with salt."

I could make no answer. In order to avoid the accusing eyes of those left to walk near me I stared up at the leaves of the great greenwood. All the trees were changing their colours; the light opening out golds, bronzes and browns: no two shades were the same but every one was touched by the jaundice of my desire to hurt my father. Shame forced me to march so far staring upwards I developed a crick in my neck. When I risked a glance at Bert's companions they had lost interest in me which was exactly what I had hoped for: if the earth could have gaped and swallowed me up that would have been even better.

"Your behaviour interests me."

It was Ham, his expedient lack of enthusiasm for my company seemingly forgotten.

"I had not judged you to be of such a selfish nature until now," he continued. "My observations led me to believe you possessed a certain supple coolness of temperament, an ability to stand back and examine your own motives and ideas. Now I see a different person altogether."

"That is only because you can make yourself as cold as ice at will!" I snarled at him. "Perhaps you weren't born but got blown through a window in a blizzard."

I was taken completely off-guard by what happened next. Ham, whom I had already classified as a coward and a weakling, grabbed an unstringed bow off a man alongside him, seized me by the hair and proceeded to thrash me angrily. The archers did not break their step, nor did Ham stand still in order to administer the beating. As I was flogged — so certainly with justice — we all continued our advance on the home of Hood. When, later on, Bert came back to patch up our quarrel, he found me a rueful, contrite youth who knew his place among men of larger growth. No one told him what Ham had done to me, nor did I. It was better to accept this discipline and subjugation as necessary; a need I had refused to recognise until now — and I enjoyed the improved standing Ham now had amongst these men of action as a result of his entirely unexperimental and non-academic outburst of wrath. If such an eccentric and intellectual stranger could suddenly become *one of us* to a mob of rough, ignorant outlaws who lived by robbery and terror, violence required no further advertisement than its performance, as far as I was further concerned. No longer would I waste my time with the moral questions which physical force arouses in the minds of those who contemplate the state of the world. From now on, having been drubbed by a philosopher of such reputation, I would give violence an equal place with reason as a means of proving one's case.

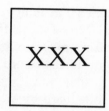

XXX

Now there were many much-used paths and tracks in the forest; the multi-coloured carpet of fallen leaves from the great, contorted oaks, soaring beech, birch and ash swept aside by traffic. The path we were marching along was as wide as a highway, beaten to a red dust beneath the trees, and I saw the ruts of cartwheels. As we progressed more people mixed with our company, many of them women and children.

My glances of enquiry at my father brought no response. He gave many greetings as we walked along, side by side, but he did not introduce me, nor did the folk who joined the column take any interest in my person. Now we were in this part of the greenwood all attempts at stealth were abandoned as unnecessary and the crowd began to chat, glad to be home.

The women and children had come to meet their menfolk returning from their mission to abduct Ham, Angel and myself: I must confess that I was surprised to find these silent, highly-trained and disciplined archers to be family men. Now, here they were, their children on their shoulders, strolling along under the trees as if on their ways to a fair. It was too pleasant to be true, as was the sheen on my father's skin, the gleam in his eye (the white of which was far too white), and the overfirm strength of his grasp on my shoulder.

In my anxious, exciting world this open cheerfulness and security were not to be trusted: they portended something treacherous. There was danger or deception here. The jollier the outlaws became, the more apprehensively I viewed the situation. Their decreasing alertness was matched by my increasing watchfulness. With my skin still tingling from Ham's thrashing and my senses responding to some unspoken suffering within my father I was fully awakened to every possibility. It occurred to me I could be cast in the role of sacrifice: I had recently read about the religious practices of the Carthaginians who offered up their most promising children to their god, Baal, so the Roman historian Livy would have us believe of them. The light of noble sacrifice in Bert's eyes need not have been dissimilar to that of a Carthaginian father choosing the most troublesome of his sons to take to the altar.

We climbed up a gentle hill which brought us out of the oak forest into a saucer-shaped valley full of slender birch and ferns. Through the pale-barked trees I could see a lake gleaming below us with the bowed, familiar shapes of willow around its shore. As we approached the edge of the water I saw that there was an island in the lake which was thick with evergreen. As I was examining it Bert tugged me to follow the company which had taken a left fork in the broad grass road through the ferns. After a few hundred yards we stopped in front of a low timber building with a sod roof.

"Here we are," Bert said.

I stared at the dwelling. Suddenly I had no desire to enter this place. I looked at the crowd as it flowed on through the trees.

"What about Ham and Angel?" I asked. "Where are they going?"

"They're staying somewhere else."

Much of the confidence had drained from Bert's face. I could see he was nervous. He pulled me towards the door of the house.

"Give it a chance," he said, a note of pleading in his voice.

"Give what a chance?"

The door opened and a skinny, carrot-haired woman with prominent teeth stepped out, drying her hands on her apron.

"This is my wife," Bert said hoarsely.

I could not speak. The woman eyed me warily, a corner of her thin lips lifted in a half-snarl.

"Your wife?" I said, trying to keep the fear out of my voice.

"Yes, son."

I nodded dumbly. The woman shifted her feet and seemed to shrug. I could hear other people in the house. My heart tightened. Oh, no, don't let there be children! So soon? Her children? My mind raced on. Bert could hear the noise as well. He had turned crimson. I feared the worst.

The entrance filled with women, all staring at me curiously. There were all shapes and sorts. Some of them were laughing. I smiled with relief. They were obviously the wife's friends or relatives.

"These are my other wives," Bert said hollowly; then he commenced to introduce each one of them by name, his voice fraught with embarrassment.

I burst out laughing at this stark imbecility. The women joined in, nervously encouraging my mirth as if it were a better alternative to whatever reaction they might have imagined I would have. Bert knew me better and his glance was full of apprehension as he picked up the coldness of my real response. When he had laboured through the list of names he ushered the women into the house and shut the door upon them, then turned to face me.

"So," he said briskly, "now you know."

"What do I know?" I said with icy control. "That my father is a clown? But it's not even a joke, is it?"

"It's no joke," he replied with a mixture of doggedness and defiance (though a pain-filled glitter deep down in his eye conveyed that he might wish it were). "I'm properly wed to all of them."

"Someone's taken your wits away," I snapped, alarmed at the fury welling up inside me. "I think your mind's gone."

"The Arabs have several wives if they feel like it; why shouldn't I?" Bert said, trying hard to smile.

"Since when did you become an Arab?"

"I'm not, by nature, a *monogamous* man . . ." he said with a pedantic air like a child reciting by rote, but I refused to let him finish. I will not record the terrible insults which I poured upon him as they shamed me even then, as I was saying them. Bert went deep red and I saw the strain of keeping his temper blazing in his eyes.

"Steady on, son, steady on," he murmured, his hands clutching at his clothes to keep them off me. "I can explain how all this came about. Give me a chance."

"Why do you suddenly need one wife, never mind five?" I yelled at him. "You never bothered before. I don't even know whether my mother is alive or dead. That's how much you've cared about wives!"

"Are you going to listen, or not?" Bert said with a display of long-suffering patience, folding his arms and stepping back a pace. "Some of us in the scheme have two wives, some three, some four. There's one poor fellow has seven!"

"Can you tell me why?"

"To find out which works out best. And I can tell you, I don't think it's five."

At last he smiled. The famous sunrise rose out of his mouth and illuminated the space between us.

"Are you telling me it's an experiment?"

Bert nodded and the smile went away. I saw the indignity and miserable subjection lurking in his apologetic glance.

"What are they trying to prove?" I asked, struggling to keep my head clear. "That life is utterly impossible?"

"There is a perfect number," Bert replied. "So Hood says."

This struck home. The perversion of a pure mathematical concept, deprived of its true meaning, angered me beyond restraint.

"Hood is a charlatan! A perfect number in Mathematics cannot be reflected in human affairs. He is playing with ideas. He is using you to amuse himself! Have you no pride?"

Bert stiffened. I watched the colour creep up his cheek and braced myself for the blow but none came. It would have been welcome if it had for I needed a sign I could still talk to this deluded creature, my father.

"Yes, Hedric, I've got pride," he said finally. "Pride enough to push back the barriers of knowledge. If you can do it, so can I."

"Ah," I said with a sigh, "I see."

Here was something sad. My father had allowed himself to be used in this heartless way out of envy for me. If I could be at the forefront of knowledge he must be there as well. But it remained hard to forgive his absurdities and lack of proper logic: for every condition there is a cause; for every cause an originating cause. When Bert had entered Sherwood he had been very vulnerable and disillusioned. He had felt the whole world was against him; easy meat for Hood. Now it was my duty to bring my dad face to face with his own shortcomings and to encourage him to remedy them. But what did I have to offer him in place of Hood? Nothing, except a life lived out through me.

These discussions took many days and I will not detail the advances and retreats of our battle: Bert saw himself as a brave servant of Hood's intellect, a man at the spear-point of progress. I saw him as Hood's victim: a chained sexual ape. Whatever the rigours and dangers of my education it was designed to bring me up in a real world where men of authority — my mentors, The Four — would find a prominent place for me. Bert believed (with some good reason) their power to be arbitrary and corrupt. This would contaminate any eminence or success I achieved. True glory was to be found in Hood's hidden forest laboratory where dedication and sacrifice were appreciated. On being asked why such a high-minded and altruistic society had to have a covert existence — in fact to be outside the law — Bert replied that these were the best conditions for the revealed truth as the

273

boundaries between it and the decadent system which threatened it were kept clearer this way.

"But do you still hold true to our faith?" I demanded of him on the evening of my third day in Sherwood as we walked by the lake shore. Even as I asked the question I had guilt in my own heart because I knew how damaged my own had been after Oxford.

"And what faith is that?" Bert replied, employing a tactic of his that I had often despaired of during our arguments — answering a question with a question — then looking pleased with himself.

"What I am living now is a *life*, Hedric, not a faith. Can I expect a child to understand this? Especially one who has been spoilt and pampered to the degree you have of late. I will not try to teach you any doctrine. I will not give you books to read that will infect your mind. All I ask is you do as I did when I first came here, broken-hearted, a fugitive, a failure, rejected by you, by my craft, by my religion: I kept my mouth shut and watched. I was penniless and afraid. Maurice Welbilove got me here through his influence and he had sworn an oath for my good behaviour and my trustworthiness. I was treated with respect. I was consulted. No one took me for granted. They gave me shelter and hospitality. By the time I was asked to make my contribution to Sherwood's well-being they'd won me over."

"What do you mean, 'they'd won me over'?" I screamed, making the willow-warblers scurry from their perches to go twittering out over the lake. "You'd been softened up, then bribed, now you're being exploited!"

"Hood has changed me. I see things clearly now. Open up your heart to him," Bert said with a gentle hand on my forearm, his big head inclined towards mine, his eyes appealing.

"Don't look like that," I pleaded, "not you. I can't stand it. Tell me this is all a sham."

"I believe in what Hood is doing," he replied.

"You sound like a Cretin!"

"Everything has to be planned if Man is to be saved. We cannot leave the future to chance. By trial and error and thought on the highest level, we can be saved."

"I do not wish to be saved!" I shouted. "I wish to be a great architect, to serve the Gods by completing their Creation. If that is not enough then . . . then . . ." Angrily I groped for words. "I don't want to live."

Bert walked down to the lake shore and stood with his feet close to the water. I saw thousands of red pebbles beneath the soles of his boots, pebbles that stretched down into the clear water and along the shore. I clutched my own pebble in my pocket as Bert crunched a few steps along then pointed out to the island. I could see a low, black boat being rowed away from it.

"Hood is leaving us for a while. When he returns I'll ask him to meet you. It is a privilege afforded to very few but he has heard of your . . ." here he paused and I was glad to suspect the resurgence of his old mockery (oh, let it be a chink in his armour! I prayed) ". . . your notability amongst kings and their masons and minions. He has not seen fit to meet me, but then, I was not such an elevated personage when I arrived. Did I arrive? No, I *crawled* into Hood's realm. . . ."

Bert's shoulders slumped as if he were recalling the ignominy of his entry into Sherwood. He kept his eyes on the boat and the steady flash of its oars in the sun.

"He is alone most of the time, in contemplation. I am satisfied to believe that once in a while he takes the time to contemplate *me*."

"All he'll contemplate about you is what a gullible fool you are," I insisted. "I don't accept that you really go along with all this. I know you too well, Dad. He must have threatened you. . . ."

"No, not once. Even in the first few weeks when I was often in trouble, he helped me."

"That is obviously his strategy. . . ."

"So, you have an answer for everything. But then, you always had, Hedric. Don't imagine I'm merely biding my time to escape. Sherwood is a better place to be than the outside world, even with five women I don't want. . . ."

"Aah!" I said happily. "You've found out that much. I hope you've told them the experiment hasn't worked."

Bert grimaced and turned away. I felt my attention drawn to the distant boat which was now approaching the shore. Where Hood would actually land was shielded by a promontory so I could not see him leave the vessel. There were four figures outlined against the lake's surface as the boat glided along: three of them were plying the oars and one sat at the stern. As they were a quarter of a mile away I could not distinguish their features.

"So, Dad," I said with mock thoughtfulness, "after all your years of agonising and arguing with yourself you've ended up in the service of a great thief. That's all Hood is, no matter what you think of him. He's intellectually dishonest as well as commonly dishonest. At least that means he's all of a piece. I wouldn't like to think you venerated a man of no integrity. . . ."

Bert turned his back. I saw the tendons in his short neck spring into position for an outburst.

"Don't talk to me as if I were a lump of dung," he said with surprising control. "I can still teach you a few things. At the moment you think you're top-notch. That is an illusion. Don't make yourself a slave to your own mind."

"That's preposterous," I replied with a brief laugh. "We are all what our minds can make of us."

"You speak for yourself," Bert replied with bitterness. "Mine has done me few favours."

A horn was blown further along the lake shore where the boat had now landed.

"Hood's gone. I can't wait until he returns before we start to deal with you. The Green Parley will have to advise me . . ." Bert muttered, tugging at his wispy black and grey hair. "Oh, son, son, three months is all it took to contaminate you. What happened to all I taught you? Why did you forget it so quickly? Never mind. We will make a true man of you, somehow."

"What is a true man, Father?" I asked. "Can you define him for me? Is it supposed to be you?"

Unable to answer except with a glance of dumb, defeated suffering, Bert stumbled away through the ferns towards the settlement, leaving me alone. When he had gone I sat down on the grass, grieving in one part of me, triumphant in another. Being put beyond the reach of my beloved father was a strength — and it would be tested, that much I knew — but it also put a space between us that all his new-found, obstinate conviction would not be able to bridge. Much would depend on the tolerance exercised by Hood: if the great outlaw demanded total obedience from his flock — amongst which I was now numbered — then I would have to dissemble cleverly to avoid his displeasure. This was a prospect that did not alarm me as I had studied the playwrights and had picked up the arts of acting and rhetoric. Just as I could argue against Hoodism — whatever that might be once I had disentangled its essential nature from my father's confused ramblings

276

—I could also find arguments in its favour, as one can for all the works of the Evil One should the need arise. One doubt remained, however: would I be able to convince Bert that I had accepted this new way of life in all sincerity? I might have to prevaricate for days in order to make my escape. The Four would have their myrmidons scouring the country looking for me as well as keeping an eye open for Ham and Angel, but they would never find me here. Within a month they would forget their miraculous young mason and find another protégé: someone else would go to Paris in my place! The daze created by my reunion with Bert cleared from my mind and I became fully aware of what he had put at risk — my whole future. Whatever this weird life in the greenwood meant to him it could never be anything to me. I had tasted the larger world and, even in disgust and fear, had found it formidably fascinating. Beside it Hood's domain was a mere cottage garden.

A heron flew down and alighted on the lake shore, stepping delicately over the pebbles until it found a perch in the water. Lowering its head it pointed its beak downwards and went still, suddenly unleashing the coiled power in its neck, shooting its beak deep into the water and coming up with a wriggling fish. Then it walked out of the water and stood beside me, so near that I could have touched it, and began to swallow its prey. The guttural noises which the heron made while the fish was going down were clearly audible. By this time I had reasoned it out that the bird did not realise I was a live thing because I had been sitting so still. However, when the heron cranked its long neck round and examined me from top to toe as it gulped, its dagger-sharp eyes boring straight into mine from beneath its pointed crest, I felt the hair rise on the back of my neck. This wild, naturally apprehensive creature did not care that I was close. Had my significance shrunk so far? I jumped up, waving my arms, and the heron took off; yet even in its haste those wide grey wings seemed to flap with dismissive disdain.

"It is a trained bird," a familiar voice said behind me. "People on the other side of the lake have taught them to catch fish then return to disgorge their catch."

It was Ham, standing with his arms folded as he watched the heron's stately passage over the lake. There was a wistful look in his eyes.

"Hood must have heard about it from the Chinese. They train

277

cormorants this way. I mentioned the practice in my examination of the relationship between magic and education. The souls of birds, as Pythagoras implies and Old Robert insists, have an eternal existence. Why shouldn't they have? They are alive. . . ."

I linked my arm with his while we walked along the shore a while, heading towards the place where I had seen the boat land. I told Ham everything that I had witnessed and what my father had told me.

"He has obviously become some kind of bucolic sectarian with a strong admixture of criminality thrown in," Ham mused. "I had heard rumours that Hood had abandoned his old plain-man's unquestioning Christianity by the end of the last century and had taken up certain Egyptian practices . . . what was it? Something to do with a more concrete afterlife . . . no matter."

"No," I said emphatically, "it is more to do with women. My father has five wives here."

Ham laughed shortly and rubbed his hands together.

"Ah, that does not preclude the land of the Nile. Their marriage practices were extremely complex. Are any of these women related to your father by blood?"

"No," I hastened to tell him, "they're all strangers but he accepts domination from them, I believe. His new happiness, as he calls it, is partly set to their account."

Ham and I rounded the promontory that had shielded the boat's landing place and saw the vessel lying drawn on to a small beach of pure pink sand. There were many footsteps around it but no other sign of life. The oars were neatly stacked in the well of the craft and a white rope went from the bow to a broken willow which stood near the water's edge.

We stood and looked at the boat. As a means of escape it immediately recommended itself but to where would we row it? All the forest was Hood's. As the thought slipped away I began to admire the craftsmanship that had gone into making the vessel. It was low, long, slender and shallow, made of flawlessly fitted flush timbers which were of a wood I could not identify. I felt the urge to sit in it. First, I looked around to see if we were being observed, then climbed over the gunwale and sat on one of the rower's benches.

Ham watched me, his eyebrows raised.

"The boat is an aquatic apparatus not designed for work on dry

278

land. The friction between the vessel and the road renders it impractical even as a form of sledge . . ." he said drily.

But I was not listening. I had caught a whiff of a perfume I knew well. It lingered in the boat where someone had sweated as they plied an oar. His face loomed up in my mind, vast, smooth jowls glistening. I saw that firm, perfect mouth and heard him puff as he climbed the Guildford High Street in search of strange wines and stranger food, sweat streaming down his neck.

Master Henry de Reyns had been one of the three oarsmen who had rowed Hood from the island.

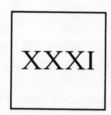

XXXI

My discovery was immediately put into doubt by Ham who did not find the idea of perfumed outlaws impossible; indeed he considered it to be a positive probability.

"It fits perfectly. Hood's reputation, apart from his cruelty and ridicule of the King's law, is that he only robs the rich. This makes sense as to rob the poor is, by definition, a profitless enterprise. Where else will one find perfume but amongst the possessions of the rich? The second stage is to do with the dispersal of the goods which he steals: it is alleged that he gives them to the poor which, in this case, might include his own followers, hence your scented oarsman."

"There is sweat on the bench," I said. "Master Henry is fat. He sweats at the least exertion. The other benches are dry."

"There is a fat, scented outlaw. Rumour has it there is a monk as old as Hood himself who is his confessor and one of his inner circle. Does the idea of a monk wearing perfume amaze you? I could introduce you to thousands who do it to protect their noses from the stench of their brethren."

As he spoke, Ham rocked the boat with me in it as if it were a cradle. His smile was indulgent but I saw I had set him thinking.

Moments later Bert reappeared, breathless and flushed. His reaction when he saw who accompanied me was loud and violent.

"Get away from my son!" he roared, his eyes bulging.

"Certainly, sir," Ham said, shifting a step backwards. "I would prefer to keep as far away as possible from him as he has brought me nothing but trouble. However, I must tell you that he is an exceptional scholar."

My father grabbed me by the arm and hauled me out of the vessel, barking my shins on the rowlocks.

"If I catch you poisoning his mind again I'll kill you!"

Ignoring Bert's clumsy threat Ham sat down on the grassy bank and twined his fingers together.

"Tell me, Herbert," he said. "Something eludes me and you may be able to help me with it. I am anxious to know this. It concerns Sherwood's basic industry and is a vital question: when one robs from the rich to give to the poor, do the poor one gives the riches of the rich to then become rich and therefore robbable?"

Bert let out an oath that I recognised from his previous store of blasphemies and raised his hand.

"Don't play games with me, egghead!" he growled at the end of his imprecations, lowering his arm. "I'm a match for you. You know nothing of our life here. We don't waste our bloody time here nit-picking or tie ourselves in knots for exercise, like you."

"Only asking, Herbert, old fellow," Ham said in a placatory tone, leaning back on his elbows. "The doomed must keep a hold on their curiosity about life to the very end: indeed, it may be that the end is the most interesting phase of our existence. . . ."

"Don't you know when to keep quiet?" Bert seethed, pacing round the relaxed figure who, to my eyes, seemed to have come upon fresh reserves of courage in himself.

"The time to keep quiet is certainly not during any terminal experience. After you have murdered me I will, perforce, be silent, on this plane at least. These ruminations of mine are essentially a tidying-up of loose ends . . . aaah . . ." he lay back, full length, his hands behind his head and looked over the lake. "It is all so beautiful here. But will the beauties of heaven be anything like this? Bestow a thought on that subject, Herbert. May our beauties not be abominable ugliness to God? Should we be astonished to find that the divine mind works to a pattern in contradistinctive contradiction to our own? We may have it all wrong. Heaven may be nothing but a gilded pig-sty."

Hurriedly I put myself between Ham and Bert as I saw the colour racing up my father's neck and cheeks; old, familiar warnings that Bert was getting lost and mad.

"He's talking for the sake of it, Dad," I said, one hand on Ham's white head as he nodded and babbled away, "don't listen. He can't help himself. . . ."

It was the right thing to say: my little act of conciliation worked. Bert's upper lip curled and he appeased his indignation with no more than a light kick at Ham's outstretched leg.

"Your head is a prison, Bacon," he concluded, "but you're not keeping my child in it."

Then he walked away, pulling me with him. When I looked back I

281

saw Ham still lying on the grass staring over the water to the island, his pale head shaking.

It was a huge, cellular community there in the deep forest, settlements radiating out from the lake which was their centre and, in the form of Hood's island, seat of ultimate government and power. To begin with I was only interested in Bert's house and the five women but as the weeks went by I turned my attention to the wider scope offered by Hood's secret state and began to study it.

Sherwood lies in the heart of England; a vast forest domain which covers most of the middle shires. Nominally it is the King's, held by brother dukes and earls in fief from him, but their authority only exists in the documents of the land exchequer: this giant territory which is at the centre of the country, worked, and may still do so for all I know, on a separate system: Hood's law.

From what I could see all forms of family, economy, education and worship were permitted provided that Hood's law and authority went unquestioned. This meant that the small settlements had local powers which were tolerant of every shape and shade of opinion and Hood's authority expressed none — its essence was enshrined in its first cause — resistance to the royal power. Beyond that Hood needed no further philosophy and could allow self-expression, free choice of religion, and many local variations. People drawn into the forest could eventually find their own niche within this flexible framework, or so it was claimed.

The real Sherwood was something different: because of Hood's status as a heroic protector of the oppressed he was not subject to either criticism or resentment of his authority: to do so invited the suspicion that one was on the King's side. Hood was always seen as a man running great risks for his people: to make these risks more acute and dangerous was, in Sherwood's terms, plain treason. Although there was no law of treason none was required. Anyone who was guilty of opposition to Hood's methods or wishes was, in effect, declaring himself to be a King's man and therefore deserved death as an enemy in war for which no judicial process was required. Such people were simply taken into the forest and cudgelled to death.

The existence of Hood's Sherwood would not have been possible without the staple food — venison. Sherwood's deer were semi-domesticated and, with pigs and small forest cattle, intensively farmed. Many decades ago the Sherwood husbandmen had weaned their beasts off grass and on to leaves and ferns as their main grazing. The meat and milk of these animals had a distinctive taste which I can recall to this day; a darker, gamier flavour which always had a touch of smokiness.

What the forest could not provide was bread: and the amount needed to feed the fifty thousand people which I estimated to be the population of Hood's domain, was far too great for the small fields and glades of the forest to produce. So bread was banned. Oats were grown for winter horse-fodder but restricted to that use, and yeast could only be used for the fermentation of fruit wines. The only substitute was a flour made from acorns and beech nuts which was made into pancakes. These were fried in pig-fat with herbs; a delicacy which I never took to. During my time in Sherwood it was bread I missed more than any other thing.

The élite of the forest were the archers. Each man's bow was cut from trees on Hood's island and no other source of yew was allowed to be used. Bert was not one of their number but the opportunity to be trained in archery was held up to him as an inducement. He knew that until he could join the bowmen he would be employed on menial tasks — at that time he was a junior keeper of a pigeon-loft, occasional mason and general labourer. Most work other than that of the bowmen was interchangeable and could be varied by choice, providing some aptitude could be shown.

About the time I decided we must escape Bert made it known to me that my abduction was not entirely due to his suggestion. A member of his Green Parley had been contacted by Maurice Welbilove with news of my impending departure from Guildford. When Bert was given the information his reaction had not been to ask Hood to capture me; that decision had already been taken. The idea received Bert's unquestioning support and gratitude but he should have investigated further. Once in the forest and safely ensconced in Bert's ready-made "family" I would have expected to receive some special notice from Hood or his lieutenants — surely my kidnapping could have had some greater purpose than to satisfy a pigeon-keeper's paternal yearnings? Instead I was designated as an apprentice coal-miner, the lowliest of occupations in the greenwood, and, had it not suited my purposes to accept, my chagrin would have been made known to Hood himself.

Also I received more notice of Hood's plans for my humiliation when on the tenth day after my arrival the Green Parley delivered a short, coarse-featured girl who suffered from a speech defect to Bert's house. She was called Flossy and came from Doncaster. Her instructions, poor child, were that she was to offer herself as my betrothed. Taking pains not to insult her I sent her away but not before my father and I had a confrontation. He claimed that the greenwood custom was for boys and girls to be given experience of love from the time that they became capable. My retort to this was that I had been through that already. This silenced Bert but he was not certain, suspecting bravado on my part. If he had been able to see into my mind he would have encountered Lucy and the questions: was she acting upon someone's orders when she seduced me? And was she chosen for this task because she had already been my father's paramour? Where did the experiments stop?

Each evening I returned from the open-cast coal diggings which were about two miles from the lake, ate at Bert's house, then claimed an hour for myself strolling in the greenwood. The labour of digging coal did not worry me. My body had developed to be much like my father's, short, strong, and powerful, ideally suited for pick- and spade-work. My companions at the shallow top-seam mine were cheerful and good-natured enough but they did not tax my intellect, nor did the mining use up any of my mental resources. Ham would meet me by the lake and a whole day's energy of thought would come pouring out, not only in our plans for escape but in enquiry into the true nature of Hood. This, we both agreed, was no longer that of the legend.

As the days advanced into November there was a last blaze of hot weather. All the leaves had fallen but the heat was that of high summer. The people of Sherwood swam in the lake among the floating golds and browns of the dead leaves, I amongst them. From the water Hood's island did not seem so far away and I conceived the desire to go there. It was forbidden but Ham thought that even if I were caught I could use the hot weather as an excuse for having swum there for fun. Hood was still away from the forest and, unless he had left guards behind, I was unlikely to be caught anyway; thus Ham reasoned, being unable to swim that distance himself owing to a childhood weakness in his lungs, but deeply interested in what the island might reveal.

Bert was away that night, having been given some white cutting work with the Cistercians at Rufford Abbey a day's march away, monks with whom Hood had an easy and convenient relationship, it seemed. Bert was due back by Sunday as he had work at Newstead, a priory of black Augustinian canons in the forest which often called on the skills of Sherwood, being as familiar with the clandestine régime of Hood as they were with the outside world when it came to services they needed.

As the people left the shore and darkness came down upon the lake I remained in the water, hiding myself in the tangle of a floating branch. Then I struck out for the island, counting the stars as they came out, starting with Venus. It was much further than I had guessed and by the time I reached the island I was glad to rest. Pulling myself on to the rocks I climbed into the shelter of the yews which reached out to the edge of the lake, then proceeded towards what I took to be the centre.

The island was sickle-shaped with an isthmus; across its neck was a tall, ivy-covered house streaked with swallow-droppings and shuttered up. It had a flower garden full of roses and the stalks of foxgloves and hollyhocks.

As I approached it I heard the horn.

There were many horns used in Sherwood, all with their own tones and notes; each signifying something specific: curfews, warnings, the rising of the sun, the infliction of punishment, the manoeuvres of the bowmen; but this horn had a deeper and darker note than all the others. It had nothing of that shrill, piercing quality of the hunter's halloo, but reverberated with a plangent, ominous melancholy, the sound of a beautiful, ecstatic pain turning to vengeance.

Hood's horn.

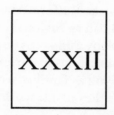

XXXII

I barely had time to slip into the cover of the yews before the shutters of the house were shaken then flung back. From my hiding-place I watched in horror as window after window was opened and candles lit by flitting servants, all of whom must have been in residence at the back of the house while I was approaching the front. By the time the front door was opened and two torches placed in holders to light the path I had counted at least seven men and three women running from room to room. What was strange was their complete silence. Later I discovered that every servant on the island was dumb, the victim of the King's savage forest laws against taking game.

It was fifteen minutes before I heard the crunch of the boat's keel on the pebbles of the isthmus shore and voices coming towards the house. From my place in the trees I could not see the party approach but I heard the whimper of dogs and immediately shinned up the nearest tree until I was well out of range of scenting. Below me I saw four hooded men, one with a brace of black greyhounds on a leash. They entered the house and the door closed behind them, but not before the dogs had started to strain towards the place where I had been standing. Before they were pulled away I saw the holder of the leash look around the clearing, then shrug.

"Probably ducks," I heard him say, then laugh.

It had gone cold. Sitting up in the tree in my sopping wet clothes, my limbs were starting to seize up and stiffen. To make matters worse, a cold wind had begun to blow off the lake. My resolve had been to wait until the company had settled in to the house then make my retreat to the place where I had swum ashore but I was shivering too much, partly with cold and partly with fear; I could hardly hold on to my perch.

I began to descend the tree. As I reached its lower branches the door opened and the shortest of the four men came out. He was no longer wearing a head-covering and his face was turned to the light.

It was Simon de Montfort. As I watched him untie himself and take a piss into a nearby bush I choked with the shock of seeing him there. I clung to the tree, my mind spinning. The degree to which my concentration had diminished in my surprise is shown by my forgetting the greyhounds which came bounding out, heading straight for my tree where they commenced to leap up, trying to get at me.

De Montfort stood very still, still pissing, and peered up at me.

"Who is there?" he called out, while two armed servants came running out of the house.

"Hedric," I said, my teeth chattering.

"Hedric who?"

I could hold on no longer. My hands had gone numb and my anxiety was so great that my blood had turned to water. De Montfort's mouth was open, ferocious as a wolf's smile. My last memory was of tumbling through the sharp branches towards the yelping dogs and his hungry, threatening blade like a soul plunging into the jaws of Hell.

There are moments that one does not expect to wake from; even those which one does not *hope* to be woken from: this was such an occasion. Before I opened my eyes I kept them shut for a long time, feeling the warmth of the fire, smelling the perfume of people, carpets and furniture, listening to voices. I was lying wrapped in a blanket, a fire very close, so close it shone through my eyelids. Someone was gripping my ankle.

"We can see that you're awake, Hedric," said a voice I loved. I responded as a child might, eager to catch sight of his beloved parent. Before I opened my eyes I knew it was Master Henry de Reyns but I did not recognise him at first.

His broad, flushed jowls were disfigured by a half-healed wound which went in a parabola from his temple to his nose. He fingered it, picking at the long scab as he stared down at me, sad and displeased. Then he bent down to whisper in my ear.

"You have disgraced yourself and our faith."

I moaned involuntarily and tried to free my ankle from his grip.

"What a stupid boy you are. I had hopes for you," he said, removing a strip of scab. "Don't I look terrible? A contest of honour, dear Hedric. Architects have their pride. The wretch insulted my Westminster. Imagine!"

I looked past him knowing what horrors awaited me: from a chair opposite Old Robert peered dimly at me, clucking with his tongue. Seated on the floor by the fire was the fourth man, his head turned away. When he slowly looked in my direction I saw the drooping eyelid of the King.

"You should have followed our curriculum more closely, child," he said with a sigh. "There is as much to learn in my second kingdom as my first, as my father John would have told you."

"You are Hood?" I asked in a shaky whisper.

"We are always Hood. My father was; his brother Cœur de Lion was; and my grandfather, Henry," the King said with a light, airy gesture. "Where better for a king who is struggling within the limitations of himself and his power to go than the greenwood? Here we think, we plan, we design, we try things out in a place not unlike Paradise."

"I see that, sire," I murmured, nodding my head as sagely as I could. "Now you have explained. . . ."

"And I can see what I'm doing to my fellow-man. That is very helpful if one stands in danger of becoming a despot," he said, glancing grimly at de Montfort. "And who wants to be a despot?"

"Sire!" I cried, trying to kneel up, clutching the blanket about me, "if I had only known."

The King shook his head.

"No, you are in the same trap as I am, boy. For which of my two worlds would you design your masterpieces? We have one mind subject to two forces, as you know from your own religion. Why should art praise one more than the other? We are the inferior of both good and evil. Shouldn't we praise both?"

I hesitated, yearning to uncover my most secret thoughts: shapes for the house of the Evil God had always haunted me. The reasoning of our brotherhood had always been that out of evil must be created good: out of stone must be created light. But the Evil God's authority was eternal and, as white cutters, we respected and loved his material, the world. From it we found the means to praise the Good God, but did not the Evil require more recognition?

"A more natural architecture is what recommends itself to me," I said, surprised at my own lofty tone which also educed an admiring chuckle from Master Henry. "Something briefer and bolder."

"What do you mean?" the King asked.

"The Pointed Style is too unnatural. It never looks as though it belongs. We have tried too hard. . . ."

288

There was a silence, broken only by the intermittent jetting of the coal in the fire. Then the King began screaming. He leapt to his feet and threw himself at me. But his blows were like those of a panicking woman, all over the place. I cowered behind Master Henry who gripped my ankle even tighter and inclined his bulk across the King's line of attack. Just as suddenly as his madness began, it ended and the King subsided back on to the floor, his chest heaving.

"You probably deserved that, you know," he muttered, wiping saliva away from his mouth on his sleeve. "Trying too hard! We intended to show you the scope of the thing, the size of our sadness. Ideas are only fruit in an orchard, pick what you wish to eat. Desires, anger, ambition — and, by God's teeth you are hot with it, boy — they cannot be governed without desires, anger and ambition . . . oh, sorry, sorry. . . ." He paused, then tried to smile. "Tell me, were we making you any wiser?"

"Oh, yes . . . yes . . ." I mumbled fearfully, my mouth numb from one of his blows. "I still want to go to Paris, find what we're looking for . . . Sire, I know I'm foolish . . . a mere child . . . I am sorry for my intrusion. . . ." I stared at him, the words drying up on my lips.

My gabbling only produced a snort from de Montfort. He looked round at Old Robert who held up his hands in a gesture of regretful agreement.

"If we let him loose he will have to be marked first," he said sternly. "No one must believe what he says from now on."

"But he is one of our brightest prospects!" the King responded bitterly. "Are not his opinions valid? Must we not take them into account? He has at least one hair on his chin! Oh, with all this genius, this duress and suffering he must be ready to help rule his king, eh? Put him into a parliament! Why not?" The King grimaced archly, then sneered. "And how did Bacon impress you?"

"A great teacher, sire!"

"He is more confused than we are. I doubt if he can recall the difference between Christ and Mahomet. My own conviction is that they were related. I am going to bathe. When I return for dinner I want this scamp gone for good."

So saying, the King got wearily to his feet and left the room. Old Robert fussed with his fingers, watching him go. When he turned to me I saw there were real tears in his eyes, not rheum. He tottered across to me and took me by the hands.

"Do not think too ill of us, boy," he quavered. "Agreement, consensus, concord — all these things seemed to be more valuable than truth. Our world is breaking up but now we see how we must let it. That way it may find a better shape by chance. Try to forgive us your pain."

De Montfort smiled from his seat by the window, his thick forearms folded over his belt. In his eyes was a kinder light than I had come to expect. It was part pity, part approval, but the remainder was a peculiar mixture of annoyance and regret.

"What a waste," he said. "I liked him."

"You would not harm me, surely?" I said as bravely as I could. "Everything you have asked of me has been performed. I did not ask to be brought into Sherwood. I was on my way to Lincoln to continue my studies. . . ."

Master Henry got to his feet and pulled me up after him. As I was dragged upright my blanket fell away from me and I stood naked in front of the three men. Their faces softened and they smiled, then Master Henry wrapped my blanket round my shoulders and led me to the door.

"On the cheek!" de Montfort called out as the door was closing. "Then people will know not to listen to him."

That is how I came to be branded with an L on my right buttock, this being as much as Master Henry could do for his co-religionist. The sight of this mark has caused much comment during my travels and has been variously interpreted as being the Roman number of my conquests in love, the brand of lechery (these suggestions were made by the same person, an Anatolian widow), a masonic sign — being similar to a set-square — an arrow pointing somewhere. Nowhere has it been reckoned to stand for lunatic and I have never enlightened anyone with this information. More to the point, I have never attempted to explain or expose The Four and what they had intended for me, or their quest to escape from the confusion of the age. To have done so until now would have cost me my life or a second branding with the L. Men make simpler choices these days, even kings. When I look upon the great works of my brothers from the time of King Henry the Third all I see is certainty: it is the same stone, the same design that betokened that earlier age's criticism of itself, and the power of the heresies, my own being a purer form of truth and one I have returned to in my fuller years. Christianity remains my walking-stick to beat off the dogs of the Inquisition but the Two Gods are my secret surety.

And so I come to the final part of my book. When it is completed I must, according to my penance, destroy it by fire to signify the death of my pride. No one will ever read what I have written, even the Abbot of Iona who imposed my penance and will supervise the incineration. In this way will I atone for my sin — one condemned by Albigensian and Christian conscience alike — and be able to live my remaining years in peace. Now that I face the writing of this ultimate chapter I realise how I have done this book for myself, how much I have left out because I am the only one to read it. May every god with a friendly word for Hedric Herbertson forgive all these omissions and inexactitudes. It was my pledge to tell the truth. The act of writing seems to make this only possible in a partial degree, the rest being fumbles and the forgeries of memory.

I am here in Kendal, close to the river, on my way north to Iona. All this country around here I know from my childhood when Bert carried me in his bag over the hills and I drank the milk of foxes. Though this book is destined for the flames, Father, guide my hand, purge my arrogance, then I may return to the world and my greatest triumphs, for the Third Style is mine, culled from the pebble I have always kept and my sight of the Göreme caves of Cappadocia in Asia Minor which I explored during my pilgrimage to Jerusalem. That Hans Seersach saw them, I am certain: but the inspiration for the style is mine and as it conquers the world of architecture it will carry two marks: ⌗ for Hedric Herbertson who will join you in the spirit when all his work is done here on earth; and L for learner, a sign which covers both of us, but I outstripped it and you never did, my darling Dad.

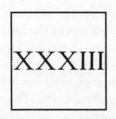

XXXIII

I stood in the stern of the boat, my breeches around my ankles so the breeze could play over my brand, and tried to listen to Master Henry as he rowed me back across the lake. That he thought I could be capable of listening to him while in the toils of such terrible pain is a comment upon his character. He had seen me bent over a kitchen table and the points of two red-hot dagger-blades pressed against my skin at right-angles to each other. He had heard me scream, seen my convulsions and smelt the odour of my seared flesh: yet here he was, applying the long oars to the water without hurry, his fishing-line trolling out over the stern. When we had got into the boat I was still weeping with the pain but that did not stop him seeing to his tackle before we embarked, showing me a little jewelled, golden fish he had bought in Venice which spun in the water, three barbed hooks fashioned from its tail fin. He rambled on about how he had come by this exotic piece of equipment, fashioned by a famous Persian goldsmith at the court of the Roman Emperor in Constantinople, what a bargain it had been, how perch, trout, salmon and pike could not resist it, how he intended to spend most of his old age engaged in the piscatorial art, and so forth. Meanwhile I struggled to digest my most excruciating shame and stem my last flow of childhood's tears. Since that day I have suffered many ignominious punishments — some justified, others less so — but there has never been one followed by such cruel indifference from a person counted as a friend. Master Henry spoke to me as if he assumed my present state of mind to be happy. When he did condescend to mention the branding it was to say that he looked upon it as a purification and I would be well advised to think of it in that way too.

"You will love that mark in future years. If you take the trouble to look at it in a mirror now and again it will remind you that you grew up in a worth-while way, not too easily, not knowing it all, not too much comfort . . ." he said, grunting as he pulled a little stronger on the left oar to straighten his course. "So few people have a useful childhood. They come out of it spoilt and soft, untried, as dependent on others as the day they were born. It is not a pure time in our lives, you know. It is all muddle and mess, strivings and strainings. Very little is clear to us. All we want to do is grow up. The attainment of age seems to be a magical triumph and we ignore the sadness of those who have got there already . . . whoa!"

Master Henry jerked at the line which was tied to his right foot. Far back in the lake behind us there was a splash.

"Is he still on? Oh, don't let him have got away . . . no . . . no. . ." he said excitedly, pulling in his line hand over hand as fast as he could until he paused, tugged at the line, then put the loops he had retrieved into the well of the boat and resumed rowing.

"Got off. Big fish, I'd say, by the feel of him. What were we discussing? Ah, childhood. There is no golden period laid down by Nature in a man's life, but only what he himself creates. You have an advantage over others, Hedric. You can be certain when you left innocence. It must be today. And you can say you are grown up when you can sit down again."

Master Henry looked at me for an answering smile to his humour but I had none. I stared at the bottom of the boat, the most bitter resentment in my heart. Under the moonlight I saw coil after coil of knotted horsehairs flowing over the gunwale as the fishing-line was teased out by the drag of the golden lure in the water. I counted the knots to keep me from hurling myself at Master Henry.

"Hedric, a few words to help you on your way. After this . . . unfortunate error on your part, let us say . . . it is not possible for us to continue our plan for your education. That must be aborted, I'm afraid, though it fills me with regret because you are a very talented young fellow, truly." He sighed in rhythm with his oar-stroke, mocking me gently. "Oh, the young, the young! Such meddlers! Never satisfied. Remember this, Hedric: one cannot only do justice to those one likes, nor injustice to those one dislikes. The aim of the law and the outlaw is *the same for all*. That is what The Four have come to acknowledge, but how, when we have to deal with people like yourself? You knew the island was a forbidden place, but you went there. Why? I know. You love the unknown. You are nosy, curious, excitable, and I adore you for it, my child. Without that spark what will become of this leaden world? It will sink into squalor."

"Are you going to let me go home?" I interrupted him, sick of his prating derisiveness.

"Home? Where is home?" he said, laughing.

"Where my father is!"

"Will you tell him what has happened to you?"

"It will be difficult not to," I replied bitterly. "This will take weeks to heal."

"Oh, he will have guessed who Hood is by now. They all have, but they would never admit it," he said genially, burying his huge head deeper in the fat of his shoulders as he pulled on the oars. "No one who has felt the harness of government on his back should be surprised that the King and Hood are the same man. But go ahead and tell your father how we have chastised you, by all means. He should have a natural interest in all you are being taught. Who knows? — he may learn something from it himself. A wise father profits from his child if he keeps his eyes and ears open. Oh, Hedric, Hedric," he sighed, beaming at me with as sweet a smile as I will ever see. "We could have been in Paris together. Paris! Then I would have shown you life. This is a crude, barbarous country by comparison, but improving," he mused, dropping to a slower stroke, his head lifted to the dark heavens. "The truth must be made plainer than Aristotle made it, or Augustine, or Old Robert. We Albigensians could be the people to draw the veil away. But will they let us? Dare they? However, they know we are an option. We may have the secret. The Cretins are so anxious to know the truth now that they will never destroy us in case we are the holders of the key . . . a key they may melt down if it suits them. . . . Ouch!"

The line had run out completely and halted, jerking violently where it was tied to Master Henry's foot. The noose of horsehair tightened abruptly, making him cry out.

"What's this? Still on?" he shouted, leaving go of the oars and grabbing the line. "He's been following us, swimming with the boat, the devil."

Far back in the lake I heard another splash, bigger than the first. Master Henry's eyes shone as he looked over my shoulder in the direction of the noise.

"My soul, what a size!" he breathed. "What a creature. Watch, boy, watch!"

Seizing my waist he forced me to turn round. I could see the ripples where the fish had jumped. They radiated out in the moonlight, bright rings dying away behind the slicing line.

"What is it?" I mumbled, not wanting to incite his callous madness further. "I can't see anything."

"Oh, a pike, a great pike!" Master Henry cried, thrills of pleasure thickening his voice. "This is the one I've been after for years." He held the line up so droplets of water sprang from it, then hauled strongly. "And I have a wonderful recipe for him passed down from the kitchen of Abbot Mellitus when he first built Westminster on the Isle of Thorns. To begin!" He paused, holding the line aloft so water droplets sprang from it, then reached forward to haul in again. "Empty and scale the biggest fish you can find. Wipe it dry and give it a few slashes across its sides, then stick it with *lardoons*, anchovies and slices of *cornichon*. Fill up the belly with a sausage meat stuffing seasoned with tarragon, aromatic pepper, a laurel leaf, a sprig of thyme, fennel, cloves, nutmeg . . . whoops! Not so fast, Lucius!"

I could see the horsehair line biting into the fat of his fingers as the fish sounded. Master Henry pulled the line away from where it had become embedded, wrapping a corner of his cloak around the hand to protect it.

"Did I mention two whole eggs? We'll need those for the binding. . . ." The line swung through the water until Master Henry was leaning over the side, his hand being pulled directly downwards. "He's under the boat. Pray there are no rocks or weeds down there! Then, Hedric, we lay the pike on two stones in front of a wood fire on top of strongly glowing embers. It must get well-cooked and smoked at the same time. Let it roast, turning frequently, for half an hour." The line tugged him so hard his whole hand went into the water, tearing the fabric of his cloak. "Ah! After this combat he will taste delicious. Did I forget the chervil? When you are serving him up, pull out the central bone which will bring all the side bones with it in one stroke, then cut him into steaks. The wine for pike is . . . wait!" He jerked the line, testing. "I think he's sulking down there, Hedric. A big boy like that, sulking. How perverse. . . !"

The line moved upwards from the depths, Master Henry hauling in as fast as he could to keep it taut.

"I can feel he's tiring. This is his last run. Then he will surrender," he crooned, sweat glittering in his eyebrows. "It is nearly over."

The fish burst out of the lake, tail thrashing, long, lean body twisting and bending in desperate efforts to shake out the lure stuck in its prognathous jaws. I held my breath, my pain forgotten for a moment. Long after it was gone back beneath the surface in a shower of spray I saw it hanging there, half in splendour, half in grim voraciousness, the fabulous lure glittering in the corner of its mouth.

I stared back over the wake of the boat towards Hood's island which was a lumpen darkness. What fight had I put up in that kitchen full of cooking smells as they branded me for life? What display of indignation had I mounted? Nothing but screams and whimpers.

With my head hung low I watched for the pike, hoping it would jump again. Master Henry had gone quiet. When I looked for the line in the water it was nowhere to be seen; then I encountered Master Henry's eyes. They were fixed on my poor brand, exposed to him in all its glory as I turned to see the fish. Tears were pouring down his magnificent cheeks and into his scar of honour as if it were a culvert. His shapely lips trembled.

"He broke me," he said, holding up the end of the line, "and he's gone off with my lure from Byzantium."

"What would the wine have been, had you caught him?" I asked with barely disguised insolence, my spirits rising.

"Oh, something dry and sharp and slightly acid," he replied morosely, his eyes telling me how he understood my enjoyment of his loss and the fish's escape. "I'll be back for him, never fear. Meanwhile, we'd better get you *home!*"

He snatched up the oars and pulled, deliberately making me stumble and sit down as the boat jerked forward. I cried out with the pain as my brand came into contact with the bench. It was not until we were near the shore that I realised how far I had been able to forget my own agony during the pike's battle for its life.

As Master Henry had seemed so unconcerned about Bert's possible reactions to what had occurred on the island I was surprised to be released from the boat once we had touched the shore. Master Henry told me to go back to Bert and tell him whatever I wanted.

"It is of no consequence what he thinks," he said dismissively. "Let him get as angry as he likes."

"Why don't you come and tell him yourself?" I retorted, pulling my breeches up and wincing. "If you're not afraid of your own brother mason, your own brother Albigensian. . . . Why don't you try to explain. . . ?"

"You have learnt nothing, have you, Hedric? I am appalled at your lack of common sense," he muttered angrily, settling himself back at the oars as I crawled painfully over the side and let myself down into the shallow water. "Your life has been spared. Go out into the world and make a living. Forget all this . . . ambition. It will make you unhappy as well as impudent."

I stood up to my waist in the water, glad of the soothing cool on my throbbing wound, watching the boat slide away, the bulk of my tormentor moving to and fro as he plied the oars.

Man's nature is one thing, one's own is another. Although I have had some success at anticipating the moods and thoughts of others in my time, I have never ceased to be astonished at what my own mind and emotions will come up with at certain moments. As Master Henry rowed away out of my life, for I never saw him again, I knew I still loved him in spite of everything he had done to me.

I crept back to my father's house through the darkened forest, my breeches and wet clothes in a bundle under my arm. On the way I met the Green Parley's watch. The bowmen demanded to know why I was out after nightfall and half-naked, sharing a few coarse jests amongst themselves at my expense. I told them I had been walking by the lake and had fallen in. They let me go, advising me to leave walking on the water to the Lord God.

When I reached Bert's house I could hear them all shouting at each other long before I got to the door. They were having yet another row — this time about me. I could hear my father's irascible roaring as it occasionally surfaced from a sea of female voices, all attacking Hedric's attitude to this, Hedric's refusal to do that, Hedric's aloofness, Hedric's arrogance, Hedric's disobedience, Hedric's aggressive nature. Bert was trying to defend me, telling the women about my lack of a mother's care, of the hardness of our wandering life together, how he had often failed as a father, of my abilities, my intelligence, my energy, my perseverance. But as the row progressed he began to edge his comments about me with criticism. He equivocated, half-agreed, conceded a point or two in my disfavour, said that he knew I wasn't easy to get along with, asked the women for more patience in dealing with me, even pity. Then he began to cajole, to coax and wheedle, begging them to help him cope with my intractable and stiff-necked superiority, my shortage of good qualities, my pride.

By this time I was pressed up against the window aperture, my heart thumping with horror as I heard him denigrate me to these strangers, these outsiders. The voice I loved more than any other was castigating me, heaping blame and recriminations on my head, but worse, talking behind my back like a loathsome old gossip at a water-pump.

"He's got too good an opinion of himself," I heard him say. "I've tried to knock it out of him but he won't be told. People have encouraged him to think too much of himself, so it's not all his fault. There've been times when I've felt like throttling him" (good-natured winning chuckles here), "but we've rubbed along somehow."

This treacherous calumny produced an appeased murmur from the women. Hearing him betray me had assuaged their bile. I peered through the window and saw him sitting by the fire, the women standing around him in a circle, shifting about with nervous excitement as they scented the kill. Bert looked up, flashing them the famous, brilliant smile I had thought was reserved for me.

"Give the lad another chance," he pleaded, coaxing them as if he had no authority left. "Help me with him!"

One of the women suggested Bert could build a hut for me a little way apart from the house. My father, grasping at anything which would get him off the hook, was quick to make an enthusiastic reply. This was a good idea, a constructive notion. He would think about it, discuss it with Hedric. Ah, there he made a mistake. She did not want Hedric to be consulted, she wanted Hedric *told*!

I retreated from the window, hardly able to stand. My heart felt as though it would batter its way out of my breast and fly away into the forest. The pain of my brand was nothing compared to what I suffered now.

I lay face down on the leaves and buried my face in my arms. What I did next cannot be described as weeping; that is too soft a word. All my blood rebelled, my flesh rose up in fearsome indignation. There were tears but they were hot and salt as if poured from scalding sea kettles. I cursed my father and all men who had pretended fatherly feelings for me. I cursed my mother. That I did not know whether she was dead or alive made the curse a hundredfold more bitter. I cursed my birth, my self, my world.

Where sleep comes from we do not know: from fonts of dreams or fatigue, from death swimming in the blood to warn us of his eventual

298

conquest; it is all a conjecture. With my being in the greatest turmoil it had ever experienced, my heart on the point of splitting, I finished my feverish maledictions and lay panting, scouring my memory for other things to execrate. Then, with the suddenness of a descending hand, I was plunged into slumber and forgetfulness.

XXXIV

I awoke under a drift of leaves, the wind having risen during the night and mercifully covered me over. For a long time I stayed under my sweet-smelling blanket, thinking through all that had happened to me the previous day. I was not sure I wanted to get up and walk back into that world. If I remained hidden in the forest then slipped away it would satisfy everyone: The Four would understand why I had fled; my father would be glad I had gone. What I would feel seemed to have no bearing on the matter, my emptiness and sadness rendering me incapable of self-interest. I had been so completely rejected by all who knew me that my spirit was numbed.

The sun broke through the lattice of oak-boughs above me. I stirred and my brand immediately began to throb. Crawling out of the leaves I tried to stand up but my legs would not hold me. On my hands and knees I shuffled over to a sapling and pulled myself up, then stood swaying, my head in a haze of pain. The clarity of my vision was affected. I watched the sunlight coalesce into a golden fog around the trees.

I must have stood there for an hour, refusing to let go of the sapling. Voices came from the nearby path as people passed along it but I did not call out. Who would be interested? I asked myself. Why should they care?

My right leg was very stiff and the area of my thigh immediately below the brand was hot to the touch. The burn itself was aflame, so heated that I dare not touch it. I did not have to be a doctor to know that it was turning septic. Before long there would be a fever. The poison would travel through my body until it reached my vital organs. Once it entered my liver, kidneys, lungs and heart I would die.

So be it, I thought. That will make them feel guilty.

Suicide has a kind of honour among the young. It is the ultimate means of drawing attention to oneself without having to endure the aftermath, or admit the puerile weakness that brought about the decision. If one has a condition that can be neglected in order to bring about death, this is a boon; especially if it involves the degree of maltreatment, contumely and cruelty mine had. I will let the brand kill me, I swore, clinging hold of my tree. When they find my body no one will ever doubt I died as a result of injustice.

All the morning, I stood there, waiting. The sun reached its meridian then began to go down: I remained on my feet, willing the poison to flow and race through. The path, which was only fifty yards away through the trees, was a thoroughfare between settlements and always busy during the day. All I would have had to do is call out and someone would have heard me. But I kept silent, grimly staring through the glades as the shadows of the great oaks lengthened.

It was one of my father's wives who found me. Her name was Beth and she was the ugliest and most unpleasant of them all. When she came waddling through the trees towards me, her arms outstretched, I groaned aloud and yelled at her to go away. Her stupid face did not respond, even when I pushed her down as she struggled to embrace me.

"Come, come our Hedric," she chided me, getting to her feet. "None of that. Your father is worried out of his wits about you. We've been searching for you all day. Where've ye been? What's happened to you? What's this? Oh, dear God, what have they done to you? He'll go mad, I tell you, he'll go mad. They've gone too far this time. . . ."

With this prattle in my ears I allowed her to lead me back to the house and Bert. When we got there he was still out hunting for me. Beth made me lie down on my side and as her sister-wives returned she displayed me like a trophy. I was an object for pity, love and care. They became indignant about my maltreatment. I lay there, having refused to say a word in explanation of what had happened, and recalled what I had heard at the window the previous night. Were these the same women? Who was it I had heard traducing my name? Ghosts? Nymphs? Or these swollen creatures with their present blandishments? I ground my teeth and waited for Bert.

When he returned it was dark. The women had tried to feed me but I had refused to eat. They had attempted to dress the wound but I had torn it away. Bert had to see it as it was.

It was a moment I had waited for.

When he entered the room the women were clustered around me cooing, offering me titbits. Bert eased them aside, looked down into

301

my eyes which guided him towards the horrifying lividness of my pus-filled wound, then knelt by my side and said cheerfully:

"You'll be all right, son. That'll heal."

He was right, of course. It did heal. My wound became not only a household concern but one that aroused the sympathetic interest of the entire Sherwood community. No one — including my father — asked how it had come about that a great L had been stamped upon my right buttock: all of them were too far gone in their acceptance of Hood's violent and arbitrary rule to question any punishment he might care to hand out. My crime was taken for granted, the appropriateness of my chastisement assumed — but I was still only a boy mutilated in the coarse of a hard life. It could have been any adventurous, mischievous child's fate.

Bert was so complacent about it even his wives thought him unnatural. He appeared to have no curiosity at all about what had happened. It was enough for him that justice had been done to my overweening pride. When I did attempt to tell him the details he only let me get as far as my swim to the island before holding up his hand to stop me. "Say no more," he said emphatically. "To go to Hood's island without authority is a hanging matter in the greenwood. You have been let off lightly." He did not even ask me what my brand stood for. As for the identity of the people responsible he made it plain that he never wanted to know.

My loyalty to Albigensian truth throughout my life has not been solely due to upbringing, nor am I an ardent traditionalist. In my faith are explanations of fortune's changes and why the blows of fate are delivered: also, it is a creator's religion, taking as its premise the unfinished and disappointing state of the original work of the Two Gods. When one's father is equally unfinished and disappointing then it is natural for the creative son to apply his talents to this inadequate parent in order to improve him. My father had reached such a point of cowed submissiveness, had accepted such a lowly role in Hood's alleged paradise, that I now felt this urge to fashion him anew. I would design him, put in better foundations, and rebuild my Bert. As with our craft, the keywords would be patience and diligence.

Ham was a regular visitor during my convalescence. Now that I had suffered so much for my ambition Bert was quite happy for my philosopher-friend to visit me: he needed no further reminder of the rewards of intellectual pride than my sick-bed. I could not refrain from telling Ham the whole story, once I had sworn him to secrecy. He affected a lack of surprise but I could tell the news shook him. If he was a prisoner in Sherwood then it was with the knowledge of those whom he looked upon as his patrons: de Montfort and the Bishop of Lincoln. As time went by he received requests from the various Green Parleys to examine and comment upon the social, political and agricultural experiments going on in the greenwood and Ham could perceive a cause for his detention. What he could not do was decide how to say anything critical about them without displeasing any of The Four. So he edged deeper into obscurantism, cloaking his meaning with recondite, unintelligible references to mystic authors, employing logic which perplexed rather than elucidated until the Green Parleys approached him no more. By the time I effected my escape, bearing my father from Hood's domain, Ham had been spirited away. The next mention I heard of Roger Bacon was during my pilgrimage to Rome. He was in Paris and in trouble. Alchemy, magic and astrology were his downfall, it is said. Ham claimed them as manifestations of divine wisdom, an opinion which enraged the Pope to such a degree that he put Ham in prison for years. I do not like to think of him in such straits but, no doubt, he made the best of it. With so much generative power in his head he would find means of continuing his life's work wherever he was. Ham could dissert upon a mouse's stool or a speck of dust. The very stones of his prison would become parts of his proof.

Our exit from the greenwood was devised with the aid of one of Hood's most outlandish experiments. Once Ham had gone The Four must have sent word that I was to be consulted in a capacity similar to Ham's, having been his disciple. There was no mention of the branding, no further admonishments or warnings; all I received were "requests" from different Green Parleys scattered throughout the forest engaged in explorative schemes on behalf of The Four. My wound had hardly healed before the first summons came. Needless to say, it provoked a comment from my father that Hood must have been led to believe I had learned my lesson. I refrained from pointing out to Bert that as far as I could see he was never "requested" to be anything more than a subject on which ideas were tested, whereas, in my case, Hood still assumed I could think. This was petty of me, I agree, but this scrap of intellectual self-respect enabled me to outwit the all-encompassing, pervasive power of The Four; an influence which, in the dark hours of my sickness, I had felt to be unchallengeable. It was everywhere; it was nowhere. All attitudes and opinions were represented in its cause. It was Christian, it was Albigensian, it was atheist when it chose to be. It would try anything, agree to anything, betray anything and absorb anything. Now, with me, it was confident I could be useful because I had been put in my place.

In my role as observer I witnessed many absurd experiments, all carried out to gorge The Four's inordinate curiosity. A humanitarian and scientific purpose was claimed for all schemes; the general good was the excuse for their cruel experimental madness. It was put out that the people came up with the ideas! True, it was the intimidated condition of their minds made such vicious wastefulness possible, but democracy had no part in the process. To my shame I must record that after my branding I made no attempt to say what I really thought of these scandalous researches and treated them as if the future of civilisation depended upon such murderous nonsense.

Hood had a particular interest in one of the most foolish of these enterprises: bat-farming. The site of the experiment was a system of limestone caves at Creswell. Colonies of the creatures had made the caves their exclusive habitat. The story was current in Sherwood that Hood had holed up at Creswell many years ago while being pursued by a lord and his followers from Worksop. While he hid in the caves his companions were the millions of bats, and they had sustained him through an entire winter. Leather from their wings had provided his boots; fur from their bodies his clothes; their meat, his food. Also he had become attuned to their language of high-pitched sounds in which he found the most beautiful harmonies of music.

When I first visited the Creswell Caves and met the pale, shrunken creatures who had been set to emulate Hood's mythical feat of survival, my orders were to comment upon the sense of space and dimension created by the environment. It had been noticed that the subjects increasingly behaved as if they inhabited a larger and loftier place than the cramped caves.

My observations bore this out: after six months of living off and with bats, subjects of both sexes lost their proper sense of spatial proportion; they took greater steps, made larger, slower gestures, kept bumping into things. Also their hair fell out, they vomited constantly, they lost all interest in sex and started making experiments of their own as to how best they might commit suicide.

It was a long-running scheme, initiated when King John was Hood. Hundreds of people had already perished by the time I arrived at Creswell upon my Green Parley's orders. I was astonished at the size of the experiment and the unreal wildness of the denizens in their ribbed boots and brown, cross-hatched fur jerkins. They had a pallor streaked with a purple lattice — their own veins, poisoned — and most were completely bald. To look into their eyes was to peep into Sodom and Gomorrah: bloodshot furies, yellow smoke, the pupils wide as a carp's mouth opening and closing as they strained for light.

The Creswell experiment had never been a success: to be sent there was a sentence of death. Half a mile away, in the forest, there was a graveyard full of those who had given their lives for Hood's whim — an inherited whim by now! Yet no one would speak up and condemn the futility of continuing the scheme. When I submitted my report I kept to my designated task: yes, the subjects at Creswell did suffer from a defective sense of spatial awareness. This might be attributable to living in a permanent state of darkness or a traceable component in the organism of the bat. I referred to Aristotle (of course); and al-Ghazzali who studied spatial blindness at the Baghdad court two hundred years ago; plus a small work by the Spanish Jew Avencebrol on the difference between divine and human comprehension of space in the universe. At the end of my report I asked if I could be allowed to return to Creswell to continue my study at some future date, taking my father with me. His wide experience of architectural forms and spatial relationships created within enclosed structures would be very useful to me.

Within three days I received an answer from my Green Parley. I was to be allowed to return to Creswell for the purposes outlined but my father was to precede me and live in the colony for a month in order to become intimately acquainted with the conditions. While he was there he would be expected to draw up a plan for extending the caves in order to accommodate the experiment on a much larger scale.

When the order came through for Bert to go to Creswell I did not inform him that it was my fault. The poor women were staggered by the decision. Life had improved of late. They were all rubbing along together much better than before. Three of them were pregnant. A new garden had been wrested from the ferns. Even I was a cause for rejoicing: my behaviour had become more tractable and generous. As a family we were growing closer, sharing the burden, building a future with Hood. To send the object of our loyalty and affection to a withering death was hardly a reward for all the good work we had put into this innovative experiment in English polygamy. So furious did the women become that they complained to the Green Parley, demanding either to keep Bert or go with him. The effect was the reduction of my father's wives from five to four. Poor, ugly Beth who had saved me from a lonely death in the forest was summarily divorced from Bert and sent to a multiple water-mill project in East Retford. In a written reply to the grievances of the remaining wives, the Green Parley quoted as their authorities two philosophers who had recommended four as the maximum number of wives a man should have: Al-Ghazzali and the Spanish Jew, Avencebrol, both influenced by Koranic law.

It reeked of Roger Bacon. Whether it was a coded message or a reminder from The Four that they knew all things and all thoughts, and could draw on the best minds whenever they wished, I do not know. The time was long past for fear or speculation. I had to concentrate on Creswell and our deliverance.

My father's departure for the caves was reminiscent of Greek tragedy: neither Aeschylus nor Euripides could have wrung more from a parting. With that intrinsic feminine genius for making-do which has kept the world hanging together since the beginning of human time, the wives busied themselves trying to make Bert happy until the day of dread. Then they deliberately undid their handiwork by unleashing their sorrow. Bert could not admit he considered himself a doomed man but this did not prevent the women indulging in an outburst of grief so strenuous it wilted the resolve of the Creswell transport when it arrived to pick Bert up. I hung back, unwilling to play-act more than was necessary, but watched my father very closely to see how he treated me at the moment when he believed himself irretrievably destined for death. He would have to say *something*.

Bert managed to disappoint me again. He said nothing.

"Look after yourself, Dad," I whispered in his ear as he climbed into the cart, the wives clutching at him in their extremities of grief. "I'll get you out of there, I promise."

"You look after yourself and my lovelies," he called out as the cart jerked forward. "Never mind me. By the time you get to Creswell I'll have answered all their questions about bats or any other bloody thing!"

For a moment I saw the old Bert, his eyes blazing, mole's paws gripping the edges of the cart, and heard his defiant laugh. Then he was gone beneath the boughs, head shaking.

That night, in a house of mourning women, the true nature of my feelings for my father emerged. For the first time in my life I was with people who needed him, had come to love him — in spite of the diminishment and demeaning he had suffered at their hands, or because of it, perhaps. Bert had reduced himself in order to survive, then he had further reduced himself in order to help others survive: from this had grown a bondage he had spent his previous life avoiding. If he would have a memorial on earth it might be this chorus of sorrow: what he had built in his career as a white cutter was no more than piles of stone, and I, perhaps, the most forgettable pile of all. As I lay on my bed in the corner of the room with the women pacing up and down, sobbing and whimpering, my dry eyes were an accusation of unnaturalness. Did I care about my father for his own sake? Or did he have to fit my inner need? I had effectively sent him to the caves in order that he be purged of his new self and his old self returned safe to me as its custodian.

Was this the manner of all sons? I asked myself as the women fell asleep, exhausted by so much sorrow. Was this Nature at work, or me? Why could I not look upon my father as a friend and cut these cords of blood? Nature has made me his superior in many things, I mused unhappily, trying to deafen myself to the moans of the dreaming women. Outside the night birds were fluting sadly.

Suddenly I sat bolt upright, clutching my head.

Or has *he* deliberately made me his superior in many things? Is that a true father's purpose?

My month of waiting to join Bert at Creswell was a sad time. His achievement as a husband and the love which had been generated in that crowded household came under attack by the worst enemy of such things: time. When it was known that my father had been sent away to the caves our neighbours in the settlement carefully and quietly let us know that they found our situation very pitiable but this did not stop men starting to hang about the house after only a week

307

had passed. Within a fortnight one of the wives was absent from her duties so often it created dissension: her shameless behaviour was emulated by another wife shortly afterwards who didn't see why she should have to cover for her sister's lewdness; from then on the whole thing degenerated into a shambles of gossip and recrimination. Only one wife kept her head, loyally refusing to be tempted. She was not the prettiest or the strongest but her quality of steadfast wifely honourableness made up for it all. Her name was Lily and I called her loyal Lily until the day I left for Creswell. It was my plan to remove my father from her arms for ever; she had treated me kindly, keeping the house decent while the other three women collapsed into self-indulgent sluttishness; she had given all her devotion for nothing and, I suspect, would have to do so again; but I had to be callous enough to walk away, leaving her in ignorance. To this day I can see loyal Lily in her apron. She stands in the overgrown garden, slight, vulnerable, sad-eyed, her hand raised in a gesture which says: come back if you can but I know you can't. If she ever found another husband he was a lucky man, if you like that sort of thing.

XXXV

The caves at Creswell lie in a limestone gorge which has a surface stream fed by subterranean waters. The settlement is strictly guarded. Over the years many desperate victims of Hood's experiments have tried to escape through the surrounding forest but have failed. Their debilitated condition, the close security at the caves' entrances, their warped visual and proportional senses have conspired to defeat them. When I arrived at Creswell I had the advantage of knowing these drawbacks. For my own part I was as fit and strong as ever I had been, having prepared myself for the ordeal; but I knew that Bert would be ill. No one could live at Creswell and retain good health. He would be a burden during our escape. I would have to nurse him into freedom.

I was given a room at the guest-quarters close by the archers' barracks and escorted in and out of the caves each day. I made no attempt to hide my interest in my father's whereabouts, thinking it would excite the suspicion of the controller if I showed such an unnatural disinclination. It was mid-December now and the state of the subjects was pitiable whereas the bats thrived. In all the major caves there had been a huge increase before hibernation and the roofs were covered, dense black folds of the creatures hanging silently over the freezing subjects. I went from huddled shape to huddled shape, coaxing comments out of them, encouraging them to talk about themselves: but all I was doing was searching for my father in their dark, terrible faces, for the controller would tell me nothing.

He had no record of Bert.

For the date on which I calculated Bert must have arrived, and a week after, there was no entry in the controller's book about my father.

In front of me he checked the roll of every cave in the system, also the entries in the burial account: not a mention of Bert. It was as if my father had never existed.

I kept my head, refusing to go further than a display of filial concern. A request for information on Bert's whereabouts was sent back to our Green Parley, the controller having assumed an error had been made somewhere along the line. His opinion was that Bert had been side-tracked into another scheme while in transit. It had happened before. The most likely culprit was a drastic longevity experiment based on Greek athleticism which was located not far from Blyth. "They get through a lot of folk very quickly," the controller told me. "It wouldn't be the first time they've stolen from our quotas."

I knew he was lying. The sufferings of my apprenticeship to the mighty had taught me always to anticipate the wilfulness of their ways. The game was still on. They were playing with me.

Bert was at Creswell. Within this vast melancholy maze he was waiting for me. The Four knew exactly where that was and that I would try to find him. It was in their power to stop me but they had let me get this far. Reading their minds I came to believe they wanted me to carry on my search and be successful: then they could dispose of Hedric Herbertson and Herbert Haroldson together and be done with them.

Dutifully I did my rounds through the caves each day: equally dutifully I reconnoitred the gorge and the forest for other places where my father might be. I was not followed, as far as I knew, nor was I harassed. The controller took the trouble to ask after my state of mind: was I worried? Had I reached the stage where I was truly independent of my father? Oh, yes, he was sure we would get some positive news soon.

When the archers came for me two hours before sunrise on my eleventh day at Creswell I was not surprised. They stood and watched me while I dressed and asked no questions when I packed my things, an indication I did not expect to be coming back. The controller was waiting for me at the gate to the guest-quarters. I think there must have been something in my step and the way I carried myself for he made no attempt at explanations but merely smiled and shrugged as he led us off towards the gorge. It was quiet there, only the running stream raising its voice. I was conscious of the cold and the millions of sleeping bats hanging up in the caves waiting for winter to end.

We entered the largest cave, walking slowly between the bat-dung-encrusted cots of the subjects. Not one stirred. They were as uninterested in our presence as the hibernating bats, lost in a numbed universe of sleep. At the back of the main cavern we descended into a narrow, water-bearing passage. We could not walk side by side. I was thrust to the front and given a torch. In this manner we wandered into the limestone for another half-an-hour, shuffling along, bending under the low roof, crawling over small cataracts in the stream, the noise of which filled the passage.

After I had descended a difficult, slippery section of a narrow waterfall I turned round and held up the torch to help those following me. There was no one there. I waited, the torch held high over my head away from the tumbling water, but no one appeared.

The message was obvious. Without being told I knew that I must continue alone.

I had not long to wait. Another ten minutes of progress down the passage brought me to where The Four had wanted me to be.

The only original source of light is God, it is argued by some: all manifestations of light are derived from this fountainhead, no matter what the form. The phosphorescence of the sea-fish and the sea itself in warm climes, is dependent on that divine supply. Moonlight, starlight, the light in a human eye or a hawk's eye are given by the Good God, it is said. It does not require the sun. In the darkest night a thing can glow from what is within it; the essence.

That marble in a lightless cavern should provide its own light is, therefore, unamazing to a philosopher but it amazes the mason. I emerged from the passage, squeezing tightly between two high, smoothed sides of rock, into a lofty dome full of the softest sublime light. Prepared for shocks as I was it was all I could do to stop myself crying out; but I managed to keep my delight and my fear in rein. As I stood at the passage entrance I could see that the light was not static: it moved and increased, as did the sounds of voices. Far above me I could detect the dawn but its light was supplemented by the stone it fell on and passed through, for the dome itself was a filigree so delicate it admitted light. As I looked upwards I saw moisture descending in pearly swathes: the dew, I said to myself, wanting to shout it out. This great work is so fine that it draws in the dew to dazzle us all.

For I was not alone by then. My comprehension had grasped the sight of men working on the towering scaffolding up the walls. I knew their functions, all the old jobs, their tools, their manner of work, their shouts and calls. That Bert was one of them I never doubted. What I could not decipher from this great scene was *the style*.

Words have their ways. As a worker in stone it has been a battle for me to use language in place of my tools and my material. To approach perfection from two directions is a privilege afforded to very few and, I fear, I am not amongst them.

What I saw there is what the world has yet to see: the Second Style of Emergence which I have now developed into the Third. As it has been a self-imposed penance that I must refrain from employing the new styles and restrict myself to old ones until my atonement is complete, no building has been constructed in either Second or Third. Once my book is finished and incinerated in front of the altar I am free to liberate the new form. Having built myself a reputation as a great architect in a style which I knew to be obsolete it is reasonable to assume wonderful times for me in the future. But first, the words. I will honestly attempt to describe what I saw. My achievement will be meagre but that is language's failing as much as mine.

The dome was a skin of pure marble tooled so intricately the suffused light appeared to come through a glass. This, however, was no more than a canopy for the central magnificence which lay below, the dome being an artificial sky over the building itself, a structure no more than one hundred and twelve feet six inches long by eighty-seven feet six inches high and wide at its highest and widest points, being in the unmistakable shape of an egg supported only where it touched the floor of the cavern at the point of its bottom curve.

There was no scaffolding on the structure. All the work was being done on the cavern walls which enclosed it. Ribbing was extended from the floor to the canopy in very fine multiple parabolas, the only feature which was reminiscent of the style current in the outside world, the First and Pointed.

I stood, entranced by the audacious beauty of the building. A few people stood by the entrance, looking across at me. I had no eyes for them, only the ravishing form, the details of which I drank in slowly, lingering over the tiny fenestration. As the veils of moisture spiralled down from the canopy swirling light glinted on freckles of glass all over the building's shell. At the point of the upper egg where its curve began to taper into the longer, the proportion of distance being three to five of its full length, there was a double excrescence of delicate, curving towers, each no wider than a man, which reminded me of an insect's feelers. They groped upwards with a jaunty, rather hopeless air which initially frustrated my total acceptance of the form: then I saw what was being done to my senses and ecstatically approved.

The people at the entrance began to walk towards me. I knew I only had a few moments before the impact of this superb creation was polluted for me in some degree. My love for it was immediate and unconditional. How it had been achieved, I knew not, except that it was the work of great genius. I strove to imprint that first impression on my mind so it could never be washed away by pain, bitterness or brutality. In its lowly, hump-backed form the egg did not resist assimilation: it slid into my spirit as though I were the nest for it. My understanding of what it meant was absolute. I did not need the architect to explain.

It was a reaction against all the great arrow-headed annoyances of the First and Pointed style, the god-threatening, the perpetual challenge of the pygmy kings and popes screaming at the heavens. The egg said, Do not hazard all happiness on finding God. Ask to be left alone by the divine. Press yourself to the earth. Scent around for self-discovery. Let the message to the Creators be: Leave us to find out what we are without you, then come again when you can see we are fit to receive you. Then we will be ready for a new style and a new beginning. The egg will be obsolete.

"You do well to tremble, Hedric," said a voice seeming to come from years ago in my life. I looked to find its owner and saw Old Robert. In the extraordinary light he seemed much younger. Then I remembered it was only a few months since we had been together in Guildford. So much had happened to me and now, this, a rebirth in living, breathing, mothering stone.

"Bow to your King," Old Robert whispered, taking my elbow, then, in a louder voice. "He is overwhelmed, sire. Give him a moment to get over it."

Old Robert sat me down on a rock, keeping hold of my hand. I looked up and saw the face with the drooping eyelid. He stared at me vexatiously, bending to speak to the short, beetle-browed de Montfort beside him.

"Do you think he's disgusted? Have we offended his aesthetic sense?" he drawled. "Surely we don't have to explain what it is, not to him. His own father was responsible for the inception of it."

"No!"

I sprang to my feet, shaking off the bishop's restraining hand. De Montfort grinned and stepped back as if to give me room.

"Why do you say no to me, boy?" the King said, archly. "Have you forgotten the manners we taught you?"

"It was not my father!" I blurted out.

King Henry waved his hand dismissively.

"Oh, there is no need to protect your father. He deserves the credit for what his imagination has achieved. Now we have built this and we can see what we are dealing with. Let us know your opinion of it, when you have a moment."

Old Robert smiled behind his hand. The King glanced quickly at him, then turned back to me.

"You should be proud of your father," he admonished me. "Now, would you like to see inside?"

I was moving before he could finish what he was saying. The effects of the canopy light on the interior through the fenestration had already excited my mind: the bracing of the continuous shell arch, how such vast contours of stone could be supported, hundreds of questions were waiting to be answered.

The King stepped aside to allow me through. As I passed him I began to run.

Many buildings decline in authority as one gets close. They require the perspective of distance and their setting in landscape. As I sped towards the egg it drew me onwards, asserting its power, changing its beauty to accommodate my nearness. By the time I reached the entrance I was within a massive, invisible embrace and there were two shapes in my mind: the one I had seen from the outside, poised in its space; the other, the form which attached my being to its flowing, rising symmetry as if I were part of the fabric, a speck of dust drawn round, over and under the lustrous, curving stone.

Then I dared not enter.

My heart hammered in my chest. My feet were made of lead. What was I doing here, so ignorant, so unborn, so weak and incomplete? This was the apogee. A thousand years of inspiration and drudgery had gone into this work. It was a marvel, so powerful it had had to be constructed in secret. Even now it had not been let loose upon the world. Once I entered it and absorbed every effect, dimension and significance then I would be irretrievably its slave. No idea of mine would ever match the Second Style now I had seen it.

The King, Old Robert and de Montfort caught up with me. Lifting his foot very carefully, the King placed it on the first of the slender marble steps, each one curved in a suggestion of the ovoid, and looked enquiringly at me.

"Shall we enter, apprentice?" he said softly, his hand held out. "Come and see what has been done."

Within a moment of going in my old self had to be expelled. All drabness and incompetence were an affront to the supreme beauty I encountered. If I could have torn out my brain and tossed it away with all its luggage of worn-out notions, I would have done.

Inside the outer shell was an inner, but it was broken open at frequent points so the struts and springings were visible. There were enough of these loopholes to suggest a mechanism with its own energy holding up the structure, a huge, cradling hand from within. Here was the God absent from the outside, holding his creation gently, skilfully, tenderly, from the inside, but as a machine made by men. The divine was a strut, a chisel-mark, a bolt, not the booming void which the arrow-heads, towers and spires of the First Style sought to plunge into.

There was no altar, no nave, no choir: it was all one. In the narrowest turn of the long end was one man working on a roped cradle. I did not have to get near to him to know that familiar, no-necked shape, the broad shoulders hunched over what he was doing, his wispy grey hair standing around his head.

"We are allowing your father to do the very last piece of work on the building," de Montfort said in my ear. "It was his idea. He has suffered for it more than most men of genius. We could not allow him to construct the major part because he was temperamentally wrong — he would never have seen it through. But, it existed in his mind first so he deserves the credit. You may speak to him now."

I shook my head violently.

"You don't want to speak to your own father? To applaud him? To congratulate him? Oh, what is this, Hedric?" Old Robert chided me. "To have conceived of such beauty is marvellous in any man."

"It was not his design," I muttered between my teeth. "He was Hans Seersach's helper. I doubt if my father did any more than clean his pens!"

"Oh, we have not forgotten the Fleming," the King interposed, striding towards the upward curve of the floor where it swung towards the end where my father was working. "Herr Seersach is always with us."

He beckoned me to join him. When I reached the place where he was standing he pointed between his feet.

315

Beneath a slab of pure quartz lay the cadaver of Hans. He wore his mason's apron. Between his pale, folded hands was a set-square; at his feet a host of hammers; poised hawk-like over his face a pair of compasses, their points driven into his eyes.

"Now it is finished and we have seen it, and all my brother kings have seen it, and the Pope, and the Emperor have seen it, and all the elders of every heresy, and the mullahs of Mahomet, every one we could think of . . ." the King said, scuffing his soft shoes on the quartz, "it has been agreed that it cannot be allowed to exist, except here. Your father has accepted the post of custodian. We will call it Hood's Offertory, I think, and be done with it. You will assist him. If, in your years here, any new notion should assail you; any new ferment, let me know through the controller."

"Why did you do this to Hans?" I stuttered, terrible indignation welling up inside me.

"To recognise the help he gave your father," the King replied, looking up at the cradle where Bert was working. "One day your father will rest here himself, but in a position of greater prominence."

I ran up the slope to the place where the cradle's ropes were tied around two great blocks of curved marble. As I struggled to untie them I looked up and saw Bert staring down at me, a chisel clutched in his mole's paw.

Old Robert was the only one who seemed to care about what I was doing. He broke into an unco-ordinated trot to try and stop me but he was too slow. The King remained where he was, standing over Hans, a puzzled frown on his face. Simon de Montfort had edged away, back down the curve, his face averted.

I freed one rope and the cradle swung down until it was hanging vertically. Bert hung on, his hammer and chisel falling to the marble floor with a clatter.

"Why?" he screamed at me. "Why?"

Then he did a strange thing. Before I could release the second rope he let go and plunged silently down, turning himself in the air in order to fall head-first and break his neck.

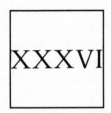

XXXVI

Thus I delivered my father from his captivity and took him from that place into another. He became a part of my self, incorporated into my nature instantly he died. When I was sent in chains from Creswell to the harbour of Whitby accompanied by four Benedictine monk-masons, Bert was with me; when I boarded ship and was manacled to the ship's hold-timbers, my father was alive in my soul. He weathered the seas of the east coast in my company, rounded the wild northern capes of Scotland in my breast, and landed with me at Iona, the King of England's condemnation on his head as well as mine. I had not been charged as a murderer in either the realm of Henry III or Hood. No attempt was made to bring me to secular justice. It was conveyed to me that my act was not accountable to the laws of Man, so much stress having been applied to my growing. The Four accepted responsibility for the murder but they could not absolve me from my sin of parricide. That was a spiritual matter. Their only plea was that my penance should be as severe as possible. The decision to send me into another kingdom and place the case before the abbot of a remote, unworldly monastery, was, I believe, influenced by Master Henry de Reyns. He was sick at the time of my father's death and had not been present at Hood's Offertory. To hand me over to the stringent mercy of ascetics smacked of my hero. He knew my spirit, how I would shoulder the worst expiative tasks and make them into great art. Let your life and your genius be one thing was his unspoken but communicated advice. Suffer, create, unite. Make up for the defects of the Gods, but avoid pride like the plague!

It was, though I am loath to admit or accept it, an act of mercy which recognised the one quality I have worthy to keep me alive: my genius. If I had been a common labourer I would have been killed, as all the men who worked on the egg must have been for they never appeared in the outside world again. The Four could not destroy the one thing in me that had value for them. Better for us all if that had been my mere humanity, my youth, even my rights, but they were not men of that sort. In their confrontations with existence they had not perceived those virtues which are not designed; the natural good which we great artists must enshrine in our creations. It is a struggle to put them there in a right way so they are neither too obvious nor too disguised; it is during this struggle we discover there is no conflict between art and truth, but a raging battle between art and honesty.

This book began in a ship. The first words were written down while we waited for the tide to take us into harbour. Since then it has been penned in corners, under trees and bushes, in churches and cells of hospitality, in rooms, alehouses, barns and abandoned cottages. Of all the labours of my life — and I have built a host of great temples to various gods, palaces, fortresses, domestic dwellings, even a hareem once in eastern Turkey — it has been the most arduous. If any writer would seek a lighter life let him turn to my profession and express himself in stone. When I have completed buildings and stood before them, gazing on the full realisation of my insubstantial dream, I have been satisfied to the point of self-veneration. Now, when I read back over what I have written, I search for those same feelings but they never come. Words are not an aid to joy. Their effect is to squeeze the truth beyond its ability to reveal its essence.

They say Iona is a sacred isle with its own light and its own weather. To be here is to be separated from the world, hidden away and uncorrupted by human desire. When I look at the sea-mist in the sun it reminds me of Creswell and the canopy. To my knowledge the egg is still there, still under the control of Hood who is now Edward, son of King Henry, a man not infatuated with architecture as his father was. He is a warrior and his Hood will be more war-like. From what I heard on the road up from Winchelsea, the blood flows in Sherwood these days. I kept well to the west of it, resisting the urge to see Hood's Offertory and my father's tomb. King Henry sent me a drawing of it to Iona, done by a brother mason in captivity at Creswell. It was Bert's mark loosed from ⊦⊣ to make a simple bed of marble ⊦⊦⊣ on which he sleeps.

Walking Iona's shores again is an odd feeling: I was a boy of fourteen when I paced them last, my only companions a few scruffy sheep and sea-gulls for the monks had been told to ignore me. The pebbles on the shore are all colours, pinks, greens, blacks, and the white cutters, layers, setters and such have used them in the fabric of the monastery. Every time I see one set into the mortar I see the glory of Hans Seersach's imagination stuck in the grey, dull, ugly mortar of this world. Once I am free of my sin I will prise him out, polish him until he shines, and show the nations the man to whom I owe a debt.

There are problems I must face in the future. My Third Style of Emergence is as bold a departure from the florid Frenchiness of the present decadent mode as Hans Seersach's was from the First. The roots of my creation are in his, although my individual perception shines through. Once it is known that a disturbing and challenging new architectural form has been let loose, the authorities will begin to question its merits and its origins. The brotherhood is not what it was, our faith having been incorporated into the Christian Church to such a degree that it is hardly visible as an independent religion. We are little more than a ring through Christ's nose now. I can expect no defence from my brother masons. They have come to dislike anyone who rocks the boat.

My plan is to produce a *fait accompli*. I have heard that Thomas Cantilupe, the old Bishop of Hereford, a close friend and ally of Simon de Montfort — slain in rebellion while I was away (I was in Ravenna when I heard the news) — had a natural daughter. Upon Cantilupe's death five years ago she inherited his fortune and spends it on building. Her interests are female, naturally, and she has helped those architects who are attempting to flatten out the pointedness of the First Style and make it rounder. This may seem to be a minor adjustment when seen against the total transformation proposed by my Third Style, but it is a step in the right direction. If I can persuade her to look at my drawings and hear me out there is a chance she will let me build my first experiment in some isolated part of her estates. Then we will invite a local churchman of known progressive views, then a minor court official or a young landowner known to be impatient with things as they are. In this way we will slowly creep up on the King.

I have another ten to twenty years of active life left in me. My health is good. I have learnt from my experiences. With some cunning and common sense I should be able to bring my Third Style to fruition before I die. Beside it all my famous achievements from Muscovy to Egypt to Tibet will be as nothing, for I will have put the world back within itself.

I worked on the interior of this abbey church of Iona for twenty months while the abbot was making up his mind about my penance. There are two arches on the northern wall of the choir, full of dog-tooth ornament. Those teeth are my work, cut out in my sorrow, day after day, my father's hand guiding the chisel along the jaws of my grief.

On the day this was completed, the abbot summoned me to appear before him; I went as I was, my hair white with stone-dust, my apron pocket full of chinking tools.

"Before God, the father of all men," he said out of a mouth pinched by fasting, "you have offended to the limit of mortal sin. To kill your father is to kill your creator and, through him, strike a blow at the Creator of all. It is not the blow that matters; God will shrug it off: it is the soul behind the blow."

As an Albigensian and a Christian, as my father and myself, I accepted his judgement. The next morning I was rowed to the Isle of Mull. From thence I began my first pilgrimage, nothing in my purse, my only means of life, my craft. Now, my three pilgrimages completed, my life's work half-done in many corners of the world, I have returned to Iona, Bert in my tool-bag, to claim my absolution.

The abbot who laid the penance on me is long dead. The present incumbent is familiar with my case, all my details having been carefully recorded when the judgement was sent to King Henry. The abbot has accepted my proofs of my journeys to Santiago de Compostella, Rome and Jerusalem.

All that remains is for me to enter the church and take my book to where a brazier is burning in front of the altar. It has enough fuel to burn for an hour, then it will go out. The abbot has told five of his choir-monks to pray for me, to give me strength because I could not finish the work yesterday and the brazier went out. It is not that I am unwilling to burn my book but I cannot find the last word.

It is not pride.